## 13

### STORY AND ART BY
# NORIYUKI KONISHI

ORIGINAL CONCEPT AND SUPERVISED BY LEVEL-5 INC.

# YO-KAI WATCH™
## Volume 13
### VIZ Media Edition

**Story and Art by Noriyuki Konishi**
**Original Concept and Supervised by LEVEL-5 Inc.**

Translation/Tetsuichiro Miyaki
English Adaptation/Aubrey Sitterson
Lettering/John Hunt
Design/Kam Li

YO-KAI WATCH Vol. 13
by Noriyuki KONISHI
© 2013 Noriyuki KONISHI
©LEVEL-5 Inc.
Original Concept and Supervised by LEVEL-5 Inc.
All rights reserved.
Original Japanese edition published by SHOGAKUKAN.
English translation rights in the United States of America,
Canada, the United Kingdom, Ireland, Australia and New Zealand
arranged with SHOGAKUKAN.

Printed in the U.S.A.

Published by VIZ Media, LLC
P.O. Box 77010
San Francisco, CA 94107

10 9 8 7 6 5 4 3 2 1
First printing, January 2020

# YO-KAI WATCH™

## 13

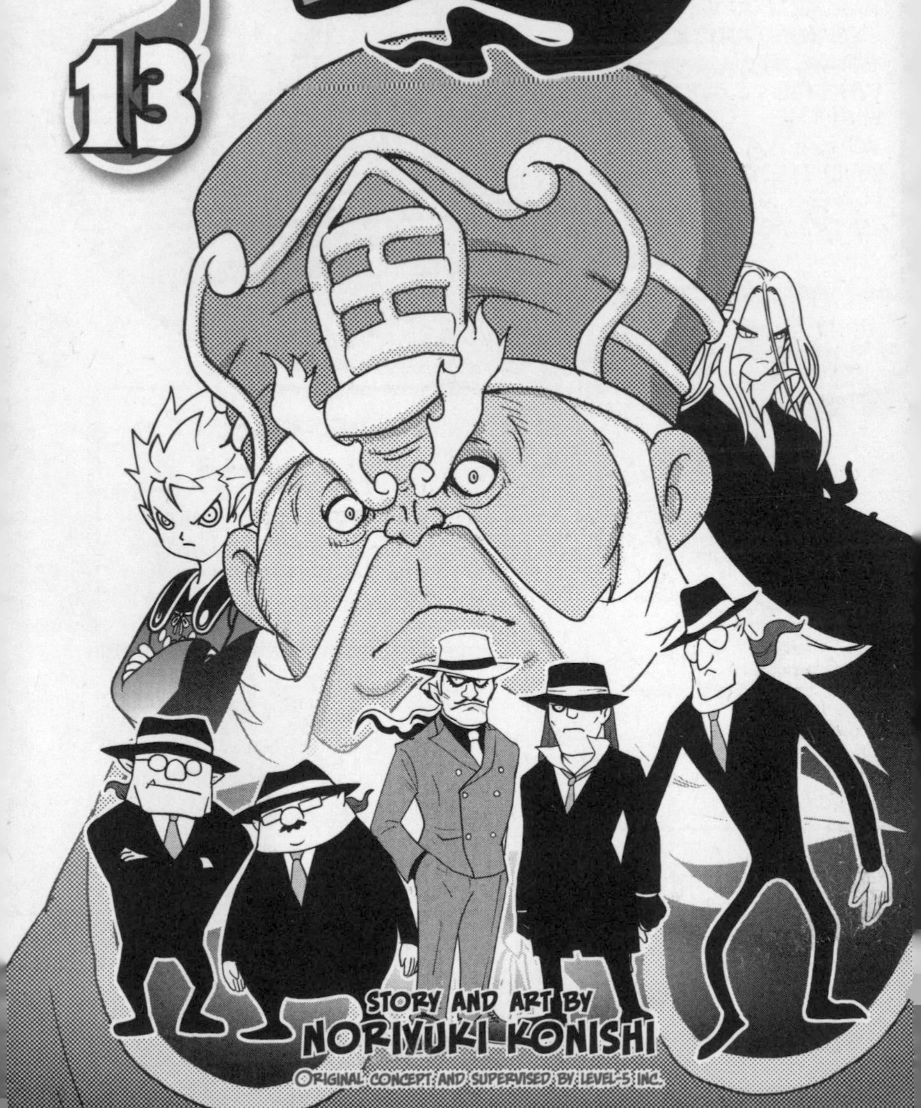

STORY AND ART BY
NORIYUKI KONISHI
ORIGINAL CONCEPT AND SUPERVISED BY LEVEL-5 INC.

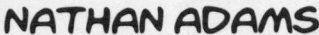

# CHARACTER INTRODUCTION

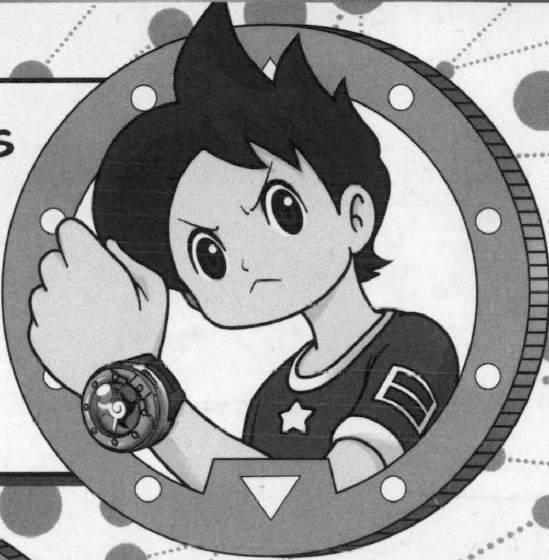

## NATHAN ADAMS

AN ORDINARY ELEMENTARY SCHOOL STUDENT. WHISPER GAVE HIM THE YO-KAI WATCH, AND THEY HAVE SINCE BECOME FRIENDS.

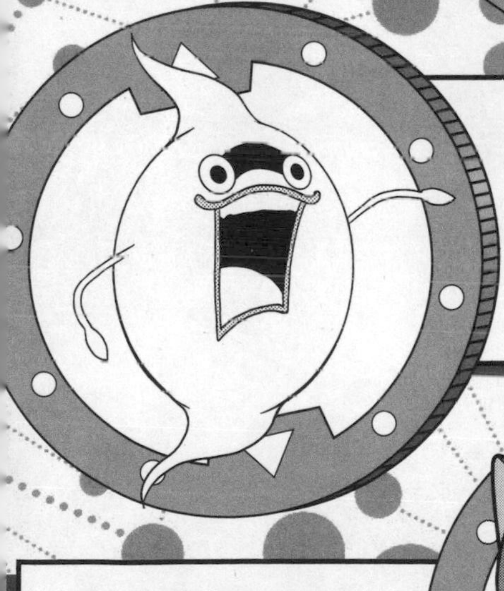

## WHISPER

A YO-KAI BUTLER FREED BY NATE, WHISPER HELPS HIM WITH HIS EXTENSIVE KNOWLEDGE OF OTHER YO-KAI.

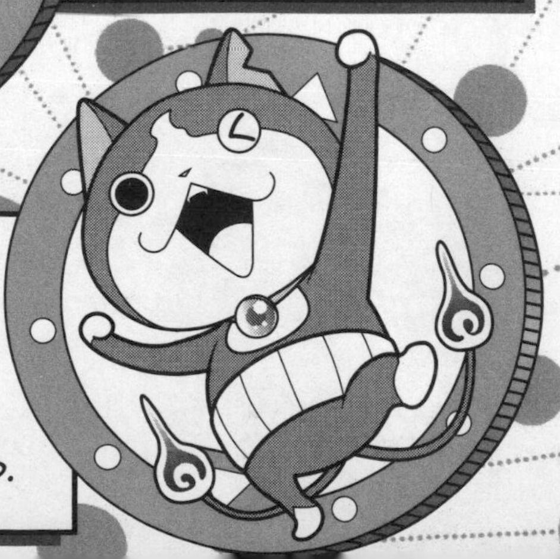

## JIBANYAN

A CAT WHO BECAME A YO-KAI WHEN HE PASSED AWAY. HE IS FRIENDLY, CAREFREE, AND THE FIRST YO-KAI THAT NATE BEFRIENDED.

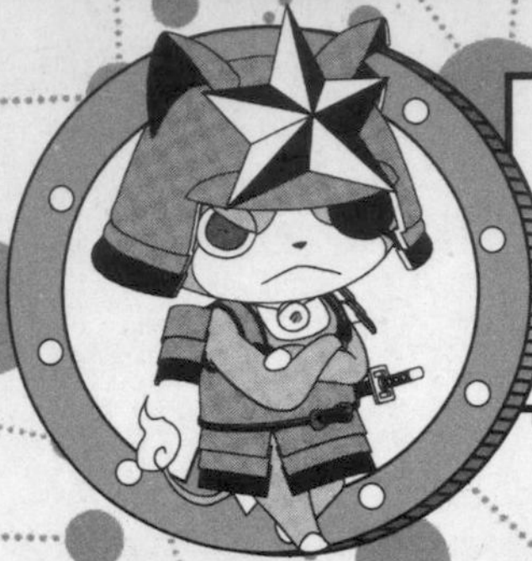

**LAST SHOGUNYAN**

A YO-KAI FROM THE WARRING STATES ERA WHO FOLLOWS THE CODE OF THE SAMURAI.

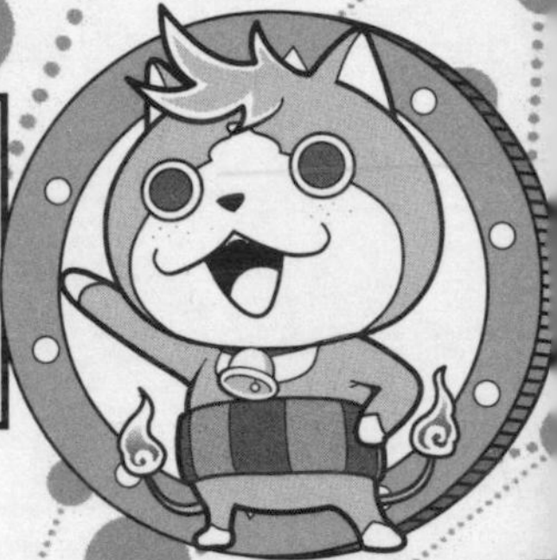

**TOMNYAN**

A MYSTERIOUS YO-KAI FROM THE LAND OF BBQ. HE SEEMS TO HAVE SOME KIND OF ULTERIOR MOTIVE...

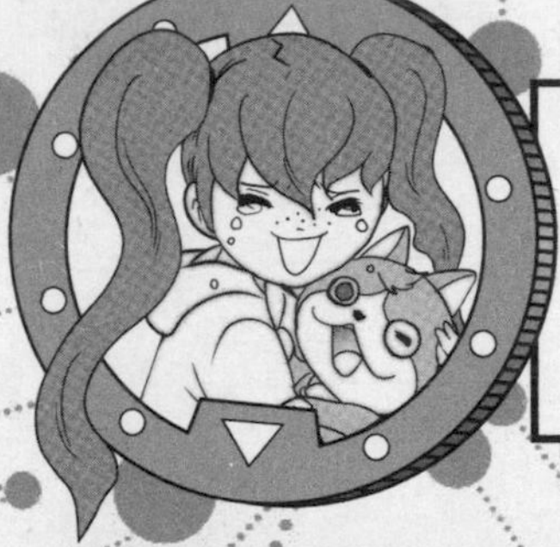

**EMILY**

TOMNYAN'S OWNER. SHE HAS BEEN IN DEEP SHOCK EVER SINCE LOSING TOMNYAN.

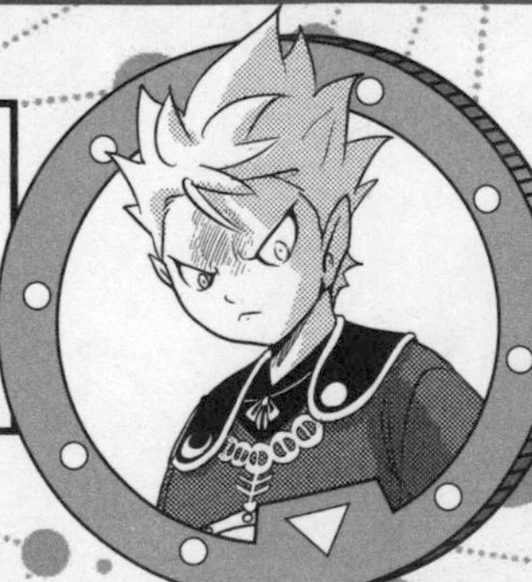

**LORD ENMA**

THE YOUNG LORD OF THE YO-KAI WORLD. WHEN HE MET NATE HE WAS IN FAVOR OF INCREASED INTERACTION BETWEEN HUMANS AND YO-KAI.

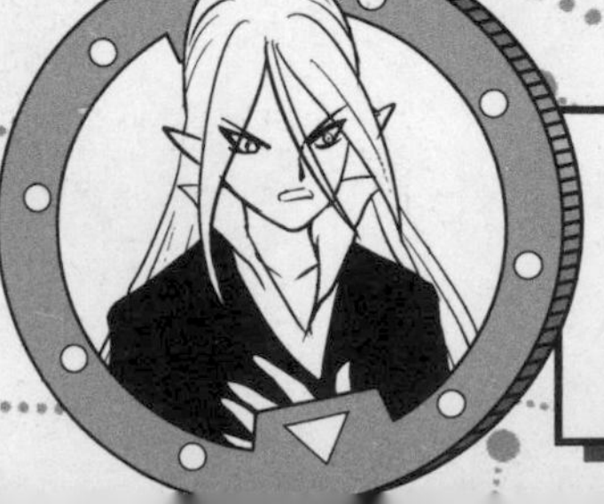

**ZAZEL**

HE WORKS UNDER LORD ENMA, WHO RULES THE YO-KAI WORLD. HE ALSO SERVED THE PREVIOUS LORD ENMA.

THE GHOULFATHER ARC 1

# THE TRUTH ABOUT TOMNYAN

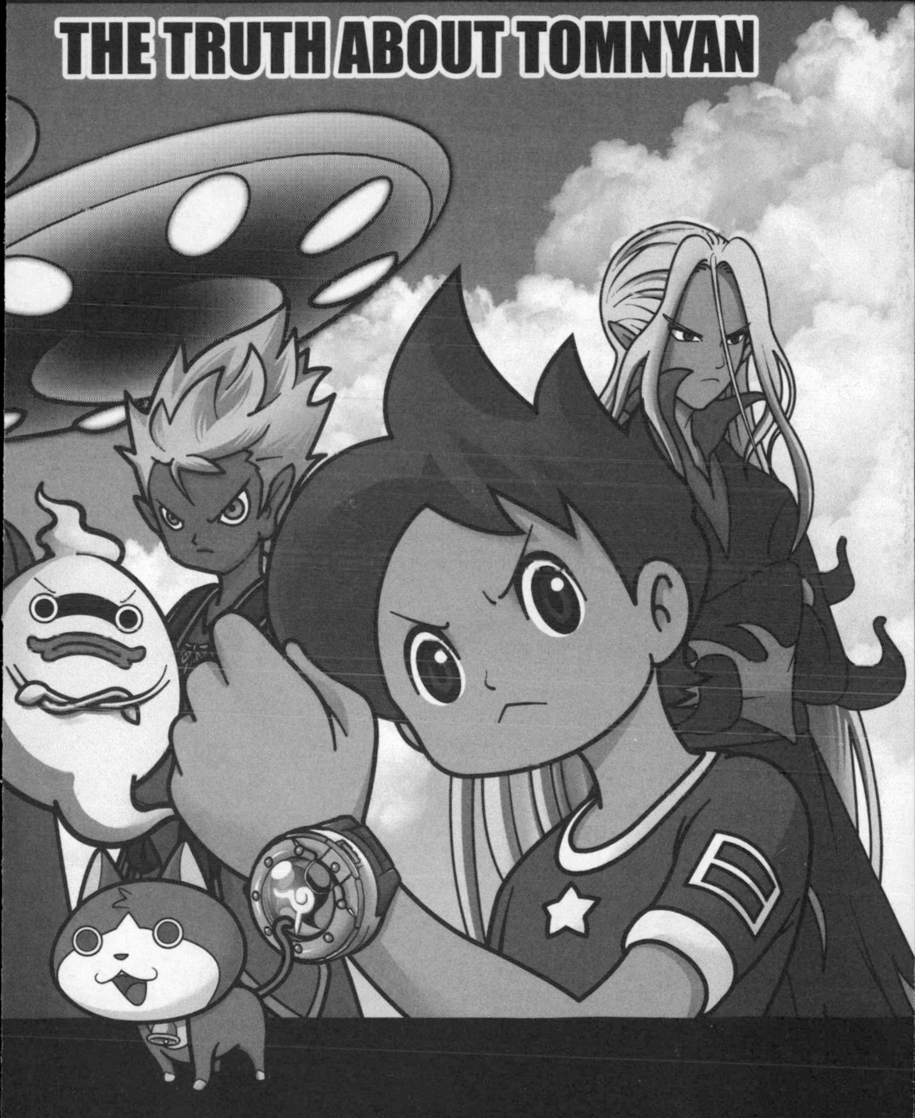

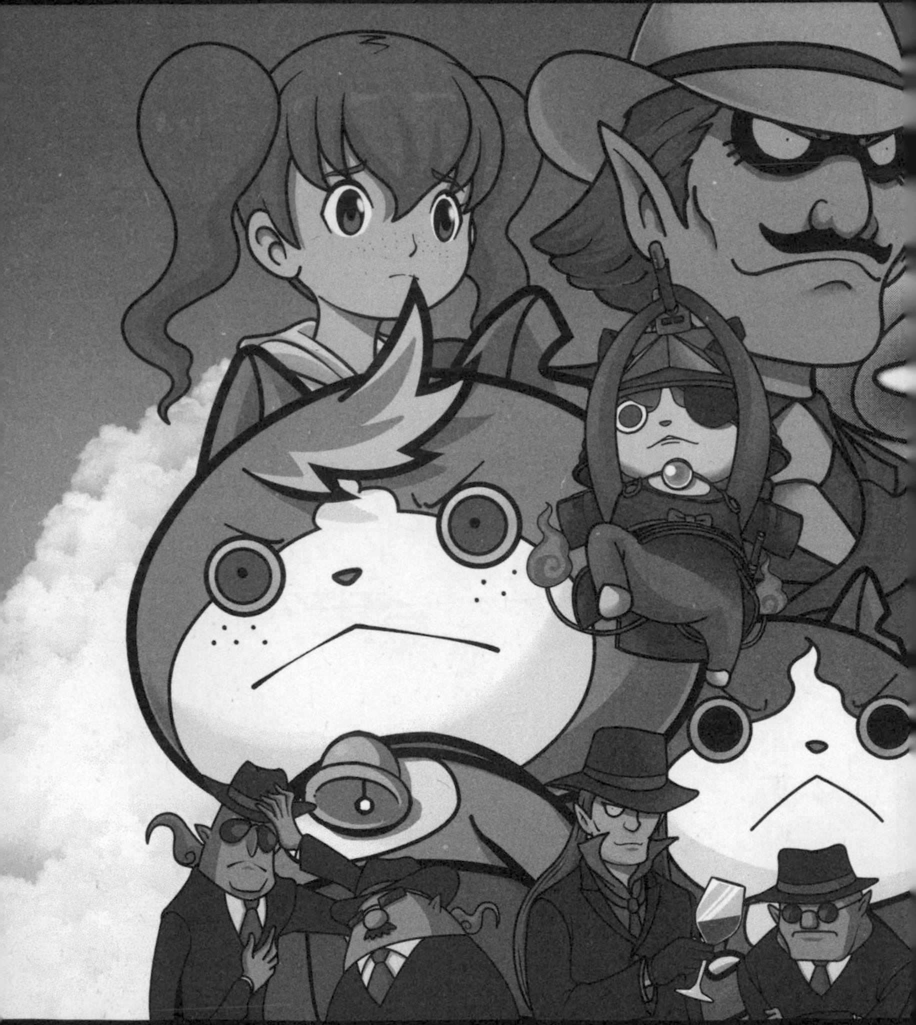

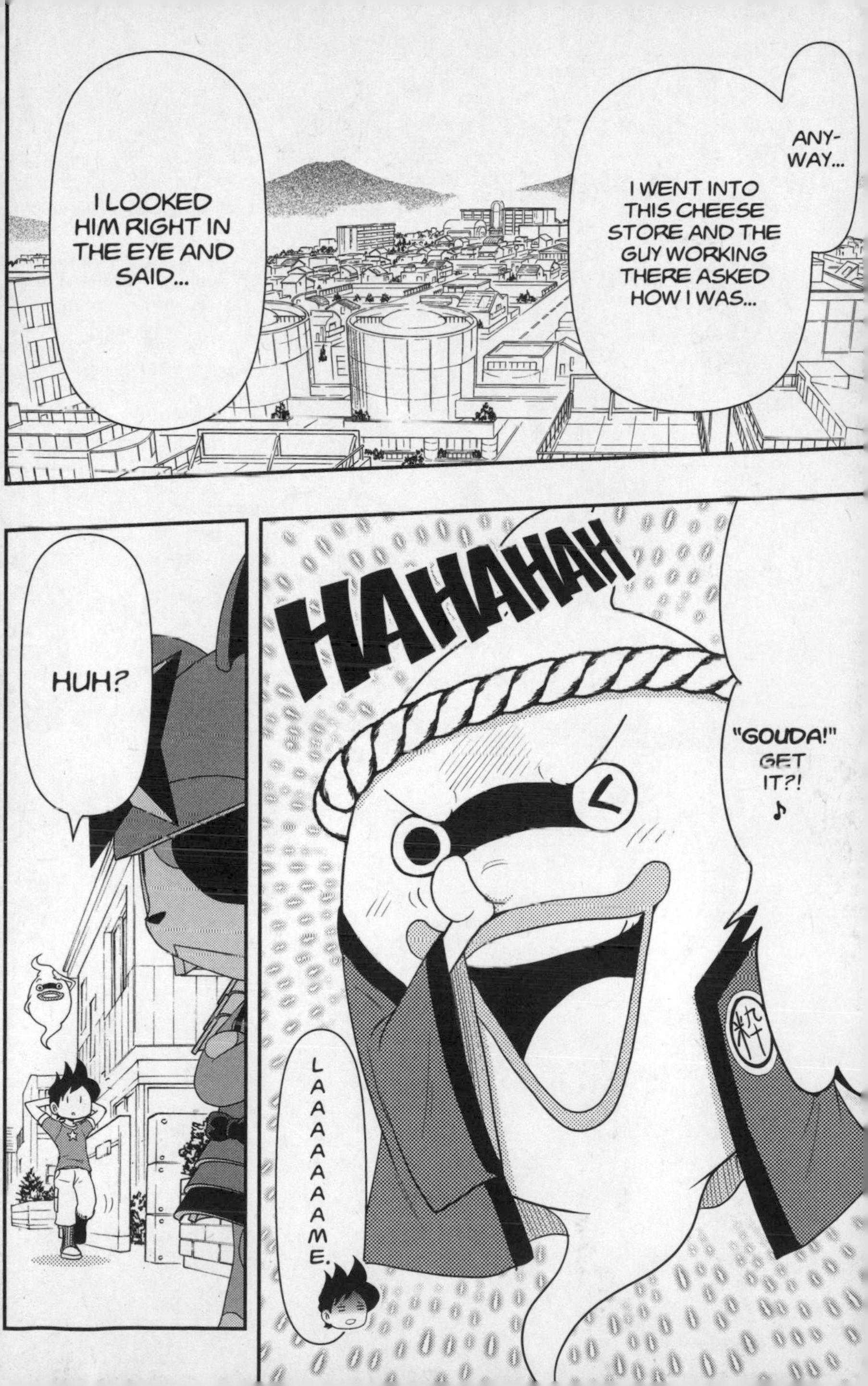
ANY-WAY...
I WENT INTO THIS CHEESE STORE AND THE GUY WORKING THERE ASKED HOW I WAS...
I LOOKED HIM RIGHT IN THE EYE AND SAID...
"GOUDA!" GET IT?! ♪
HAHAHAH
LAAAAAAAAME.
HUH?

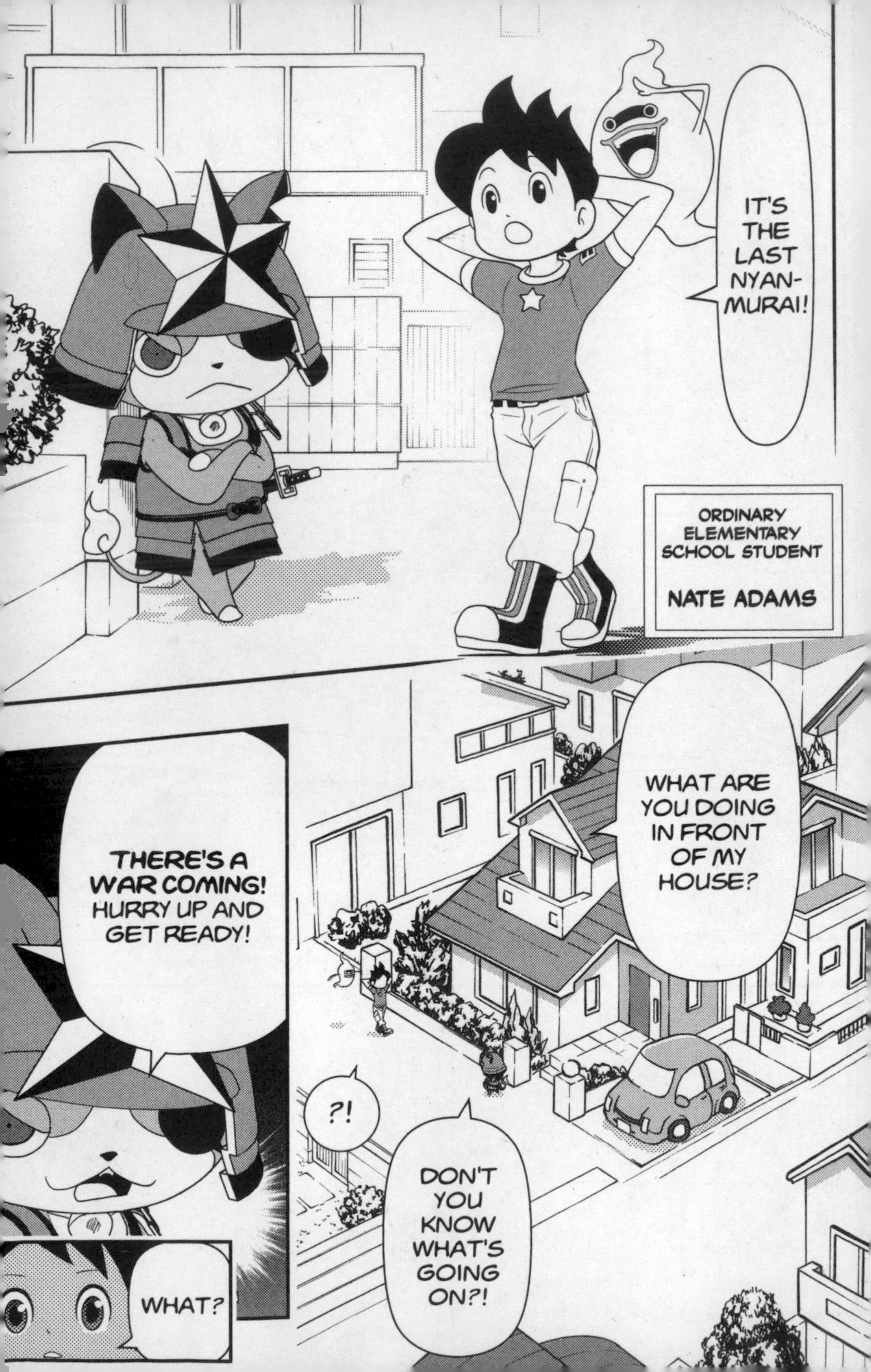

IT'S THE LAST NYAN-MURAI!
ORDINARY ELEMENTARY SCHOOL STUDENT
NATE ADAMS
WHAT ARE YOU DOING IN FRONT OF MY HOUSE?
?!
DON'T YOU KNOW WHAT'S GOING ON?!
THERE'S A WAR COMING! HURRY UP AND GET READY!
WHAT?

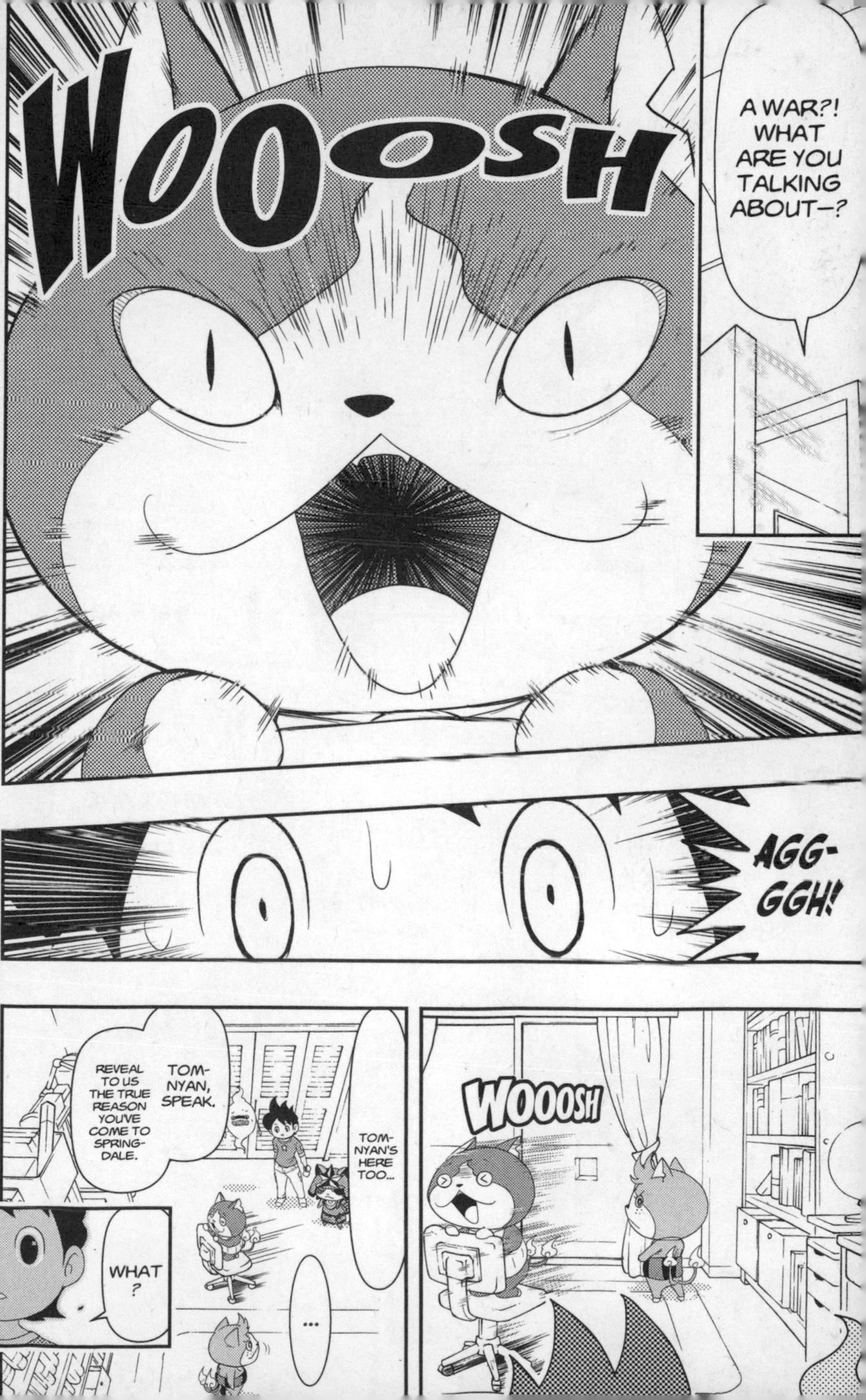
A WAR?! WHAT ARE YOU TALKING ABOUT—?
WOOOSH
AGG-GGH!
WOOOSH
TOM-NYAN'S HERE TOO...
TOM-NYAN, SPEAK.
REVEAL TO US THE TRUE REASON YOU'VE COME TO SPRING-DALE.
...
WHAT?

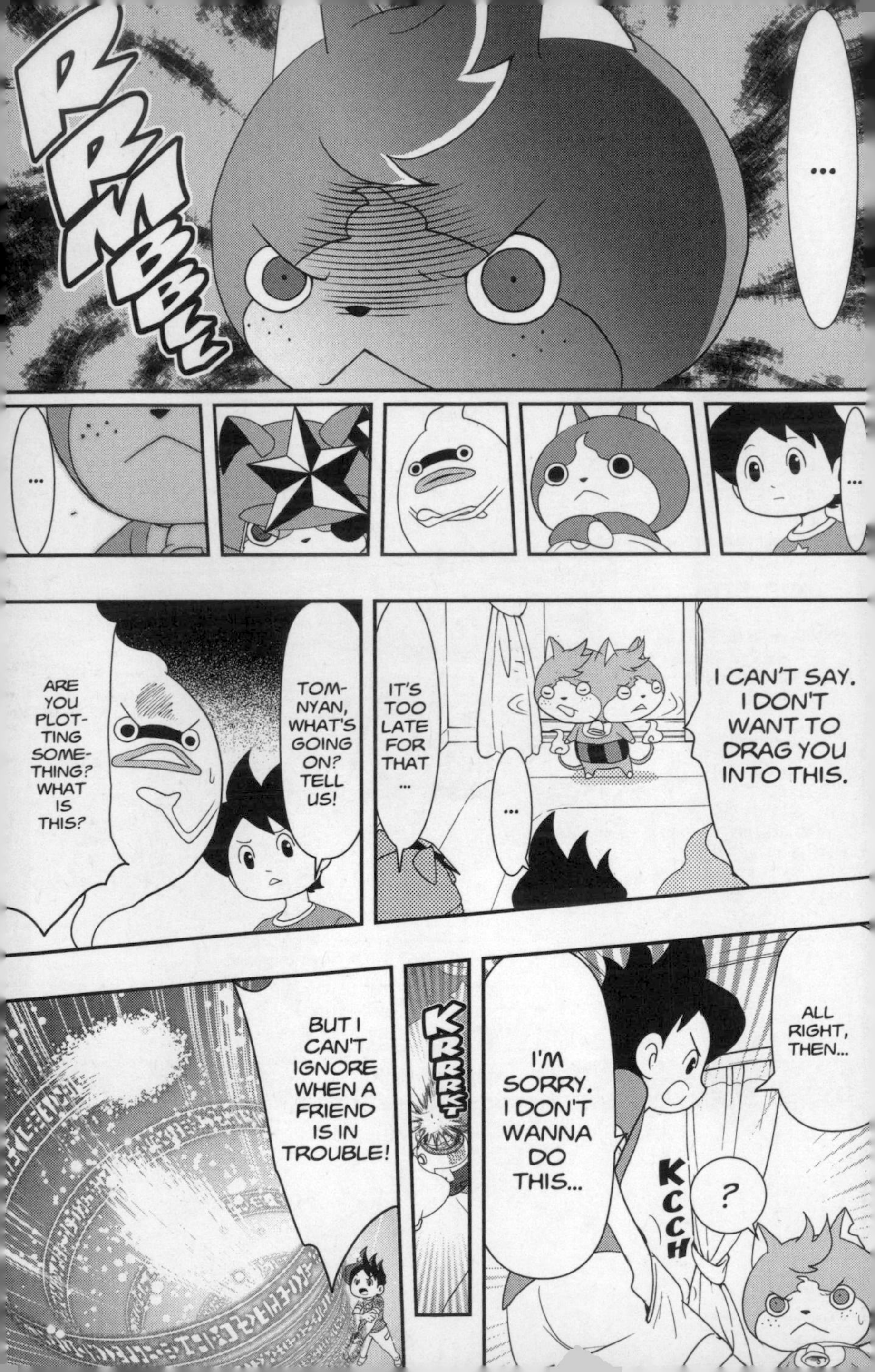
...
RRMBBLE
...
...
I CAN'T SAY. I DON'T WANT TO DRAG YOU INTO THIS.
IT'S TOO LATE FOR THAT ...
...
TOM-NYAN, WHAT'S GOING ON? TELL US!
ARE YOU PLOTTING SOMETHING? WHAT IS THIS?
ALL RIGHT, THEN...
I'M SORRY. I DON'T WANNA DO THIS...
KCCH
?
KRRRKT
BUT I CAN'T IGNORE WHEN A FRIEND IS IN TROUBLE!

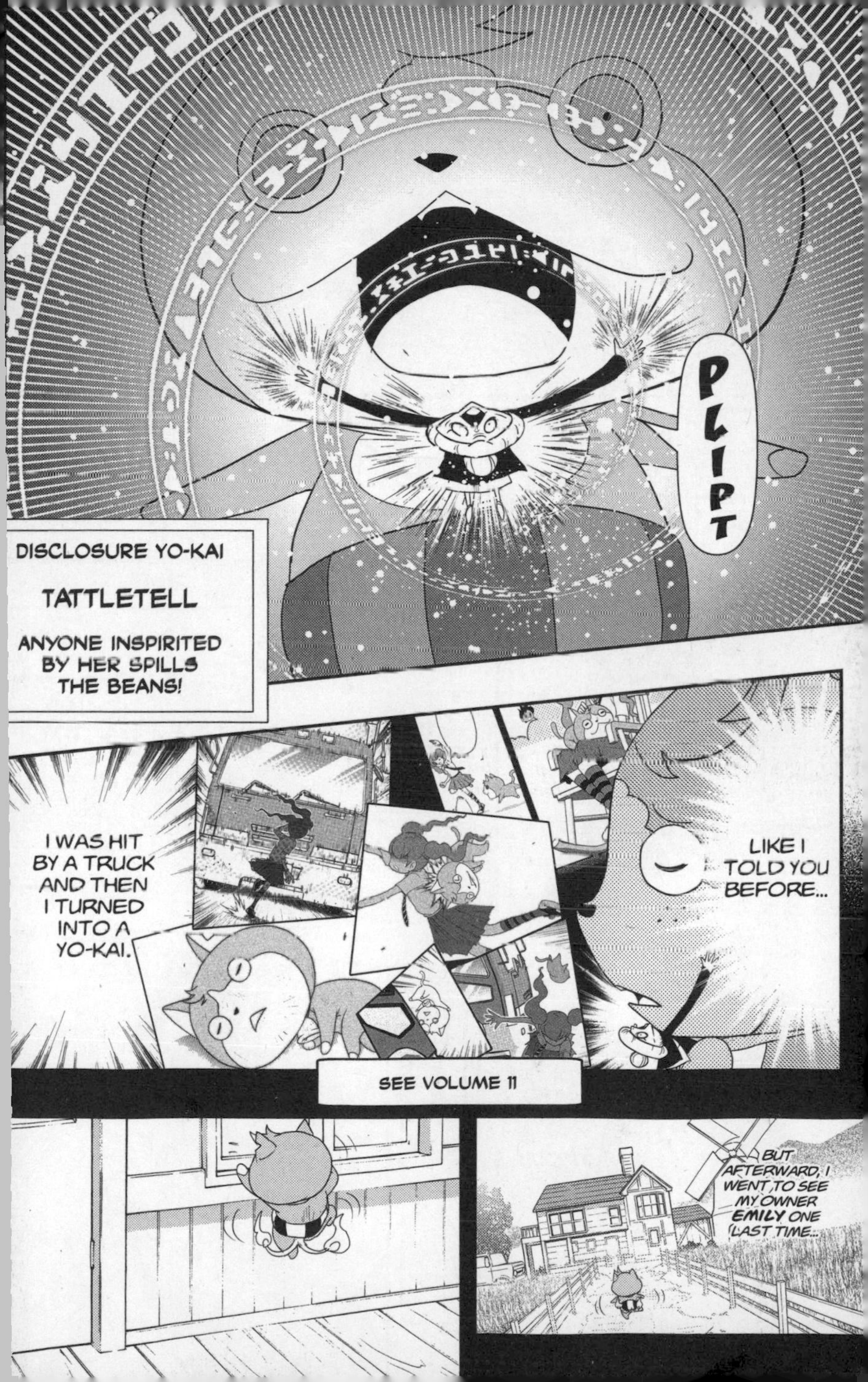
PLIPT
DISCLOSURE YO-KAI
TATTLETELL
ANYONE INSPIRITED BY HER SPILLS THE BEANS!
LIKE I TOLD YOU BEFORE...
I WAS HIT BY A TRUCK AND THEN I TURNED INTO A YO-KAI.
SEE VOLUME 11
BUT AFTERWARD, I WENT TO SEE MY OWNER EMILY ONE LAST TIME...

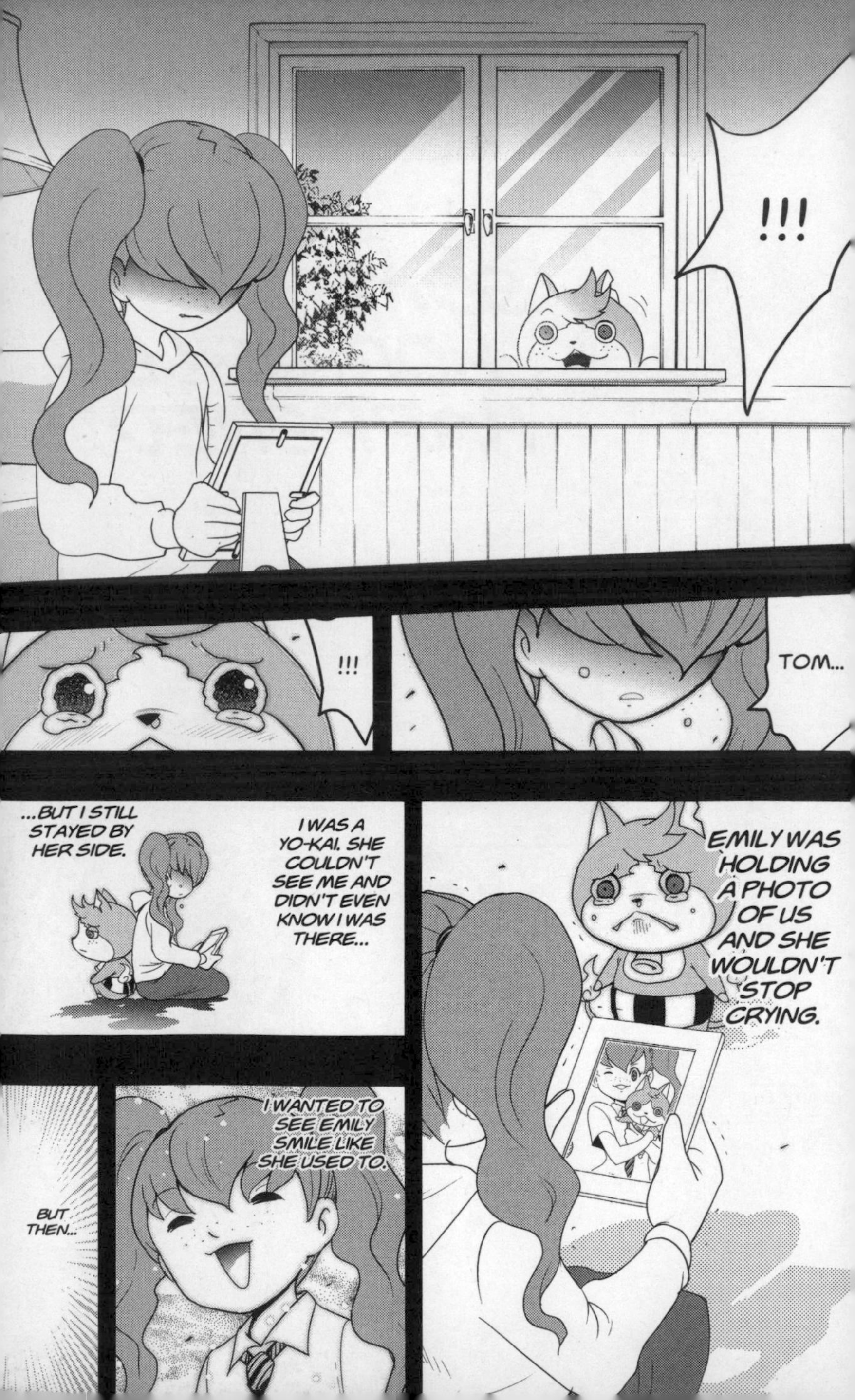
!!!
TOM...
!!!
EMILY WAS HOLDING A PHOTO OF US AND SHE WOULDN'T STOP CRYING.
I WAS A YO-KAI. SHE COULDN'T SEE ME AND DIDN'T EVEN KNOW I WAS THERE...
...BUT I STILL STAYED BY HER SIDE.
I WANTED TO SEE EMILY SMILE LIKE SHE USED TO.
BUT THEN...

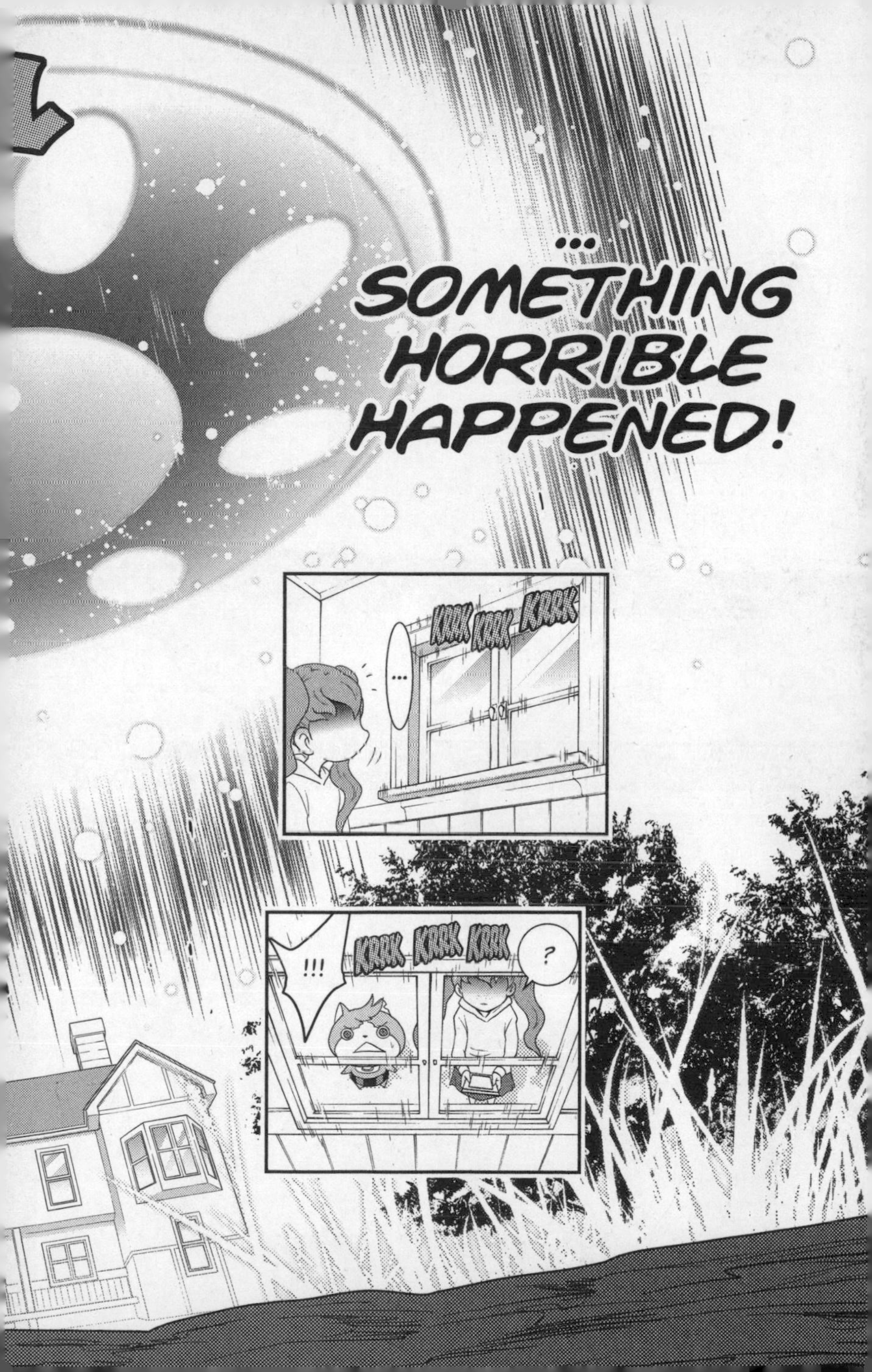
...SOMETHING HORRIBLE HAPPENED!
KRRK KRRK KRRK
...
KRRK KRRK KRRK
?
!!!

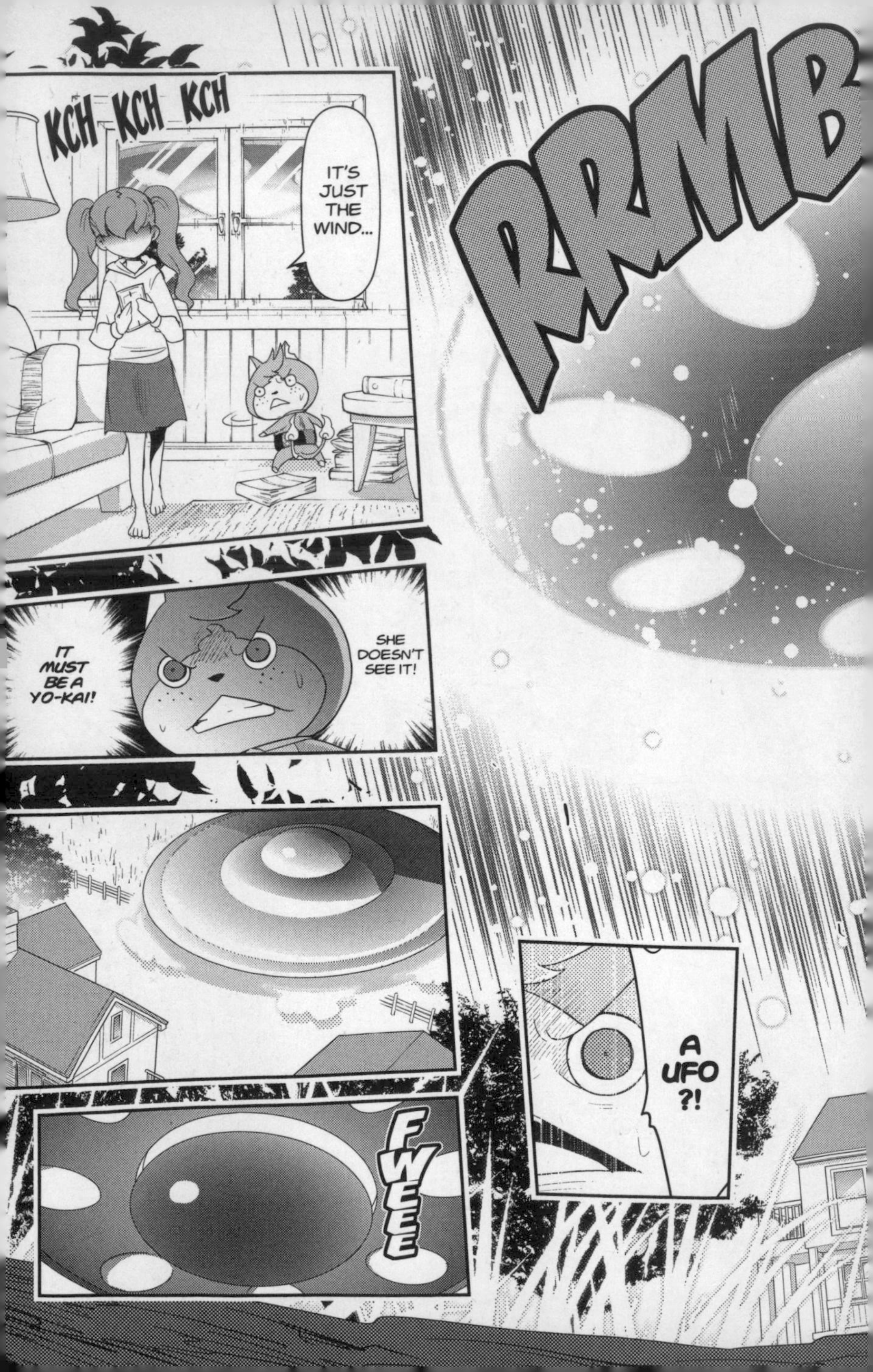
RRMB
KCH KCH KCH
IT'S JUST THE WIND...
SHE DOESN'T SEE IT!
IT MUST BE A YO-KAI!
A UFO ?!
FWEEE

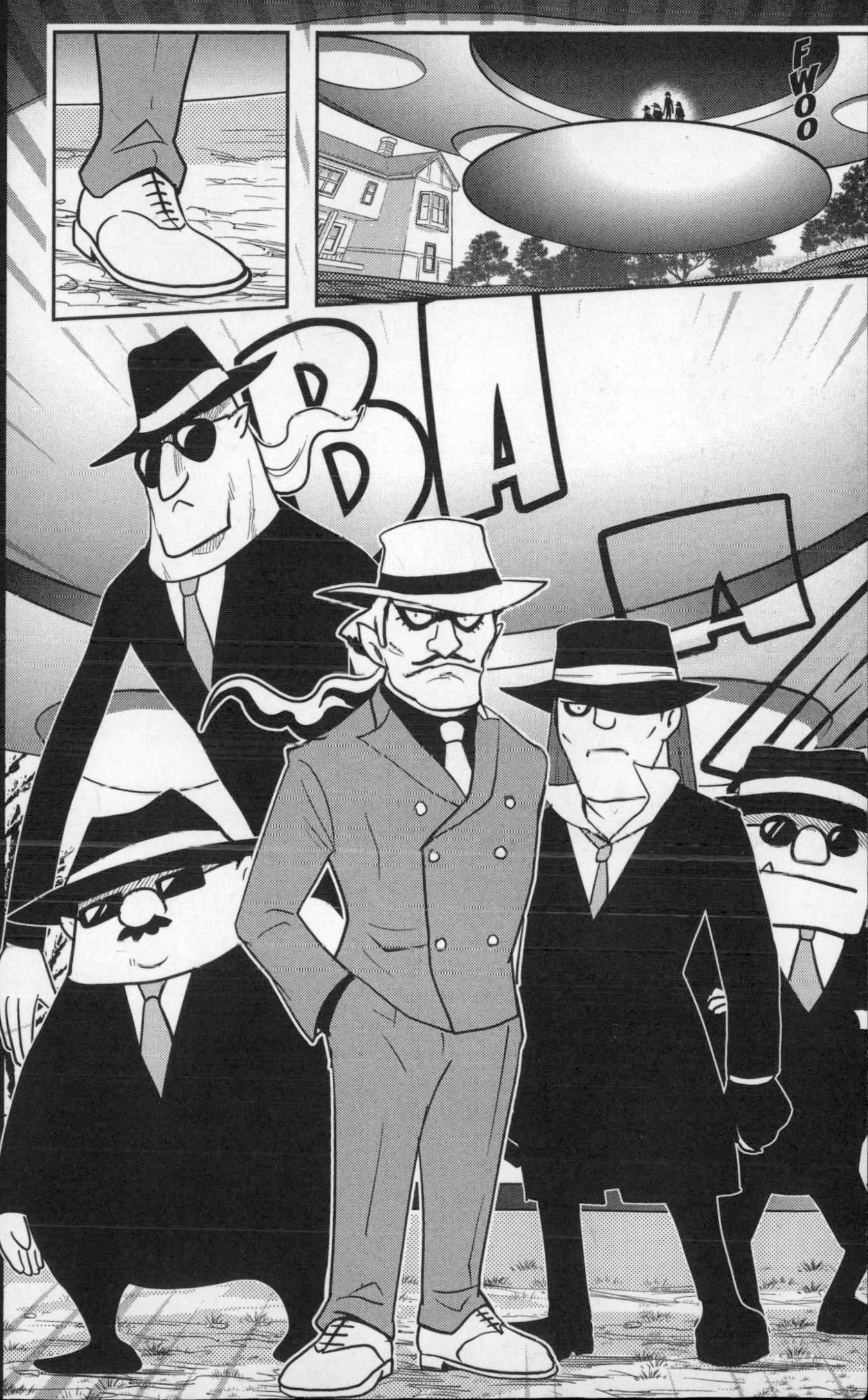
FWOO
BAA

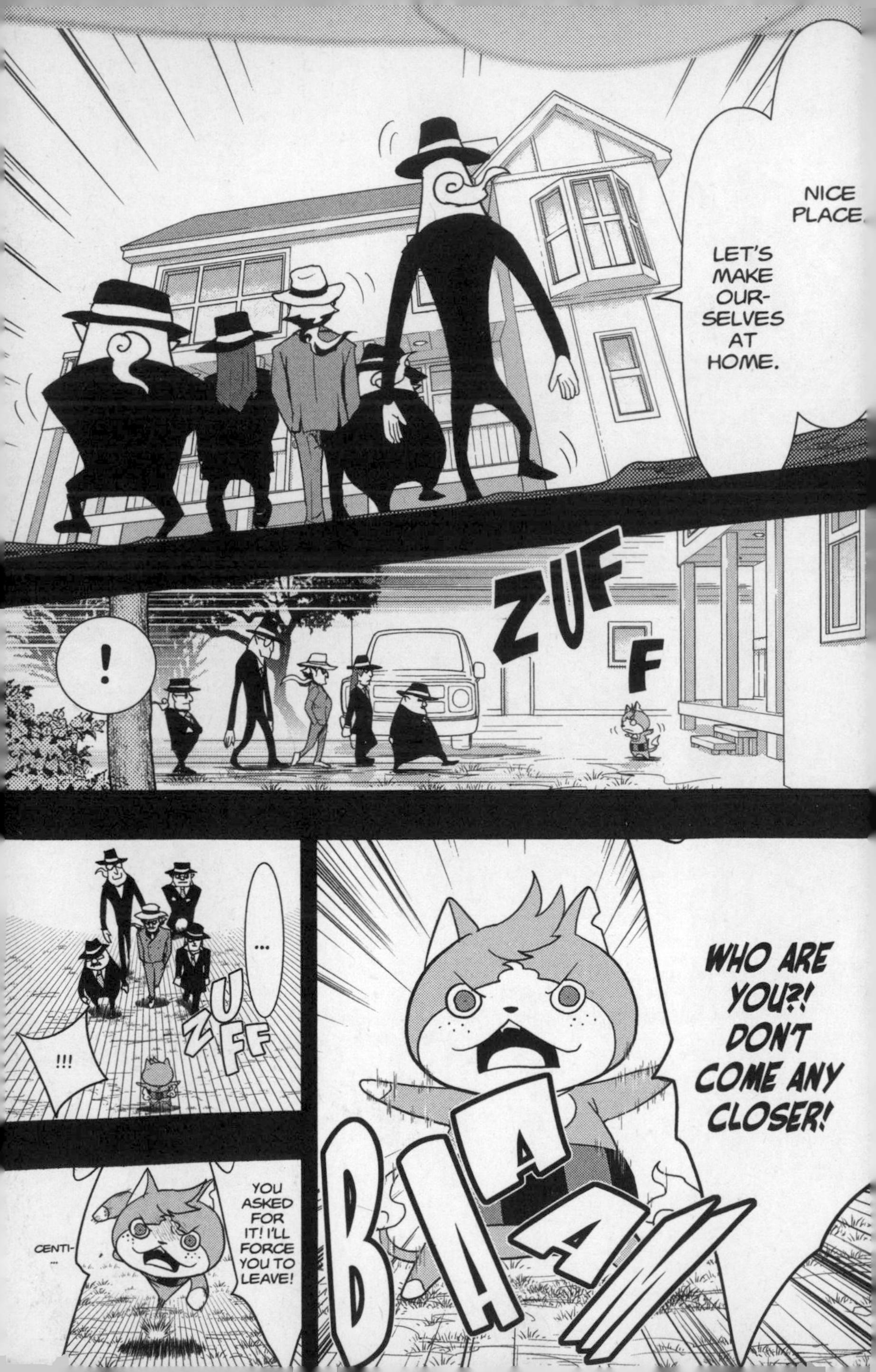
NICE PLACE.
LET'S MAKE OUR-SELVES AT HOME.
ZUFF
F
!
WHO ARE YOU?! DON'T COME ANY CLOSER!
BAAA
...
ZUFF
!!!
YOU ASKED FOR IT! I'LL FORCE YOU TO LEAVE!
CENTI-...

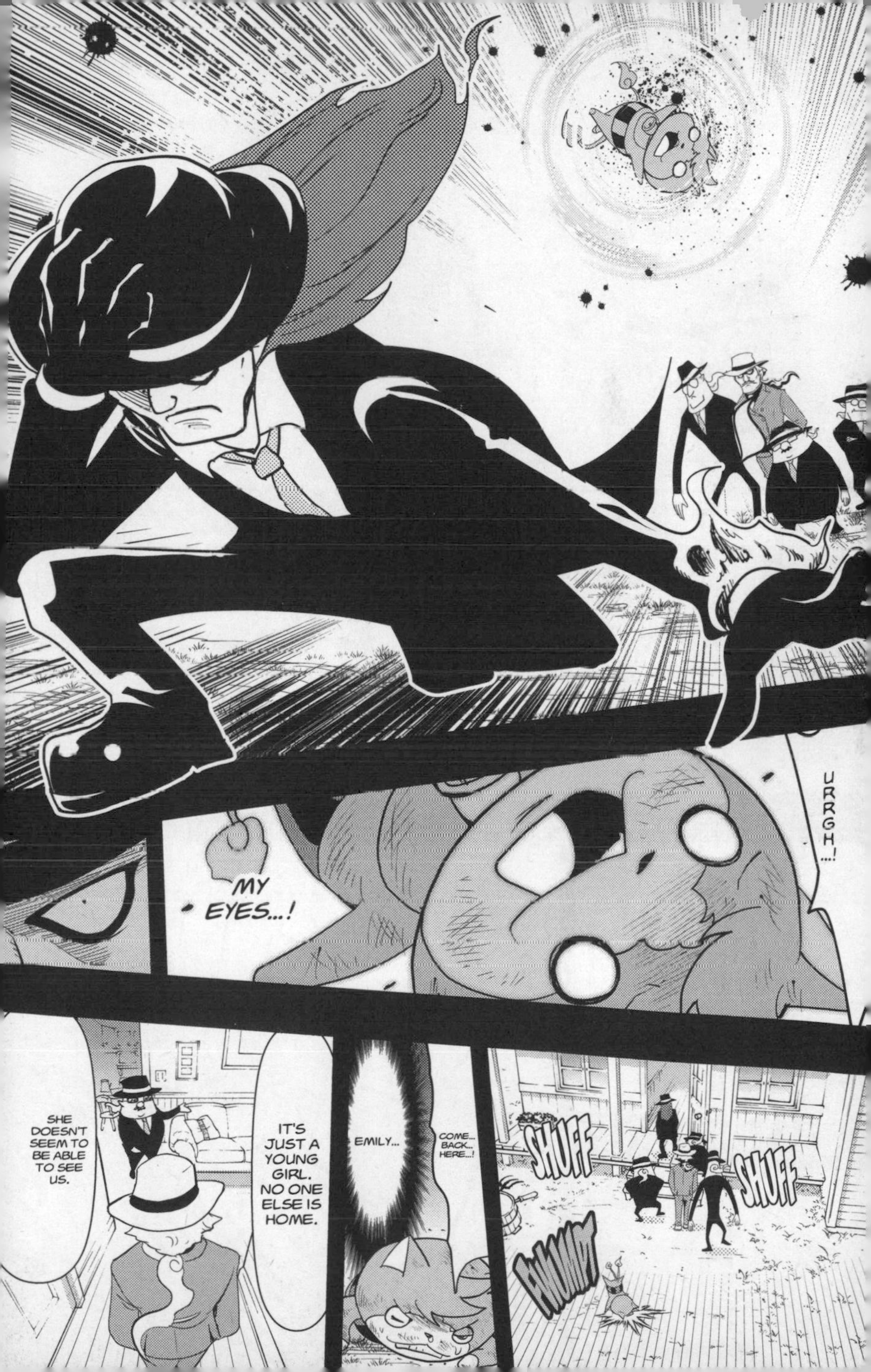
URRGH...!
MY EYES...!
SHUFF
SHUFF
COME... BACK... HERE...!
EMILY...
IT'S JUST A YOUNG GIRL. NO ONE ELSE IS HOME.
SHE DOESN'T SEEM TO BE ABLE TO SEE US.

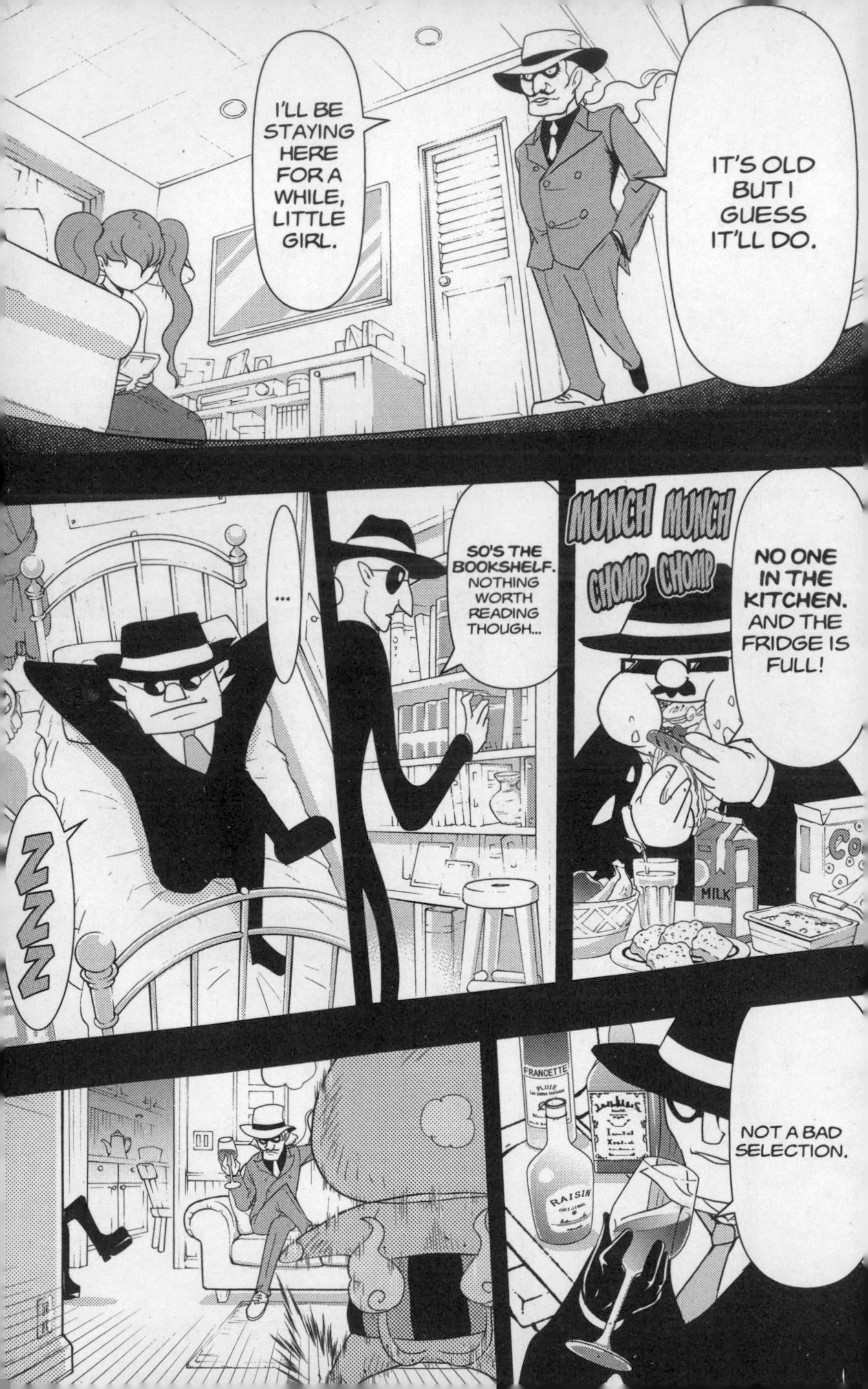
IT'S OLD BUT I GUESS IT'LL DO.
I'LL BE STAYING HERE FOR A WHILE, LITTLE GIRL.
NO ONE IN THE KITCHEN. AND THE FRIDGE IS FULL!
MUNCH MUNCH
CHOMP CHOMP
MILK
SO'S THE BOOKSHELF. NOTHING WORTH READING THOUGH...
...
ZZZ
NOT A BAD SELECTION.
FRANCETTE
RAISIN

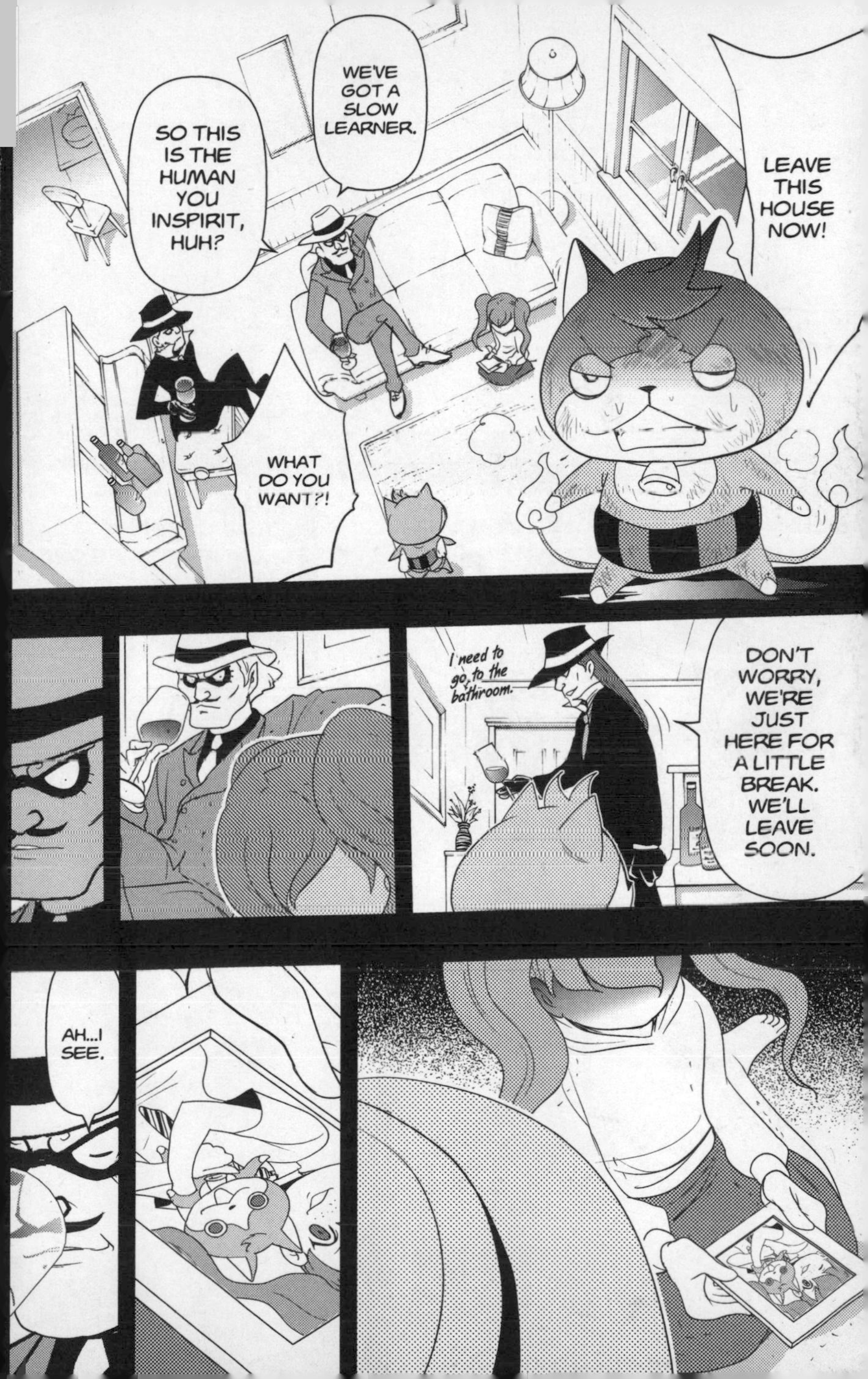
LEAVE THIS HOUSE NOW!
WE'VE GOT A SLOW LEARNER.
SO THIS IS THE HUMAN YOU INSPIRIT, HUH?
WHAT DO YOU WANT?!
DON'T WORRY, WE'RE JUST HERE FOR A LITTLE BREAK. WE'LL LEAVE SOON.
I need to go to the bathroom.
AH...I SEE.

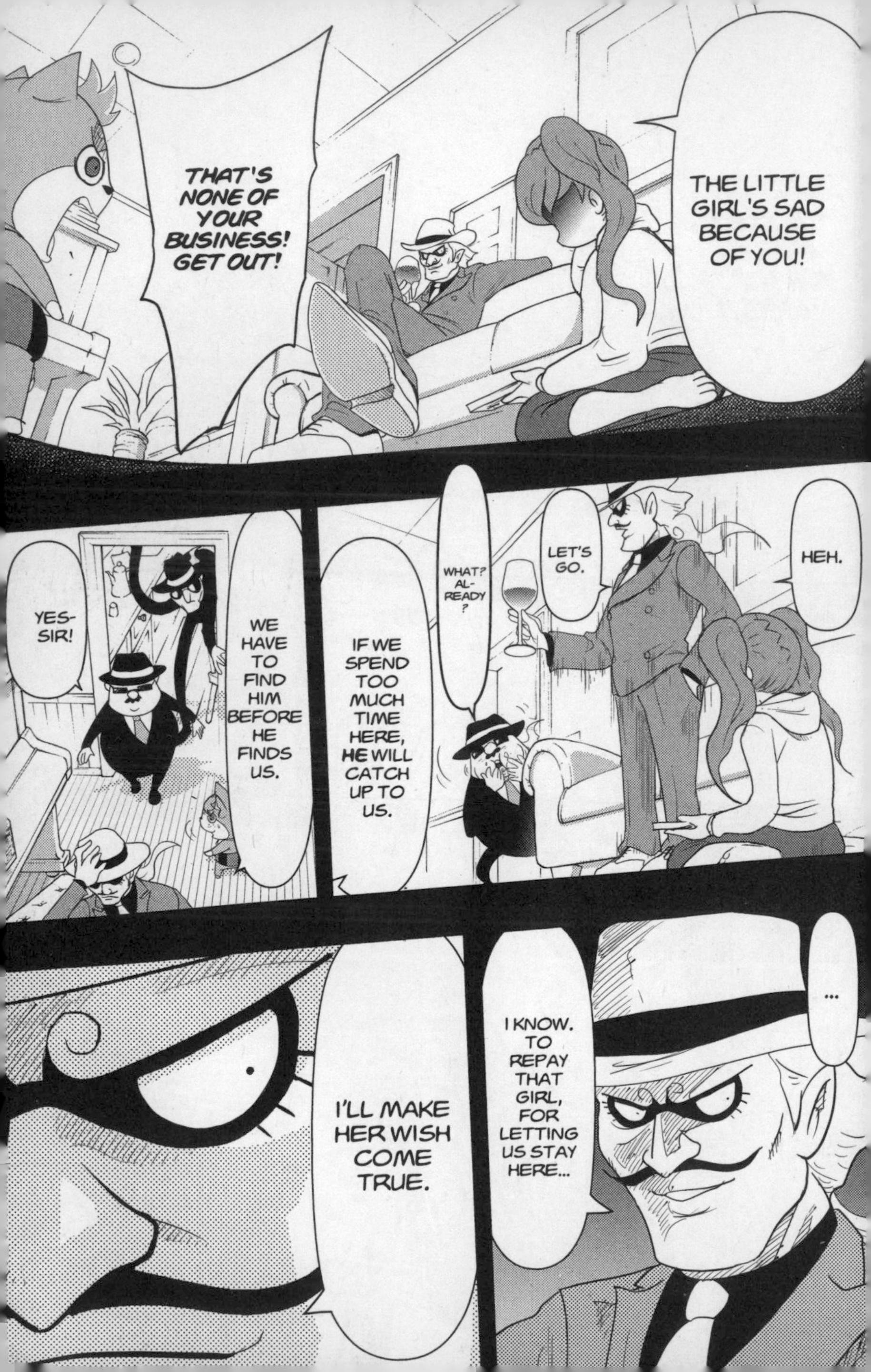
THE LITTLE GIRL'S SAD BECAUSE OF YOU!
THAT'S NONE OF YOUR BUSINESS! GET OUT!
HEH.
LET'S GO.
WHAT? AL-READY?
IF WE SPEND TOO MUCH TIME HERE, HE WILL CATCH UP TO US.
WE HAVE TO FIND HIM BEFORE HE FINDS US.
YES-SIR!
...
I KNOW. TO REPAY THAT GIRL, FOR LETTING US STAY HERE...
I'LL MAKE HER WISH COME TRUE.

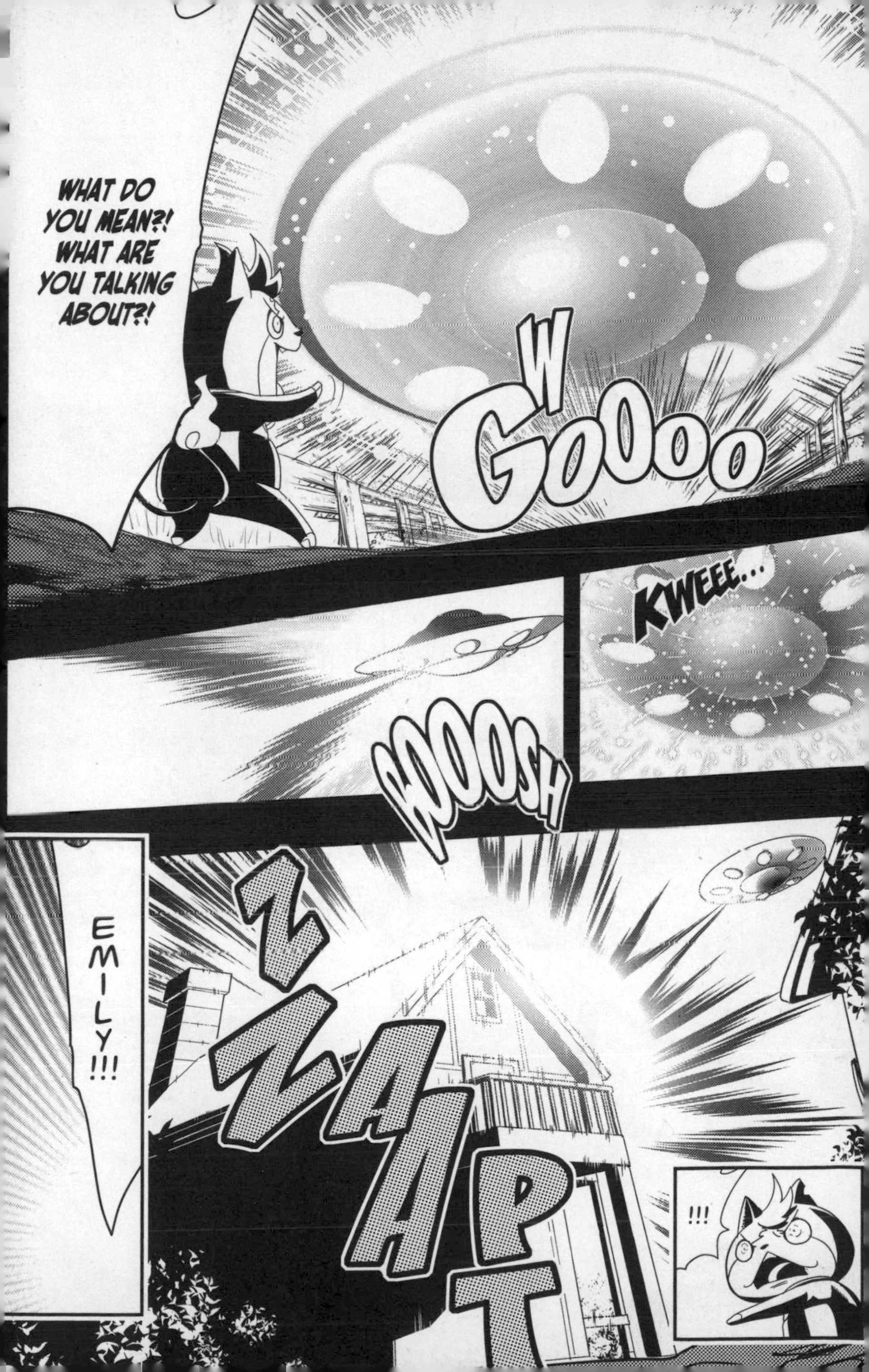
WHAT DO YOU MEAN?! WHAT ARE YOU TALKING ABOUT?!
GWOOOO
KWEEE...
WOOOSH
ZZAAPT
!!!
EMILY!!!

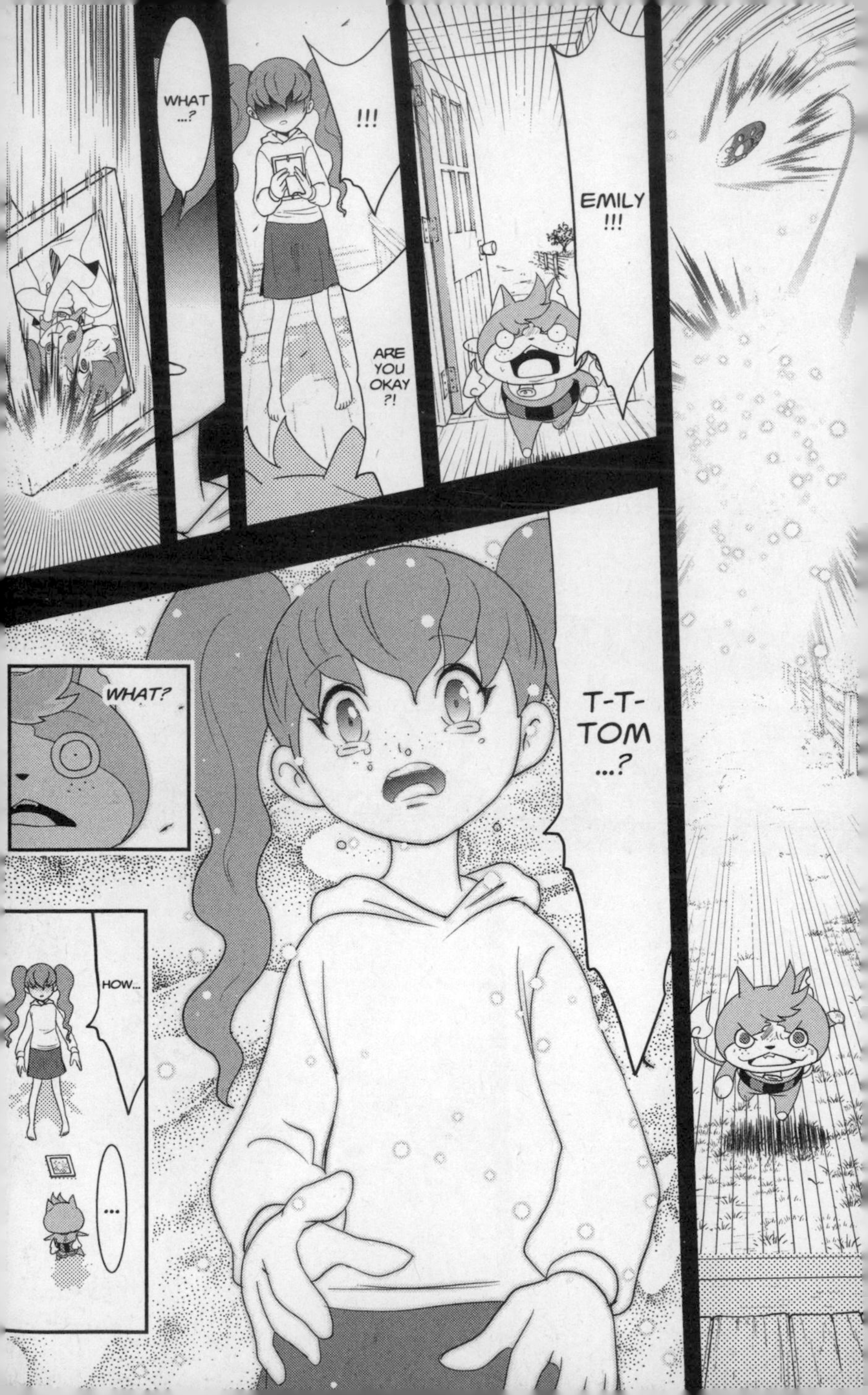
EMILY !!!
ARE YOU OKAY ?!
!!!
WHAT ...?
T-T-TOM ...?
WHAT?
HOW...
...

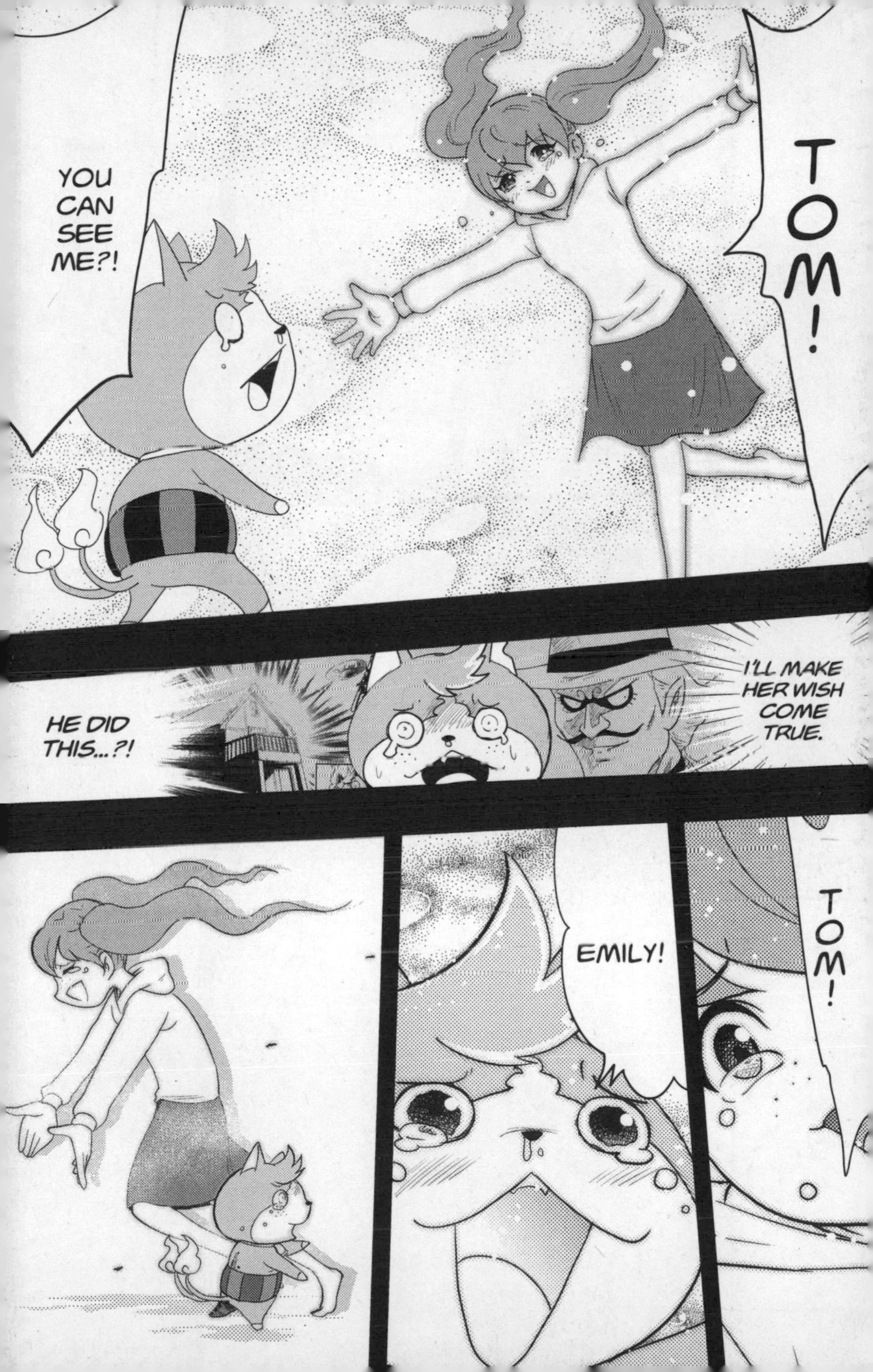
TOM!
YOU CAN SEE ME?!
I'LL MAKE HER WISH COME TRUE.
HE DID THIS...?!
TOM!
EMILY!

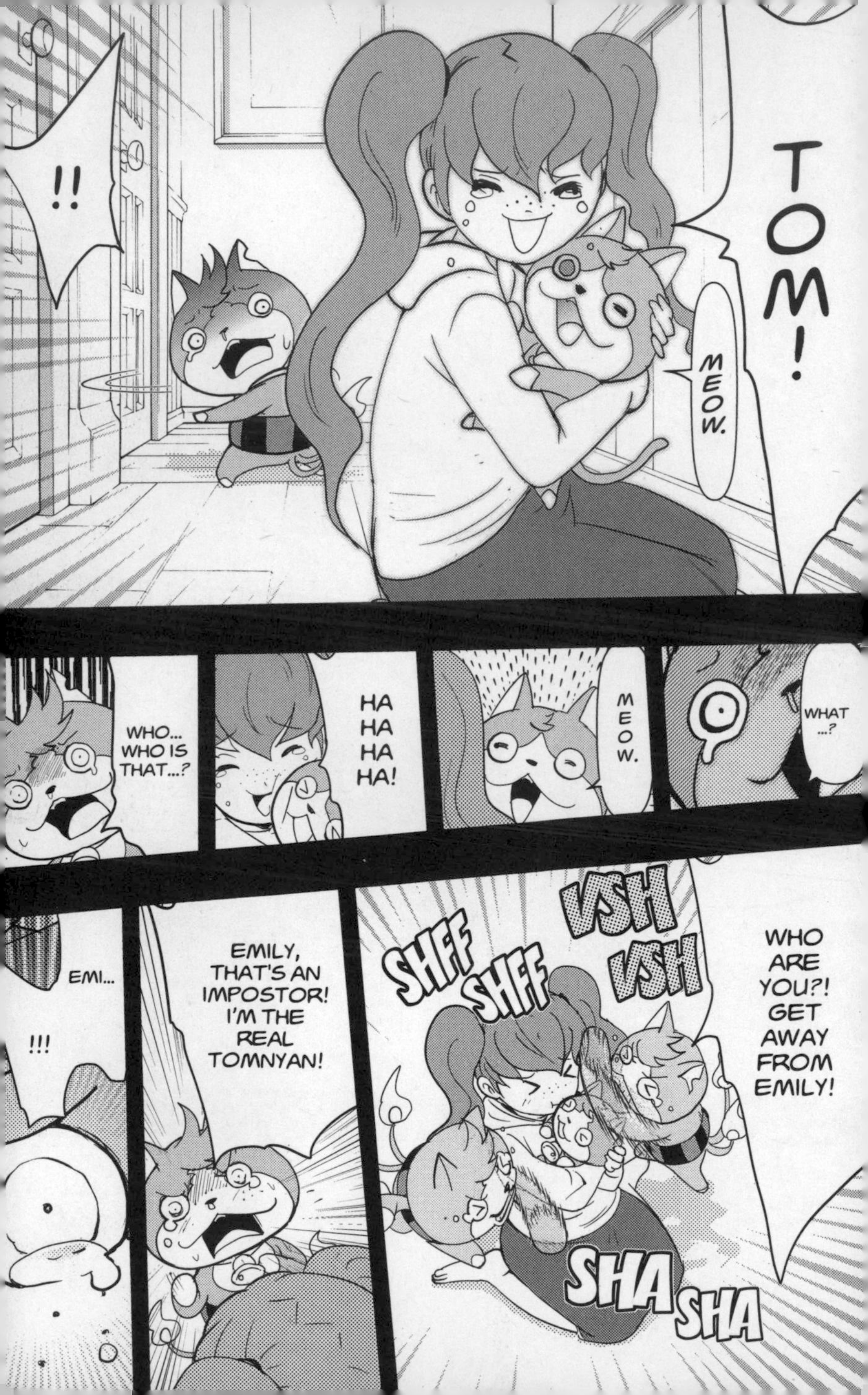
TOM!
MEOW.
!!
WHAT ...?
MEOW.
HA HA HA HA!
WHO... WHO IS THAT...?
VSH VSH
WHO ARE YOU?! GET AWAY FROM EMILY!
SHFF SHFF
SHA SHA
EMILY, THAT'S AN IMPOSTOR! I'M THE REAL TOMNYAN!
EMI...
!!!

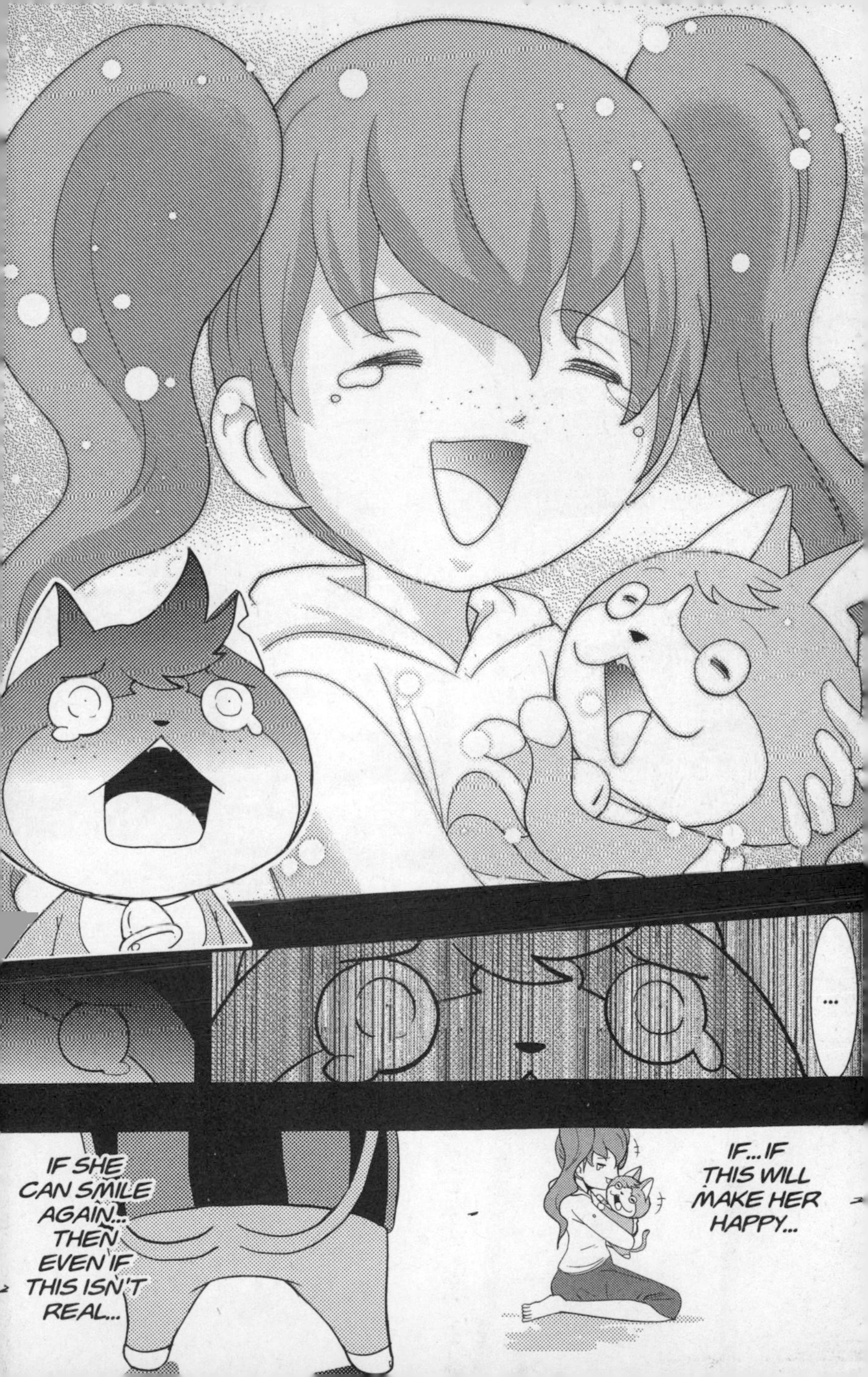
...
IF... IF THIS WILL MAKE HER HAPPY...
IF SHE CAN SMILE AGAIN... THEN EVEN IF THIS ISN'T REAL...

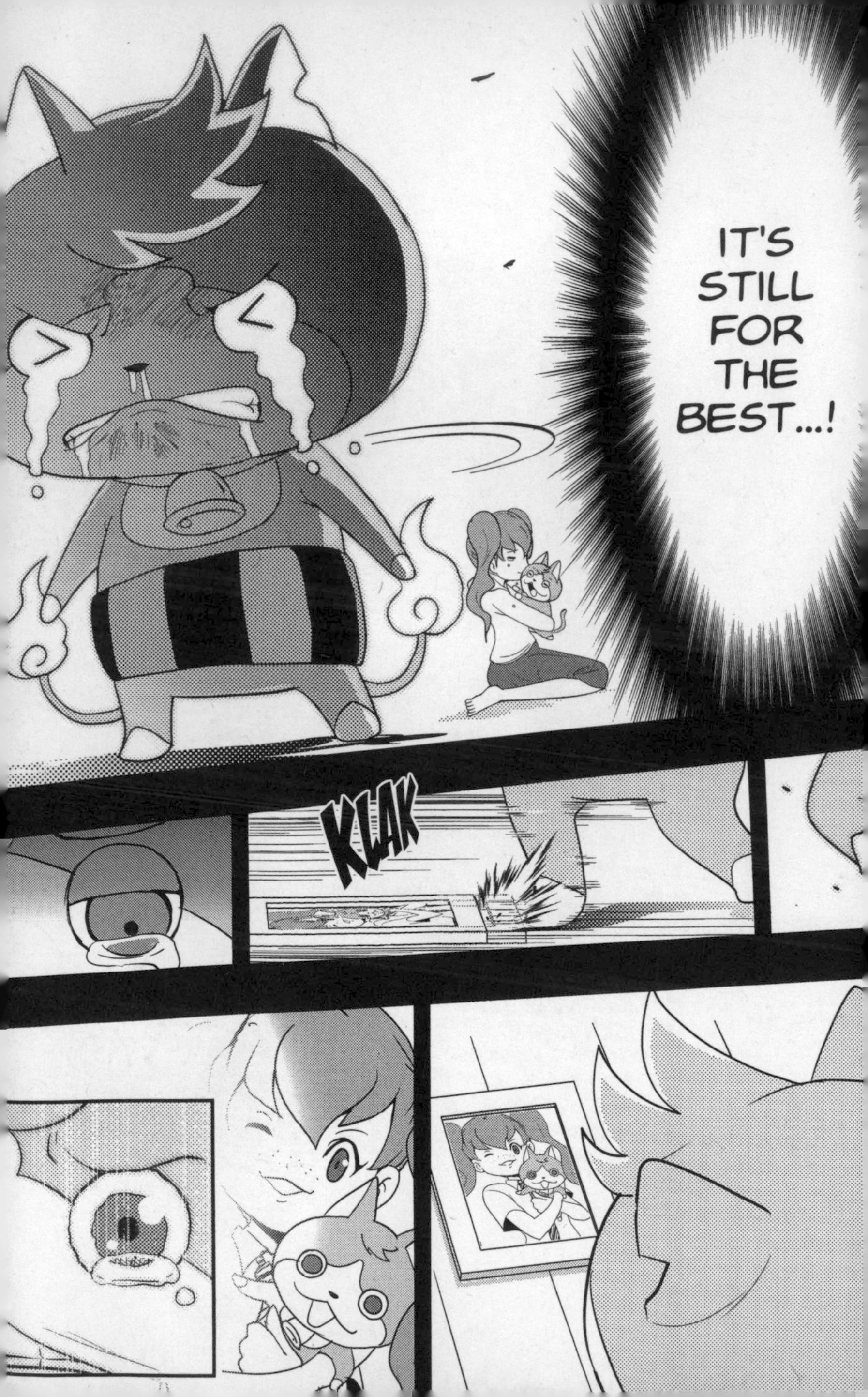
IT'S STILL FOR THE BEST...!
KLAK

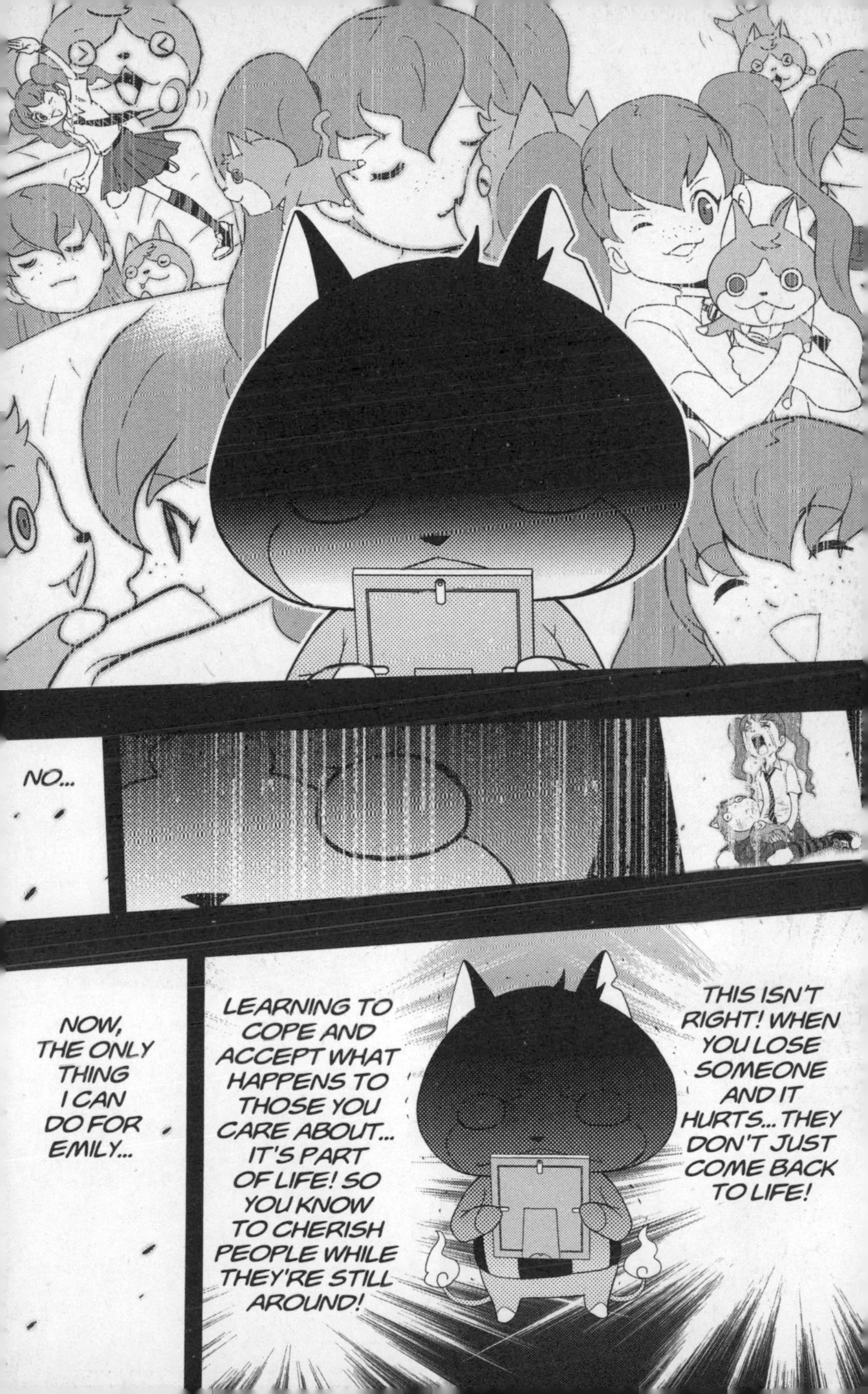
NO...
THIS ISN'T RIGHT! WHEN YOU LOSE SOMEONE AND IT HURTS... THEY DON'T JUST COME BACK TO LIFE!
LEARNING TO COPE AND ACCEPT WHAT HAPPENS TO THOSE YOU CARE ABOUT... IT'S PART OF LIFE! SO YOU KNOW TO CHERISH PEOPLE WHILE THEY'RE STILL AROUND!
NOW, THE ONLY THING I CAN DO FOR EMILY...

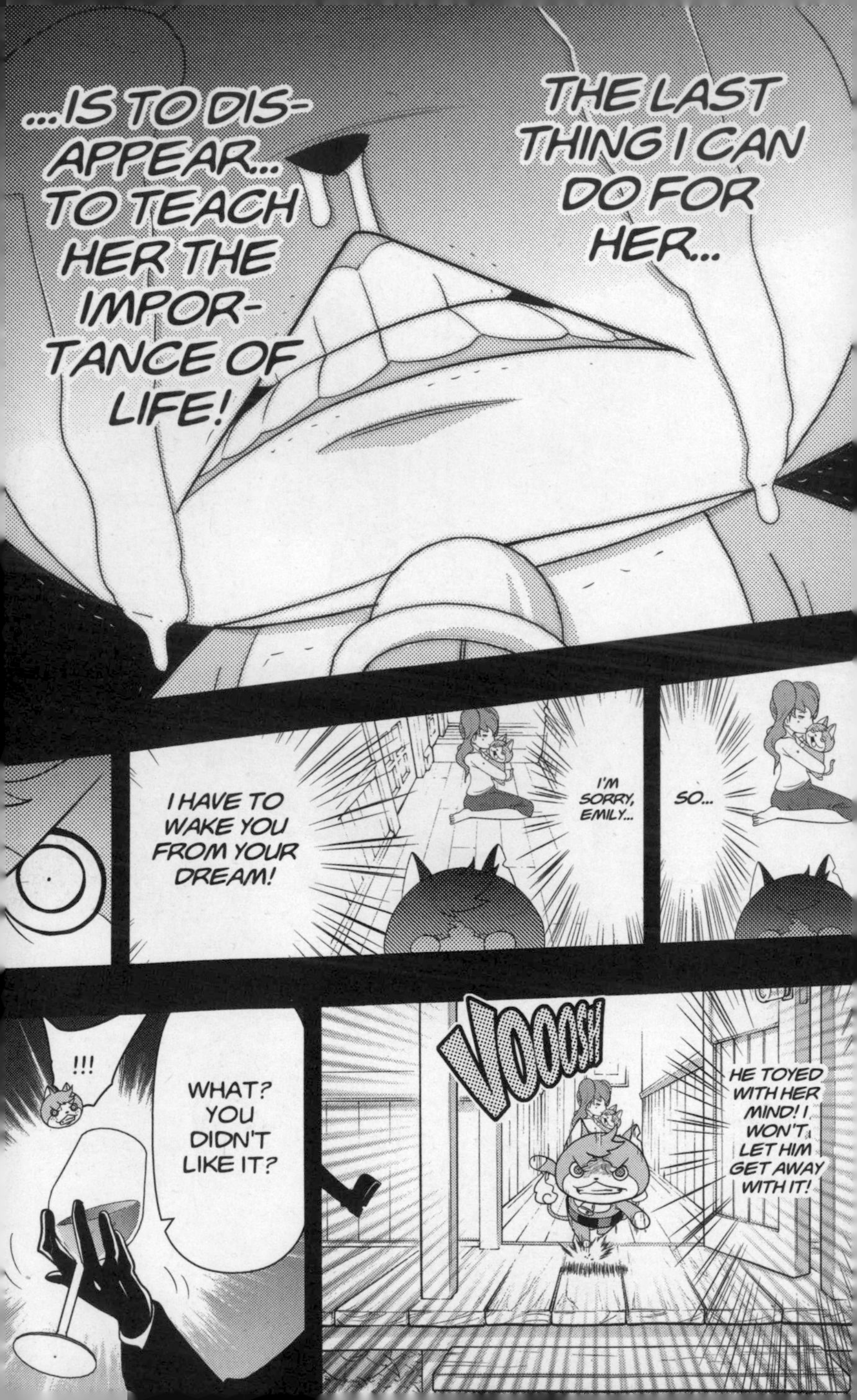
THE LAST THING I CAN DO FOR HER...
...IS TO DIS-APPEAR... TO TEACH HER THE IMPOR-TANCE OF LIFE!
SO...
I'M SORRY, EMILY...
I HAVE TO WAKE YOU FROM YOUR DREAM!
VOOOSH!
HE TOYED WITH HER MIND! I WON'T LET HIM GET AWAY WITH IT!
!!!
WHAT? YOU DIDN'T LIKE IT?

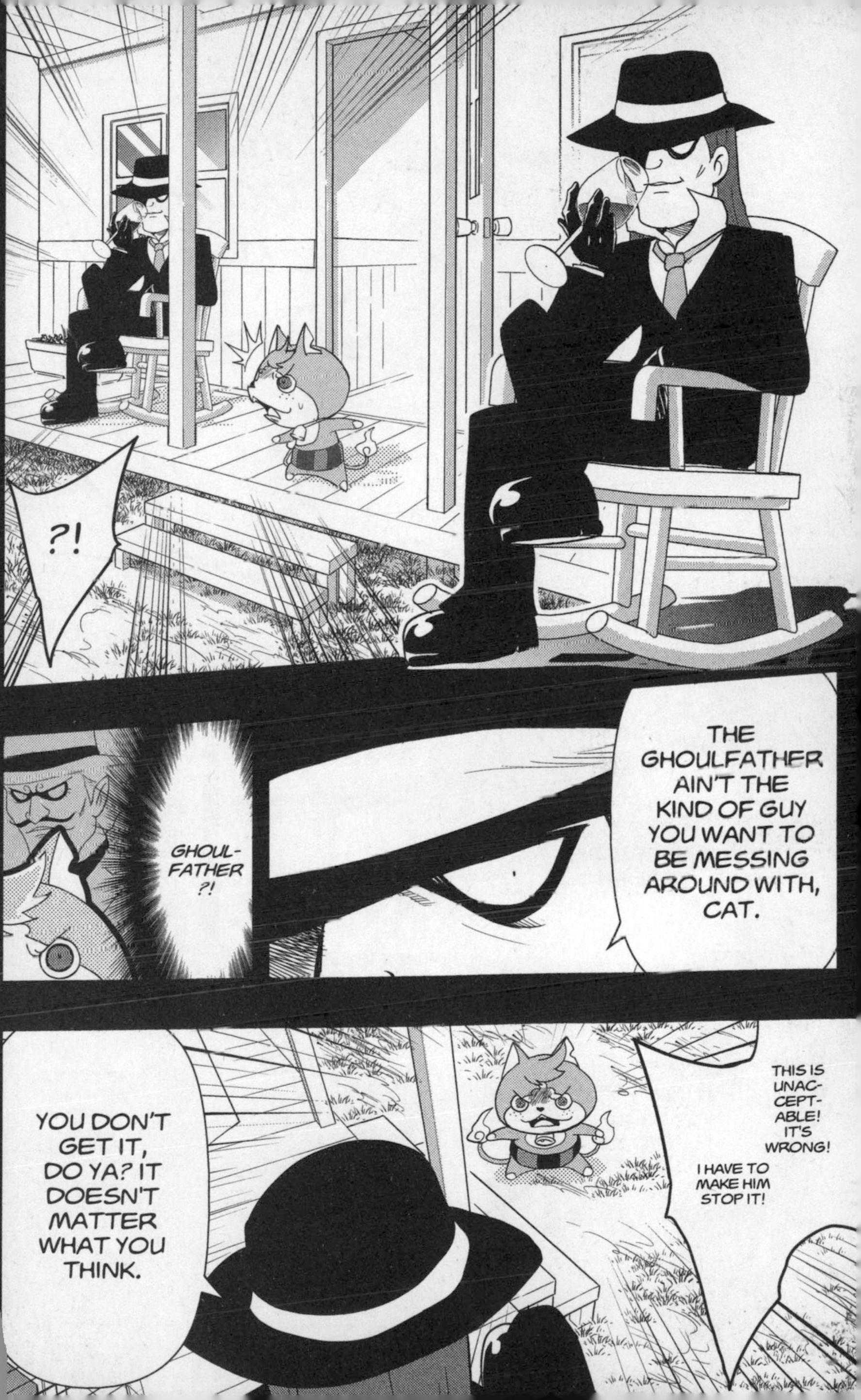
?!
THE GHOULFATHER AIN'T THE KIND OF GUY YOU WANT TO BE MESSING AROUND WITH, CAT.
GHOUL-FATHER ?!
THIS IS UNAC-CEPT-ABLE! IT'S WRONG!
I HAVE TO MAKE HIM STOP IT!
YOU DON'T GET IT, DO YA? IT DOESN'T MATTER WHAT YOU THINK.

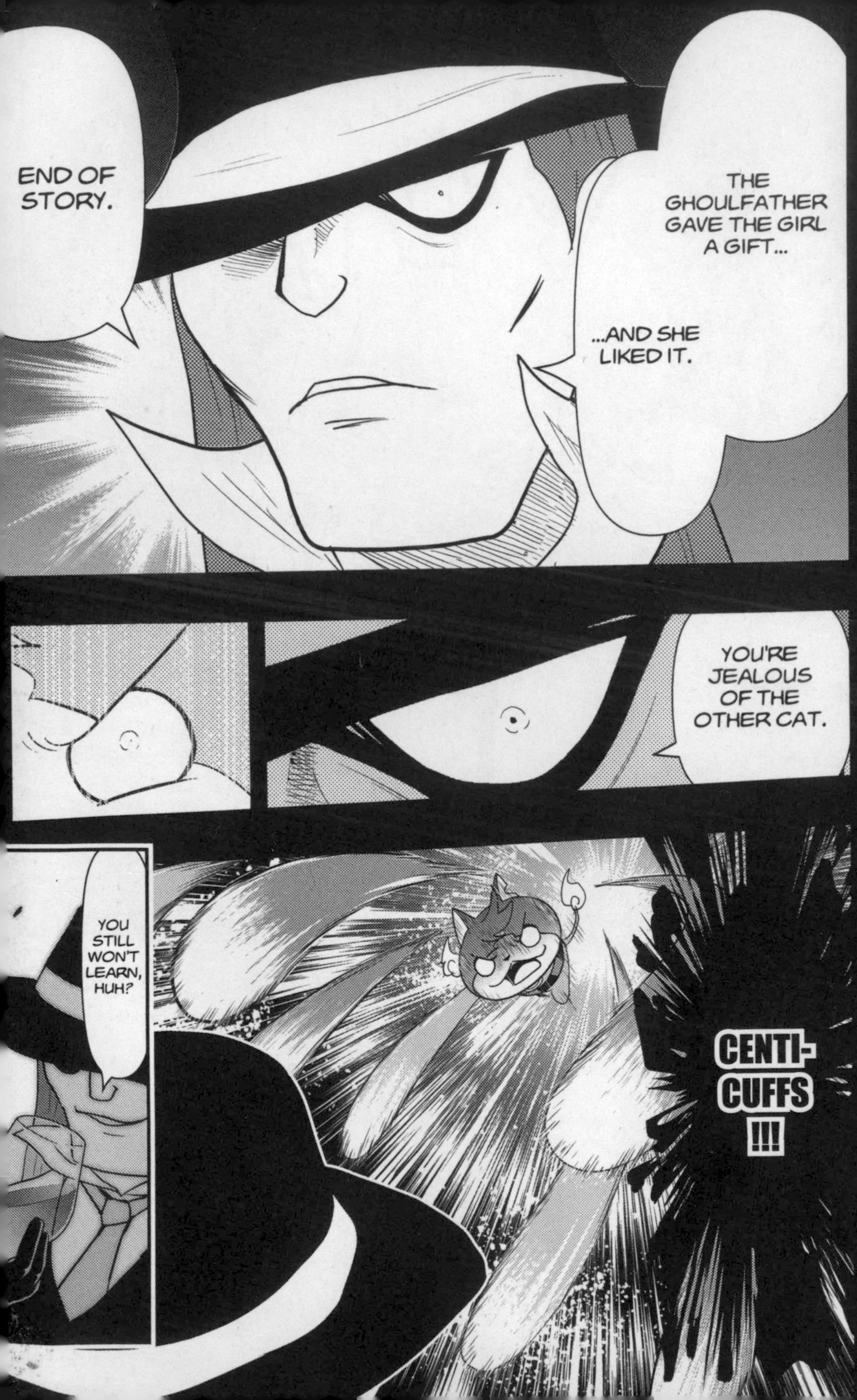
THE GHOULFATHER GAVE THE GIRL A GIFT...
...AND SHE LIKED IT.
END OF STORY.
YOU'RE JEALOUS OF THE OTHER CAT.
CENTI-CUFFS!!!
YOU STILL WON'T LEARN, HUH?

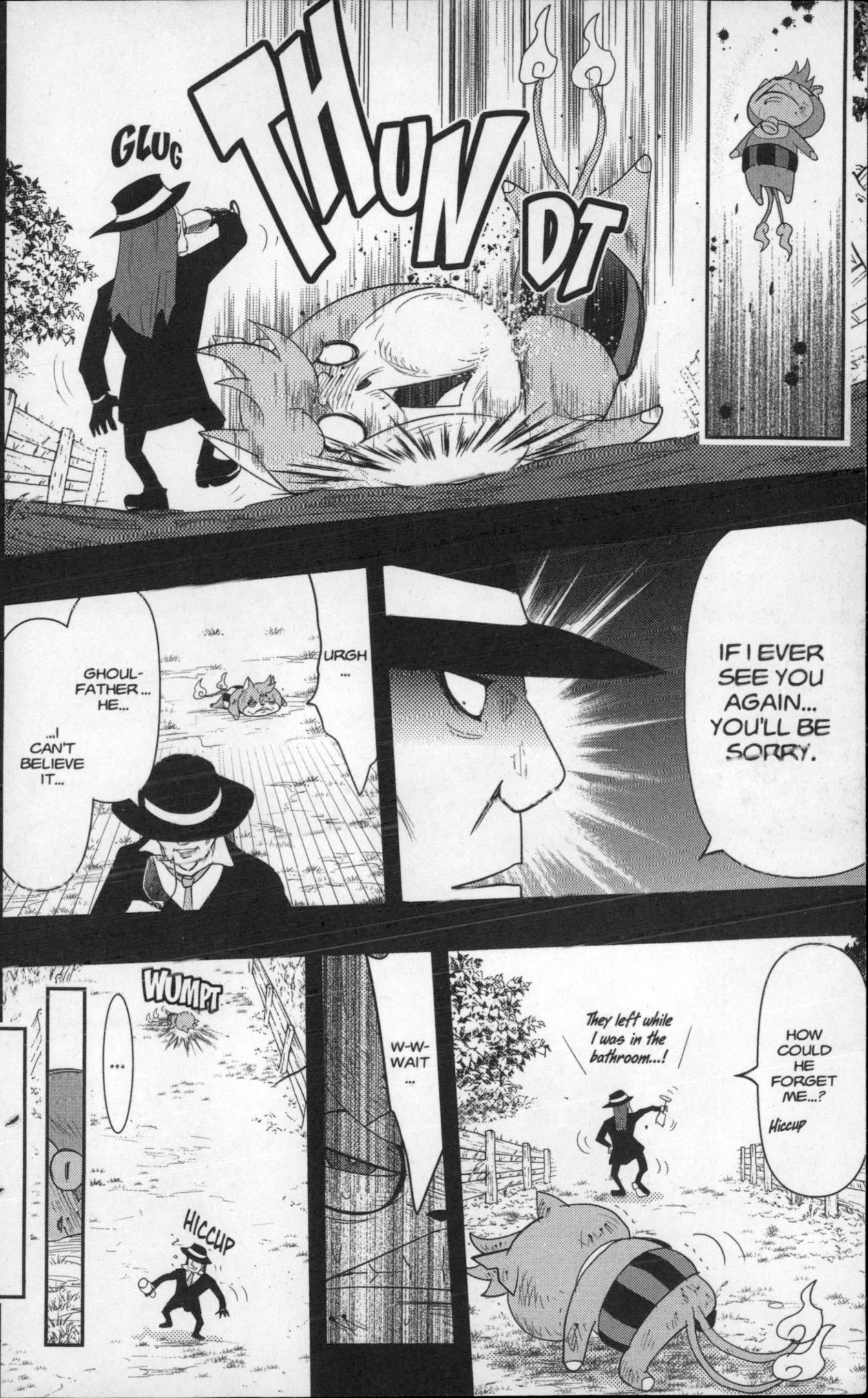
THUNDT
GLUG
IF I EVER SEE YOU AGAIN... YOU'LL BE SORRY.
URGH...
GHOUL-FATHER... HE...
...I CAN'T BELIEVE IT...
HOW COULD HE FORGET ME...?
Hiccup
They left while I was in the bathroom...!
W-W-WAIT...
WUMPT
...
HICCUP

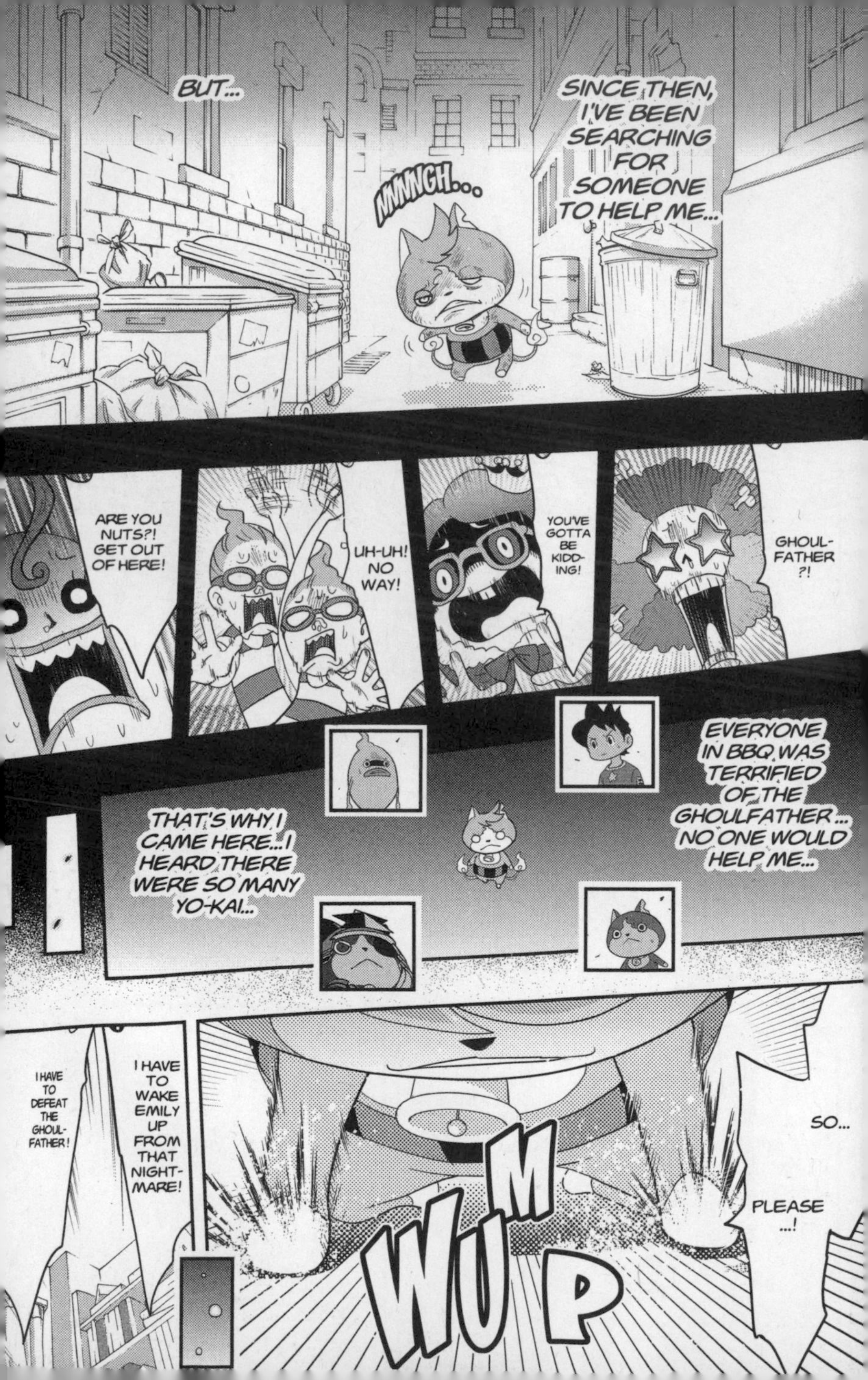
SINCE THEN, I'VE BEEN SEARCHING FOR SOMEONE TO HELP ME...
BUT...
MNNNGH...
GHOUL-FATHER?!
YOU'VE GOTTA BE KIDD-ING!
UH-UH! NO WAY!
ARE YOU NUTS?! GET OUT OF HERE!
EVERYONE IN BBQ WAS TERRIFIED OF THE GHOULFATHER... NO ONE WOULD HELP ME...
THAT'S WHY I CAME HERE...I HEARD THERE WERE SO MANY YO-KAI...
SO...
PLEASE...!
WUMP
I HAVE TO WAKE EMILY UP FROM THAT NIGHT-MARE!
I HAVE TO DEFEAT THE GHOUL-FATHER!

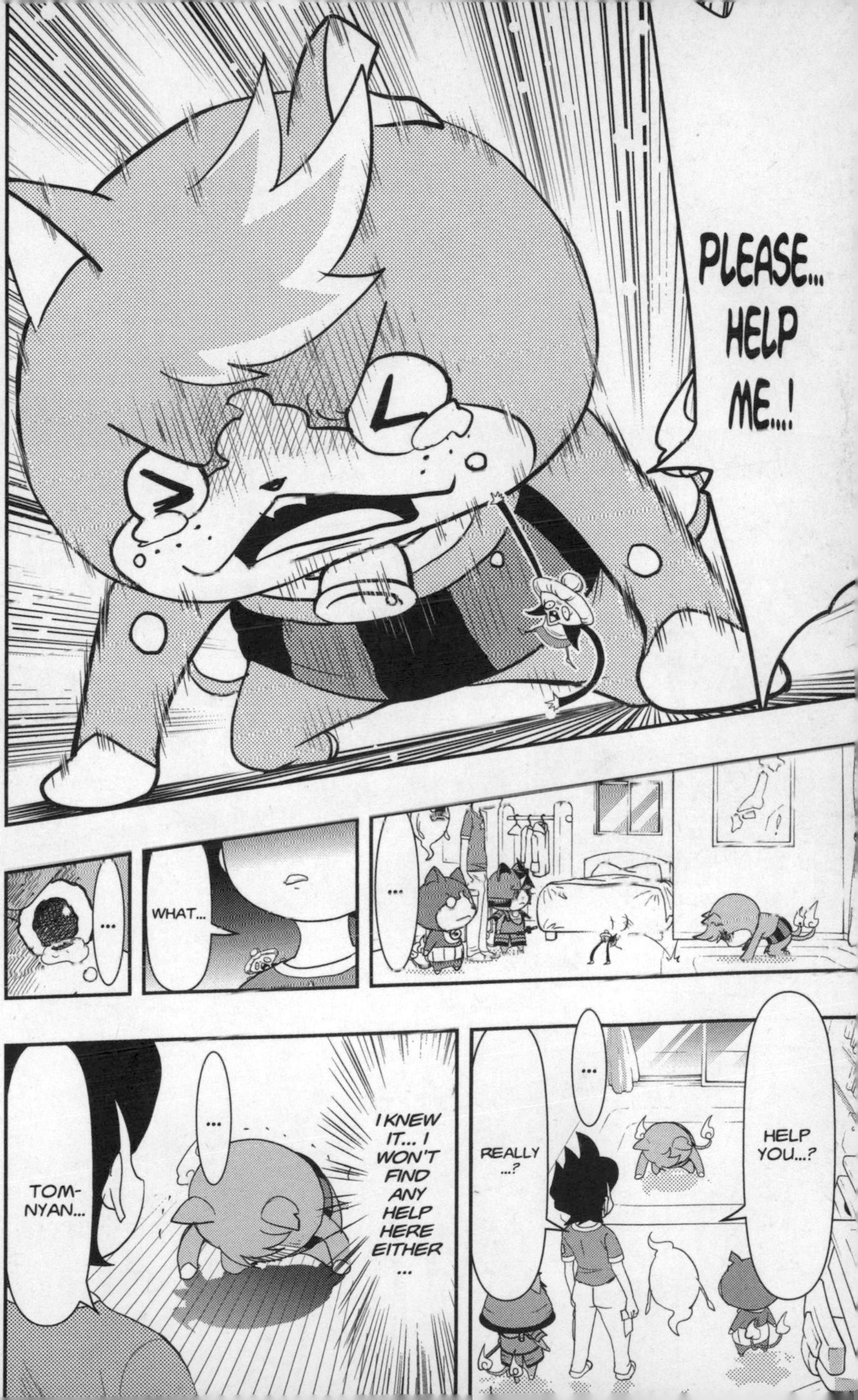
PLEASE... HELP ME...!
...
WHAT...
...
HELP YOU...?
...
REALLY ...?
I KNEW IT... I WON'T FIND ANY HELP HERE EITHER ...
...
TOM-NYAN...

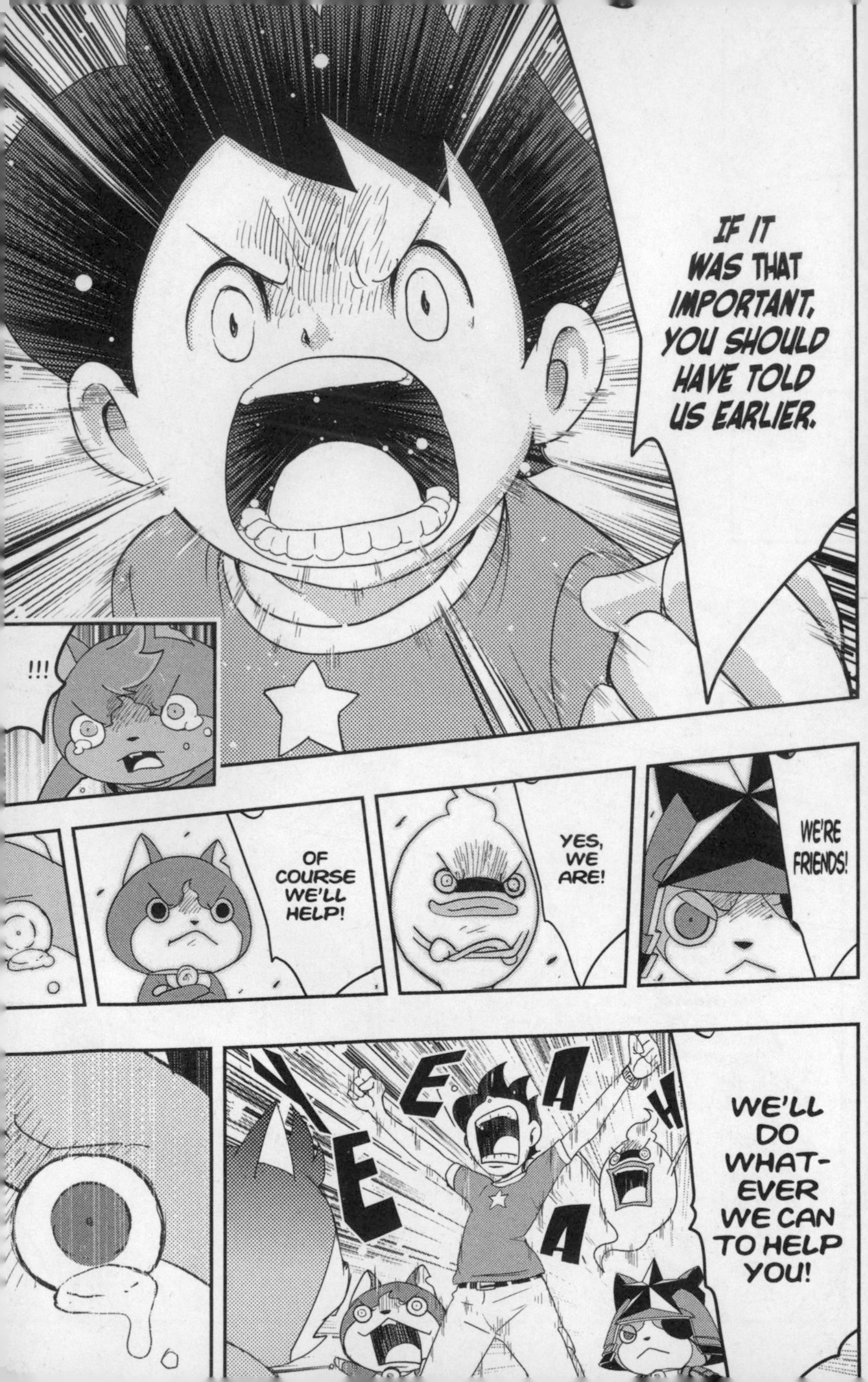
IF IT WAS THAT IMPORTANT, YOU SHOULD HAVE TOLD US EARLIER.
!!!
WE'RE FRIENDS!
YES, WE ARE!
OF COURSE WE'LL HELP!
WE'LL DO WHAT-EVER WE CAN TO HELP YOU!
YEEAAH

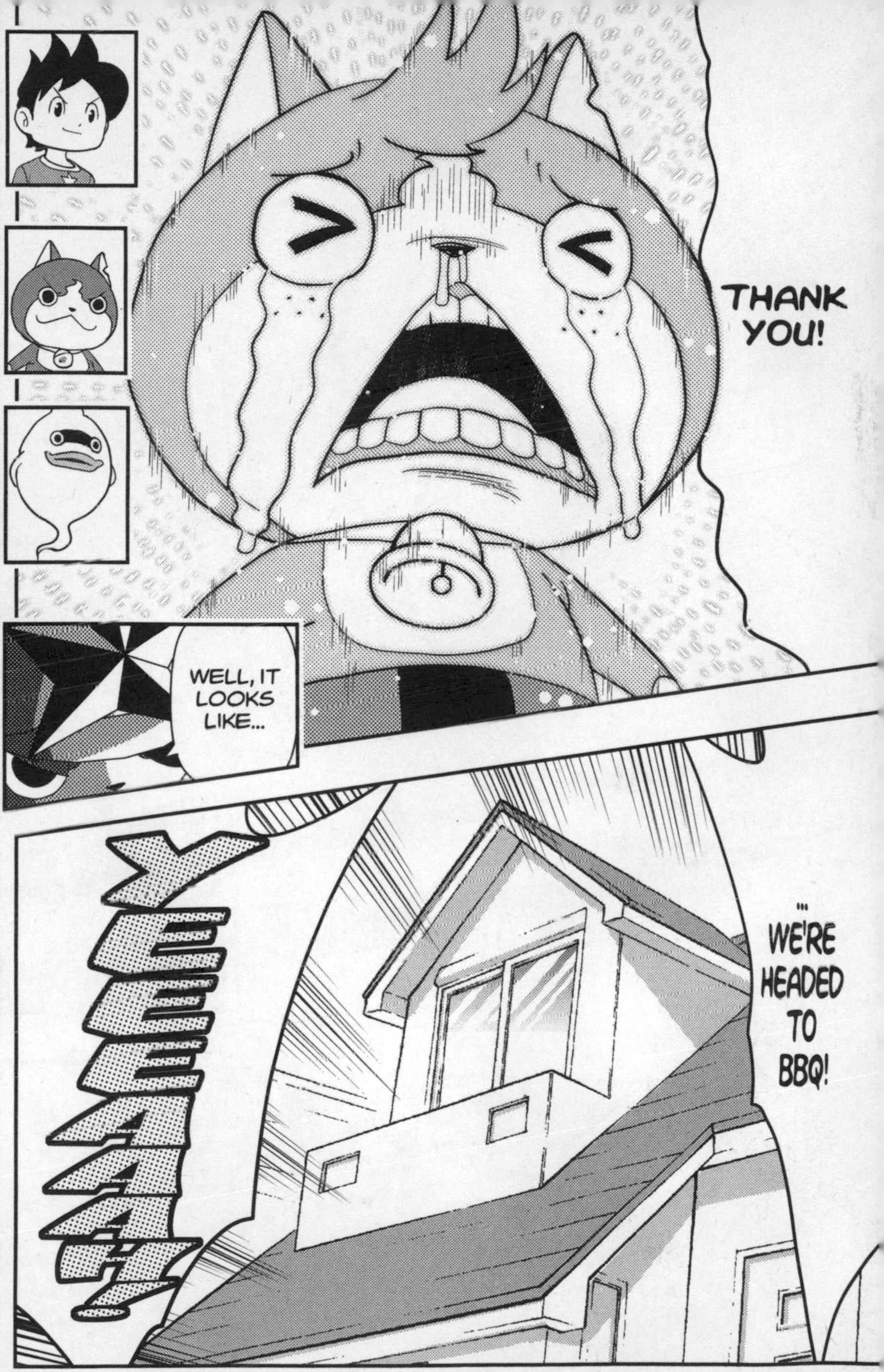
THANK YOU!
WELL, IT LOOKS LIKE...
...WE'RE HEADED TO BBQ!
YEEEAAAH!

## THE GHOULFATHER ARC ②

# THE YO-KAI WORLD FIASCO

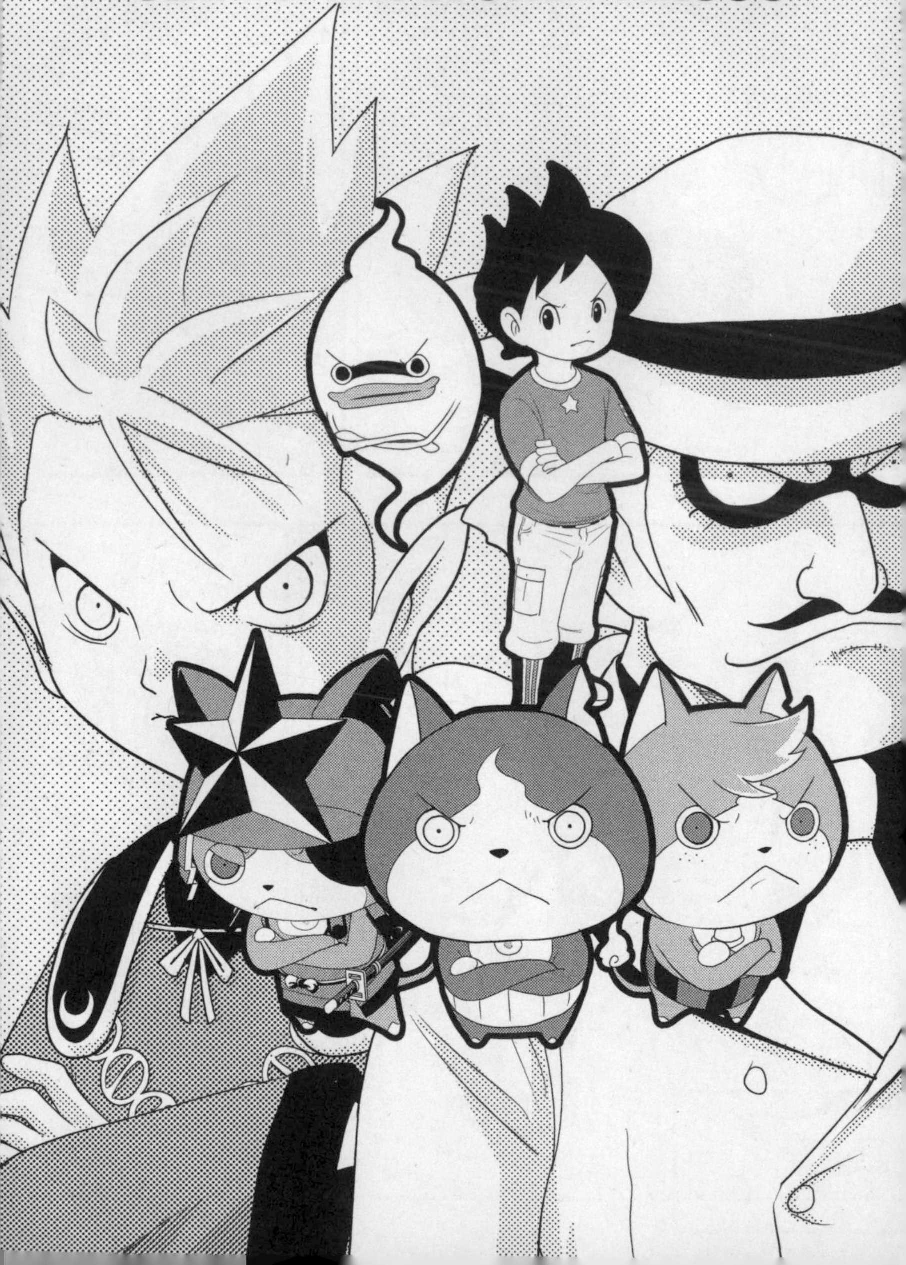

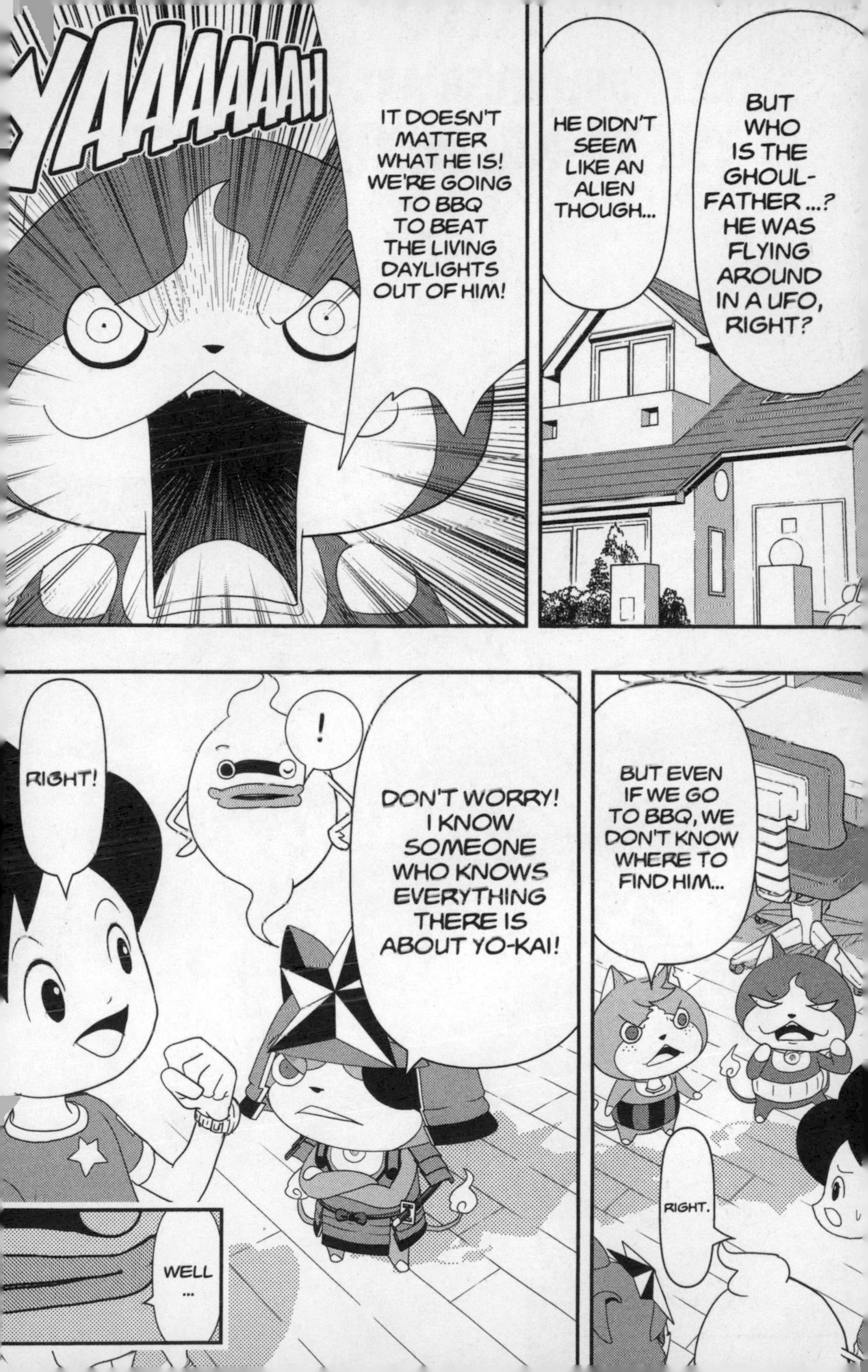
BUT WHO IS THE GHOUL-FATHER ...? HE WAS FLYING AROUND IN A UFO, RIGHT?
HE DIDN'T SEEM LIKE AN ALIEN THOUGH...
IT DOESN'T MATTER WHAT HE IS! WE'RE GOING TO BBQ TO BEAT THE LIVING DAYLIGHTS OUT OF HIM!
YAAAAAAAH
BUT EVEN IF WE GO TO BBQ, WE DON'T KNOW WHERE TO FIND HIM...
RIGHT.
DON'T WORRY! I KNOW SOMEONE WHO KNOWS EVERYTHING THERE IS ABOUT YO-KAI!
!
RIGHT!
WELL ...

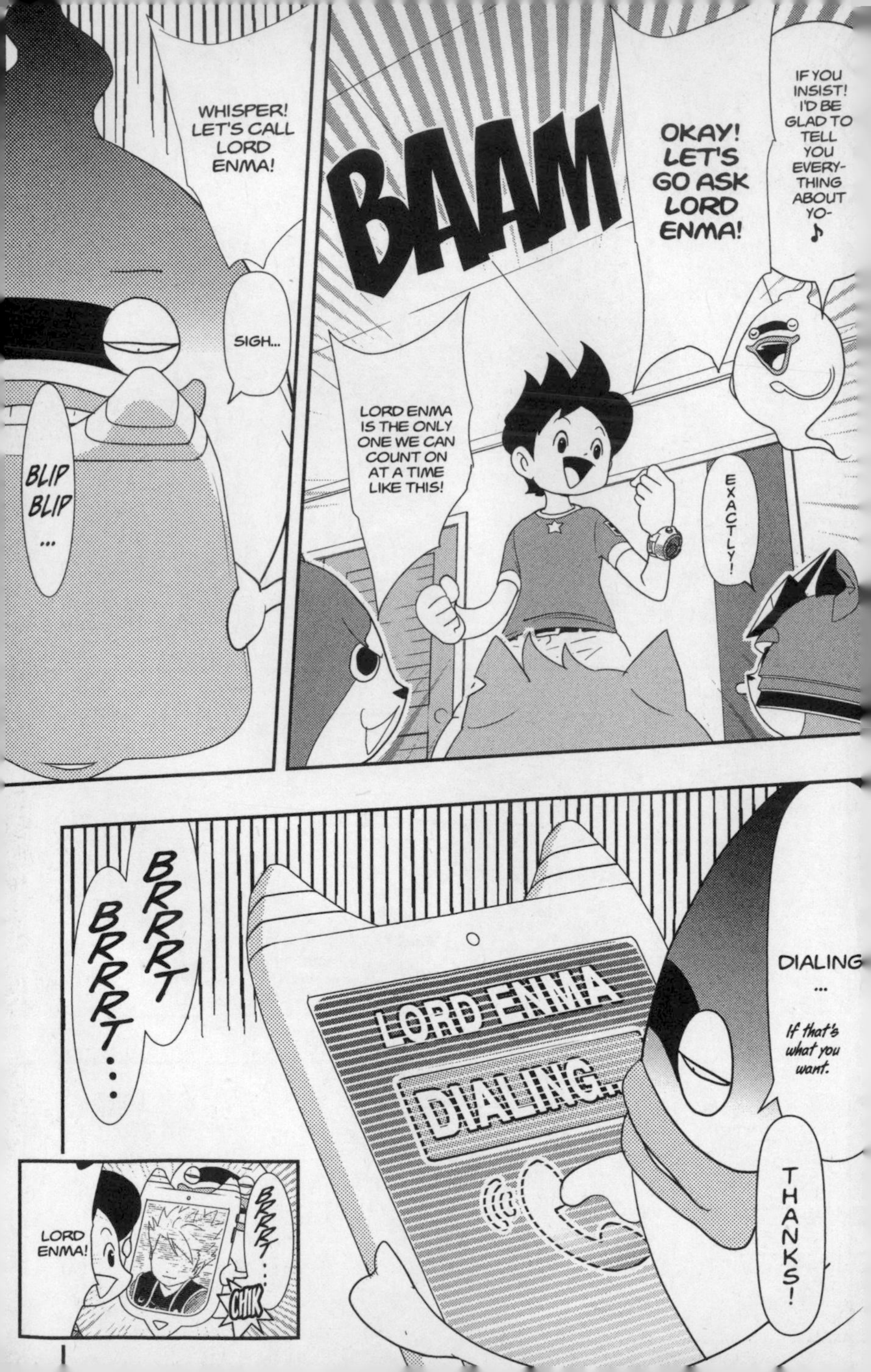
IF YOU INSIST! I'D BE GLAD TO TELL YOU EVERYTHING ABOUT YO- ♪
OKAY! LET'S GO ASK LORD ENMA!
BAAM
EXACTLY!
LORD ENMA IS THE ONLY ONE WE CAN COUNT ON AT A TIME LIKE THIS!
WHISPER! LET'S CALL LORD ENMA!
SIGH...
BLIP BLIP ...
DIALING ...
If that's what you want.
THANKS!
LORD ENMA
DIALING...
BRRRT BRRRT...
BRRRT...
CHIK
LORD ENMA!

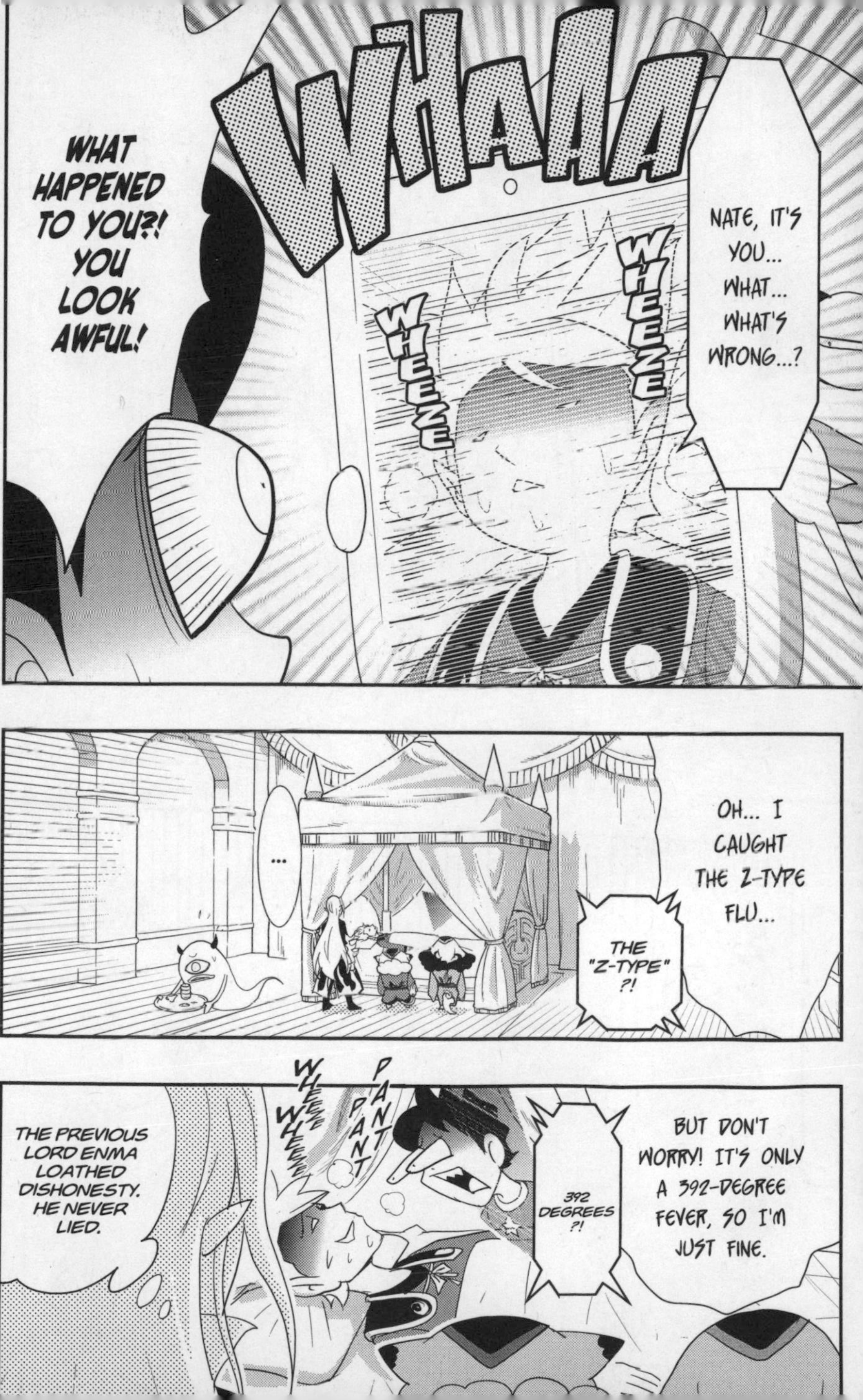
WHAAA
NATE, IT'S YOU... WHAT... WHAT'S WRONG...?
WHEEZE
WHEEZE
WHAT HAPPENED TO YOU?! YOU LOOK AWFUL!
OH... I CAUGHT THE Z-TYPE FLU...
THE "Z-TYPE" ?!
...
BUT DON'T WORRY! IT'S ONLY A 392-DEGREE FEVER, SO I'M JUST FINE.
392 DEGREES ?!
PANT PANT
WHEEZE WHEEZE
THE PREVIOUS LORD ENMA LOATHED DISHONESTY. HE NEVER LIED.

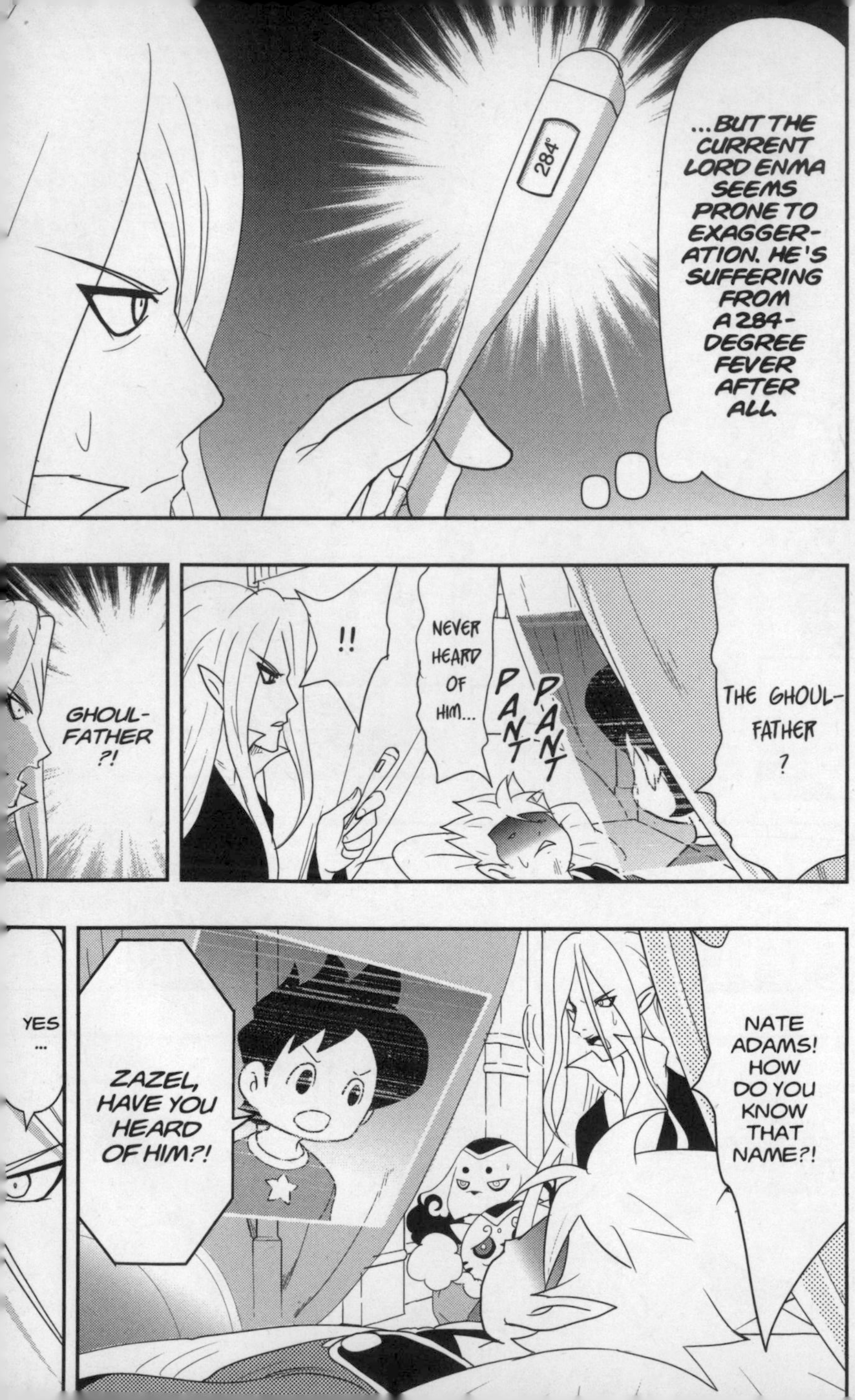

284°
...BUT THE CURRENT LORD ENMA SEEMS PRONE TO EXAGGER-ATION. HE'S SUFFERING FROM A 284-DEGREE FEVER AFTER ALL.
THE GHOUL-FATHER ?
PANT PANT
NEVER HEARD OF HIM...
!!
GHOUL-FATHER ?!
NATE ADAMS! HOW DO YOU KNOW THAT NAME?!
ZAZEL, HAVE YOU HEARD OF HIM?!
YES ...

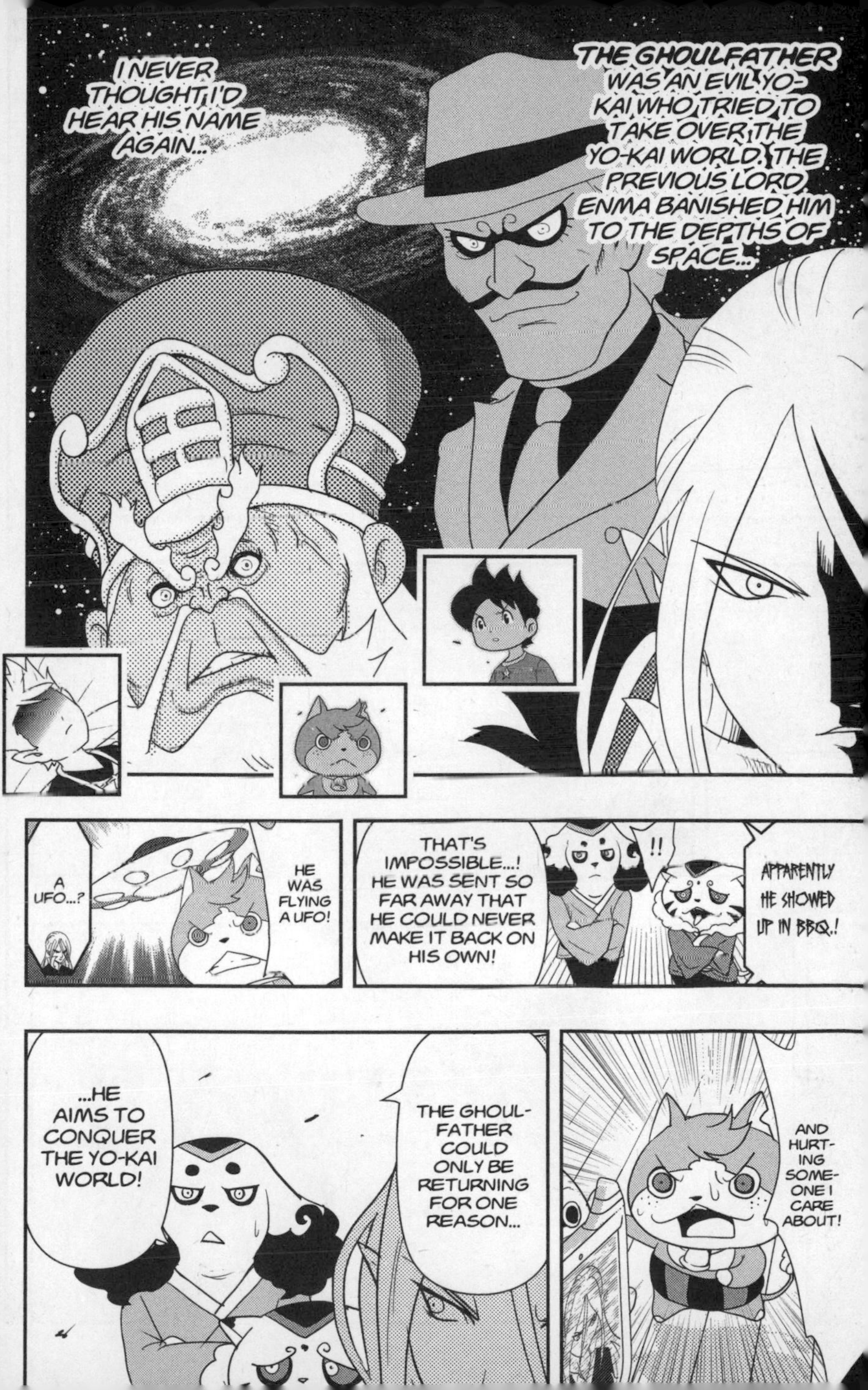
THE GHOULFATHER WAS AN EVIL YO-KAI WHO TRIED TO TAKE OVER THE YO-KAI WORLD. THE PREVIOUS LORD ENMA BANISHED HIM TO THE DEPTHS OF SPACE...
I NEVER THOUGHT I'D HEAR HIS NAME AGAIN...
APPARENTLY HE SHOWED UP IN BBQ.!
!!
THAT'S IMPOSSIBLE...! HE WAS SENT SO FAR AWAY THAT HE COULD NEVER MAKE IT BACK ON HIS OWN!
HE WAS FLYING A UFO!
A UFO...?
AND HURTING SOMEONE I CARE ABOUT!
THE GHOUL-FATHER COULD ONLY BE RETURNING FOR ONE REASON...
...HE AIMS TO CONQUER THE YO-KAI WORLD!

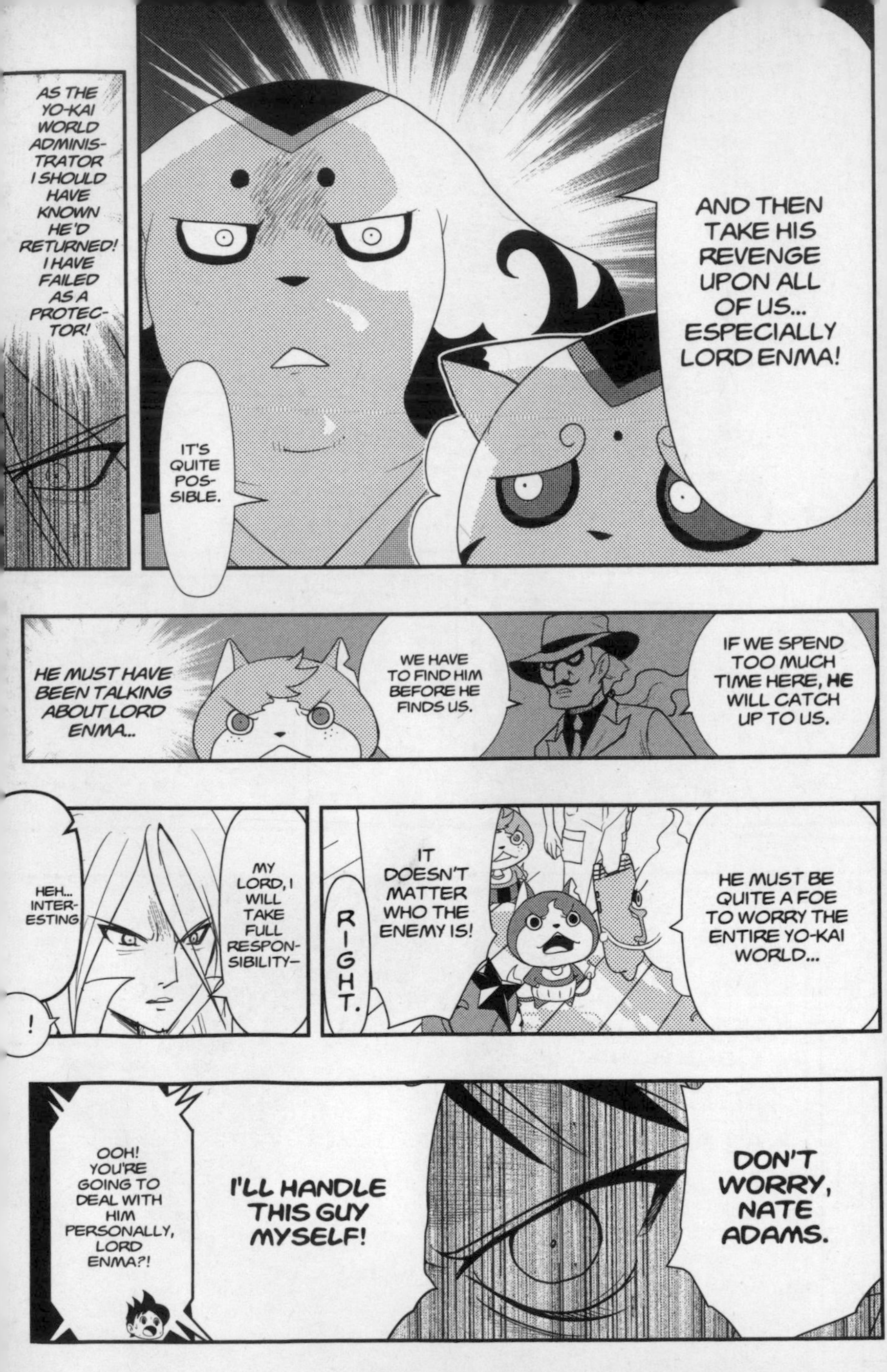
AND THEN TAKE HIS REVENGE UPON ALL OF US... ESPECIALLY LORD ENMA!
IT'S QUITE POSSIBLE.
AS THE YO-KAI WORLD ADMINISTRATOR I SHOULD HAVE KNOWN HE'D RETURNED! I HAVE FAILED AS A PROTECTOR!
IF WE SPEND TOO MUCH TIME HERE, HE WILL CATCH UP TO US.
WE HAVE TO FIND HIM BEFORE HE FINDS US.
HE MUST HAVE BEEN TALKING ABOUT LORD ENMA...
HE MUST BE QUITE A FOE TO WORRY THE ENTIRE YO-KAI WORLD...
IT DOESN'T MATTER WHO THE ENEMY IS!
RIGHT.
MY LORD, I WILL TAKE FULL RESPONSIBILITY–
HEH... INTERESTING
!
DON'T WORRY, NATE ADAMS.
I'LL HANDLE THIS GUY MYSELF!
OOH! YOU'RE GOING TO DEAL WITH HIM PERSONALLY, LORD ENMA?!

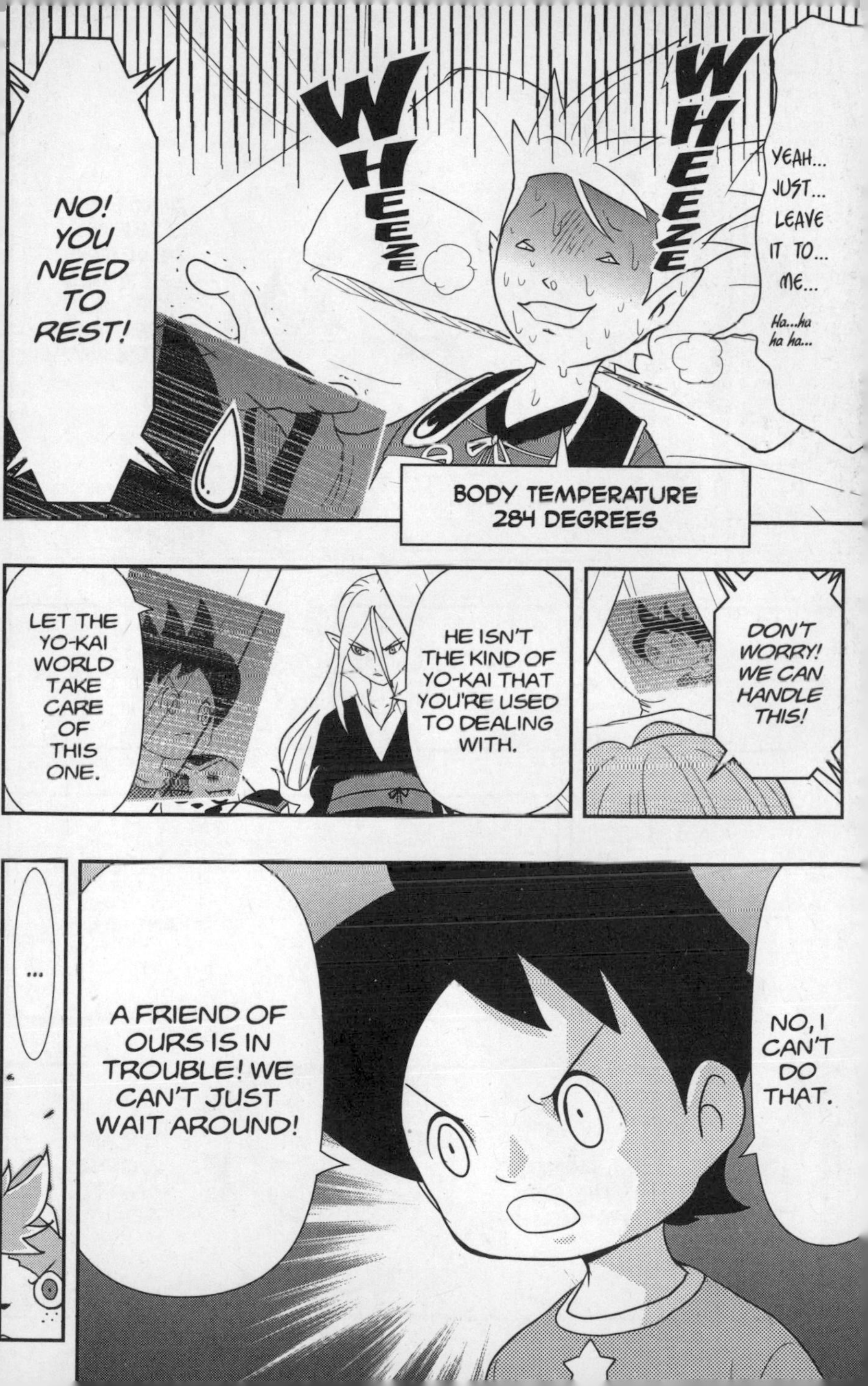
YEAH... JUST... LEAVE IT TO... ME...
Ha...ha ha ha...
WHEEZE
WHEEZE
NO! YOU NEED TO REST!
BODY TEMPERATURE 284 DEGREES
DON'T WORRY! WE CAN HANDLE THIS!
HE ISN'T THE KIND OF YO-KAI THAT YOU'RE USED TO DEALING WITH.
LET THE YO-KAI WORLD TAKE CARE OF THIS ONE.
NO, I CAN'T DO THAT.
A FRIEND OF OURS IS IN TROUBLE! WE CAN'T JUST WAIT AROUND!
...

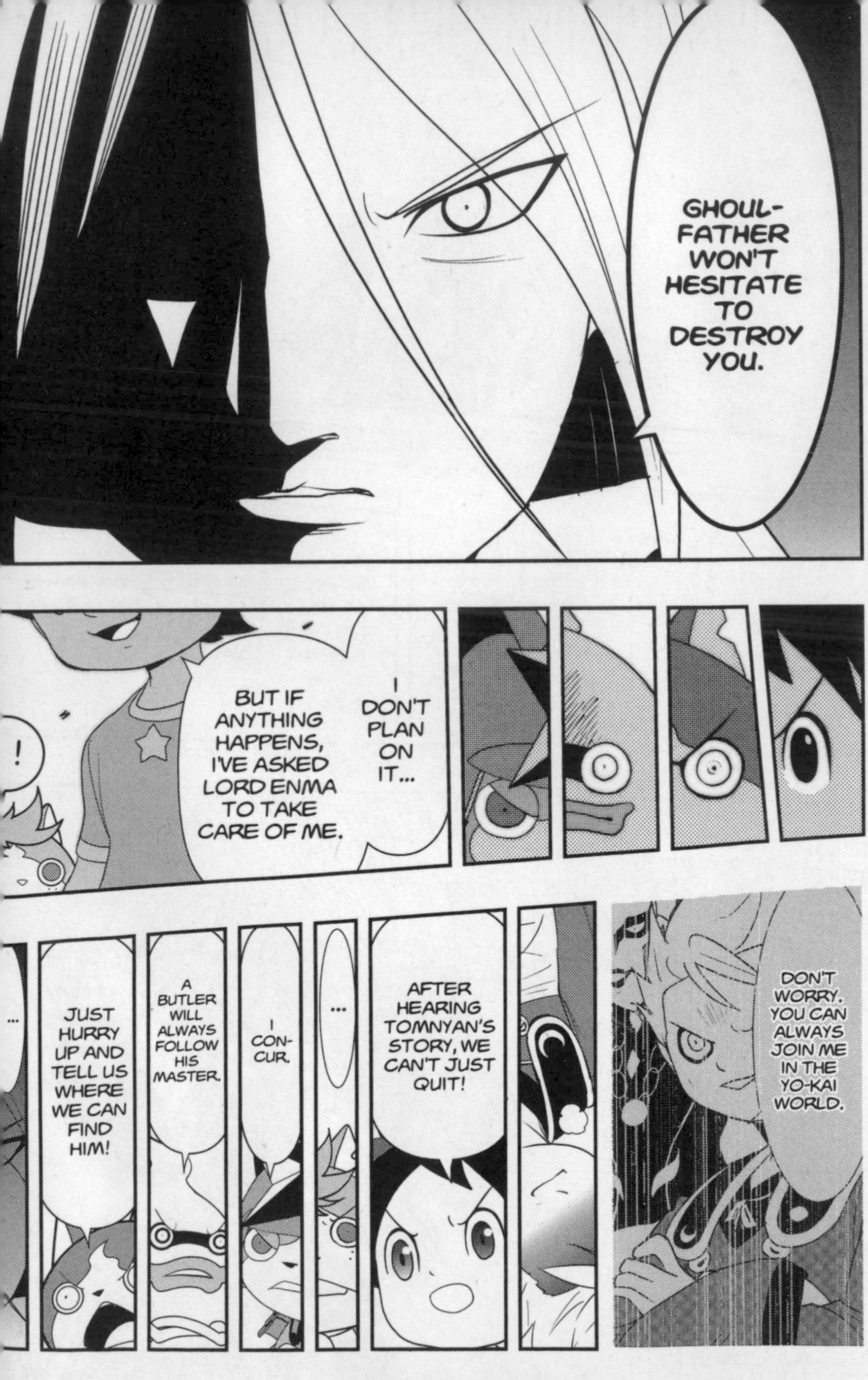
GHOUL-FATHER WON'T HESITATE TO DESTROY YOU.
I DON'T PLAN ON IT...
BUT IF ANYTHING HAPPENS, I'VE ASKED LORD ENMA TO TAKE CARE OF ME.
!
DON'T WORRY. YOU CAN ALWAYS JOIN ME IN THE YO-KAI WORLD.
AFTER HEARING TOMNYAN'S STORY, WE CAN'T JUST QUIT!
...
I CON-CUR.
A BUTLER WILL ALWAYS FOLLOW HIS MASTER.
JUST HURRY UP AND TELL US WHERE WE CAN FIND HIM!
...

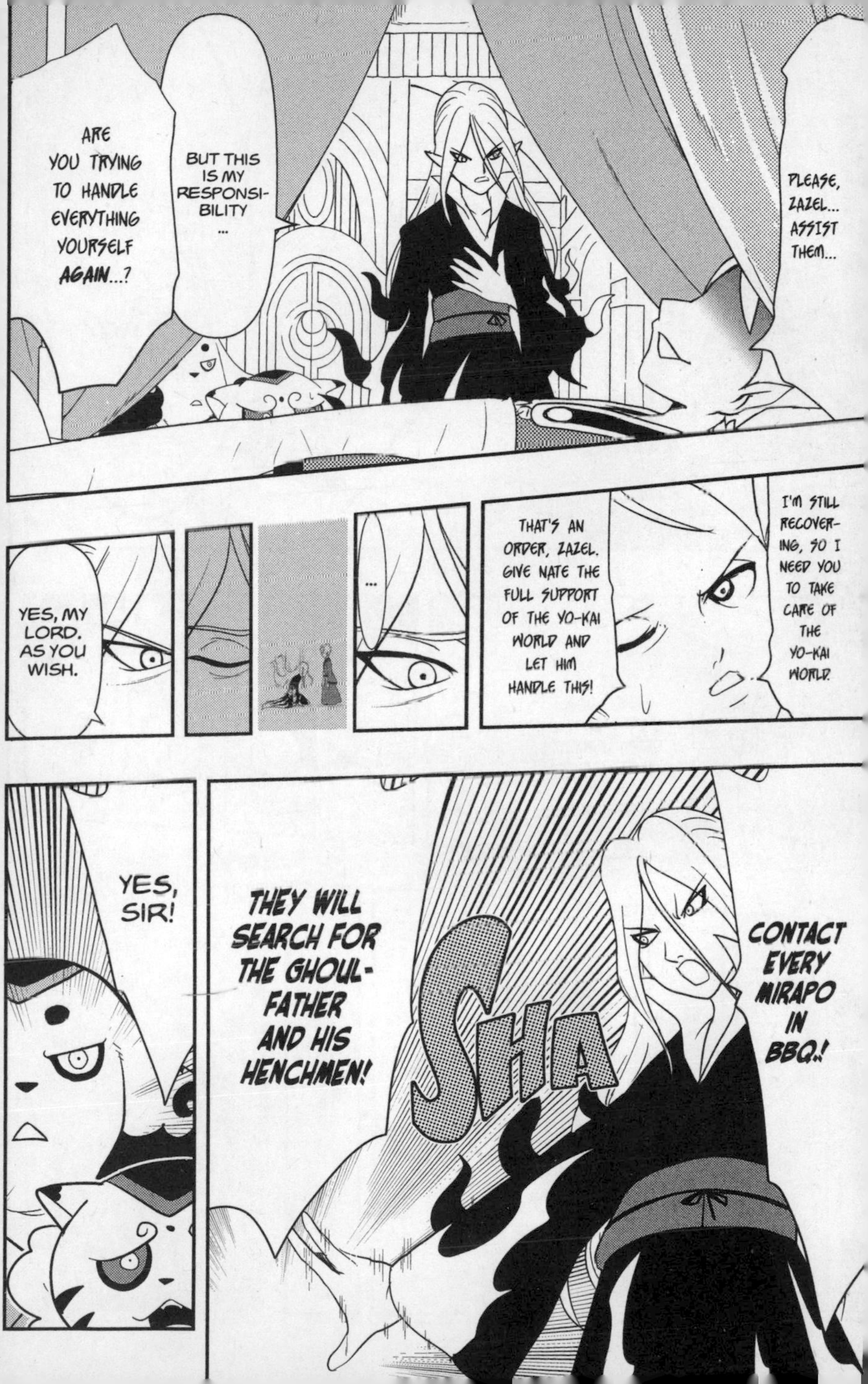
PLEASE, ZAZEL... ASSIST THEM...
BUT THIS IS MY RESPONSIBILITY ...
ARE YOU TRYING TO HANDLE EVERYTHING YOURSELF AGAIN...?
I'M STILL RECOVERING, SO I NEED YOU TO TAKE CARE OF THE YO-KAI WORLD.
THAT'S AN ORDER, ZAZEL. GIVE NATE THE FULL SUPPORT OF THE YO-KAI WORLD AND LET HIM HANDLE THIS!
...
YES, MY LORD. AS YOU WISH.
CONTACT EVERY MIRAPO IN BBQ.!
SHA
THEY WILL SEARCH FOR THE GHOUL-FATHER AND HIS HENCHMEN!
YES, SIR!

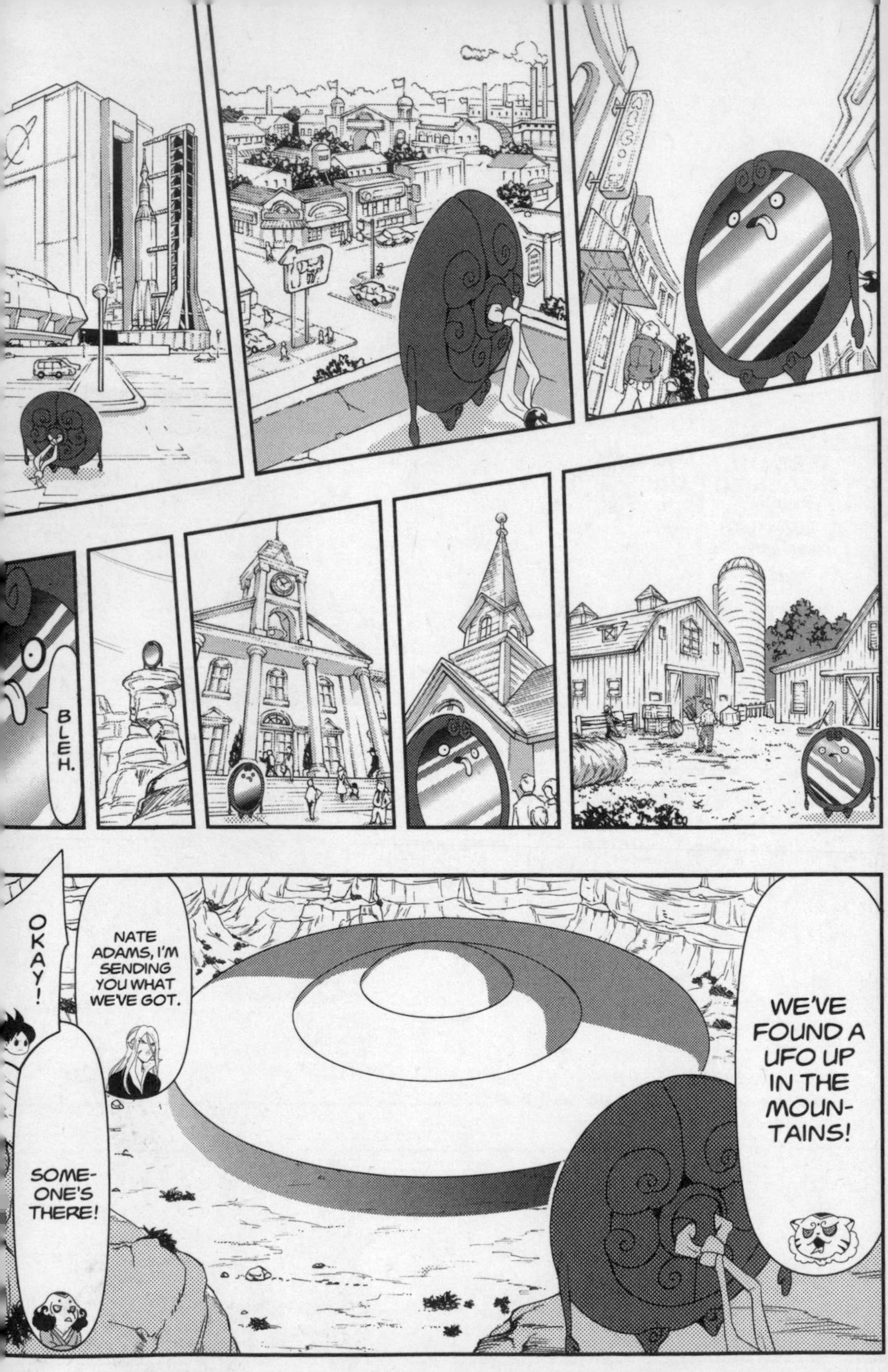
BLEH.
WE'VE FOUND A UFO UP IN THE MOUN-TAINS!
NATE ADAMS, I'M SENDING YOU WHAT WE'VE GOT.
OKAY!
SOME-ONE'S THERE!

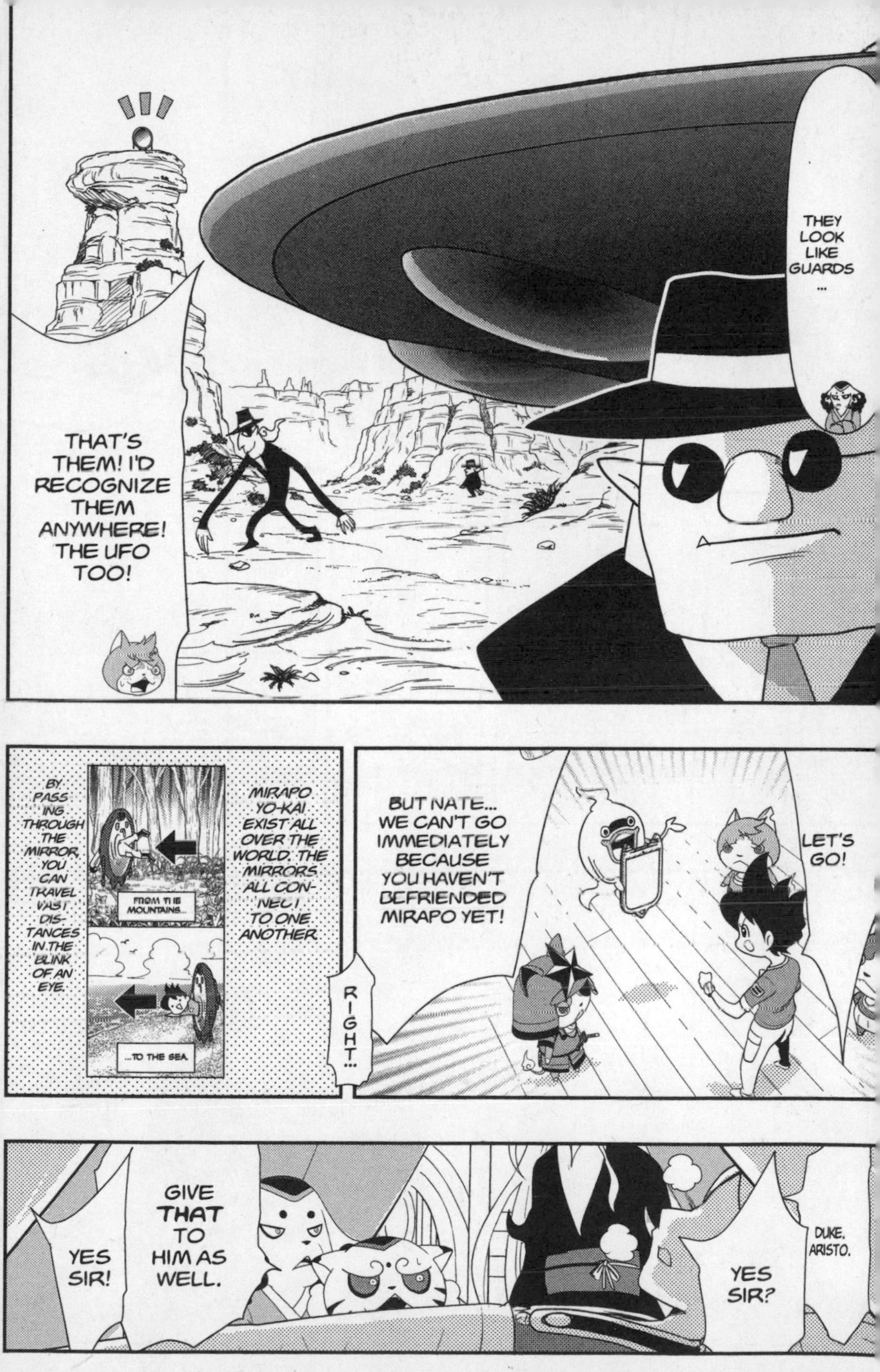
THEY LOOK LIKE GUARDS...
THAT'S THEM! I'D RECOGNIZE THEM ANYWHERE! THE UFO TOO!
LET'S GO!
BUT NATE... WE CAN'T GO IMMEDIATELY BECAUSE YOU HAVEN'T BEFRIENDED MIRAPO YET!
RIGHT...
MIRAPO YO-KAI EXIST ALL OVER THE WORLD. THE MIRRORS ALL CONNECT TO ONE ANOTHER.
BY PASSING THROUGH THE MIRROR, YOU CAN TRAVEL VAST DISTANCES IN THE BLINK OF AN EYE.
FROM THE MOUNTAINS...
...TO THE SEA
DUKE. ARISTO.
YES SIR?
GIVE THAT TO HIM AS WELL.
YES SIR!

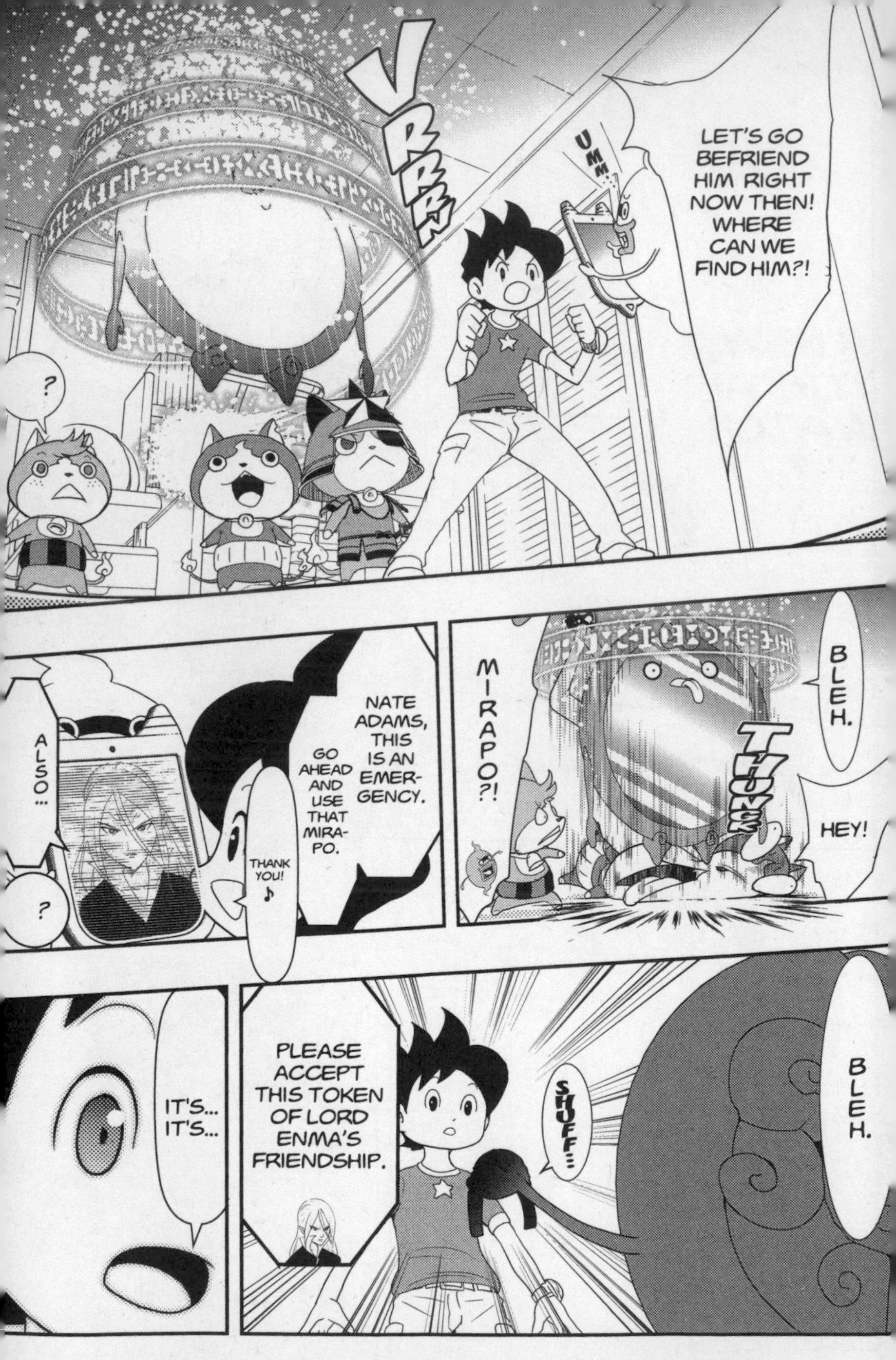
LET'S GO BEFRIEND HIM RIGHT NOW THEN! WHERE CAN WE FIND HIM?!
UMM...
VRRRN
?
BLEH.
MIRAPO?!
THUNG
HEY!
NATE ADAMS, THIS IS AN EMERGENCY.
GO AHEAD AND USE THAT MIRAPO.
THANK YOU! ♪
ALSO...
?
BLEH.
SHUFF...
PLEASE ACCEPT THIS TOKEN OF LORD ENMA'S FRIENDSHIP.
IT'S... IT'S...

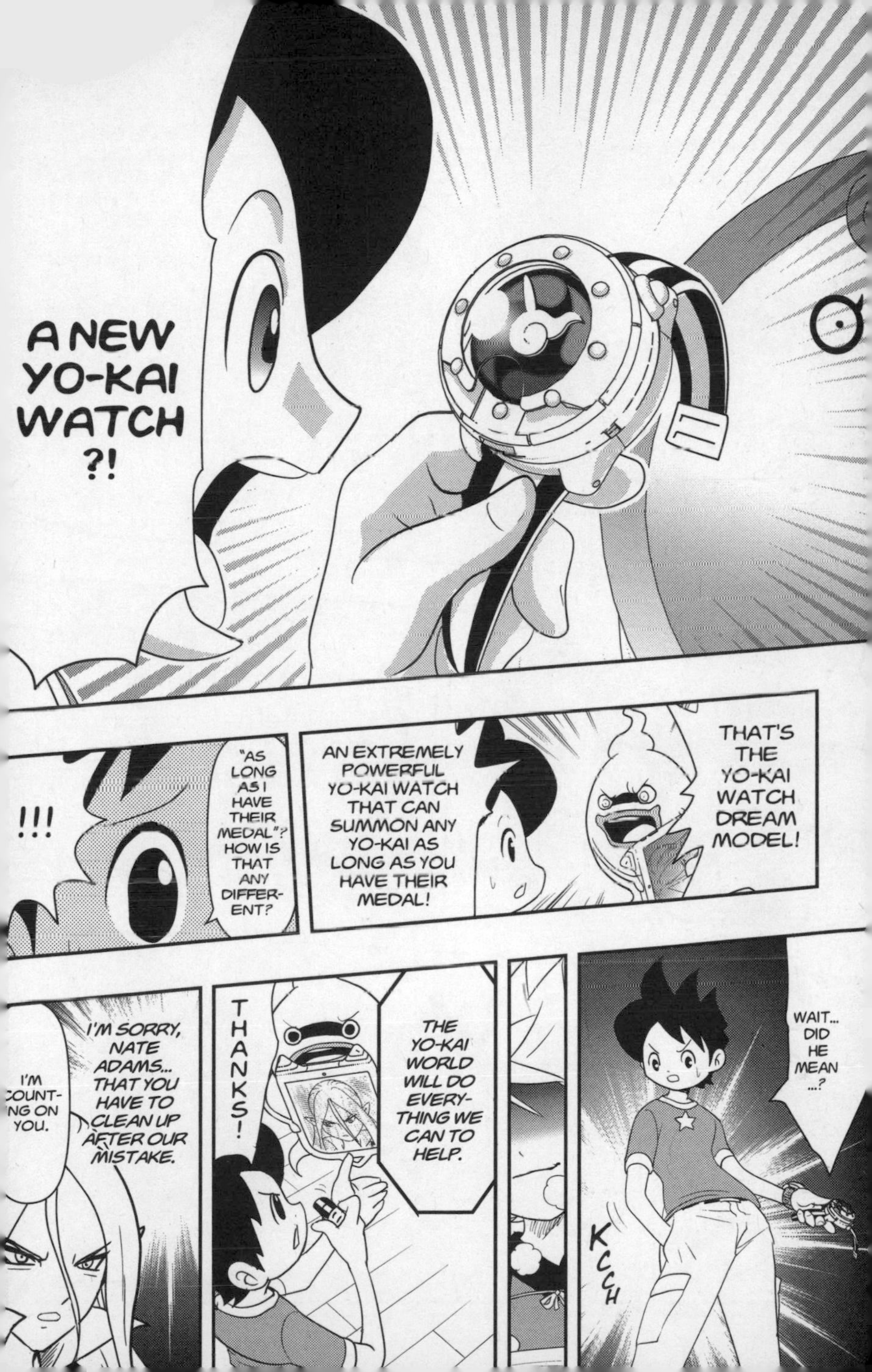
A NEW YO-KAI WATCH ?!
THAT'S THE YO-KAI WATCH DREAM MODEL!
AN EXTREMELY POWERFUL YO-KAI WATCH THAT CAN SUMMON ANY YO-KAI AS LONG AS YOU HAVE THEIR MEDAL!
"AS LONG AS I HAVE THEIR MEDAL"? HOW IS THAT ANY DIFFERENT?
!!!
WAIT... DID HE MEAN ...?
KCCH
THE YO-KAI WORLD WILL DO EVERYTHING WE CAN TO HELP.
THANKS!
I'M SORRY, NATE ADAMS... THAT YOU HAVE TO CLEAN UP AFTER OUR MISTAKE.
I'M COUNTING ON YOU.

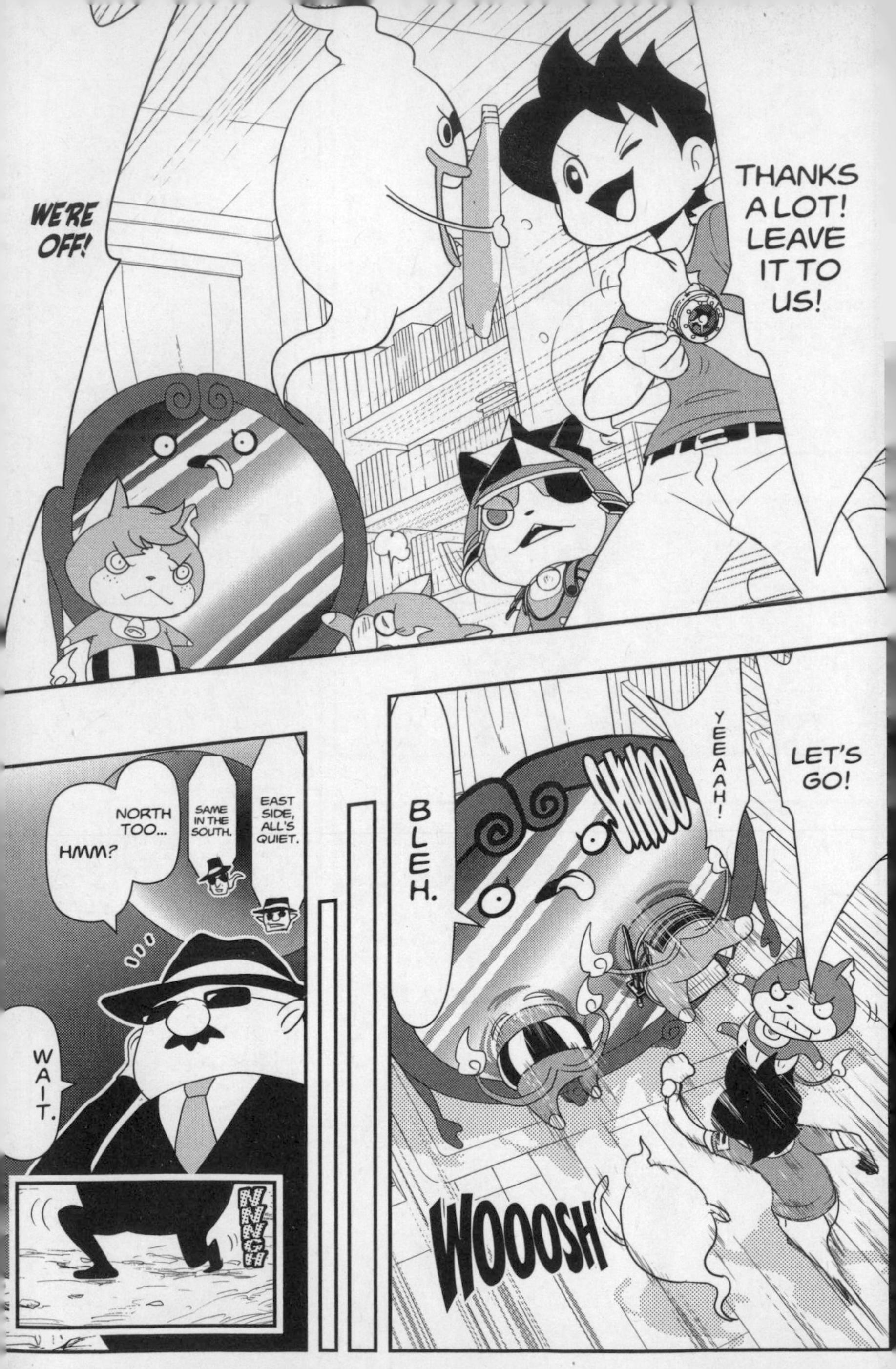
THANKS A LOT! LEAVE IT TO US!
WE'RE OFF!
LET'S GO!
YEEAAAH!
SHWOO
BLEH.
WOOOSH
EAST SIDE, ALL'S QUIET.
SAME IN THE SOUTH.
NORTH TOO...
HMM?
WAIT.
NNNGH

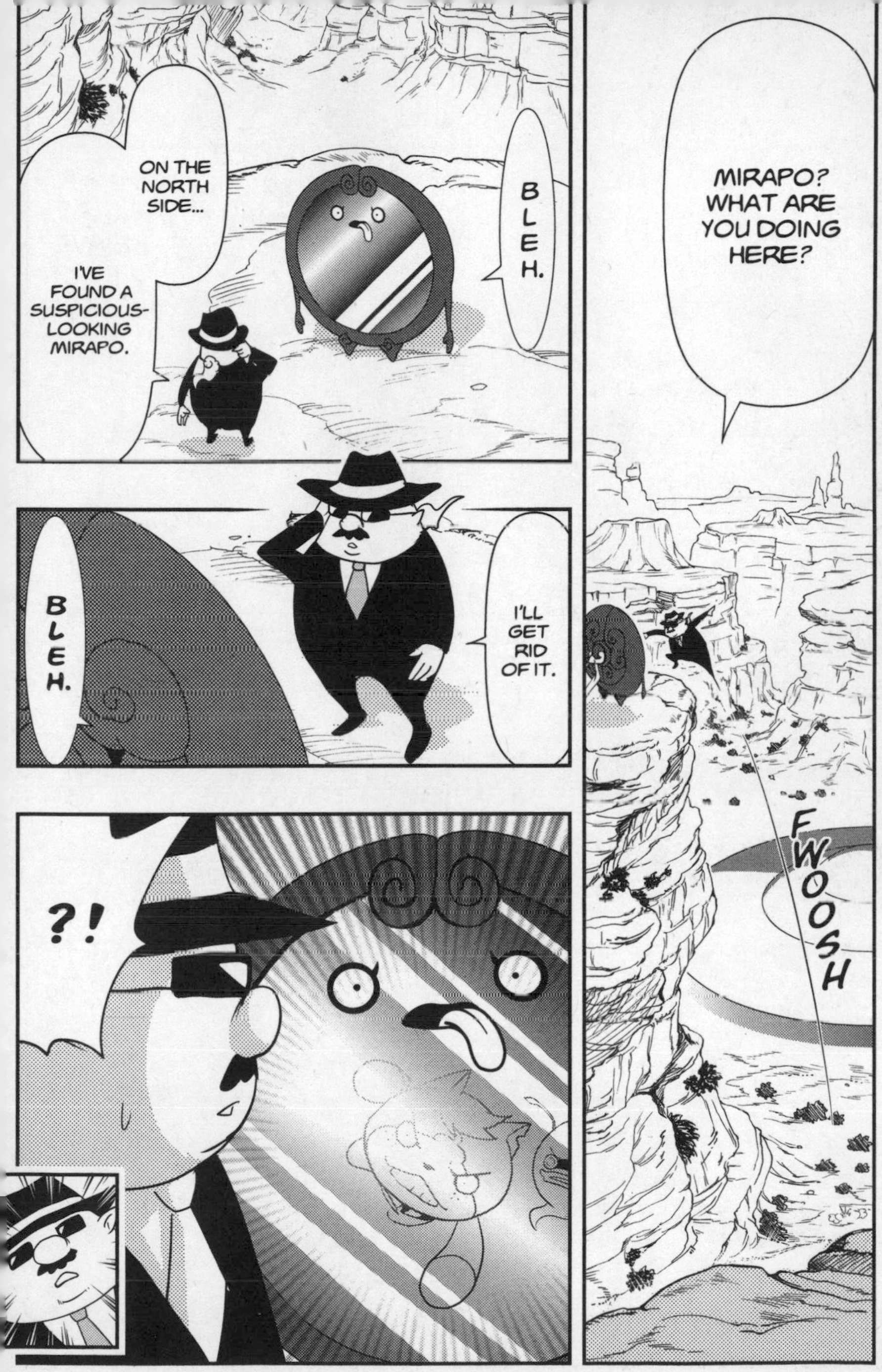
MIRAPO? WHAT ARE YOU DOING HERE?
FWOOSH
BLEH.
ON THE NORTH SIDE...
I'VE FOUND A SUSPICIOUS-LOOKING MIRAPO.
I'LL GET RID OF IT.
BLEH.
?!

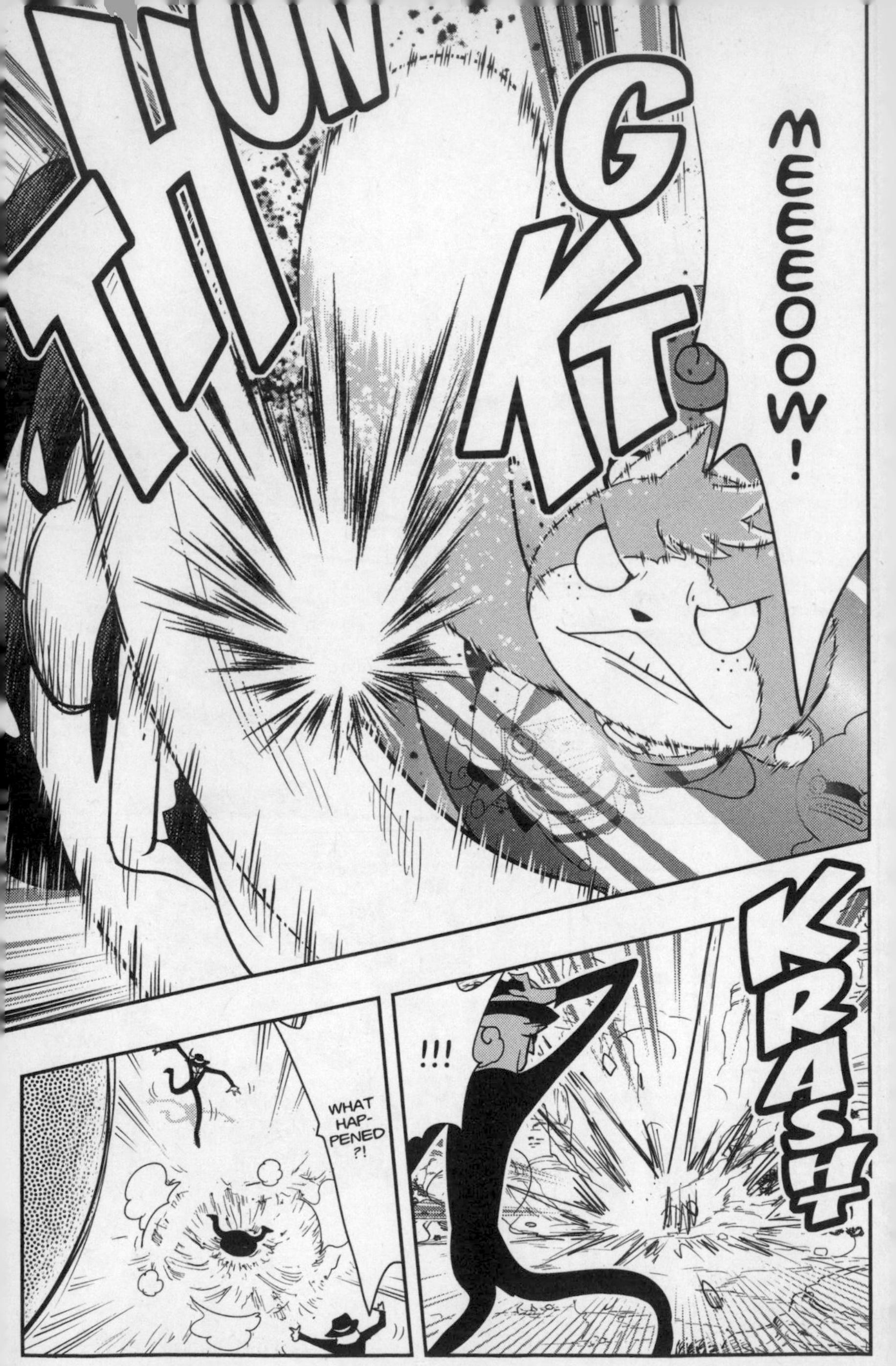
MEEEOOW!
KRASH
!!!
WHAT HAP-PENED ?!

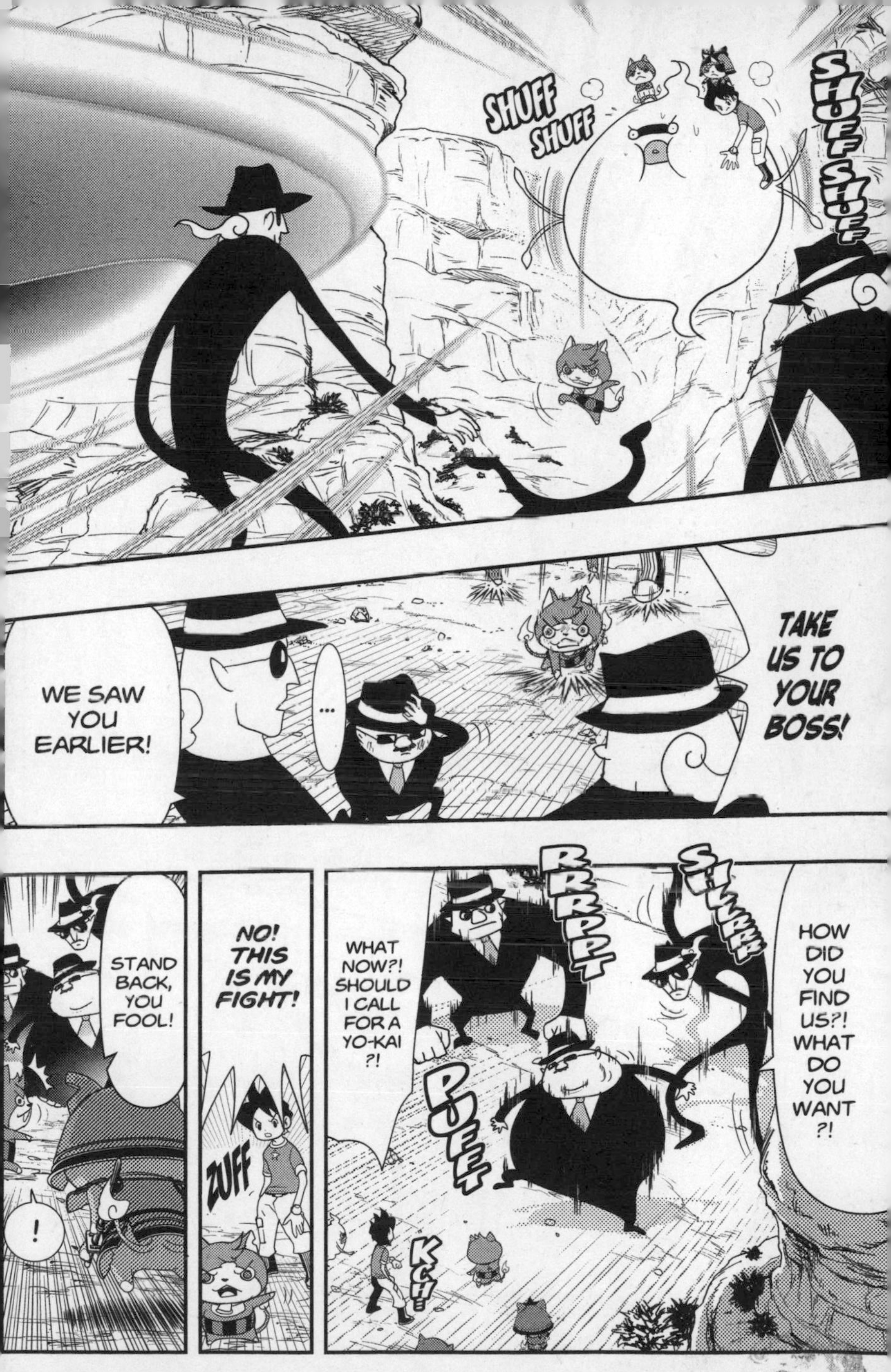
SHUFF SHUFF
SHUFF SHUFF
TAKE US TO YOUR BOSS!
...
WE SAW YOU EARLIER!
HOW DID YOU FIND US?! WHAT DO YOU WANT?!
RRRPPT
WHAT NOW?! SHOULD I CALL FOR A YO-KAI?!
KCH!!
NO! THIS IS MY FIGHT!
ZUFF
STAND BACK, YOU FOOL!
!

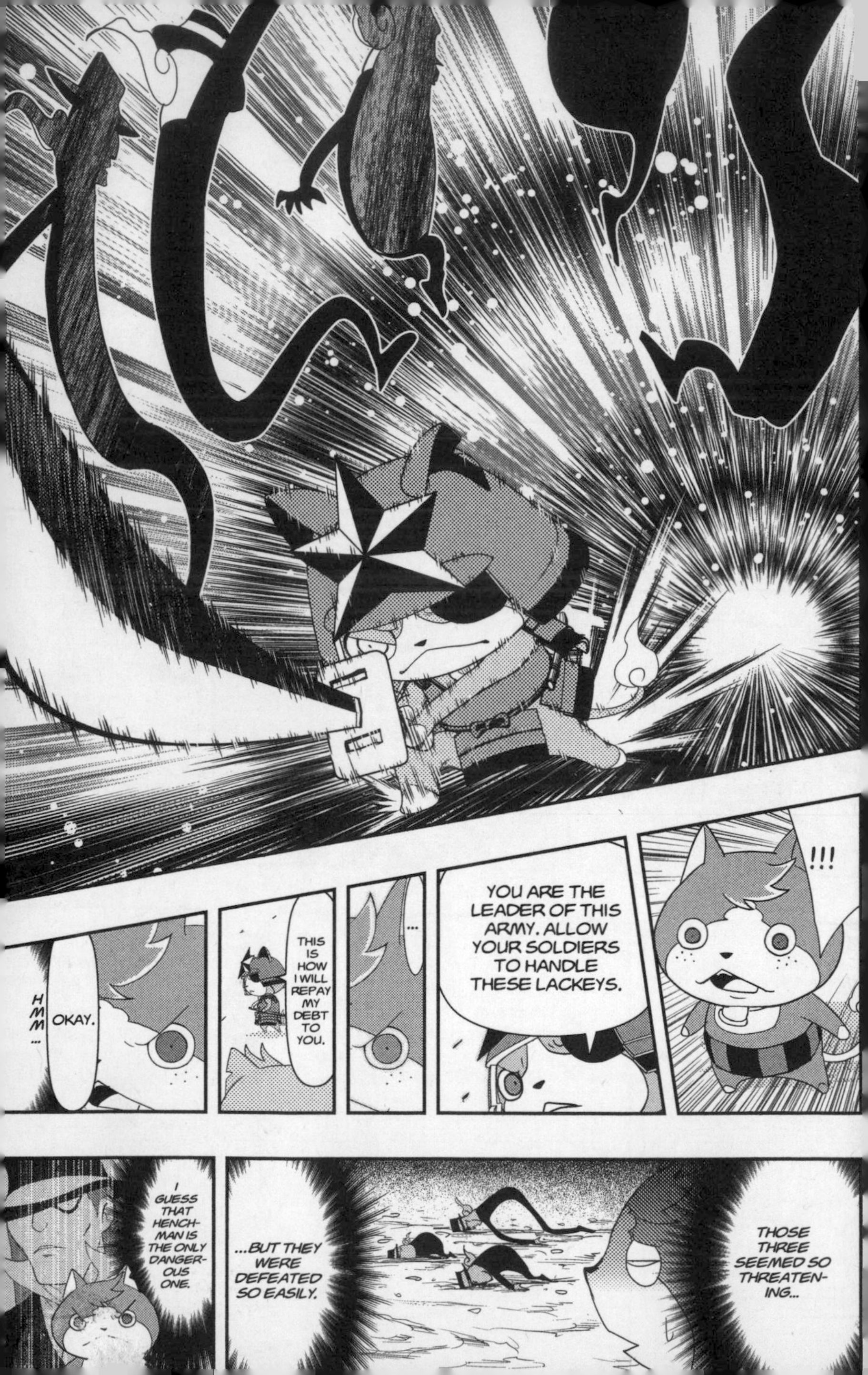
!!!
YOU ARE THE LEADER OF THIS ARMY. ALLOW YOUR SOLDIERS TO HANDLE THESE LACKEYS.
...
THIS IS HOW I WILL REPAY MY DEBT TO YOU.
OKAY.
HMM...
THOSE THREE SEEMED SO THREATENING...
...BUT THEY WERE DEFEATED SO EASILY.
I GUESS THAT HENCHMAN IS THE ONLY DANGEROUS ONE.

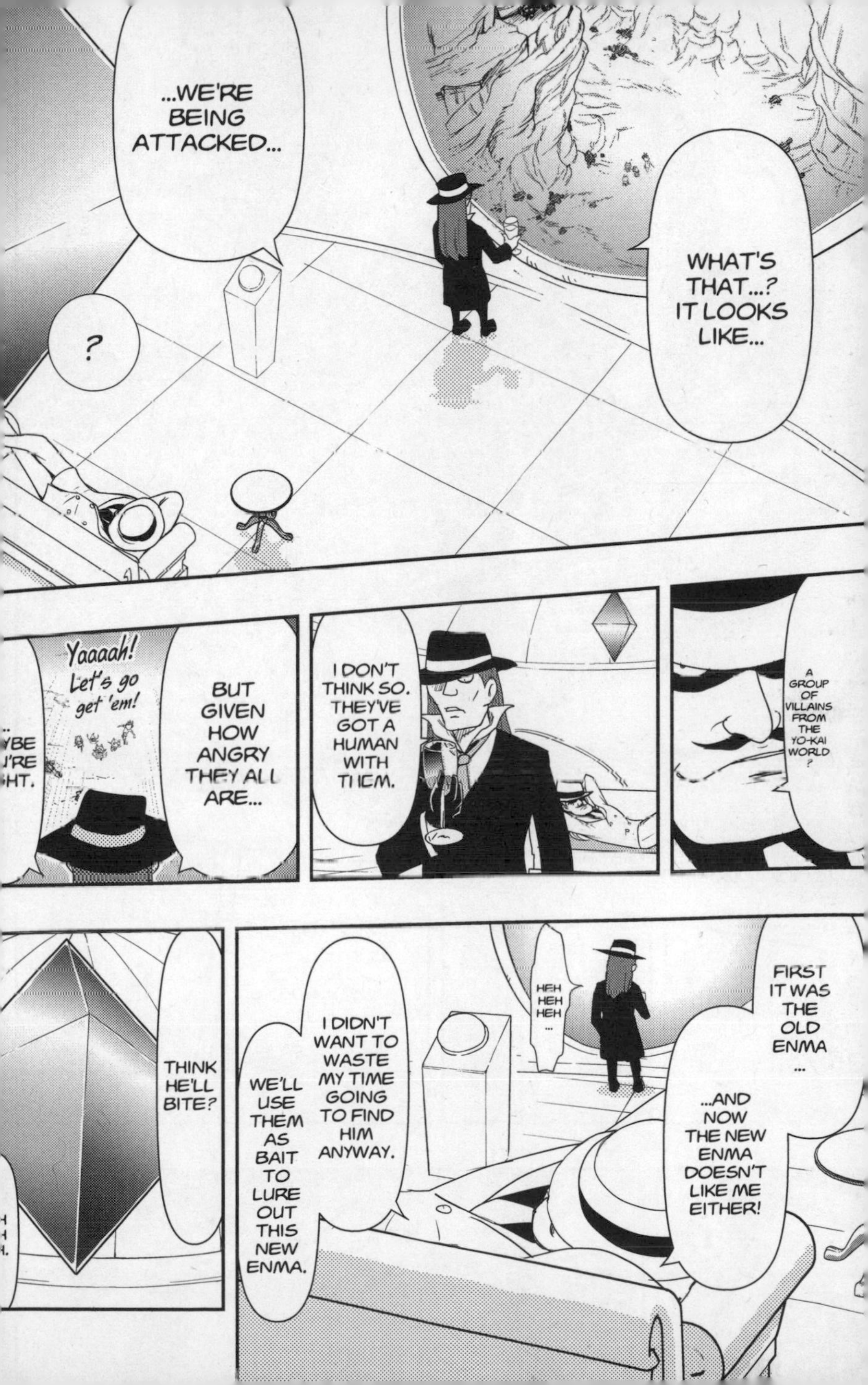
WHAT'S THAT...? IT LOOKS LIKE...
...WE'RE BEING ATTACKED...
?
A GROUP OF VILLAINS FROM THE YO-KAI WORLD?
I DON'T THINK SO. THEY'VE GOT A HUMAN WITH THEM.
BUT GIVEN HOW ANGRY THEY ALL ARE...
Yaaaah! Let's go get 'em!
FIRST IT WAS THE OLD ENMA...
...AND NOW THE NEW ENMA DOESN'T LIKE ME EITHER!
HEH HEH HEH...
I DIDN'T WANT TO WASTE MY TIME GOING TO FIND HIM ANYWAY.
WE'LL USE THEM AS BAIT TO LURE OUT THIS NEW ENMA.
THINK HE'LL BITE?

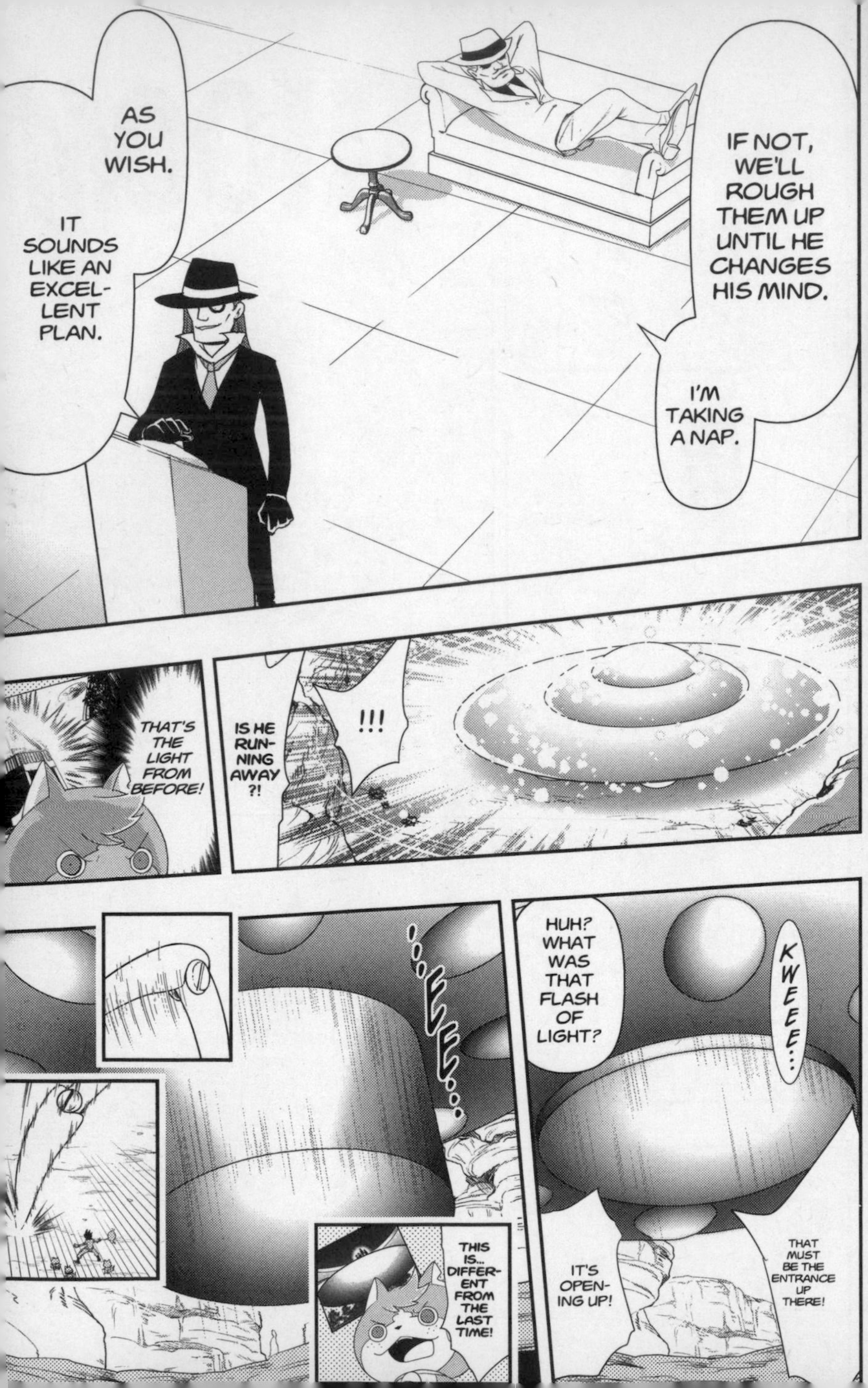
IF NOT, WE'LL ROUGH THEM UP UNTIL HE CHANGES HIS MIND.
I'M TAKING A NAP.
AS YOU WISH.
IT SOUNDS LIKE AN EXCEL-LENT PLAN.
!!!
IS HE RUN-NING AWAY?!
THAT'S THE LIGHT FROM BEFORE!
KWEEE...
HUH? WHAT WAS THAT FLASH OF LIGHT?
THAT MUST BE THE ENTRANCE UP THERE!
IT'S OPEN-ING UP!
...EE...
THIS IS... DIFFER-ENT FROM THE LAST TIME!

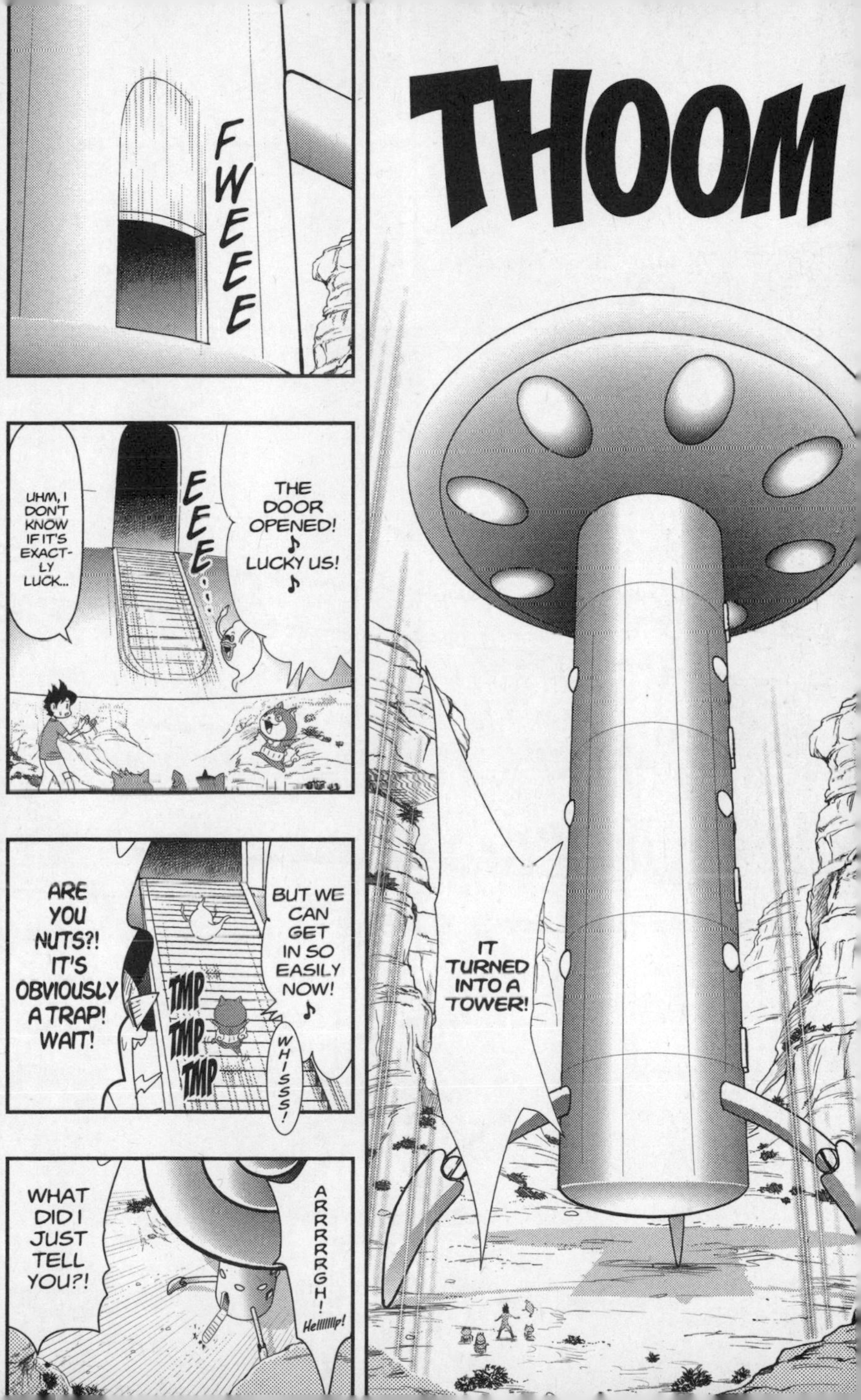
THOOM
IT TURNED INTO A TOWER!
FWEEE
THE DOOR OPENED! ♪ LUCKY US! ♪
EEE...
UHM, I DON'T KNOW IF IT'S EXACTLY LUCK...
BUT WE CAN GET IN SO EASILY NOW! ♪
WHISSS!
TMP TMP TMP
ARE YOU NUTS?! IT'S OBVIOUSLY A TRAP! WAIT!
ARRRRGH!
Hellllllp!
WHAT DID I JUST TELL YOU?!

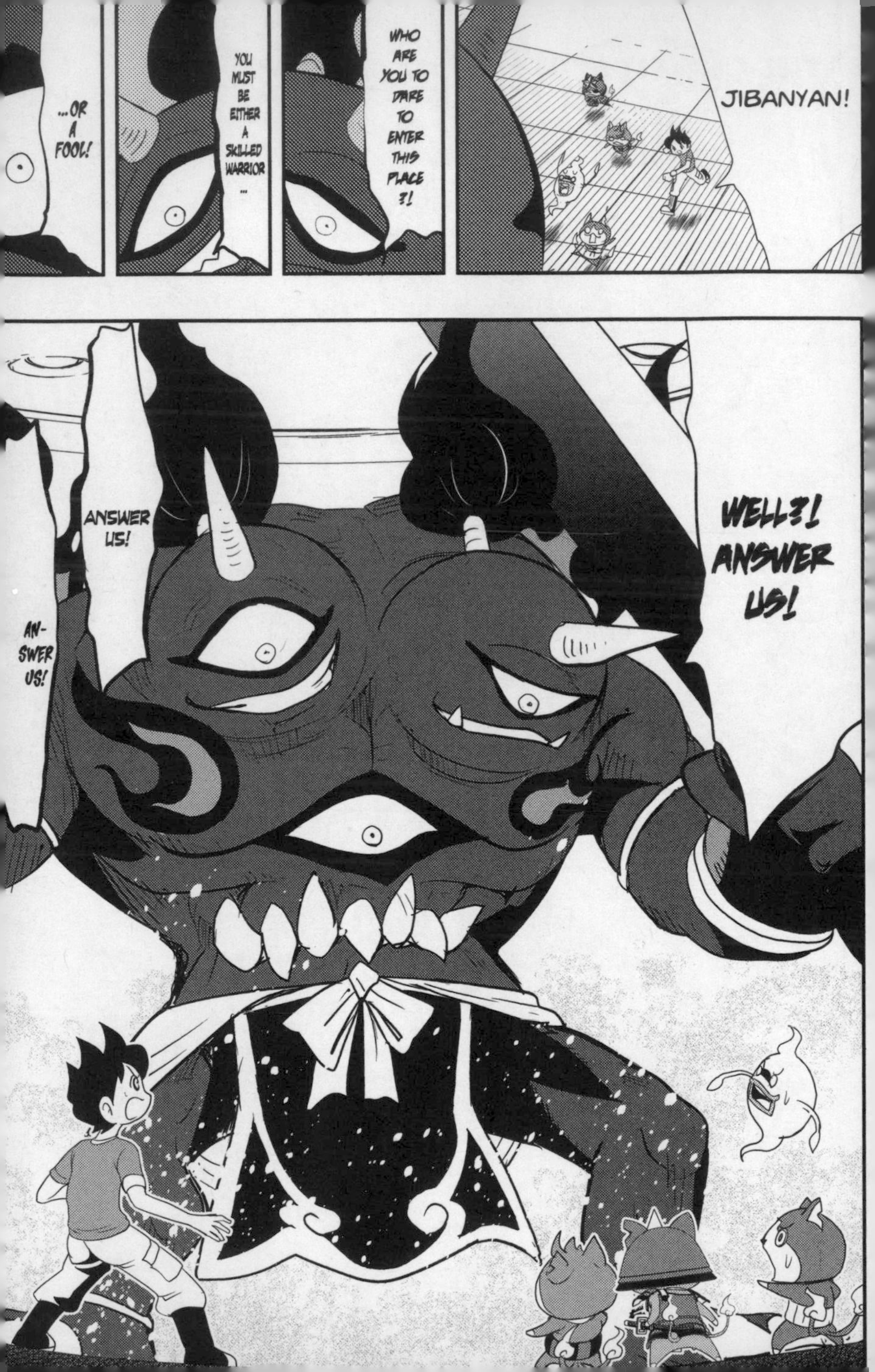
JIBANYAN!
WHO ARE YOU TO DARE TO ENTER THIS PLACE?!
YOU MUST BE EITHER A SKILLED WARRIOR...
...OR A FOOL!
WELL?! ANSWER US!
ANSWER US!
AN-SWER US!

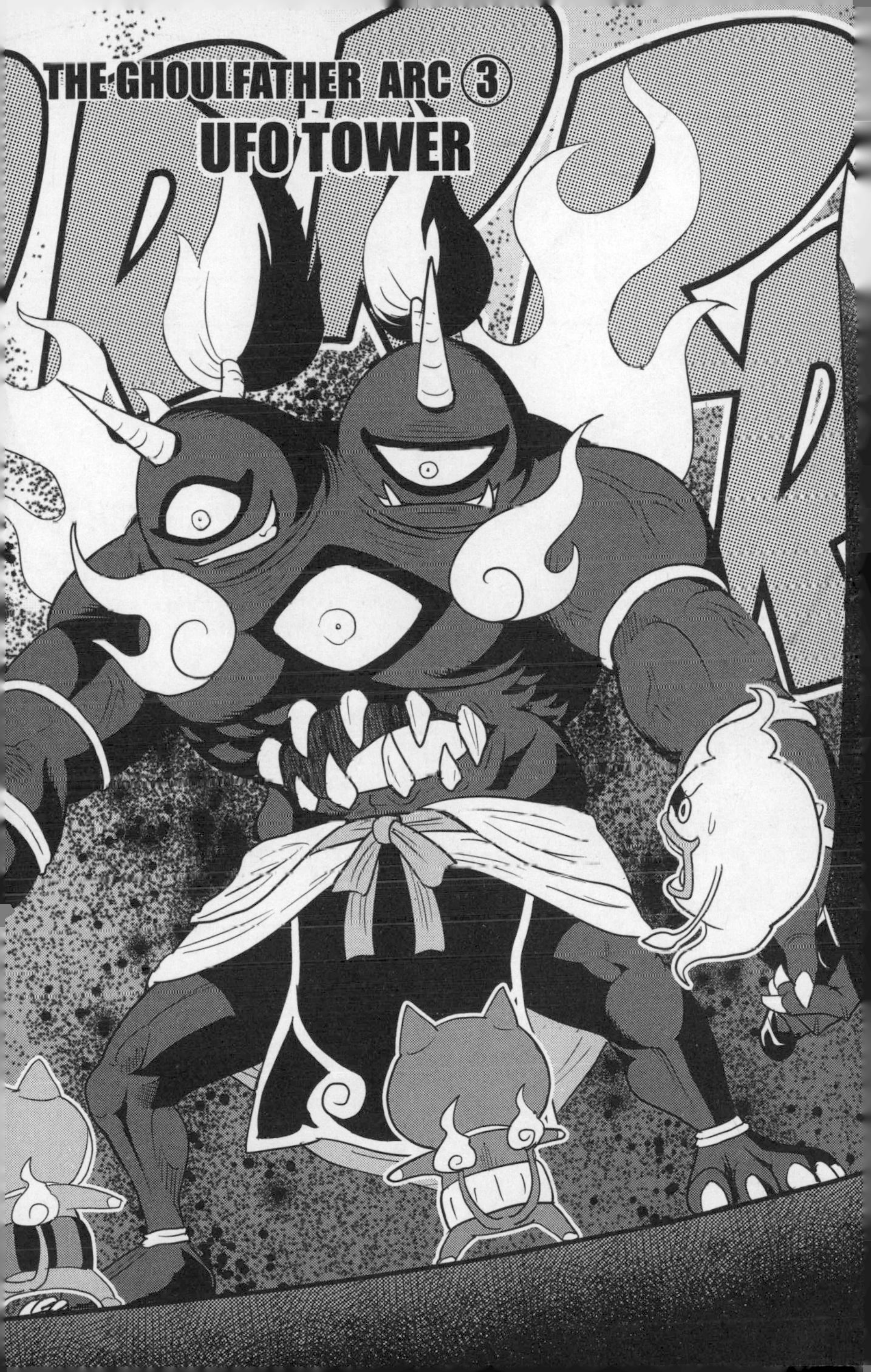
THE GHOULFATHER ARC ③
UFO TOWER

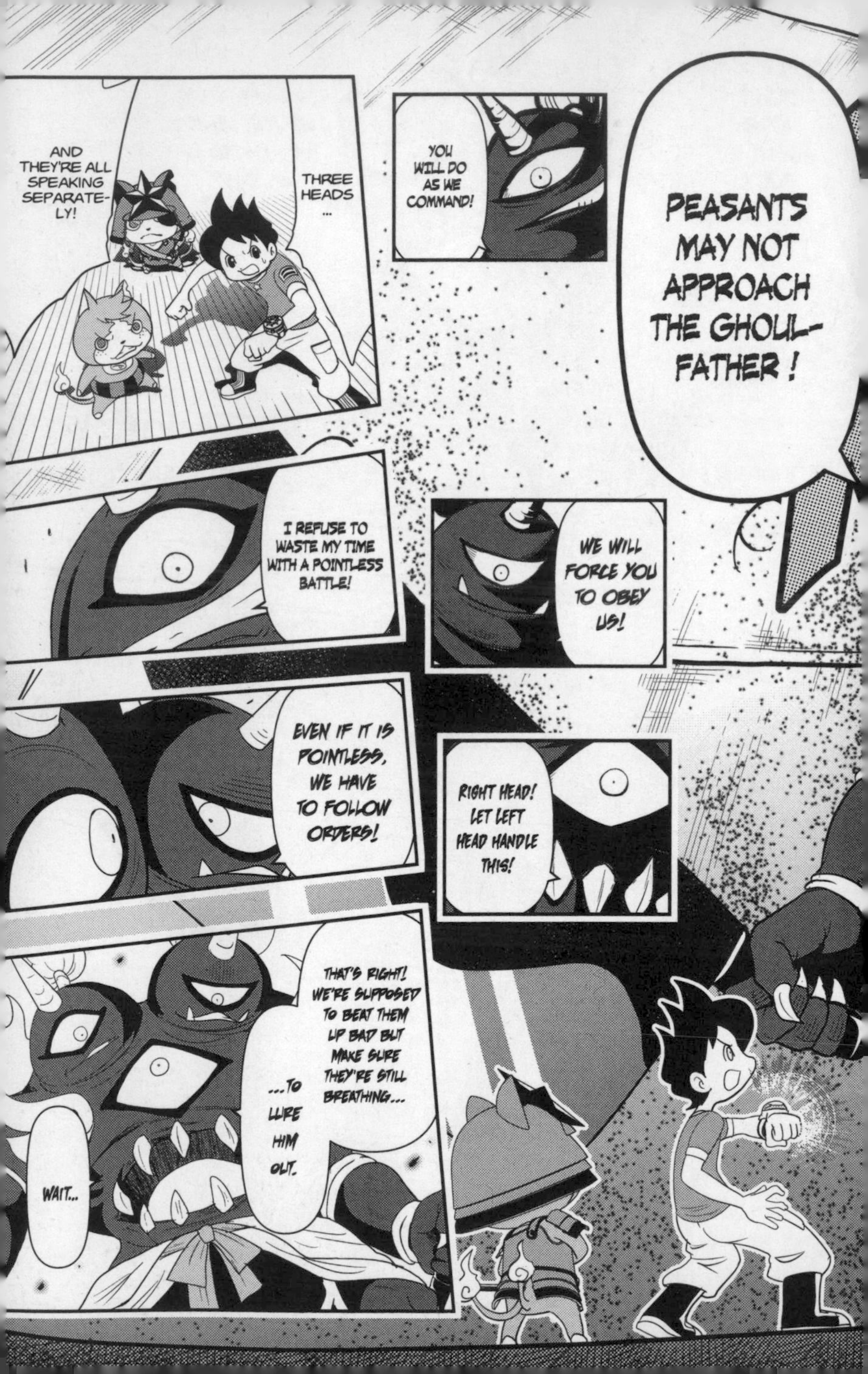
PEASANTS MAY NOT APPROACH THE GHOUL-FATHER!
YOU WILL DO AS WE COMMAND!
THREE HEADS...
AND THEY'RE ALL SPEAKING SEPARATE-LY!
WE WILL FORCE YOU TO OBEY US!
I REFUSE TO WASTE MY TIME WITH A POINTLESS BATTLE!
RIGHT HEAD! LET LEFT HEAD HANDLE THIS!
EVEN IF IT IS POINTLESS, WE HAVE TO FOLLOW ORDERS!
THAT'S RIGHT! WE'RE SUPPOSED TO BEAT THEM UP BAD BUT MAKE SURE THEY'RE STILL BREATHING...
...TO LURE HIM OUT.
WAIT...

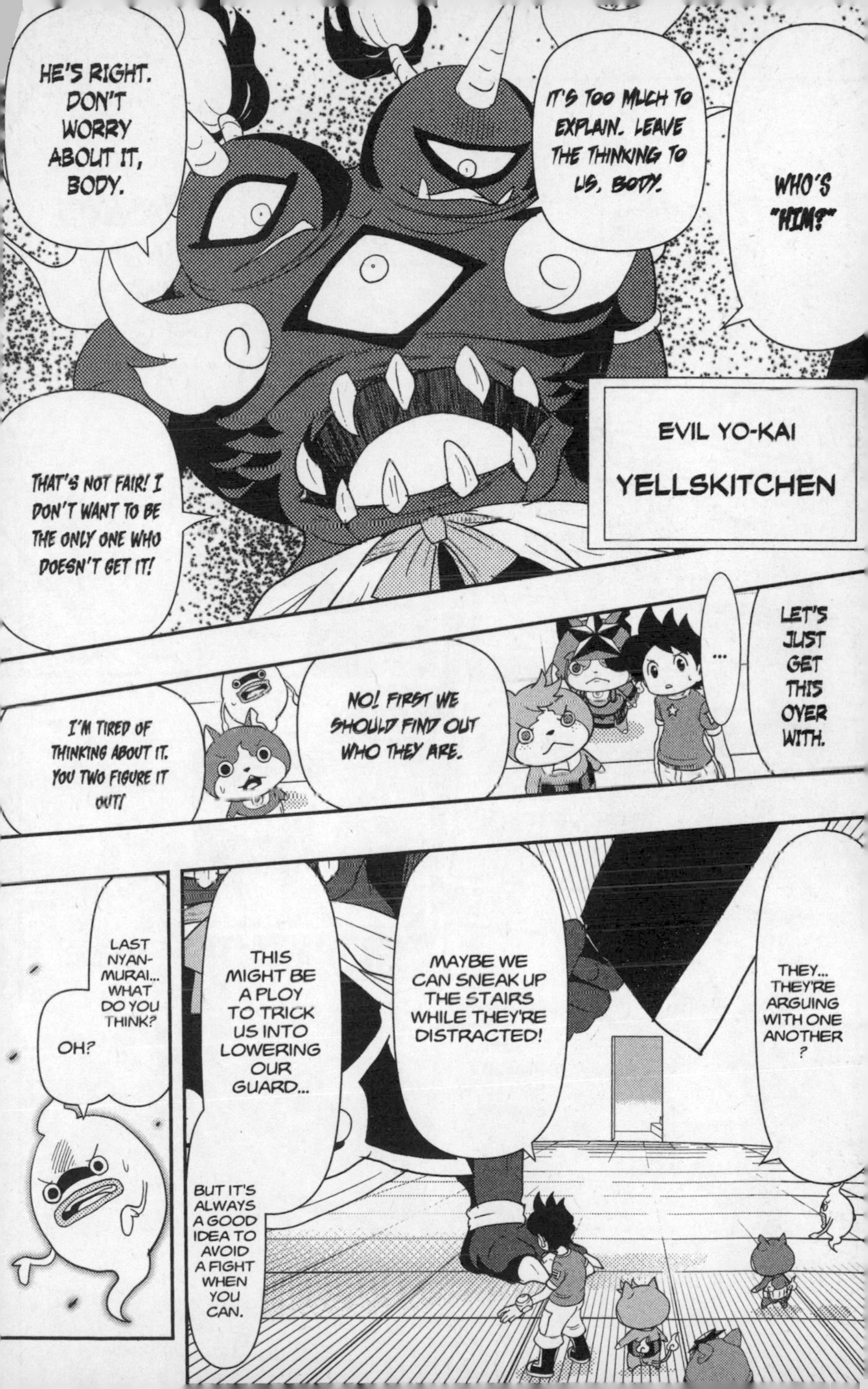
WHO'S "HIM?"
IT'S TOO MUCH TO EXPLAIN. LEAVE THE THINKING TO US, BODY.
HE'S RIGHT. DON'T WORRY ABOUT IT, BODY.
EVIL YO-KAI
YELLSKITCHEN
THAT'S NOT FAIR! I DON'T WANT TO BE THE ONLY ONE WHO DOESN'T GET IT!
LET'S JUST GET THIS OVER WITH.
...
NO! FIRST WE SHOULD FIND OUT WHO THEY ARE.
I'M TIRED OF THINKING ABOUT IT. YOU TWO FIGURE IT OUT!
THEY... THEY'RE ARGUING WITH ONE ANOTHER?
MAYBE WE CAN SNEAK UP THE STAIRS WHILE THEY'RE DISTRACTED!
THIS MIGHT BE A PLOY TO TRICK US INTO LOWERING OUR GUARD...
BUT IT'S ALWAYS A GOOD IDEA TO AVOID A FIGHT WHEN YOU CAN.
LAST NYAN-MURAI... WHAT DO YOU THINK?
OH?

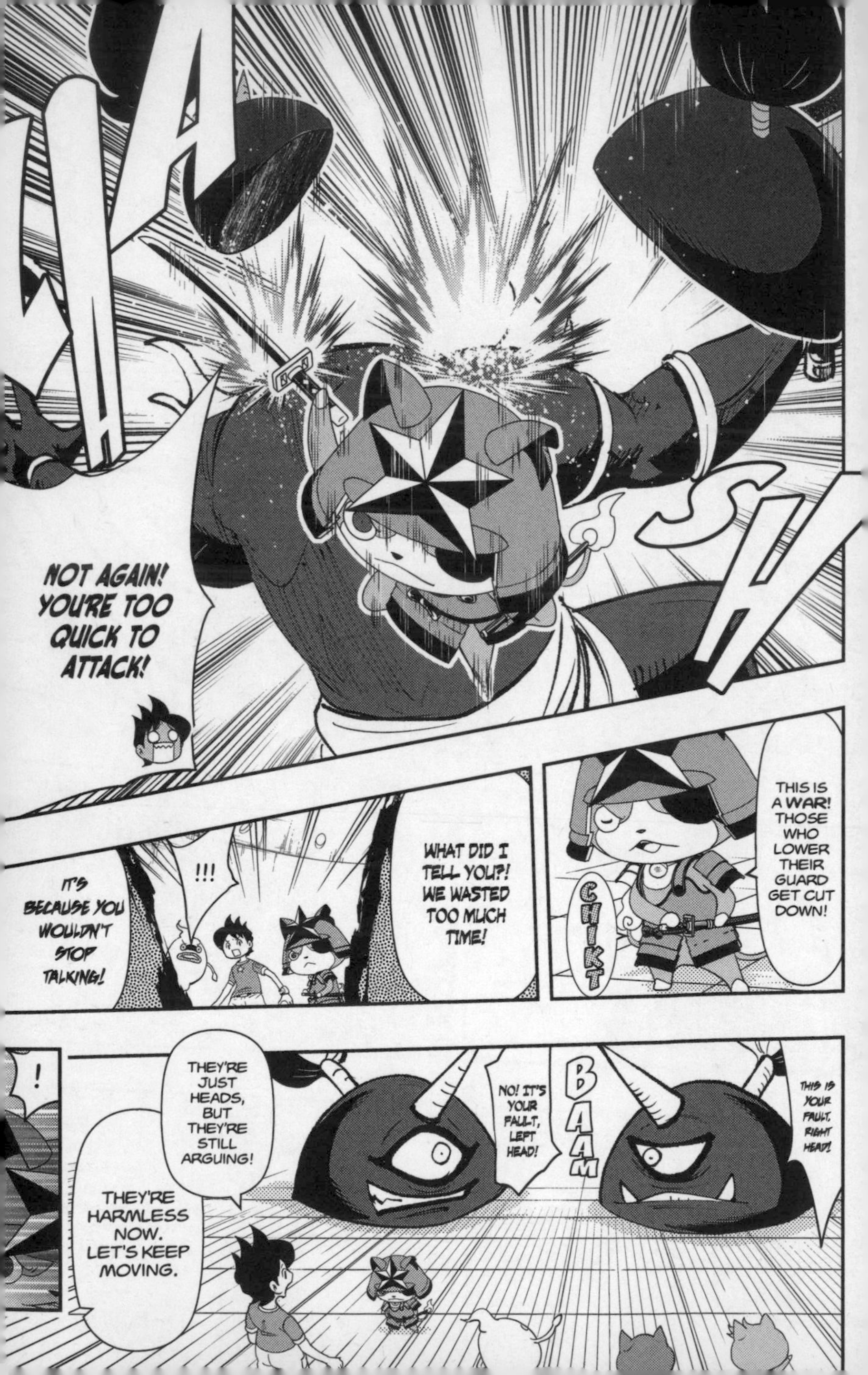
SH
NOT AGAIN! YOU'RE TOO QUICK TO ATTACK!
THIS IS A WAR! THOSE WHO LOWER THEIR GUARD GET CUT DOWN!
CHIKT
WHAT DID I TELL YOU?! WE WASTED TOO MUCH TIME!
!!!
IT'S BECAUSE YOU WOULDN'T STOP TALKING!
THIS IS YOUR FAULT, RIGHT HEAD!
BAAM
NO! IT'S YOUR FAULT, LEFT HEAD!
THEY'RE JUST HEADS, BUT THEY'RE STILL ARGUING!
!
THEY'RE HARMLESS NOW. LET'S KEEP MOVING.

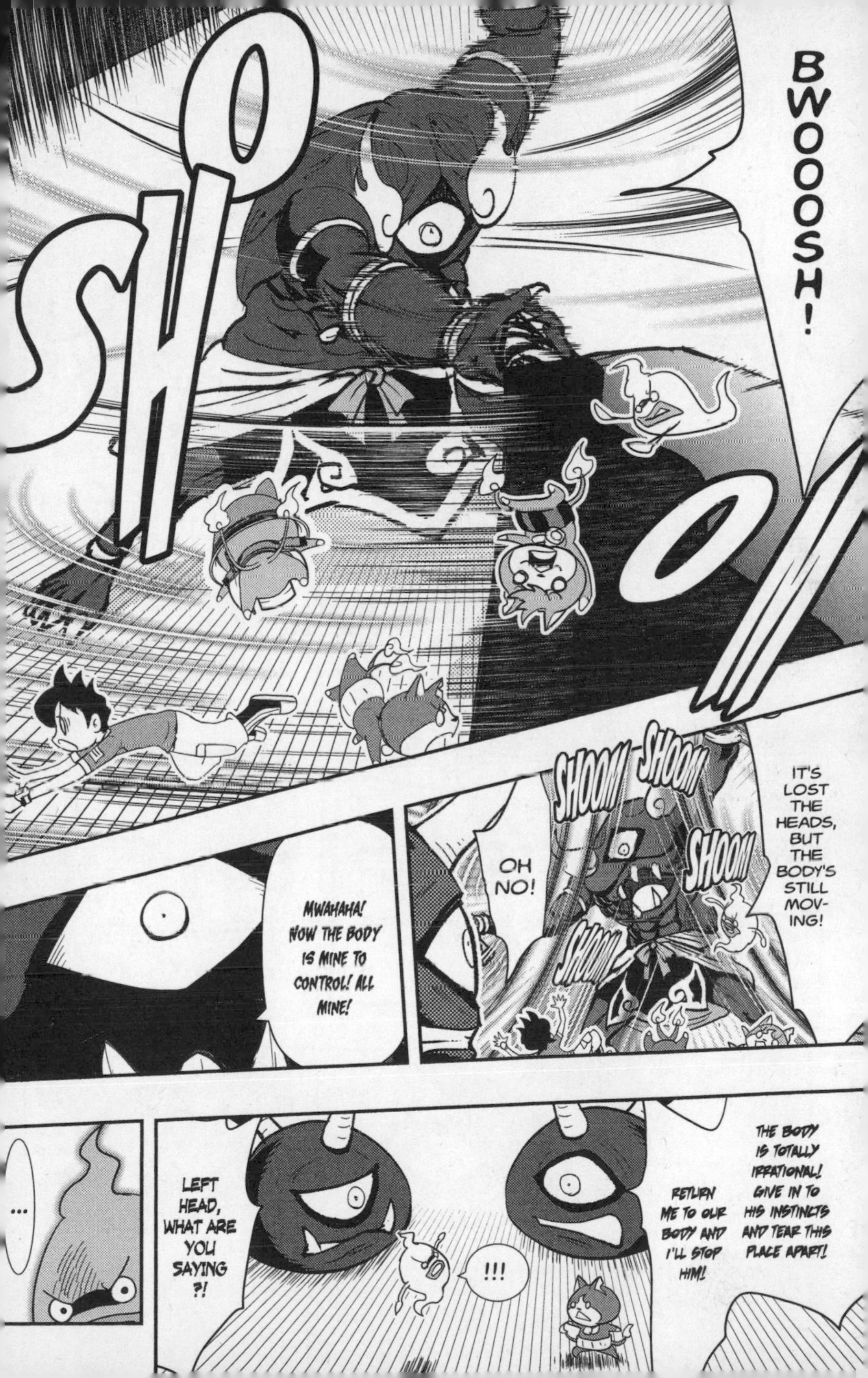
BWOOOOSH!
SHOO!!
IT'S LOST THE HEADS, BUT THE BODY'S STILL MOVING!
SHOOM SHOOM
SHOOM
SHOOM
OH NO!
MWAHAHA! NOW THE BODY IS MINE TO CONTROL! ALL MINE!
THE BODY IS TOTALLY IRRATIONAL! GIVE IN TO HIS INSTINCTS AND TEAR THIS PLACE APART!
RETURN ME TO OUR BODY AND I'LL STOP HIM!
!!!
LEFT HEAD, WHAT ARE YOU SAYING?!
...

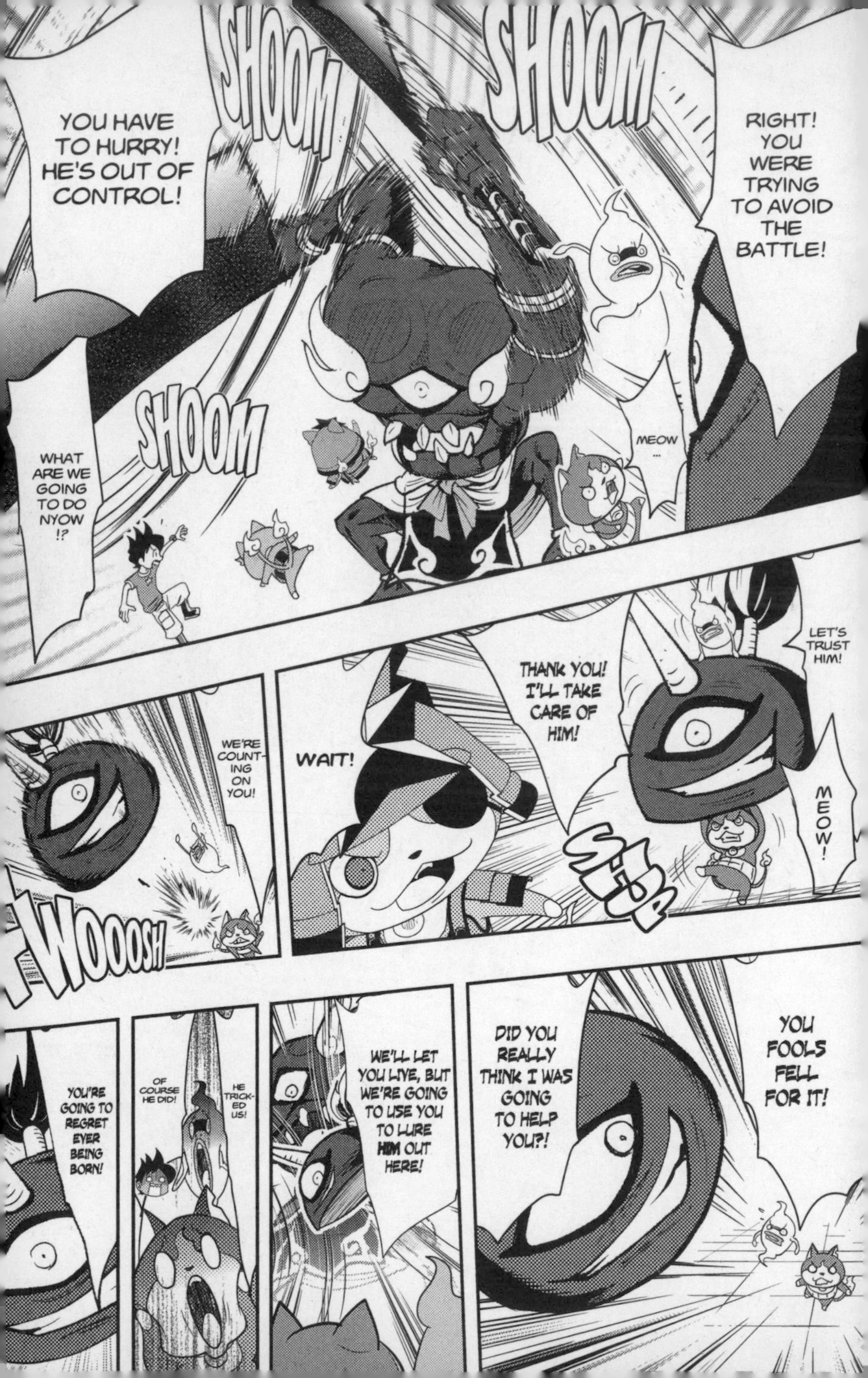
RIGHT! YOU WERE TRYING TO AVOID THE BATTLE!
SHOOM
SHOOM
YOU HAVE TO HURRY! HE'S OUT OF CONTROL!
MEOW ...
SHOOM
WHAT ARE WE GOING TO DO NYOW !?
LET'S TRUST HIM!
THANK YOU! I'LL TAKE CARE OF HIM!
MEOW!
WAIT!
WE'RE COUNTING ON YOU!
WOOOSH
YOU FOOLS FELL FOR IT!
DID YOU REALLY THINK I WAS GOING TO HELP YOU?!
WE'LL LET YOU LIVE, BUT WE'RE GOING TO USE YOU TO LURE HIM OUT HERE!
HE TRICKED US!
OF COURSE HE DID!
YOU'RE GOING TO REGRET EVER BEING BORN!

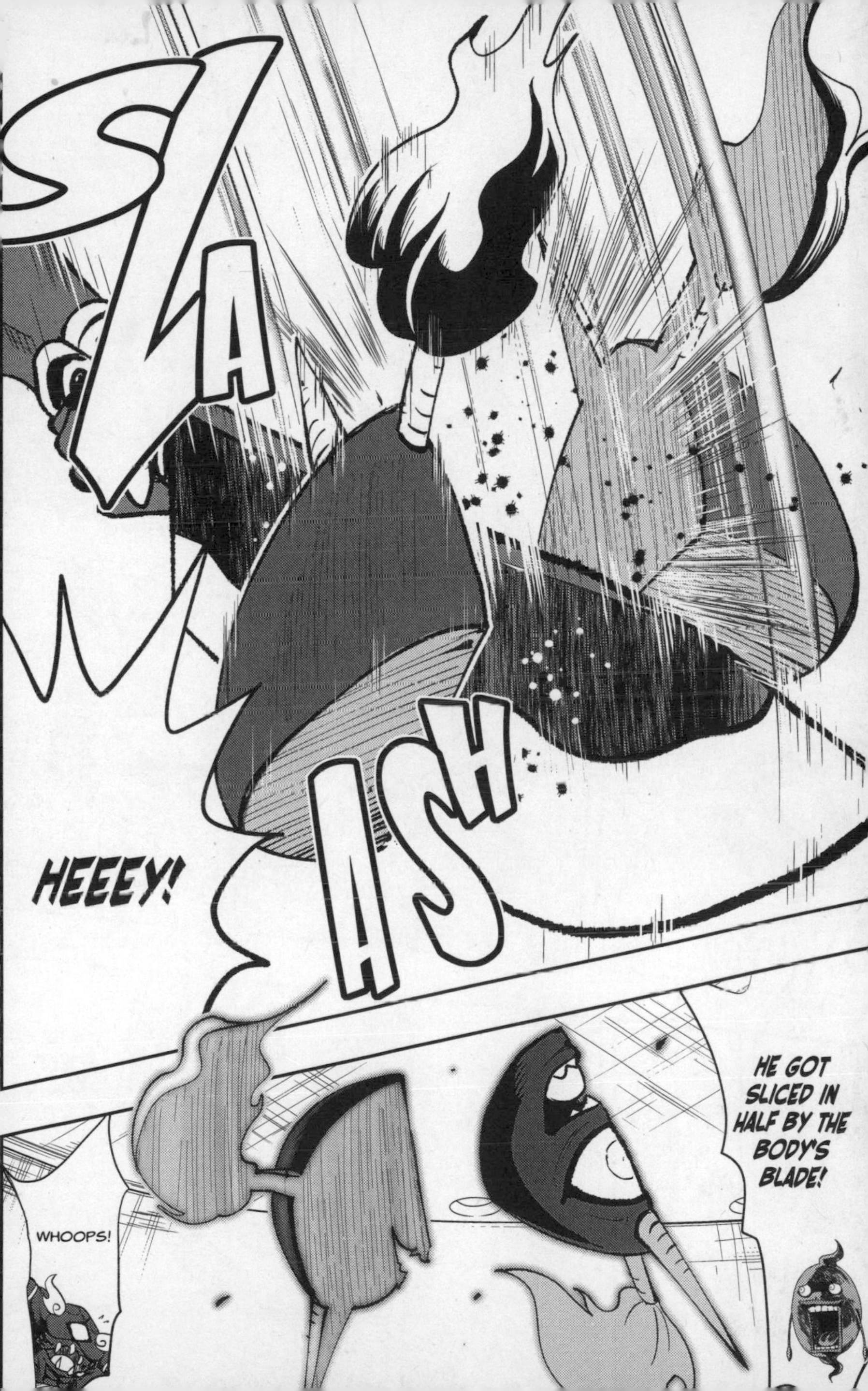
SLAASH
HEEEY!
HE GOT SLICED IN HALF BY THE BODY'S BLADE!
WHOOPS!

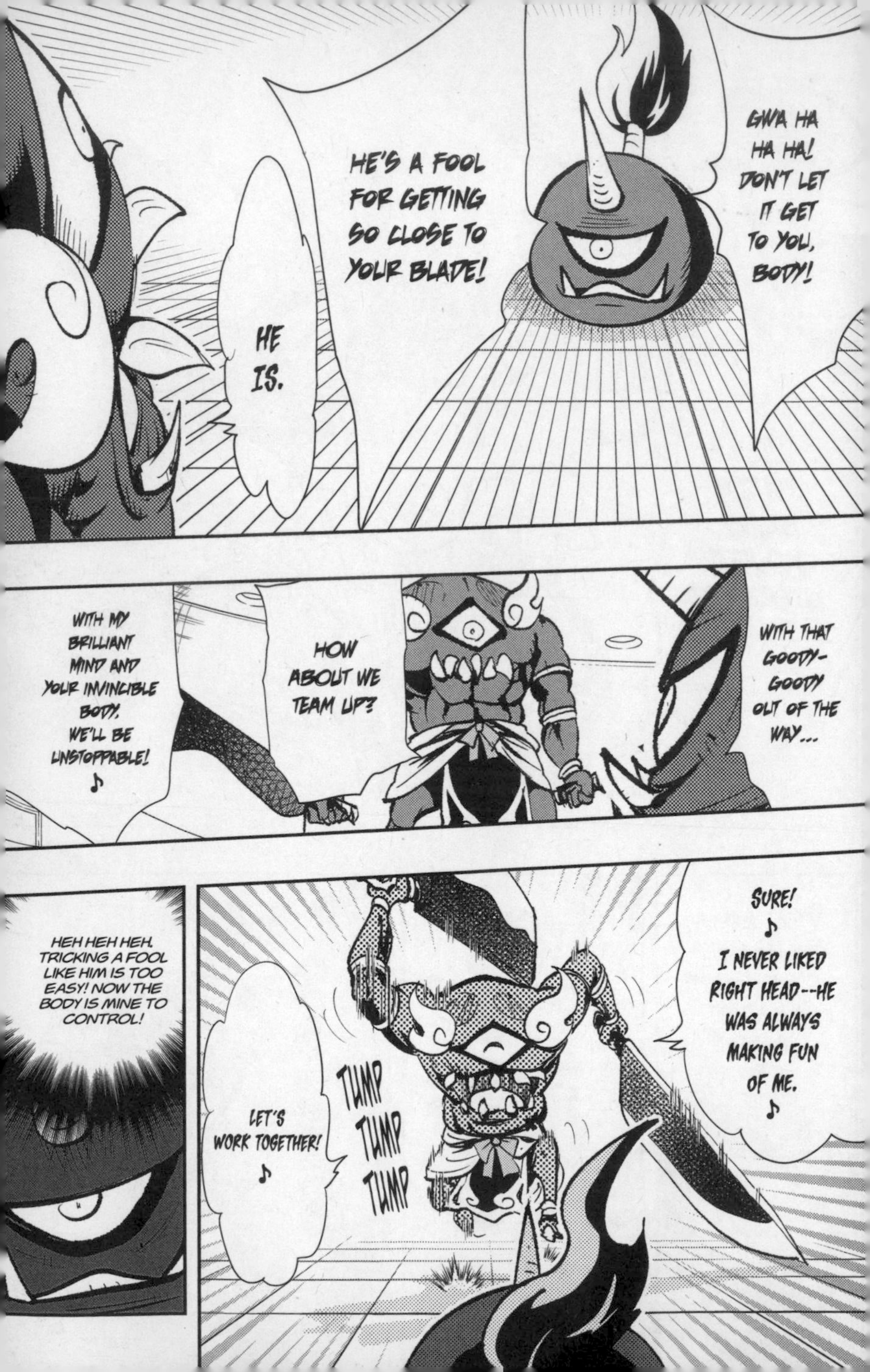
GWA HA HA HA! DON'T LET IT GET TO YOU, BODY!
HE'S A FOOL FOR GETTING SO CLOSE TO YOUR BLADE!
HE IS.
WITH THAT GOODY-GOODY OUT OF THE WAY...
HOW ABOUT WE TEAM UP?
WITH MY BRILLIANT MIND AND YOUR INVINCIBLE BODY, WE'LL BE UNSTOPPABLE! ♪
SURE! ♪ I NEVER LIKED RIGHT HEAD--HE WAS ALWAYS MAKING FUN OF ME. ♪
TUMP TUMP TUMP
LET'S WORK TOGETHER! ♪
HEH HEH HEH. TRICKING A FOOL LIKE HIM IS TOO EASY! NOW THE BODY IS MINE TO CONTROL!

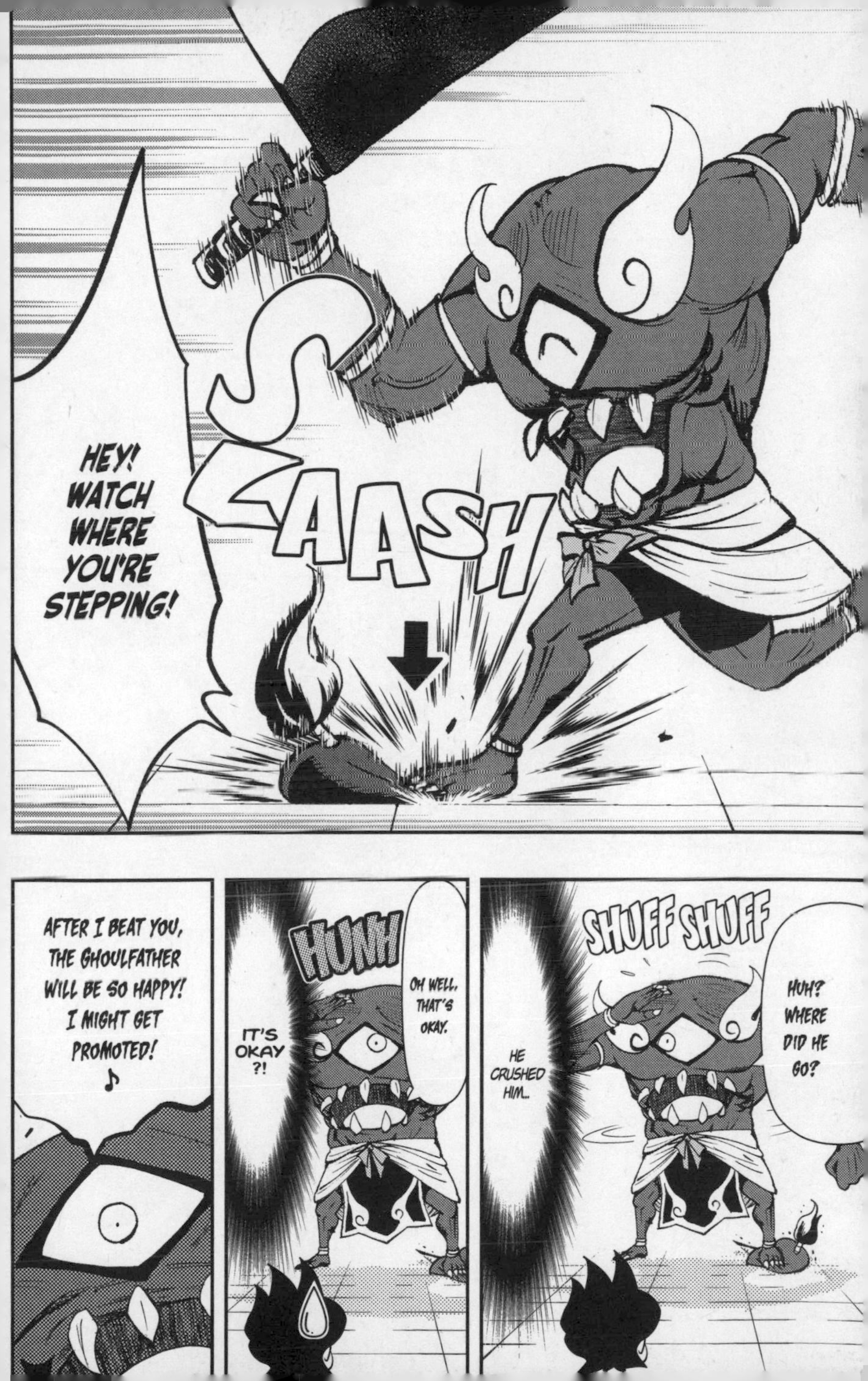
HEY! WATCH WHERE YOU'RE STEPPING!
SHUFF SHUFF
HUH? WHERE DID HE GO?
HE CRUSHED HIM..
OH WELL, THAT'S OKAY.
HUNH
IT'S OKAY ?!
AFTER I BEAT YOU, THE GHOULFATHER WILL BE SO HAPPY! I MIGHT GET PROMOTED! ♪

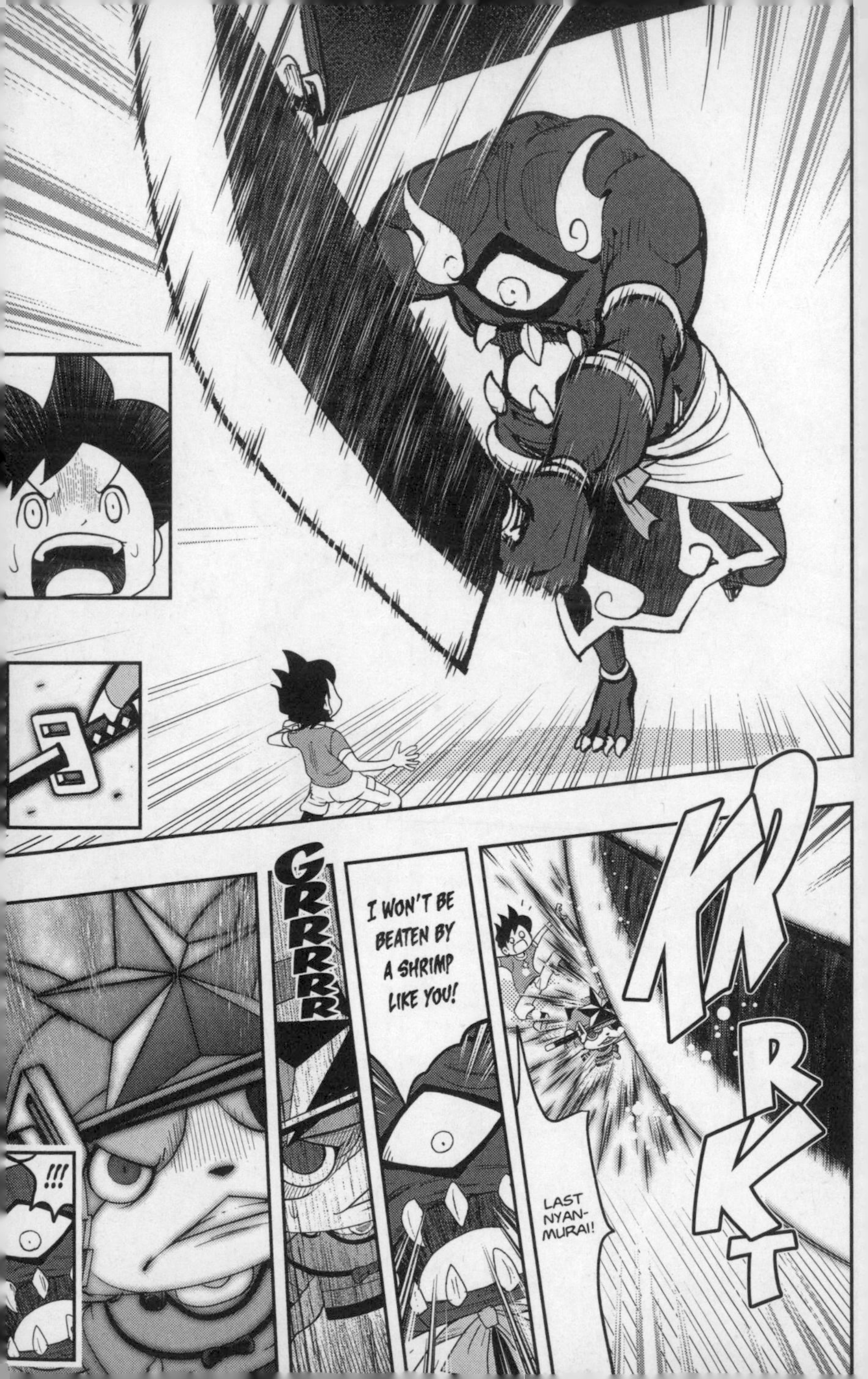
KRRKT
LAST NYAN-MURAI!
I WON'T BE BEATEN BY A SHRIMP LIKE YOU!
GRRRRR
!!!

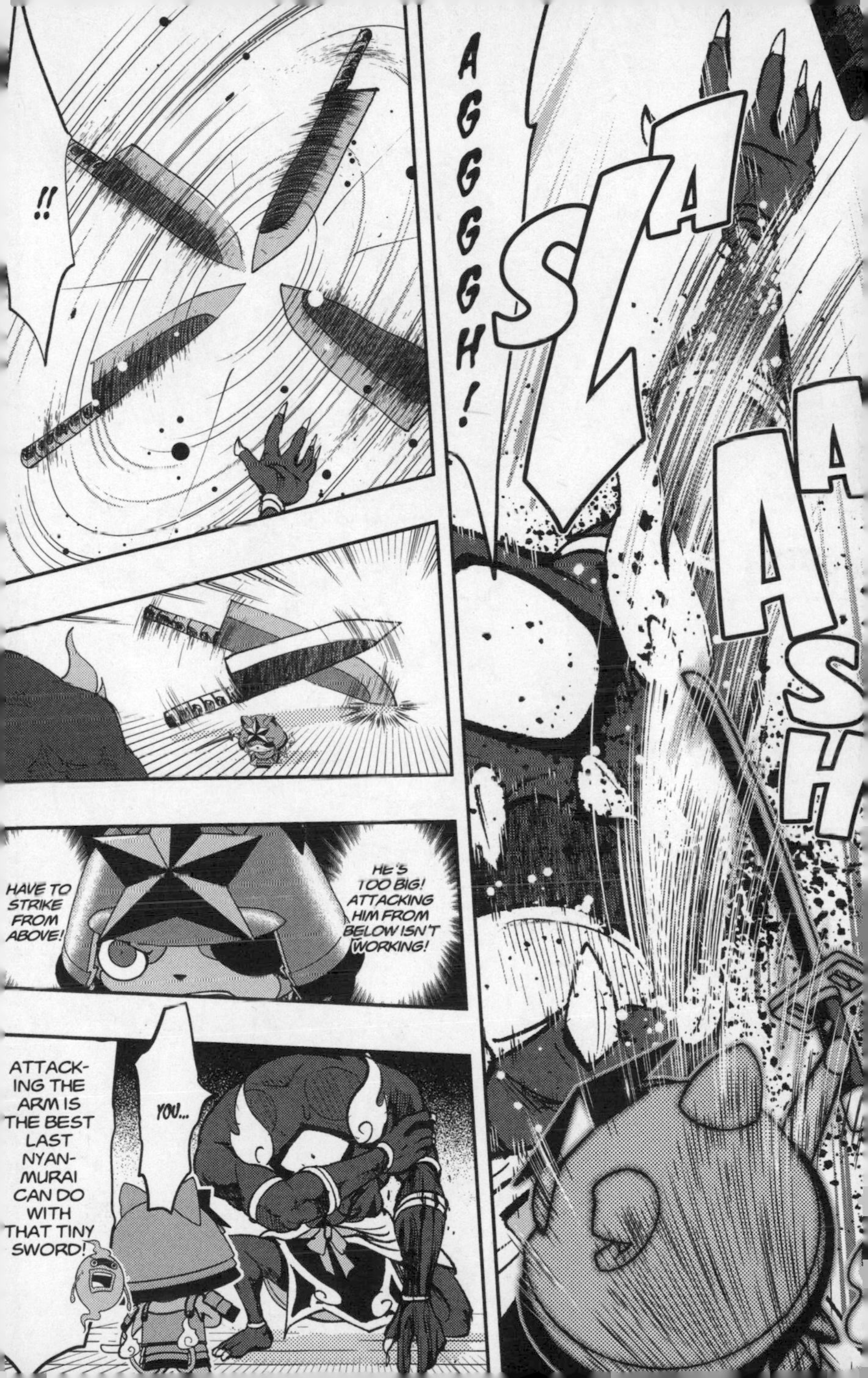
SLAAASH
AGGGGH!
!!
HE'S TOO BIG! ATTACKING HIM FROM BELOW ISN'T WORKING!
HAVE TO STRIKE FROM ABOVE!
YOU...
ATTACKING THE ARM IS THE BEST LAST NYAN-MURAI CAN DO WITH THAT TINY SWORD!

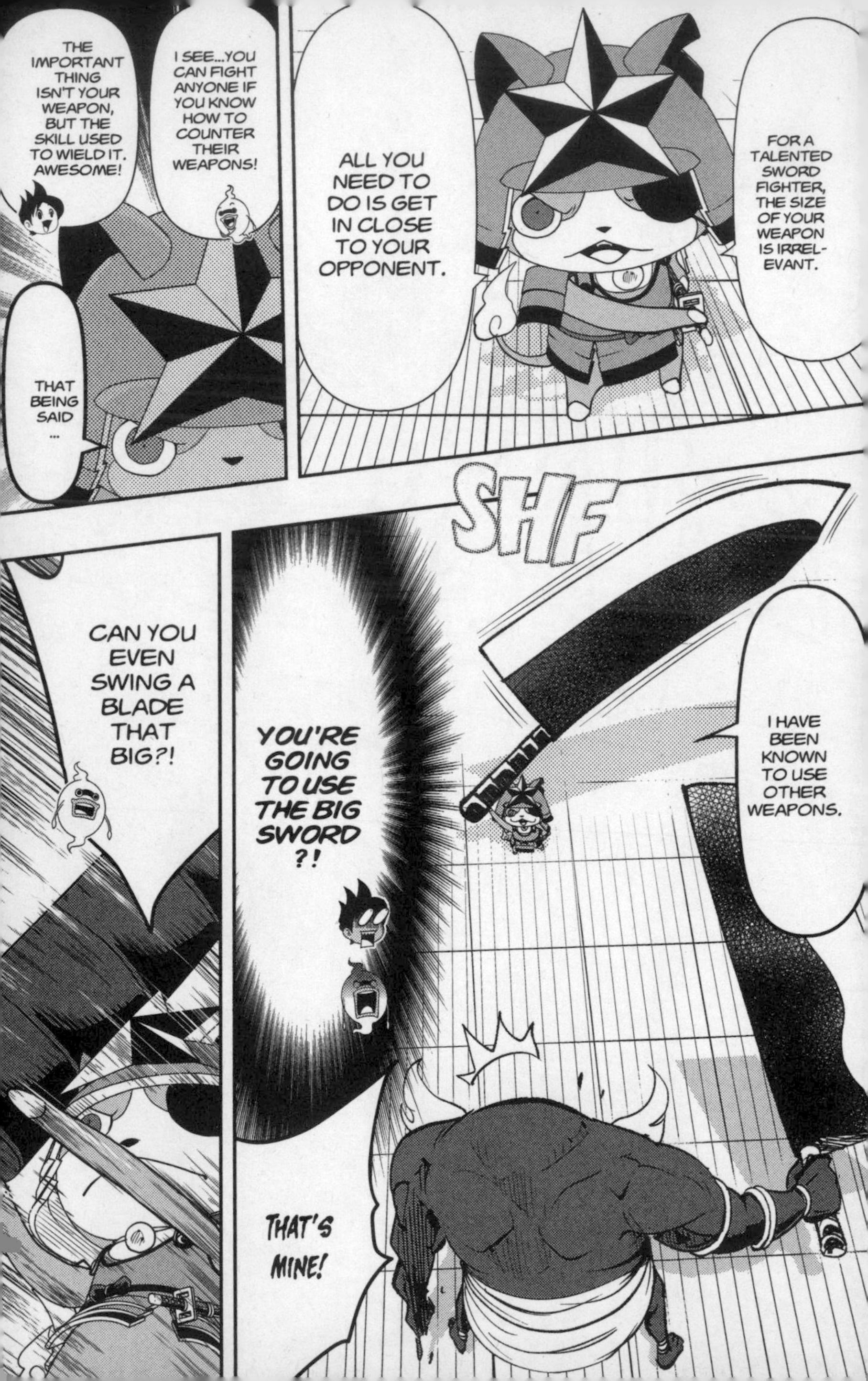
FOR A TALENTED SWORD FIGHTER, THE SIZE OF YOUR WEAPON IS IRREL-EVANT.
ALL YOU NEED TO DO IS GET IN CLOSE TO YOUR OPPONENT.
I SEE...YOU CAN FIGHT ANYONE IF YOU KNOW HOW TO COUNTER THEIR WEAPONS!
THE IMPORTANT THING ISN'T YOUR WEAPON, BUT THE SKILL USED TO WIELD IT. AWESOME!
THAT BEING SAID...
SHF
I HAVE BEEN KNOWN TO USE OTHER WEAPONS.
THAT'S MINE!
YOU'RE GOING TO USE THE BIG SWORD?!
CAN YOU EVEN SWING A BLADE THAT BIG?!

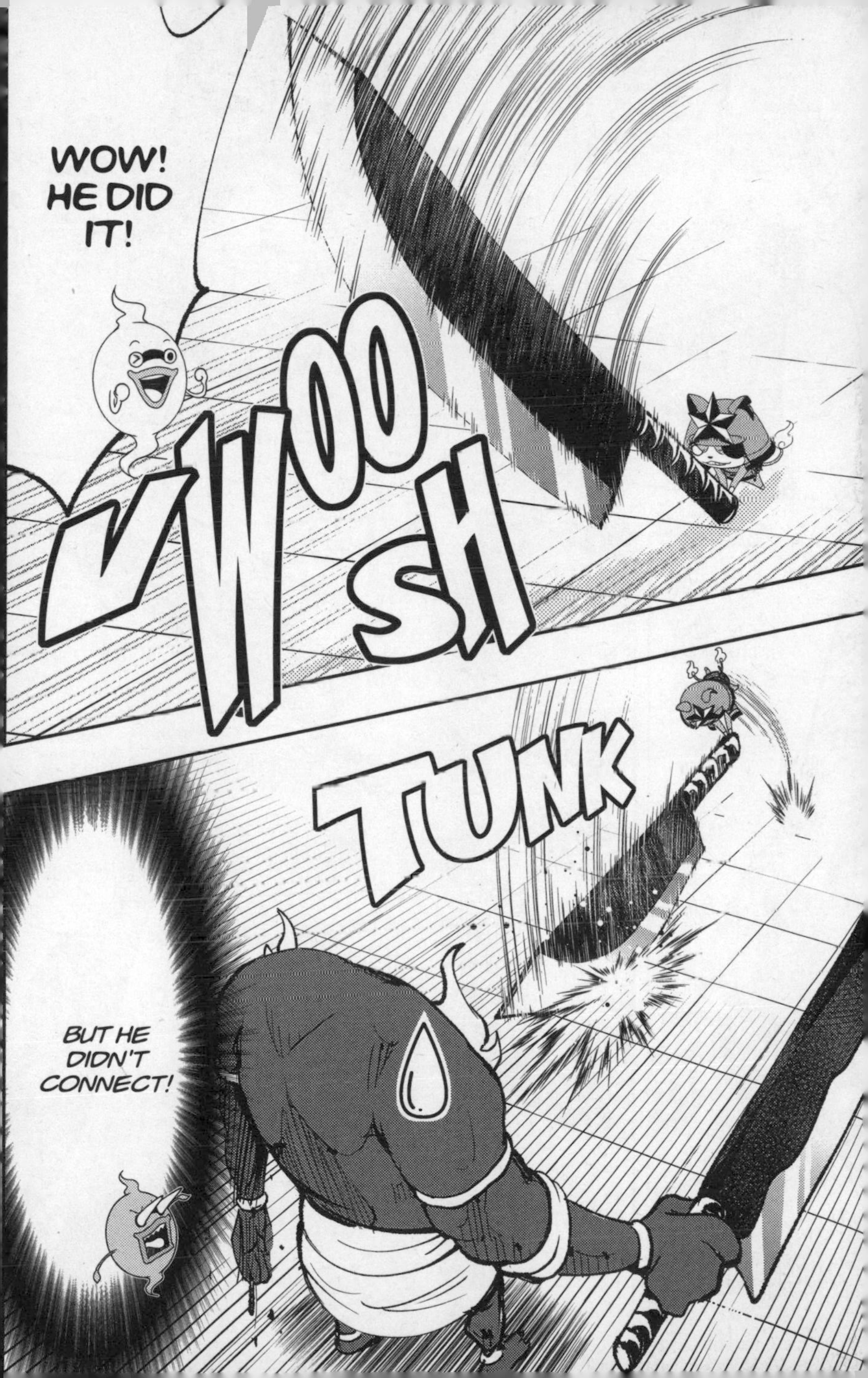
WOW! HE DID IT!
WHOOSH
TUNK
BUT HE DIDN'T CONNECT!

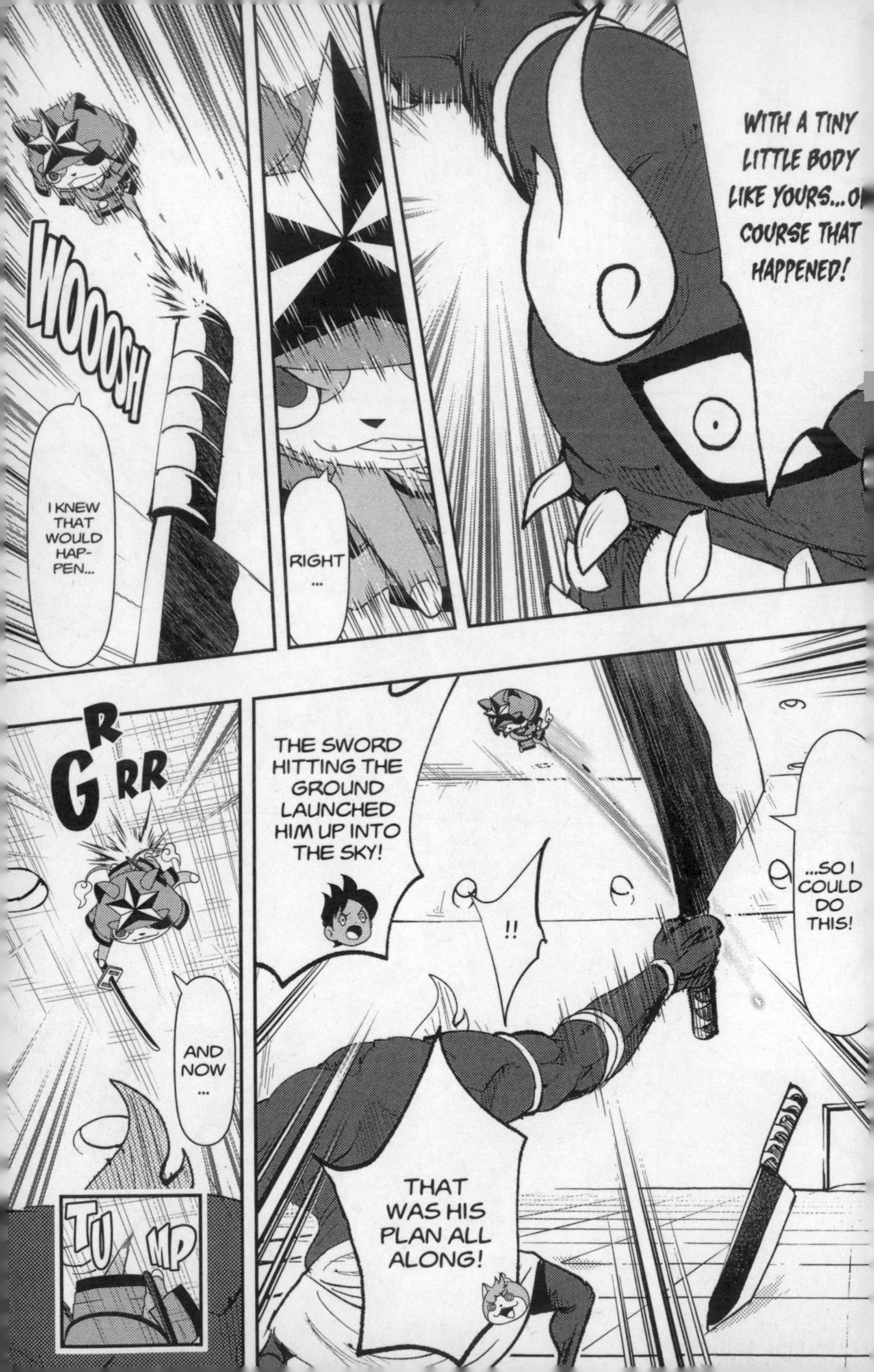
WITH A TINY LITTLE BODY LIKE YOURS...OF COURSE THAT HAPPENED!
RIGHT...
WOOOSH
I KNEW THAT WOULD HAP-PEN...
...SO I COULD DO THIS!
!!
THE SWORD HITTING THE GROUND LAUNCHED HIM UP INTO THE SKY!
THAT WAS HIS PLAN ALL ALONG!
GRRR
AND NOW...
TUMP

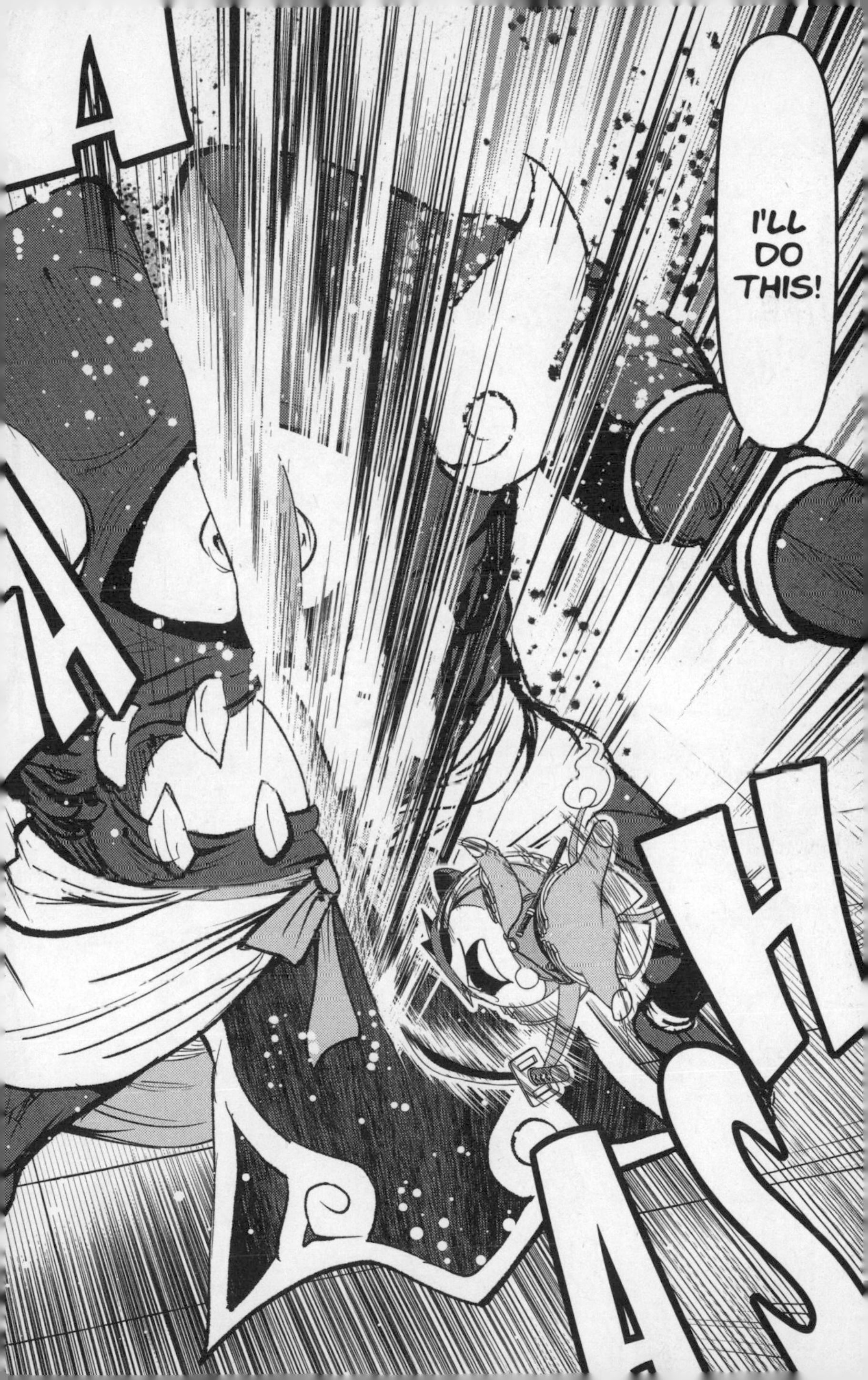
I'LL DO THIS!

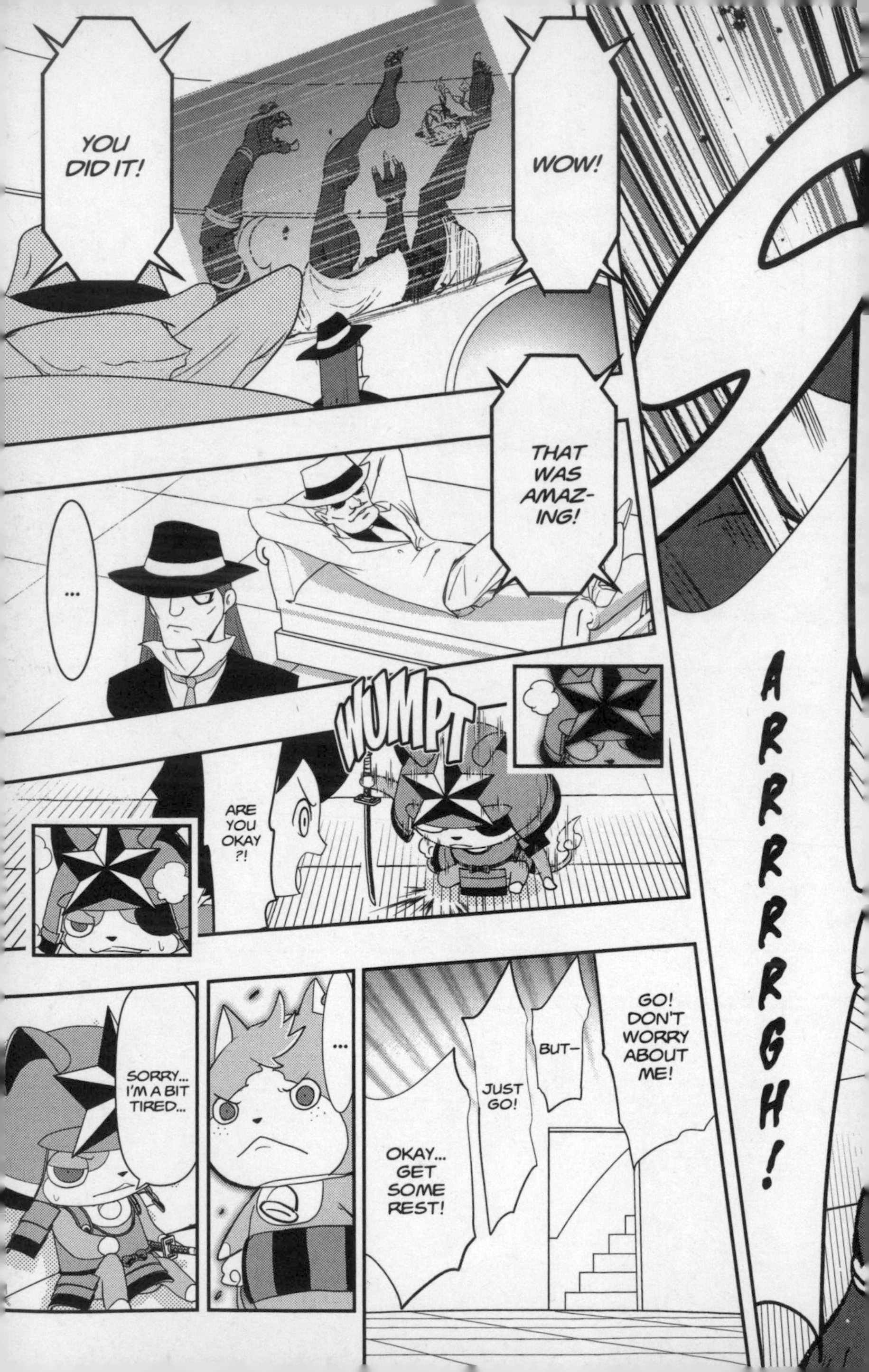
ARRRRRGH!
WOW!
YOU DID IT!
THAT WAS AMAZING!
...
WUMPT
ARE YOU OKAY?!
GO! DON'T WORRY ABOUT ME!
BUT—
JUST GO!
OKAY... GET SOME REST!
...
SORRY... I'M A BIT TIRED...

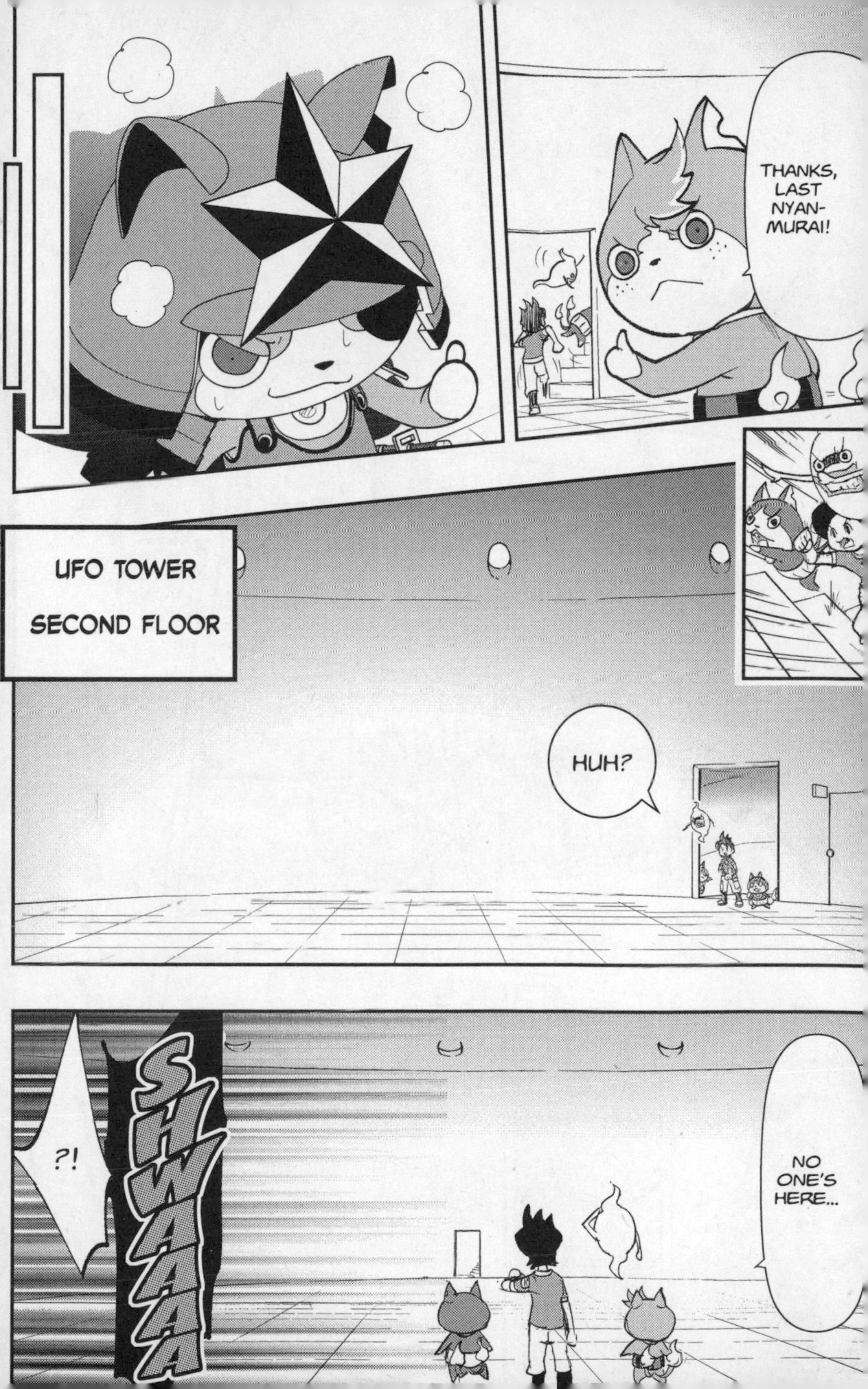
THANKS, LAST NYAN-MURAI!
UFO TOWER SECOND FLOOR
HUH?
NO ONE'S HERE...
SHWAAAA
?!

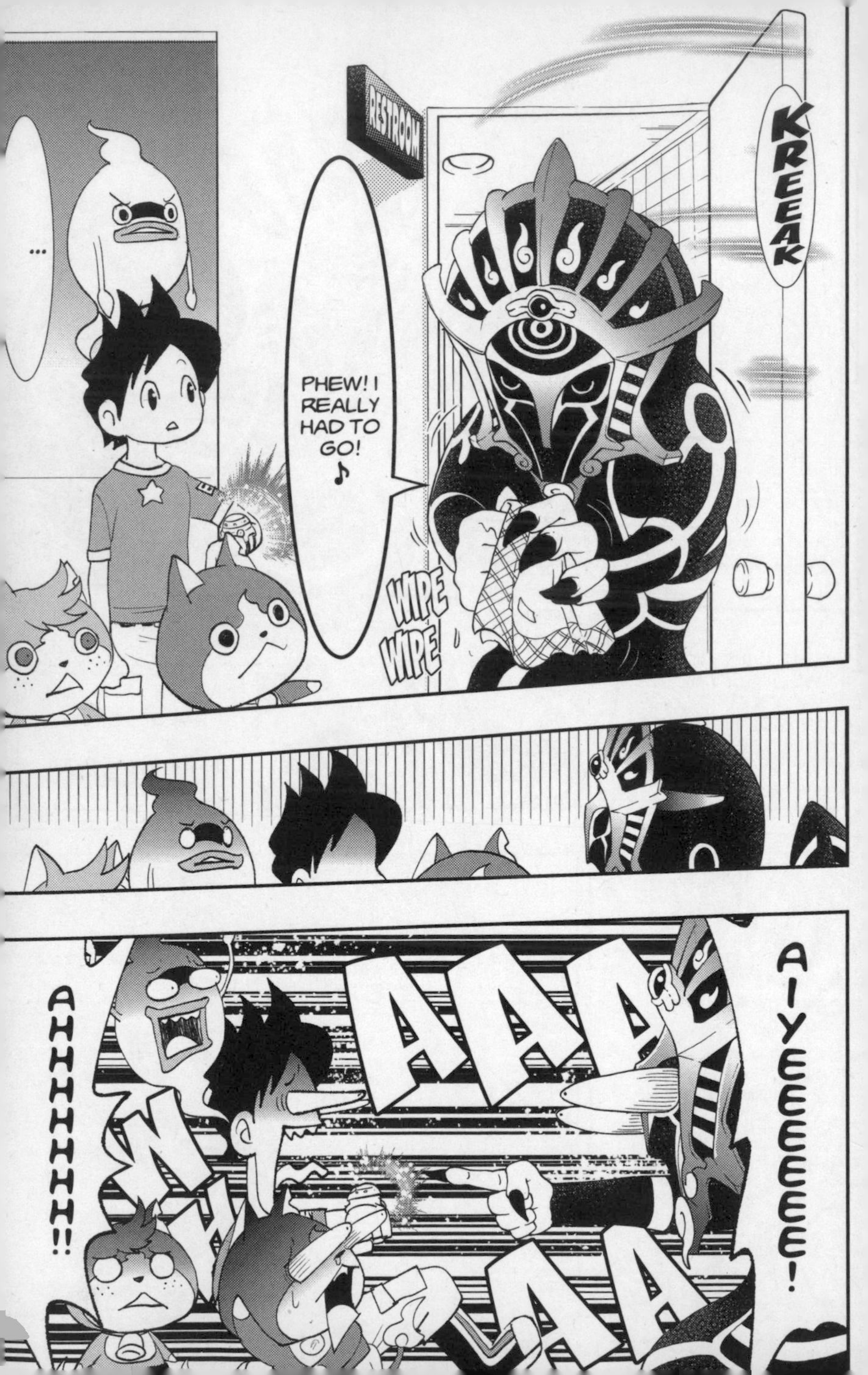
KREEAK
RESTROOM
PHEW! I REALLY HAD TO GO! ♪
WIPE WIPE
...
AIYEEEEEEE!
AAA
N
AA
AHHHHHHH!!

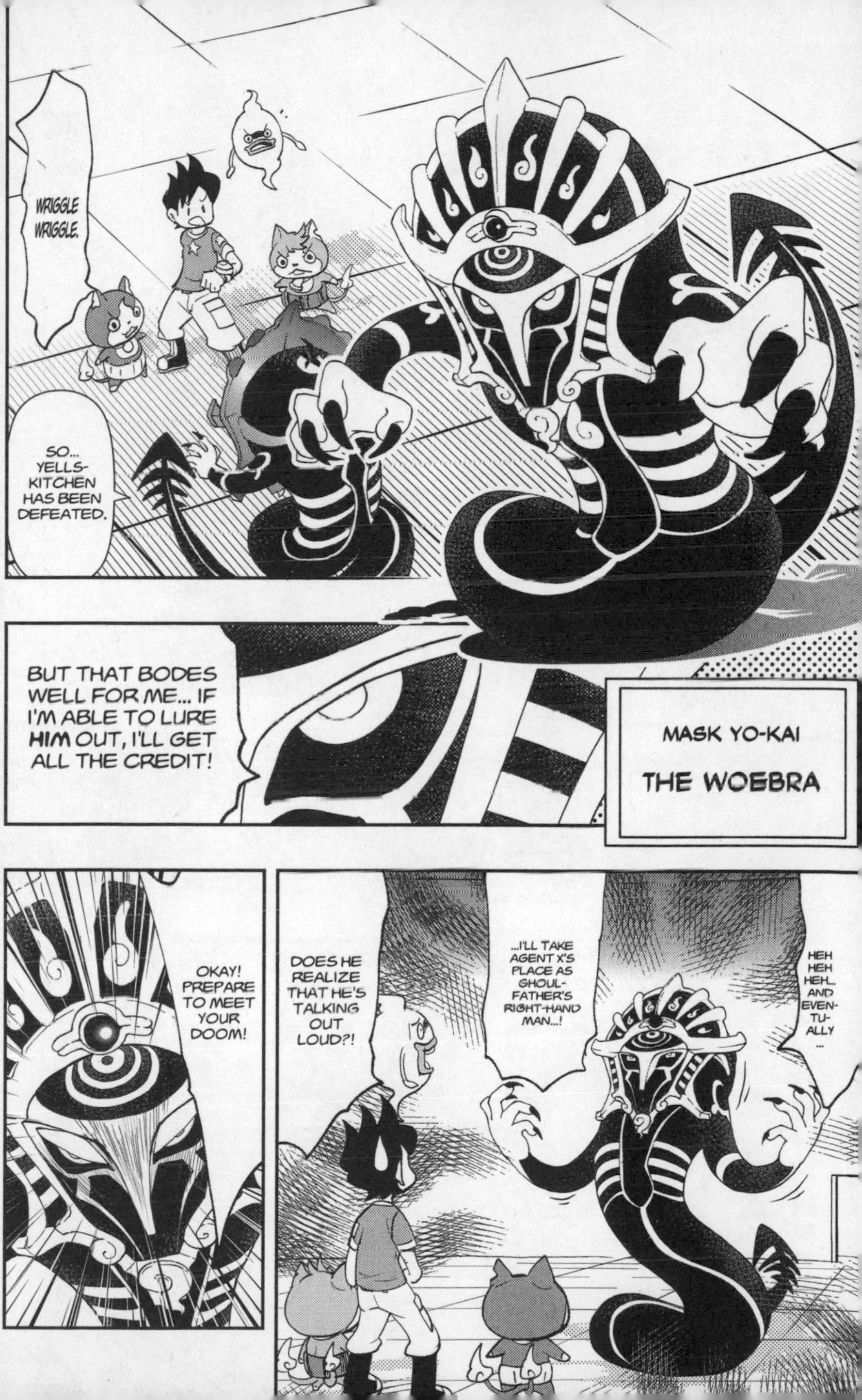
WRIGGLE WRIGGLE.
SO... YELLS-KITCHEN HAS BEEN DEFEATED.
MASK YO-KAI
THE WOEBRA
BUT THAT BODES WELL FOR ME... IF I'M ABLE TO LURE **HIM** OUT, I'LL GET ALL THE CREDIT!
HEH HEH HEH... AND EVEN-TU-ALLY ...
...I'LL TAKE AGENT X'S PLACE AS GHOUL-FATHER'S RIGHT-HAND MAN...!
DOES HE REALIZE THAT HE'S TALKING OUT LOUD?!
OKAY! PREPARE TO MEET YOUR DOOM!

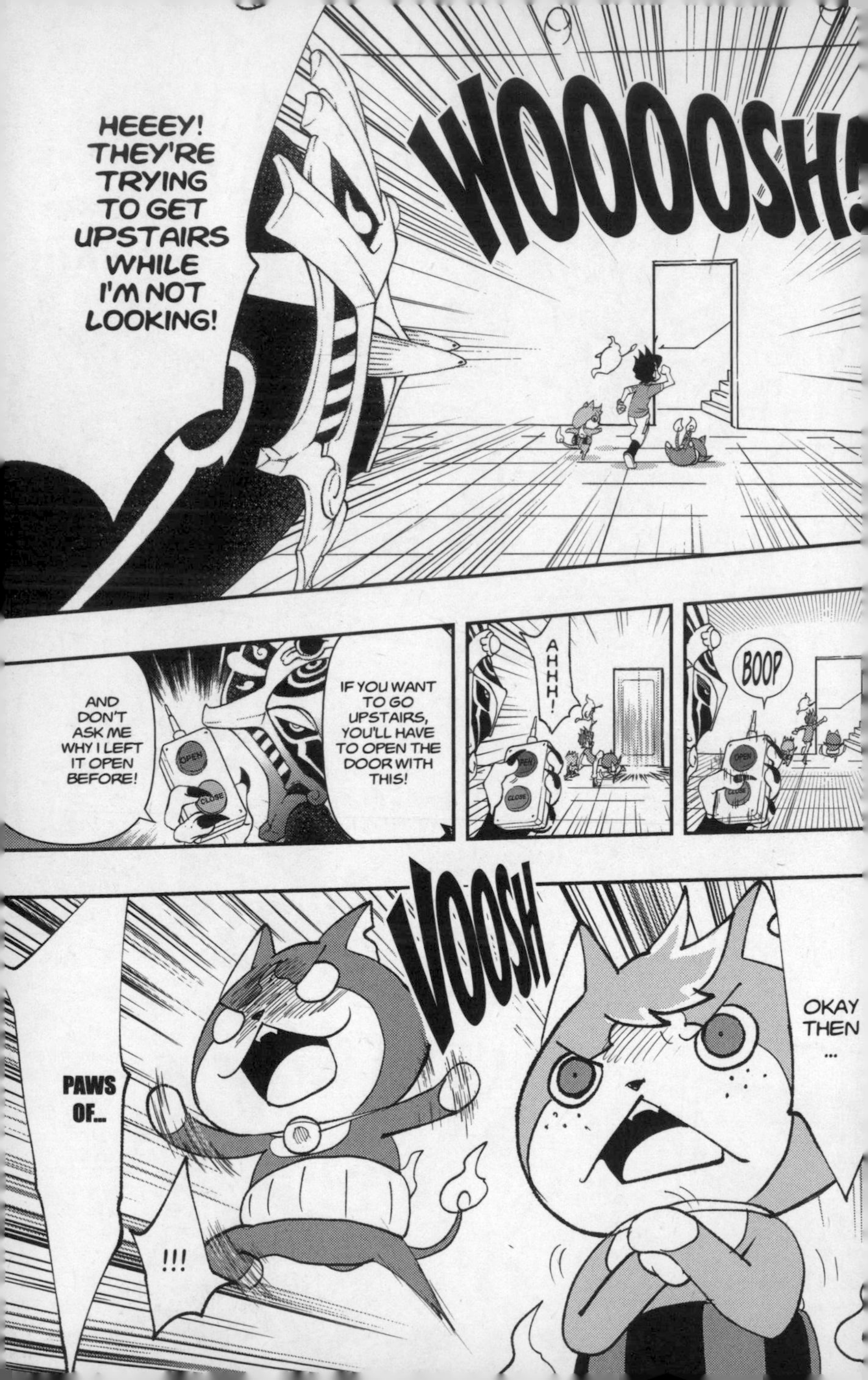
WOOOOSH!
HEEEY! THEY'RE TRYING TO GET UPSTAIRS WHILE I'M NOT LOOKING!
BOOP
AHHH!
IF YOU WANT TO GO UPSTAIRS, YOU'LL HAVE TO OPEN THE DOOR WITH THIS!
AND DON'T ASK ME WHY I LEFT IT OPEN BEFORE!
OKAY THEN ...
VOOSH
PAWS OF...
!!!

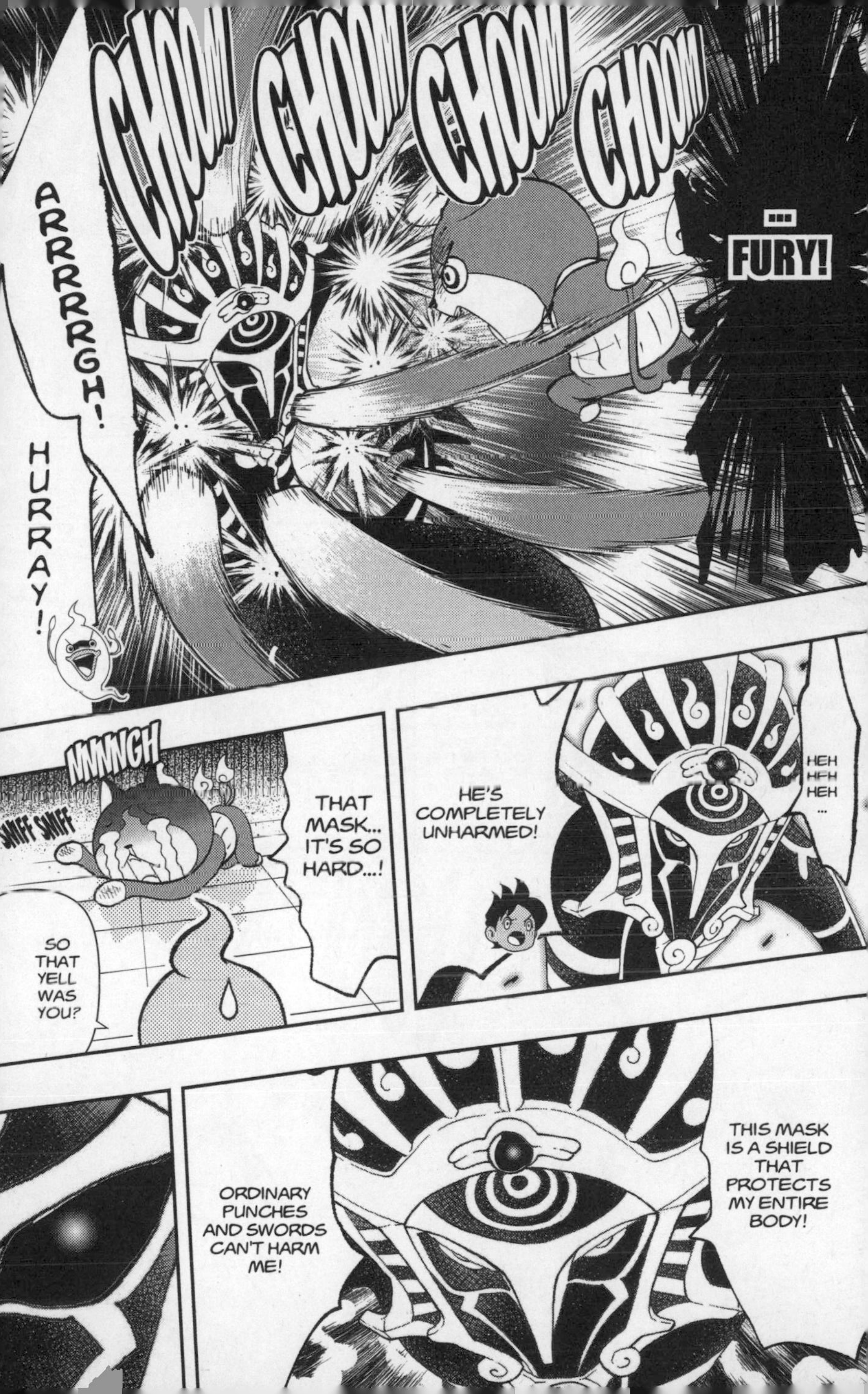
...FURY!
CHOOM
CHOOM
CHOOM
CHOOM
ARRRRRGH!
HURRAY!
HEH HEH HEH...
HE'S COMPLETELY UNHARMED!
THAT MASK... IT'S SO HARD...!
NNNNGH
SNIFF SNIFF
SO THAT YELL WAS YOU?
THIS MASK IS A SHIELD THAT PROTECTS MY ENTIRE BODY!
ORDINARY PUNCHES AND SWORDS CAN'T HARM ME!

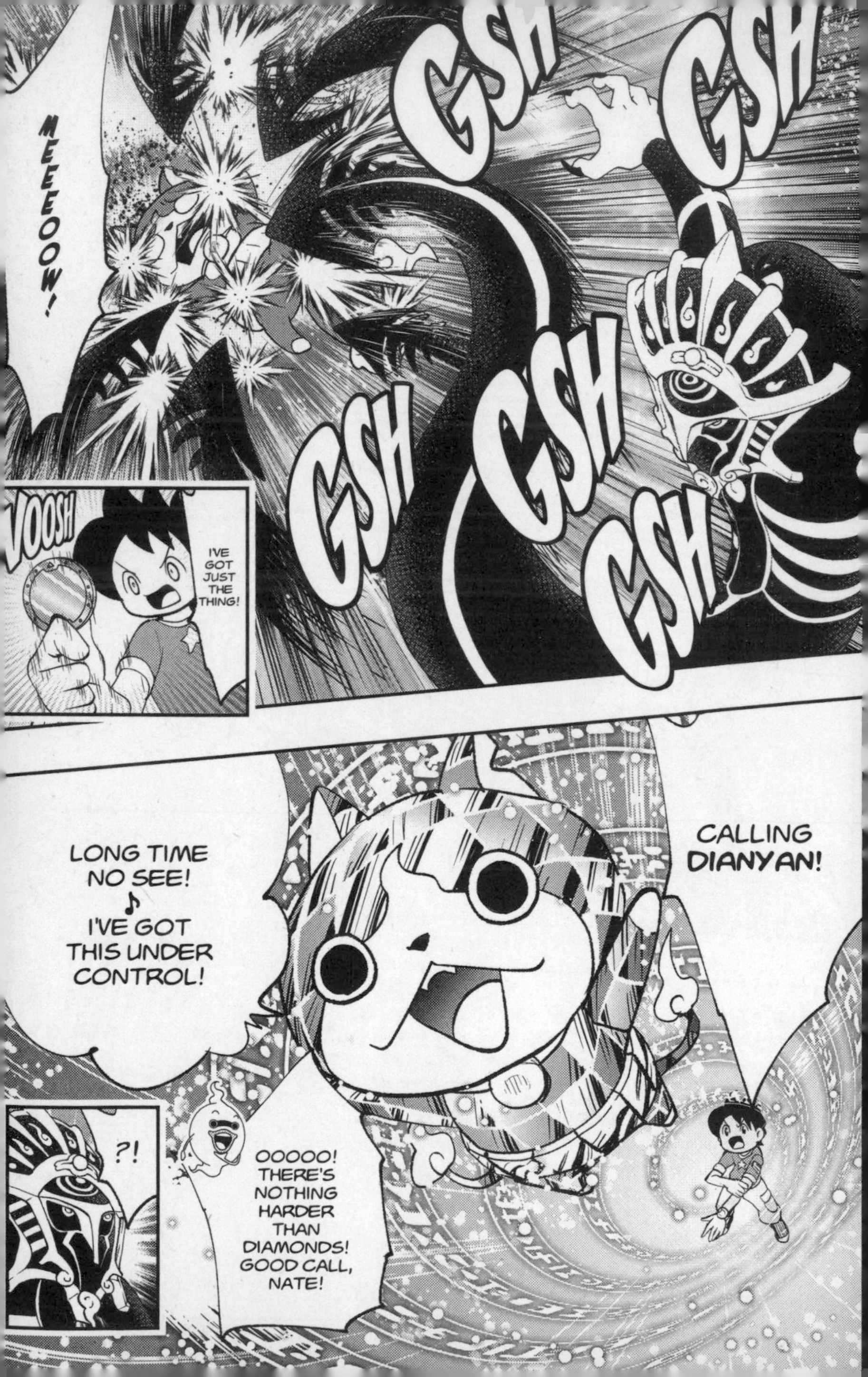
GSH
GSH
GSH
GSH
GSH
MEEEOOOW!
VOOSH
I'VE GOT JUST THE THING!
CALLING DIANYAN!
LONG TIME NO SEE! ♪
I'VE GOT THIS UNDER CONTROL!
OOOOO! THERE'S NOTHING HARDER THAN DIAMONDS! GOOD CALL, NATE!
?!

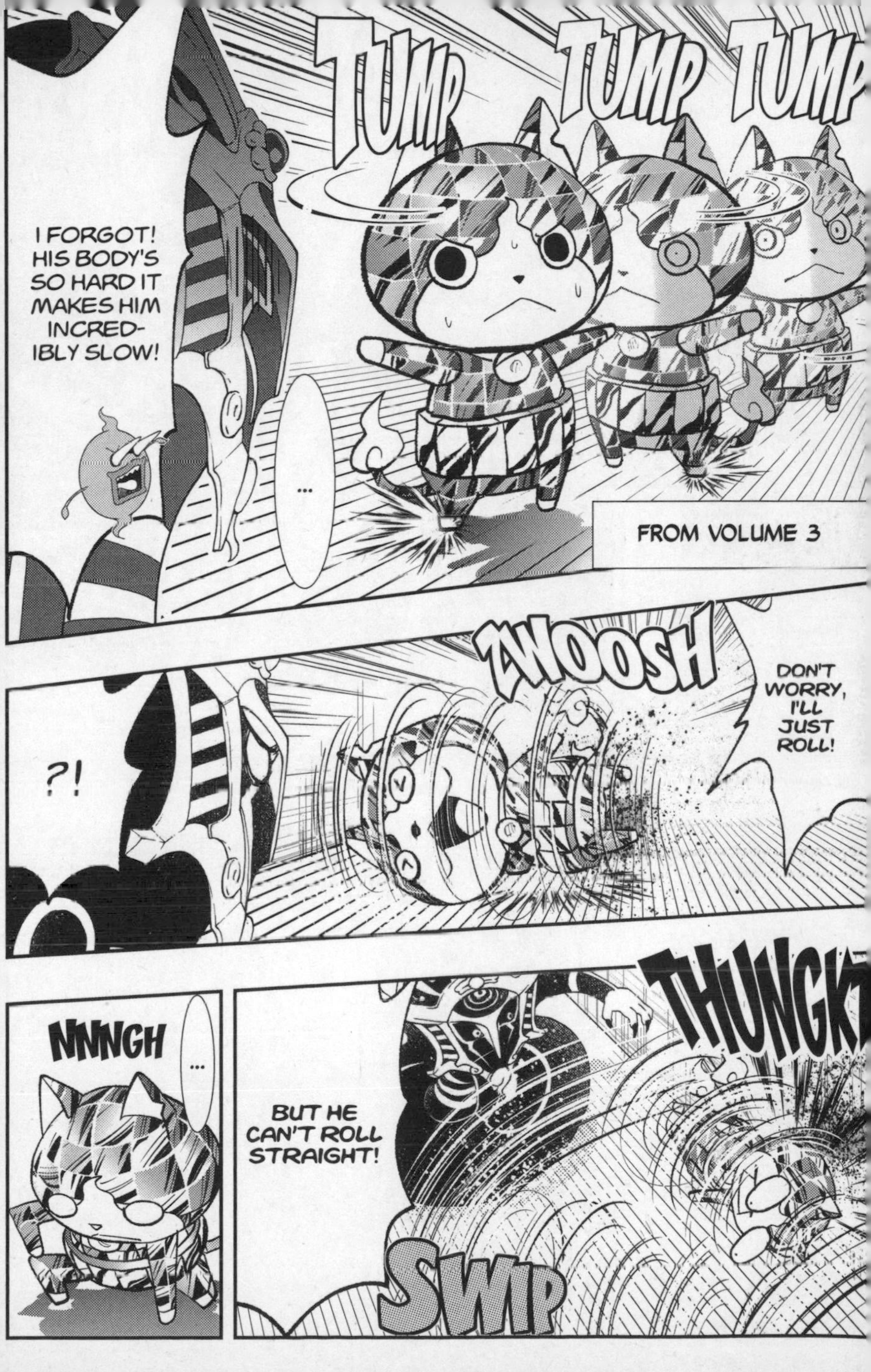
TUMP TUMP TUMP
FROM VOLUME 3
I FORGOT! HIS BODY'S SO HARD IT MAKES HIM INCRED-IBLY SLOW!
...
ZWOOSH
DON'T WORRY, I'LL JUST ROLL!
?!
THUNK
BUT HE CAN'T ROLL STRAIGHT!
SWIP
...
NNNGH

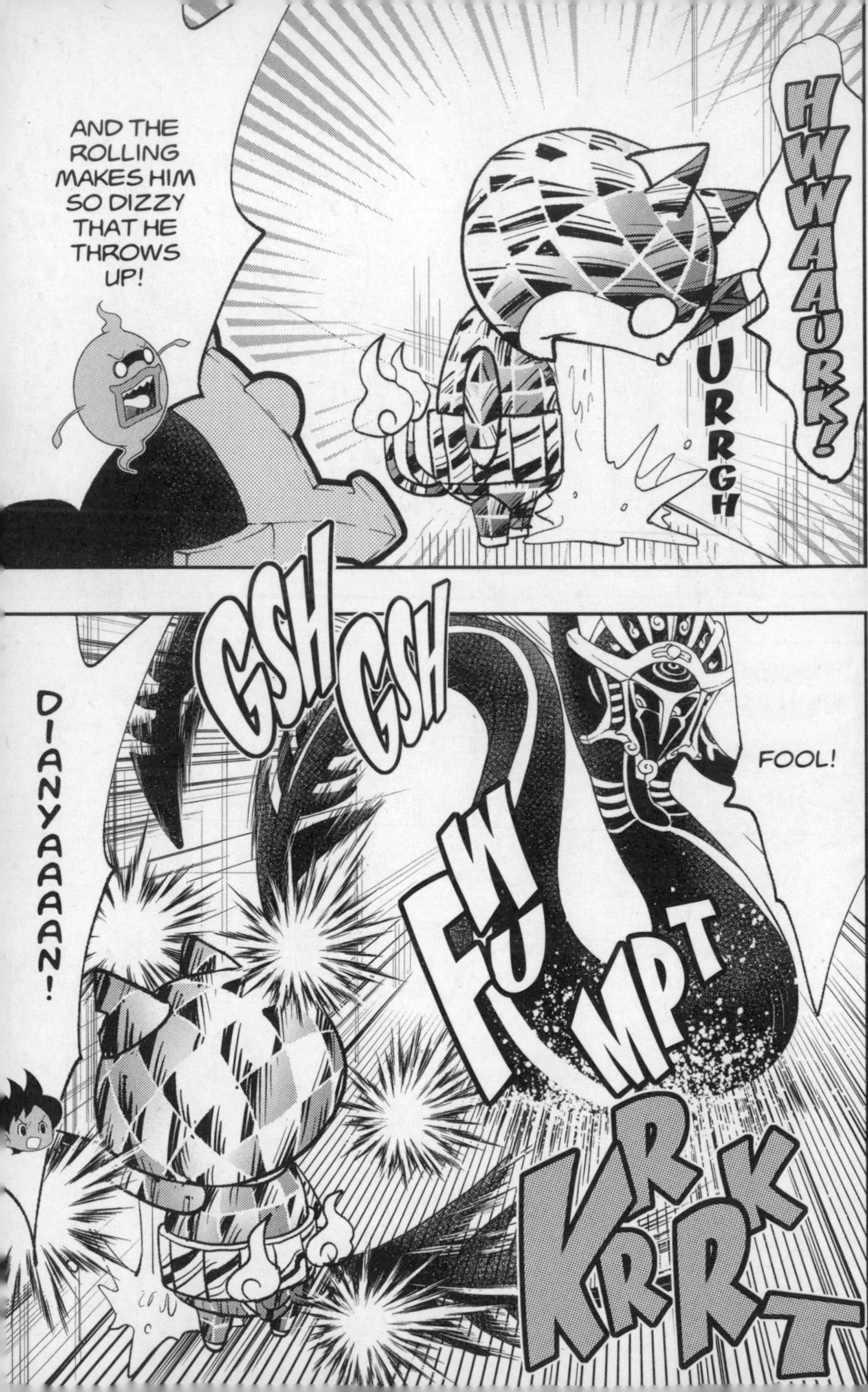
HWWAAURK!
URRGH
AND THE ROLLING MAKES HIM SO DIZZY THAT HE THROWS UP!
GSH GSH
FOOL!
FWUMPT
KRK KRRT
DIANYAAAAAN!

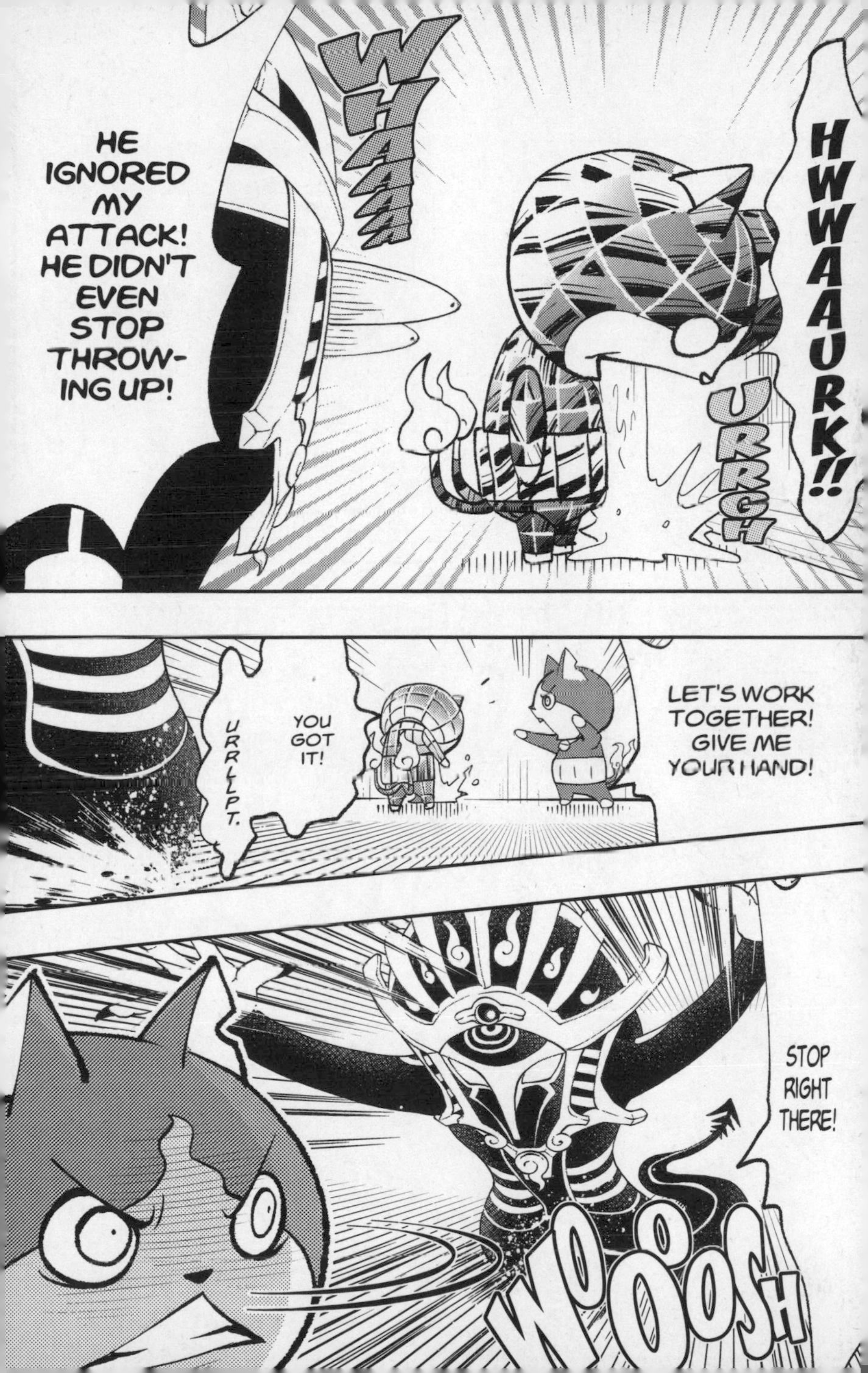
HWWAAAURK!!
URRGH
WHAAAA
HE IGNORED MY ATTACK! HE DIDN'T EVEN STOP THROWING UP!
LET'S WORK TOGETHER! GIVE ME YOUR HAND!
YOU GOT IT!
URRLLPT.
STOP RIGHT THERE!
WOOOOSH

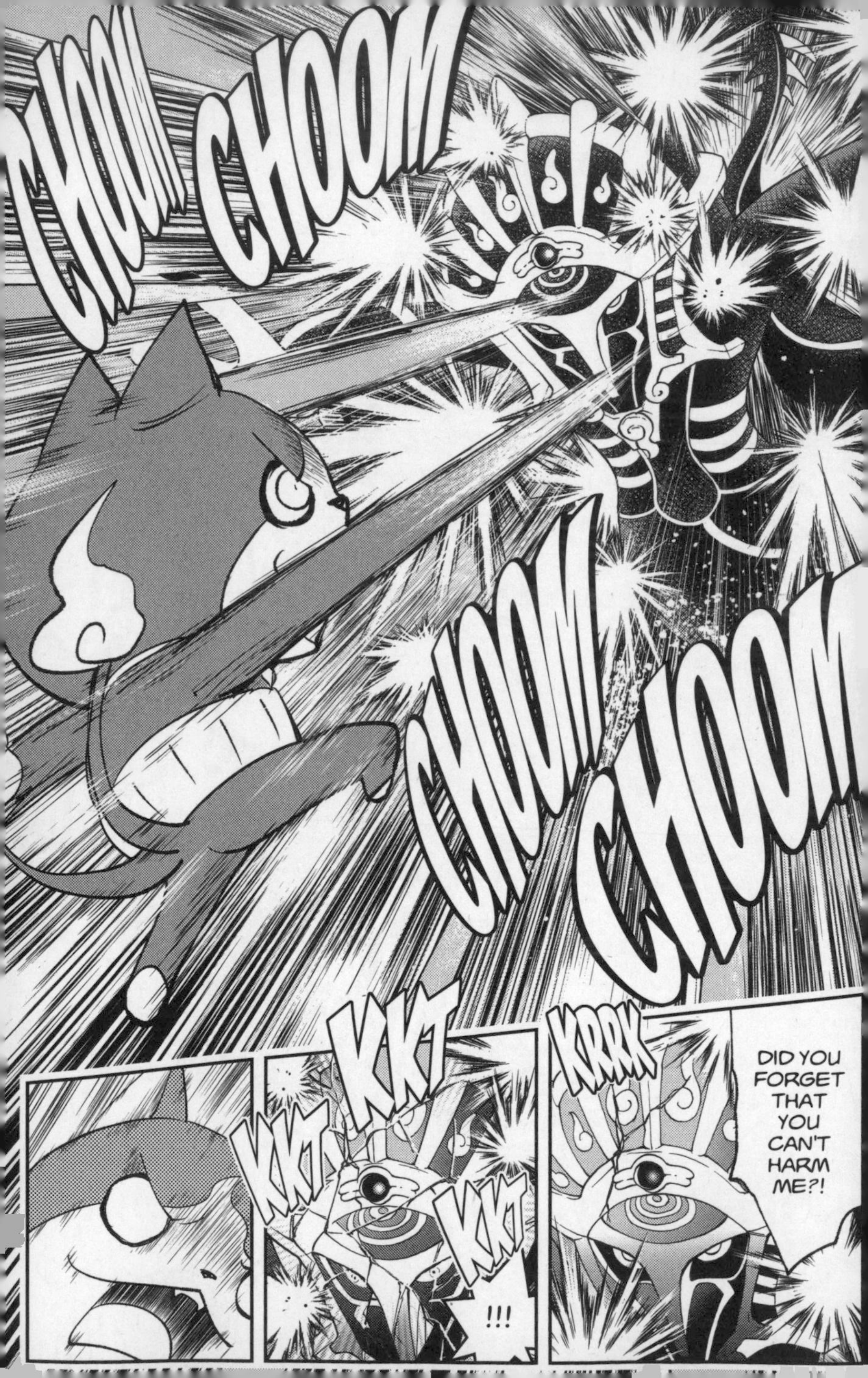
CHOOM
CHOOM
CHOOM
CHOOM
KRRK
DID YOU FORGET THAT YOU CAN'T HARM ME?!
KKT
KKT
KKT
!!!

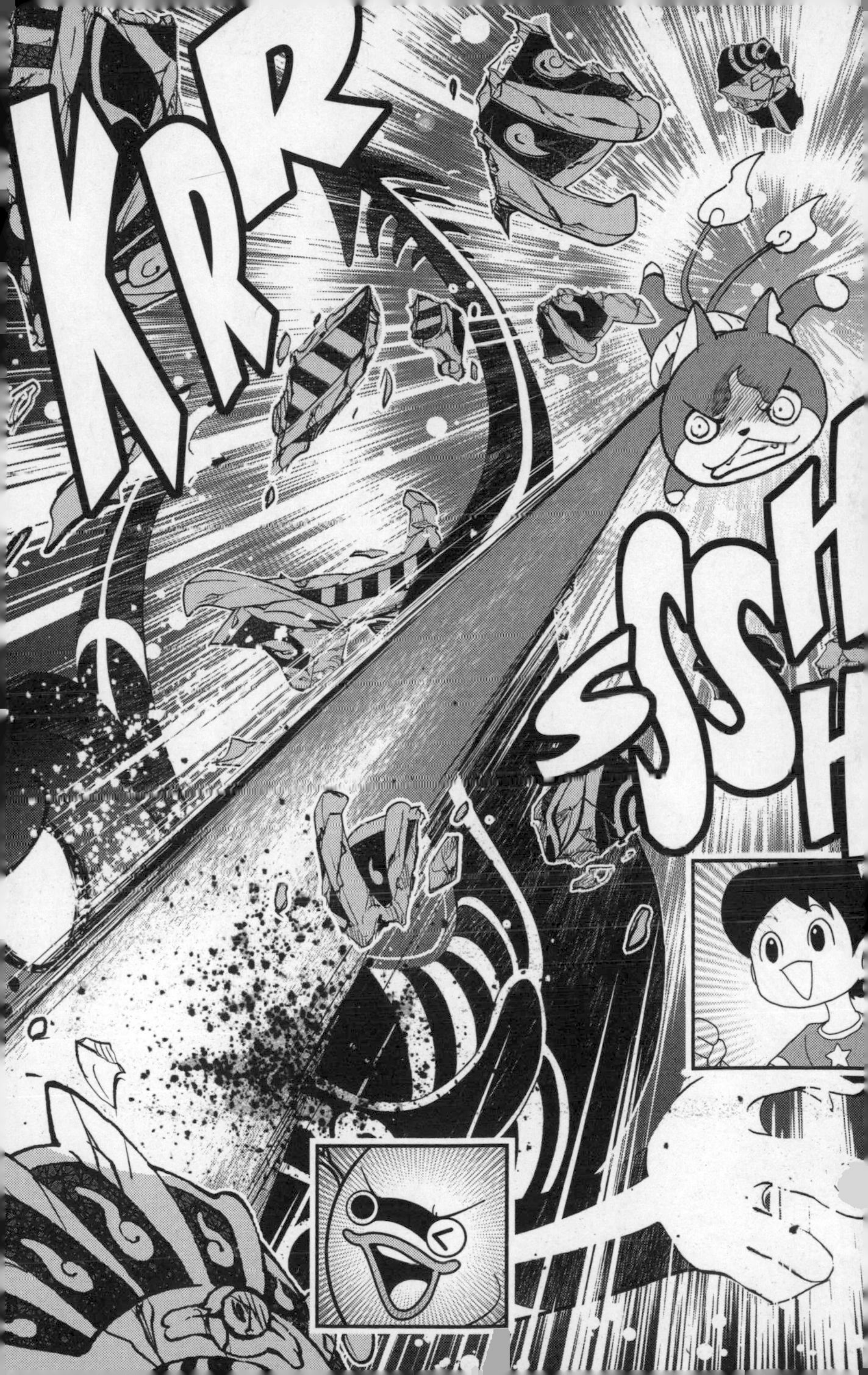
KRR
SSSH

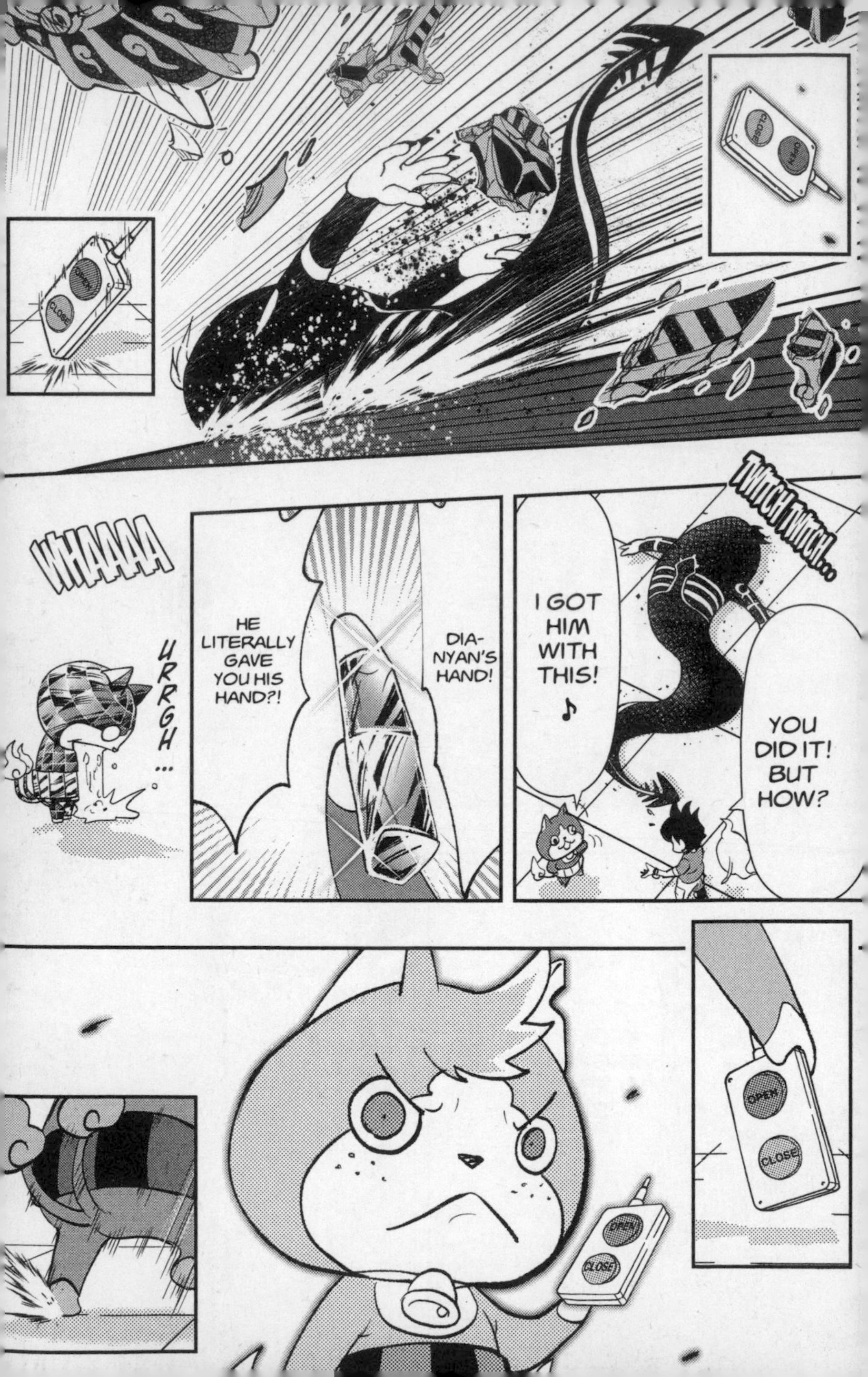
CLOSE
OPEN
OPEN
CLOSE
TWITCH TWITCH...
YOU DID IT! BUT HOW?
I GOT HIM WITH THIS! ♪
DIA-NYAN'S HAND!
HE LITERALLY GAVE YOU HIS HAND?!
WHAAAA
URRGH...
OPEN
CLOSE
OPEN
CLOSE

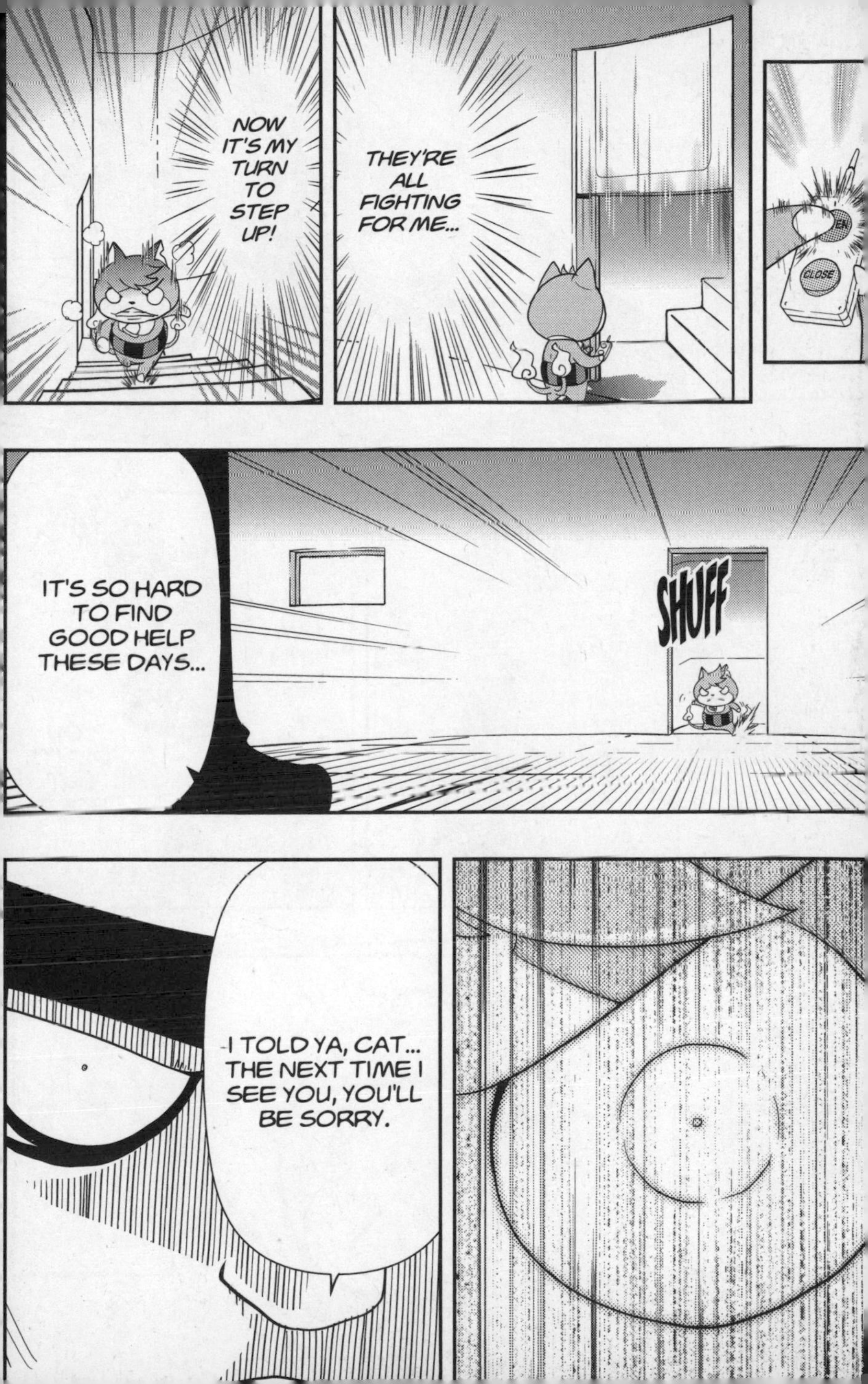
CLOSE
THEY'RE ALL FIGHTING FOR ME...
NOW IT'S MY TURN TO STEP UP!
SHUFF
IT'S SO HARD TO FIND GOOD HELP THESE DAYS...
I TOLD YA, CAT... THE NEXT TIME I SEE YOU, YOU'LL BE SORRY.

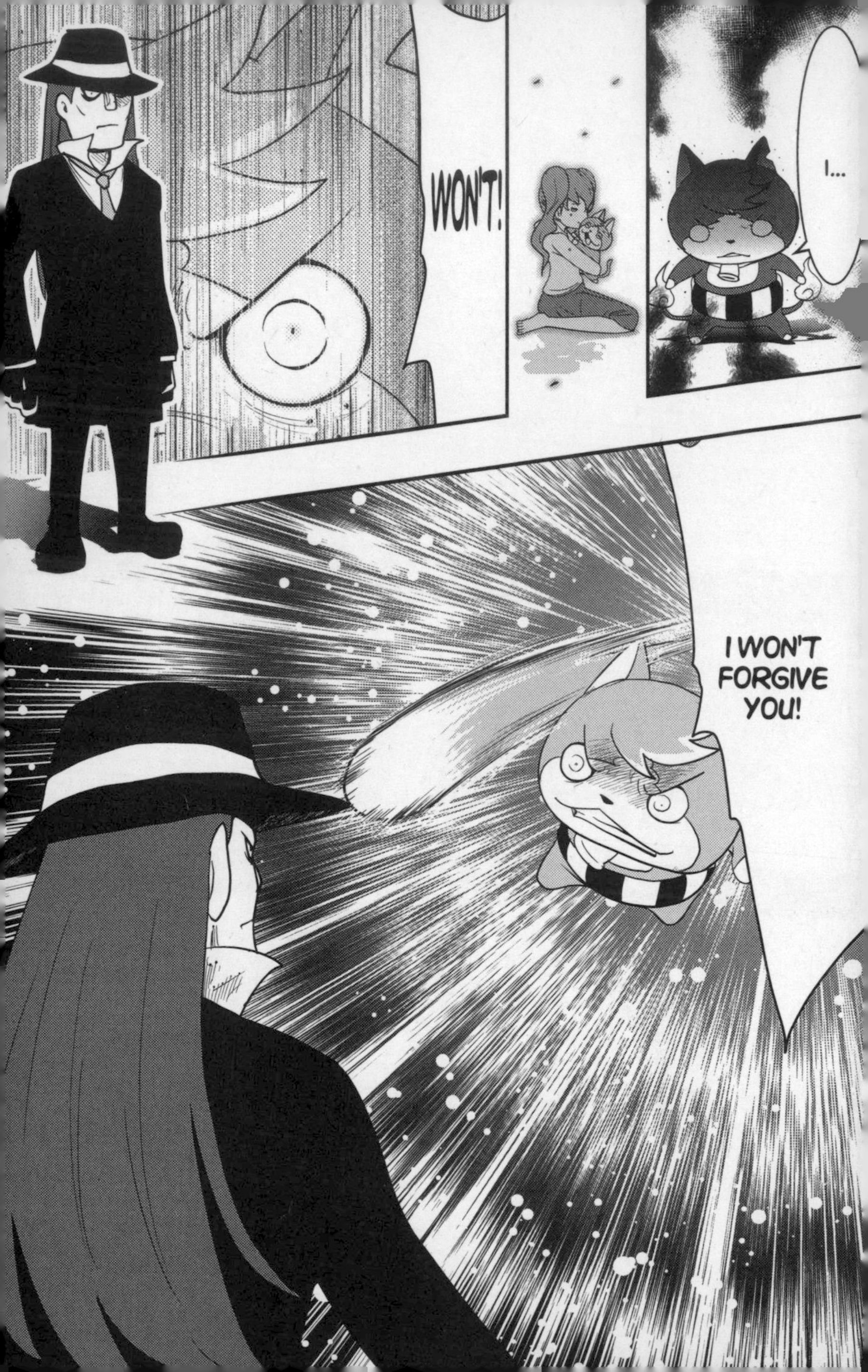
I...
WON'T!
I WON'T FORGIVE YOU!

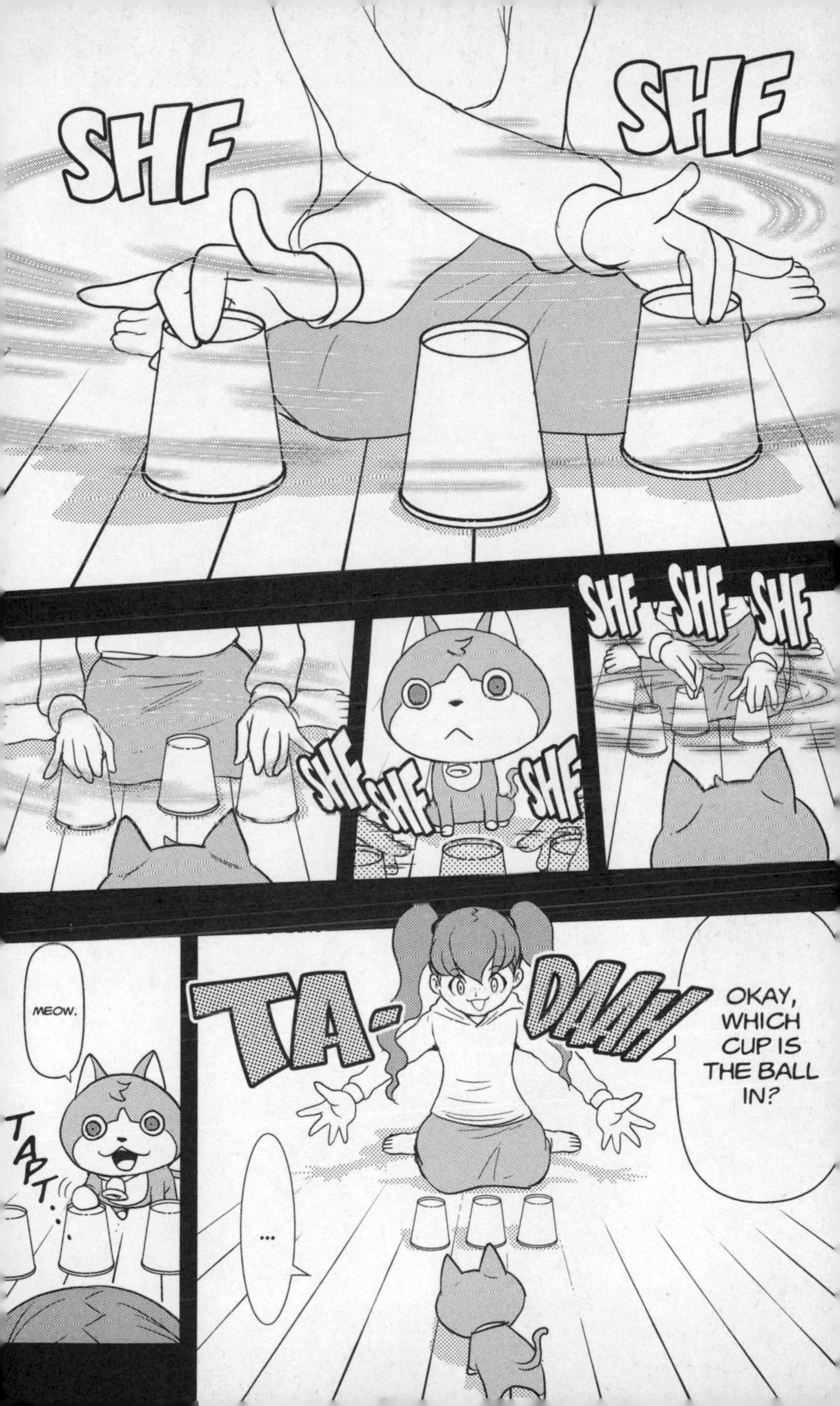
SHF
SHF
SHF-SHF-SHF
SHF-SHF-SHF
OKAY, WHICH CUP IS THE BALL IN?
TA-DAAH
...
MEOW.
TAPT...

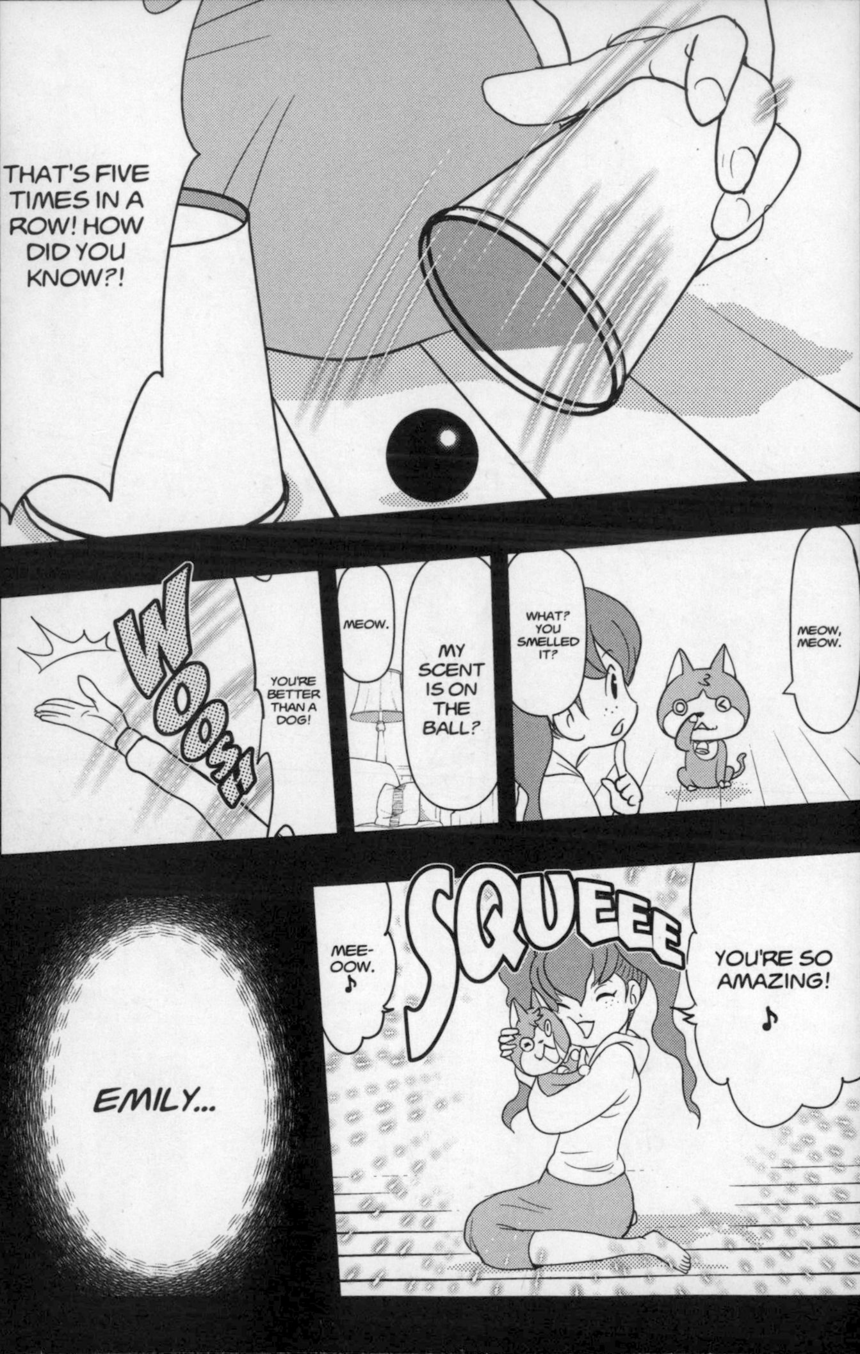
THAT'S FIVE TIMES IN A ROW! HOW DID YOU KNOW?!
MEOW, MEOW.
WHAT? YOU SMELLED IT?
MY SCENT IS ON THE BALL?
MEOW.
WOOOW!
YOU'RE BETTER THAN A DOG!
YOU'RE SO AMAZING! ♪
SQUEEE
MEE-OOW. ♪
EMILY...

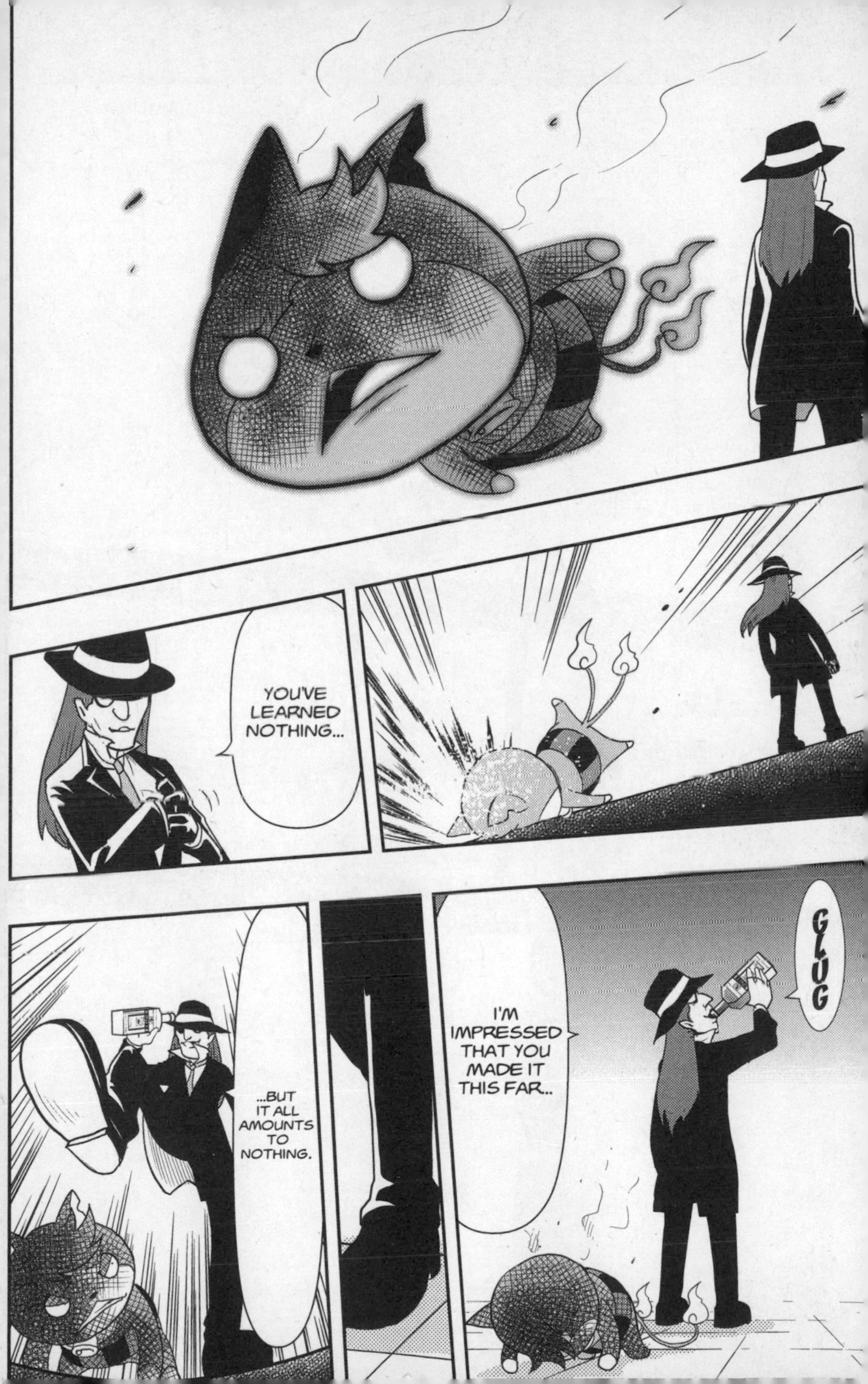
YOU'VE LEARNED NOTHING...
GLUG
I'M IMPRESSED THAT YOU MADE IT THIS FAR...
...BUT IT ALL AMOUNTS TO NOTHING.

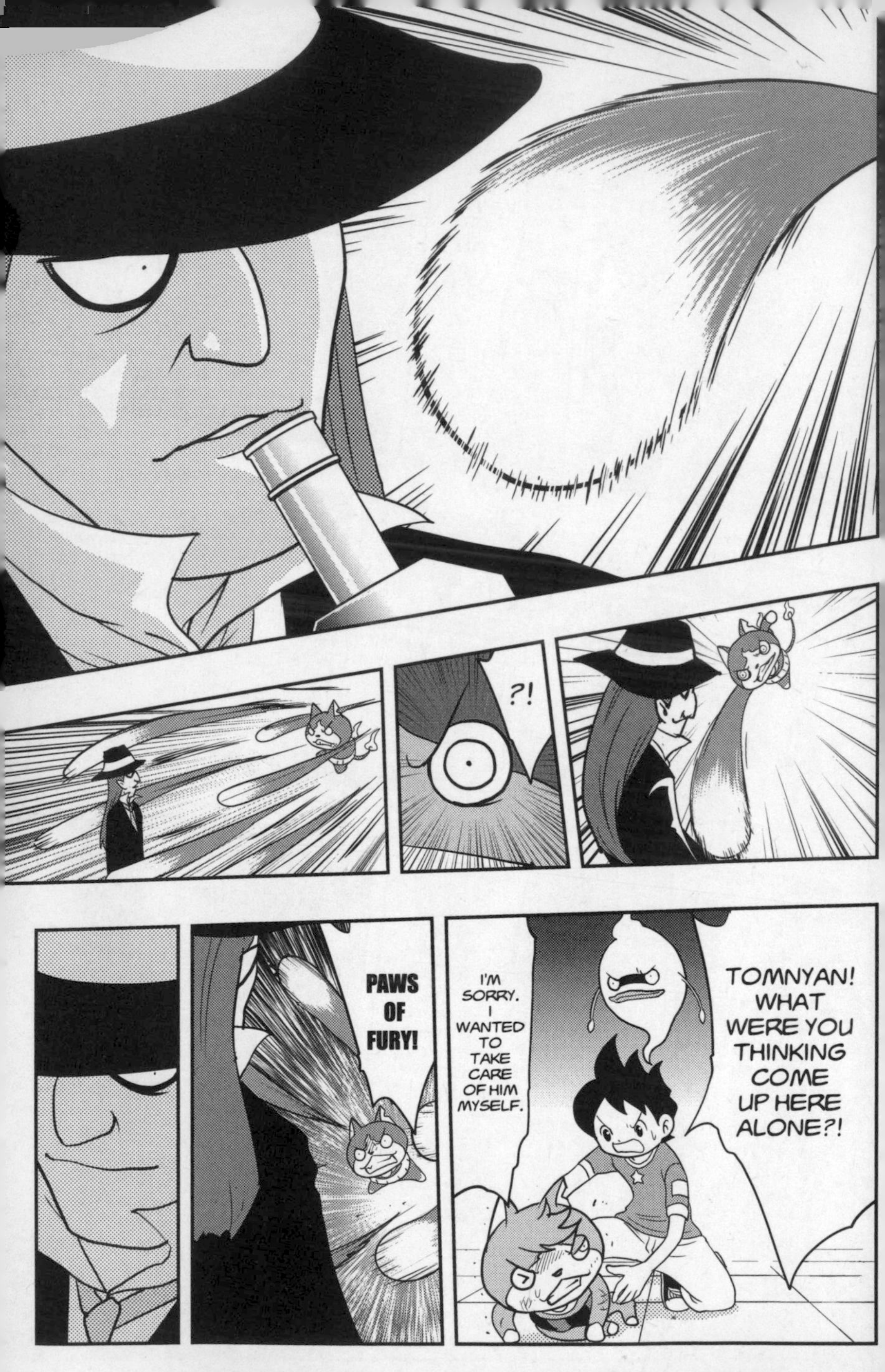
?!
TOMNYAN! WHAT WERE YOU THINKING COME UP HERE ALONE?!
I'M SORRY. I WANTED TO TAKE CARE OF HIM MYSELF.
PAWS OF FURY!

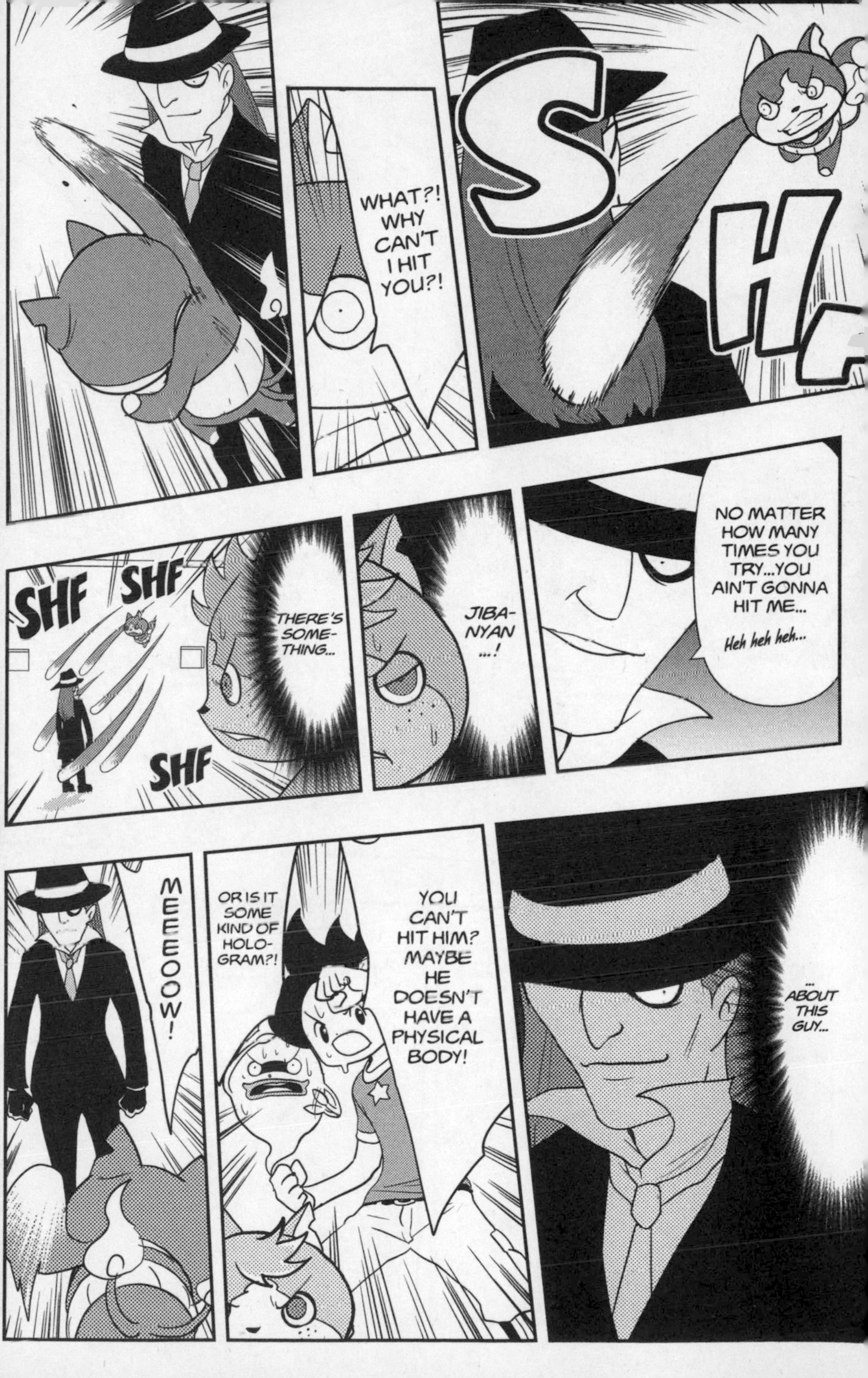
SH
WHAT?! WHY CAN'T I HIT YOU?!
NO MATTER HOW MANY TIMES YOU TRY...YOU AIN'T GONNA HIT ME...
Heh heh heh...
JIBA-NYAN ...!
THERE'S SOME-THING...
SHF
SHF
SHF
...ABOUT THIS GUY...
YOU CAN'T HIT HIM? MAYBE HE DOESN'T HAVE A PHYSICAL BODY!
OR IS IT SOME KIND OF HOLO-GRAM?!
MEEEOOOW!

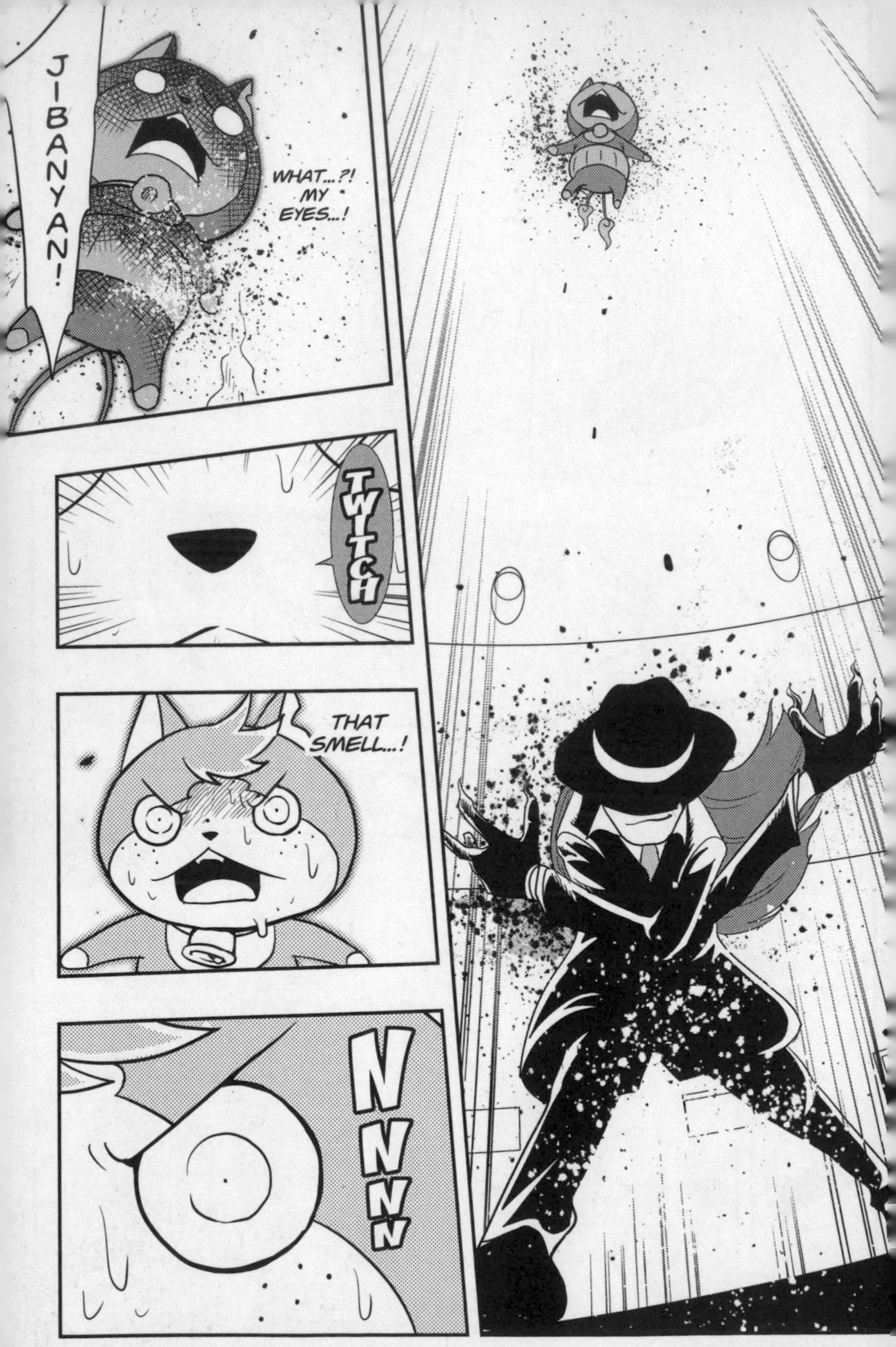
WHAT...?! MY EYES...!
JIBANYAN!
TWITCH
THAT SMELL...!
NNNN

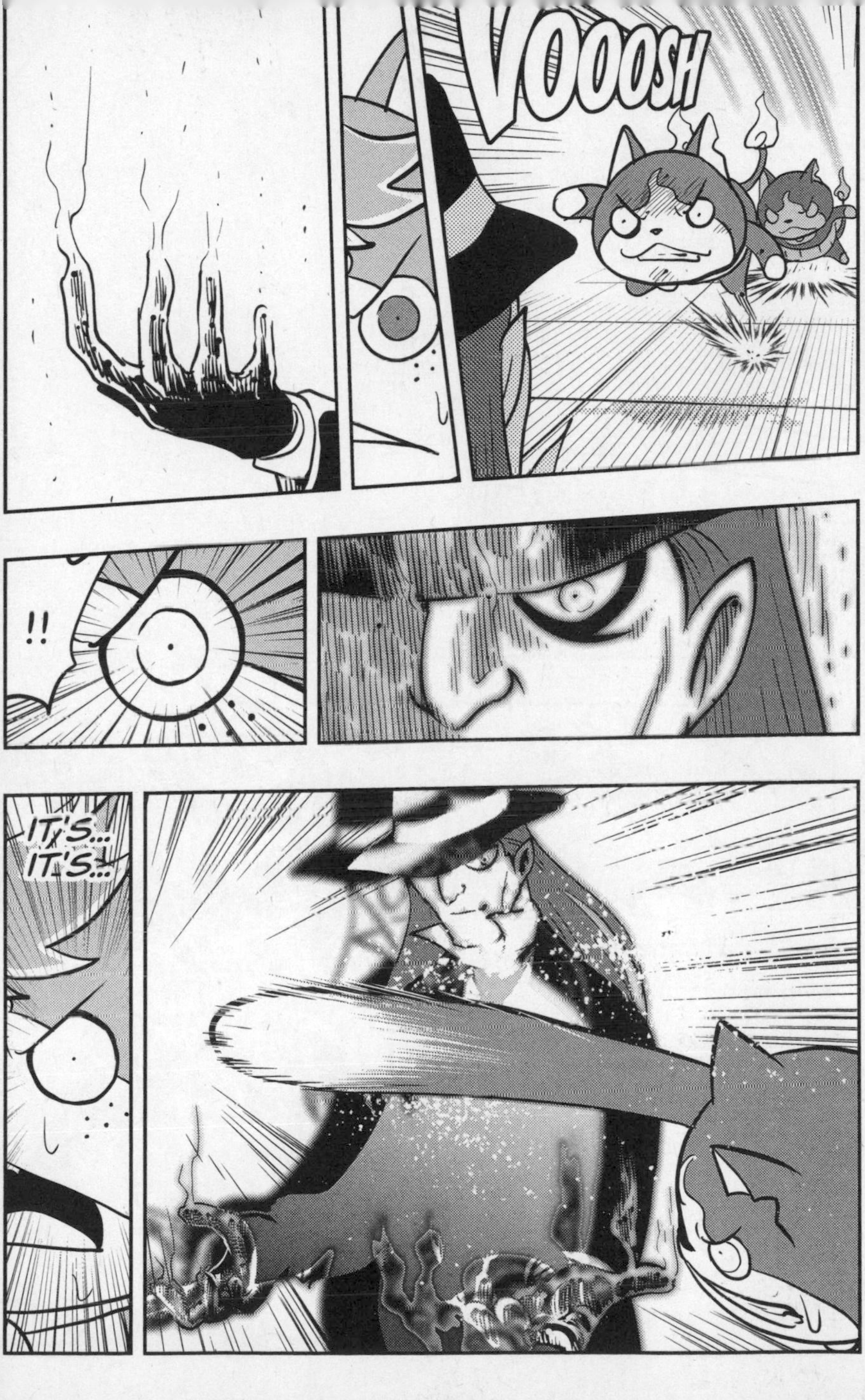
VOOOSH
!!
IT'S... IT'S...

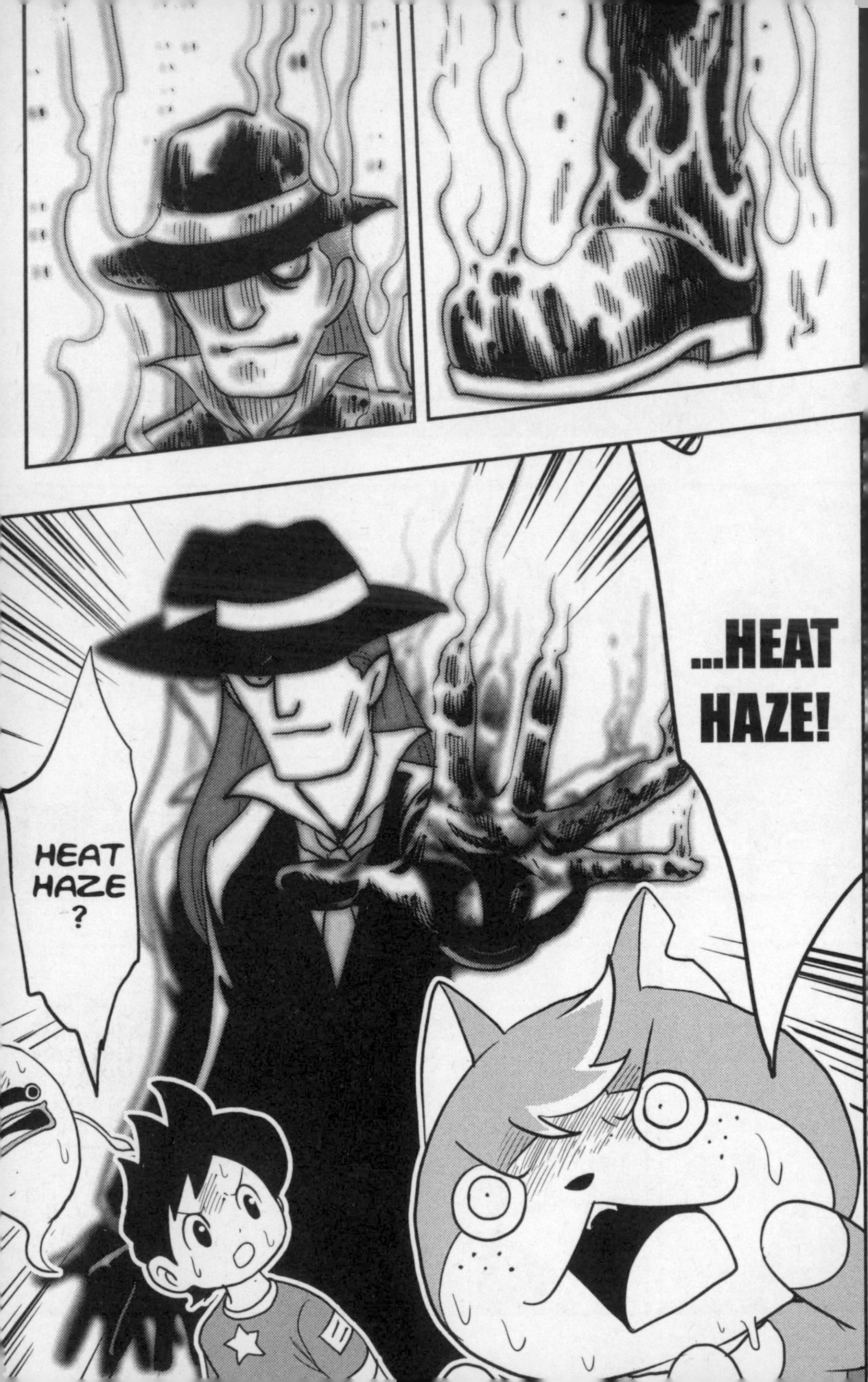
...HEAT HAZE!
HEAT HAZE ?

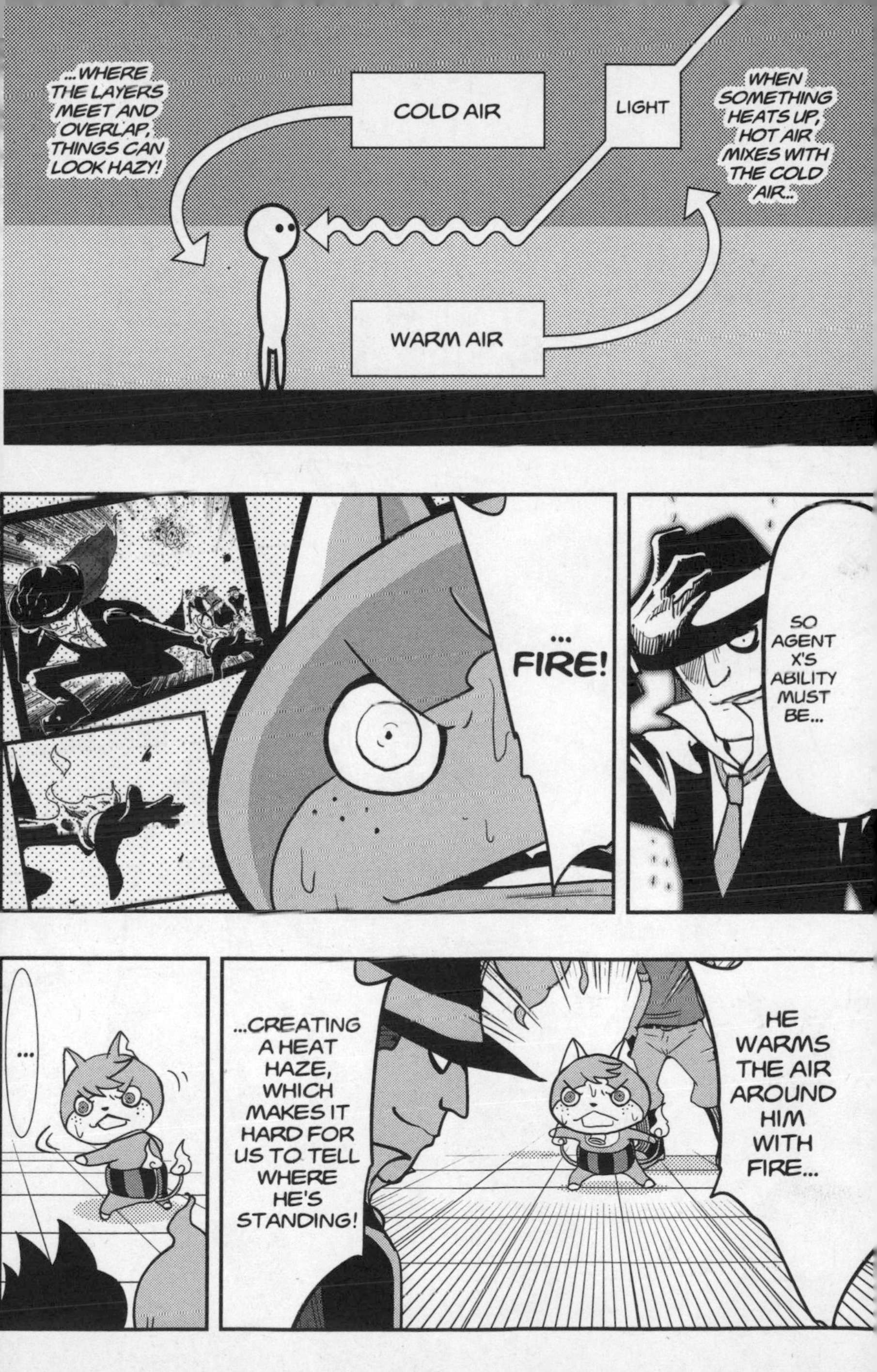
WHEN SOMETHING HEATS UP, HOT AIR MIXES WITH THE COLD AIR...
LIGHT
COLD AIR
WARM AIR
...WHERE THE LAYERS MEET AND OVERLAP, THINGS CAN LOOK HAZY!
SO AGENT X'S ABILITY MUST BE...
... FIRE!
HE WARMS THE AIR AROUND HIM WITH FIRE...
...CREATING A HEAT HAZE, WHICH MAKES IT HARD FOR US TO TELL WHERE HE'S STANDING!
...

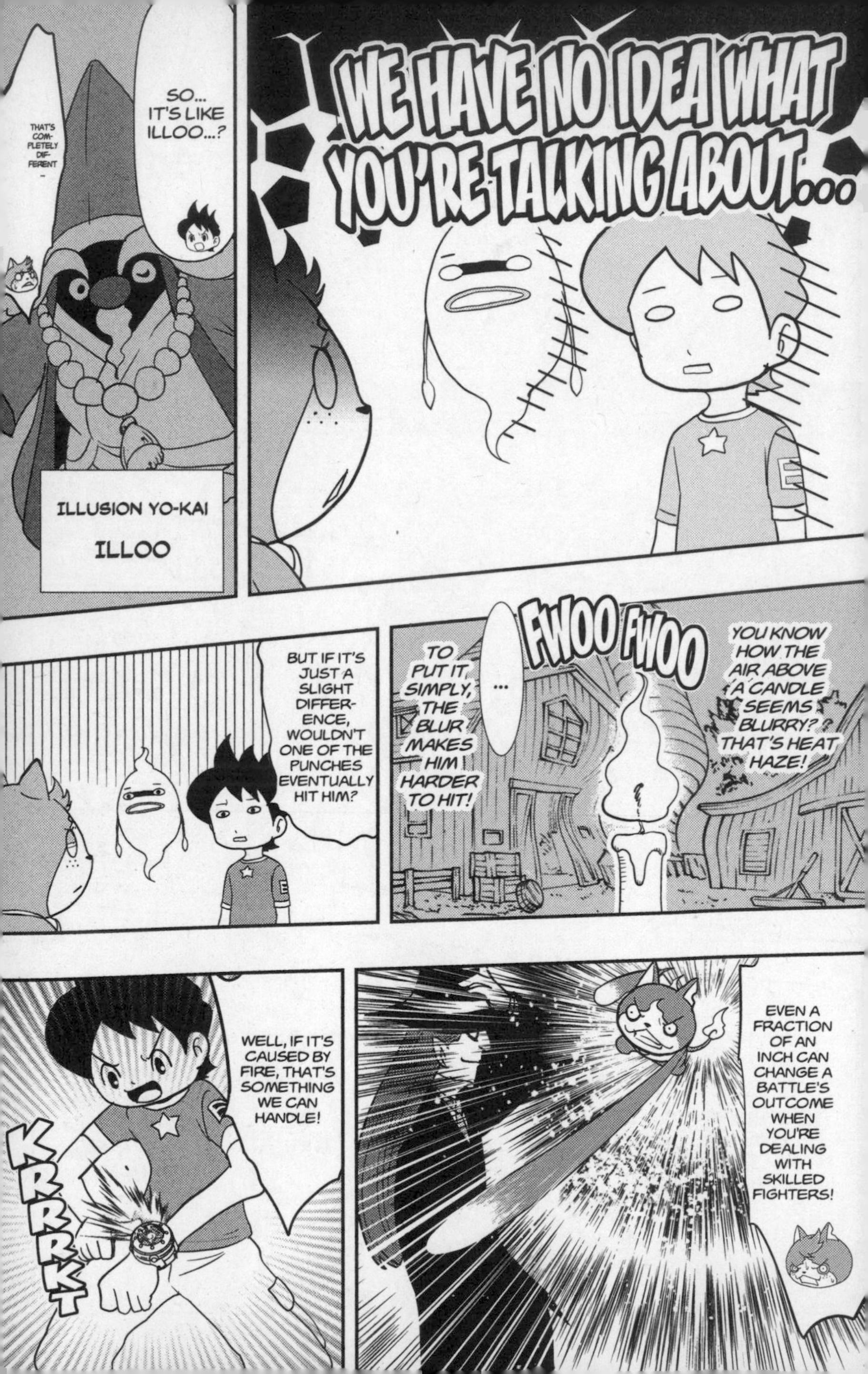
WE HAVE NO IDEA WHAT YOU'RE TALKING ABOUT...
SO... IT'S LIKE ILLOO...?
THAT'S COMPLETELY DIFFERENT
ILLUSION YO-KAI
ILLOO
YOU KNOW HOW THE AIR ABOVE A CANDLE SEEMS BLURRY? THAT'S HEAT HAZE!
FWOO FWOO
...
TO PUT IT SIMPLY, THE BLUR MAKES HIM HARDER TO HIT!
BUT IF IT'S JUST A SLIGHT DIFFERENCE, WOULDN'T ONE OF THE PUNCHES EVENTUALLY HIT HIM?
EVEN A FRACTION OF AN INCH CAN CHANGE A BATTLE'S OUTCOME WHEN YOU'RE DEALING WITH SKILLED FIGHTERS!
WELL, IF IT'S CAUSED BY FIRE, THAT'S SOMETHING WE CAN HANDLE!
KRRRKT

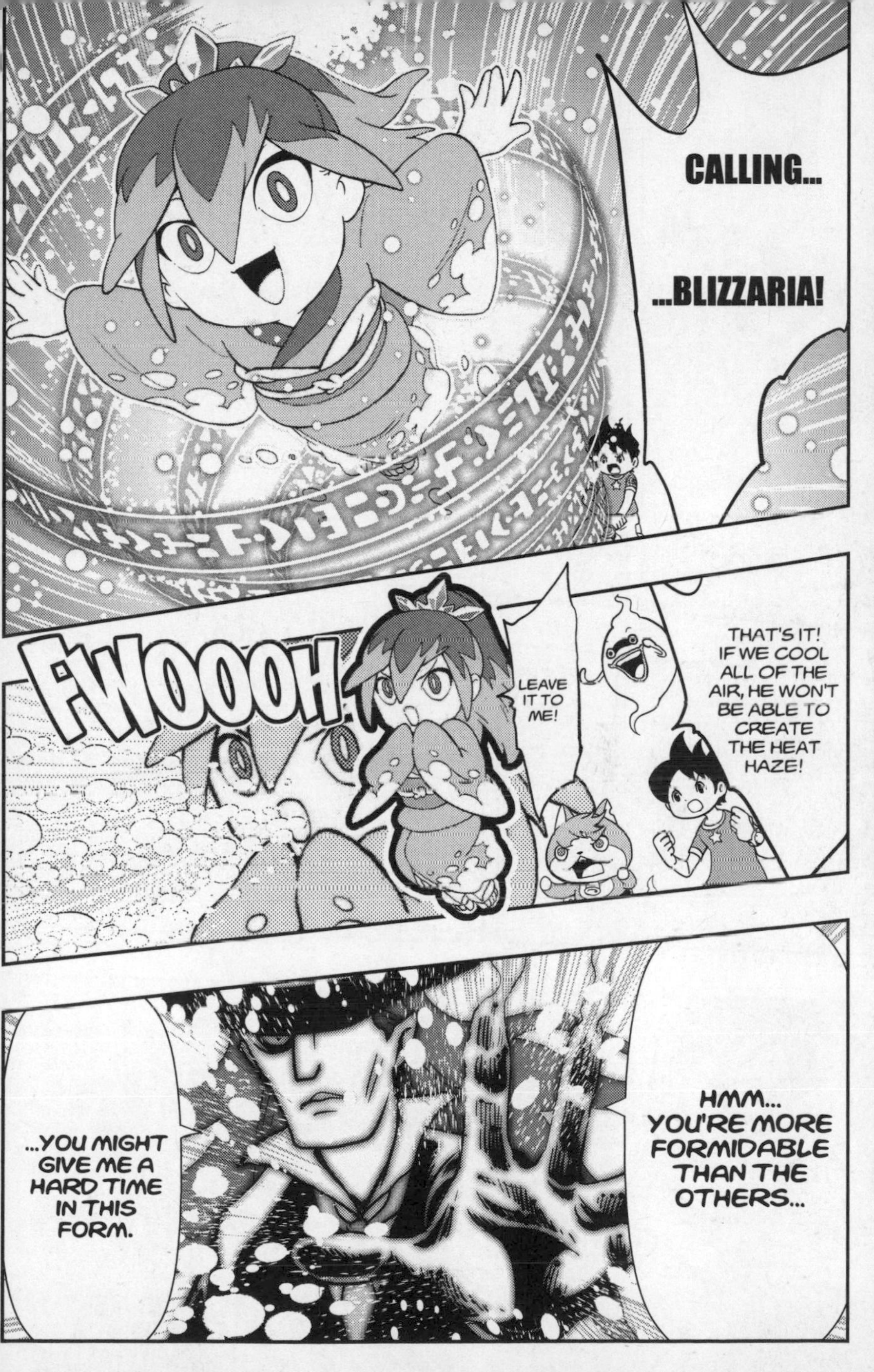
CALLING...
...BLIZZARIA!
THAT'S IT! IF WE COOL ALL OF THE AIR, HE WON'T BE ABLE TO CREATE THE HEAT HAZE!
LEAVE IT TO ME!
FWOOOH
HMM... YOU'RE MORE FORMIDABLE THAN THE OTHERS...
...YOU MIGHT GIVE ME A HARD TIME IN THIS FORM.

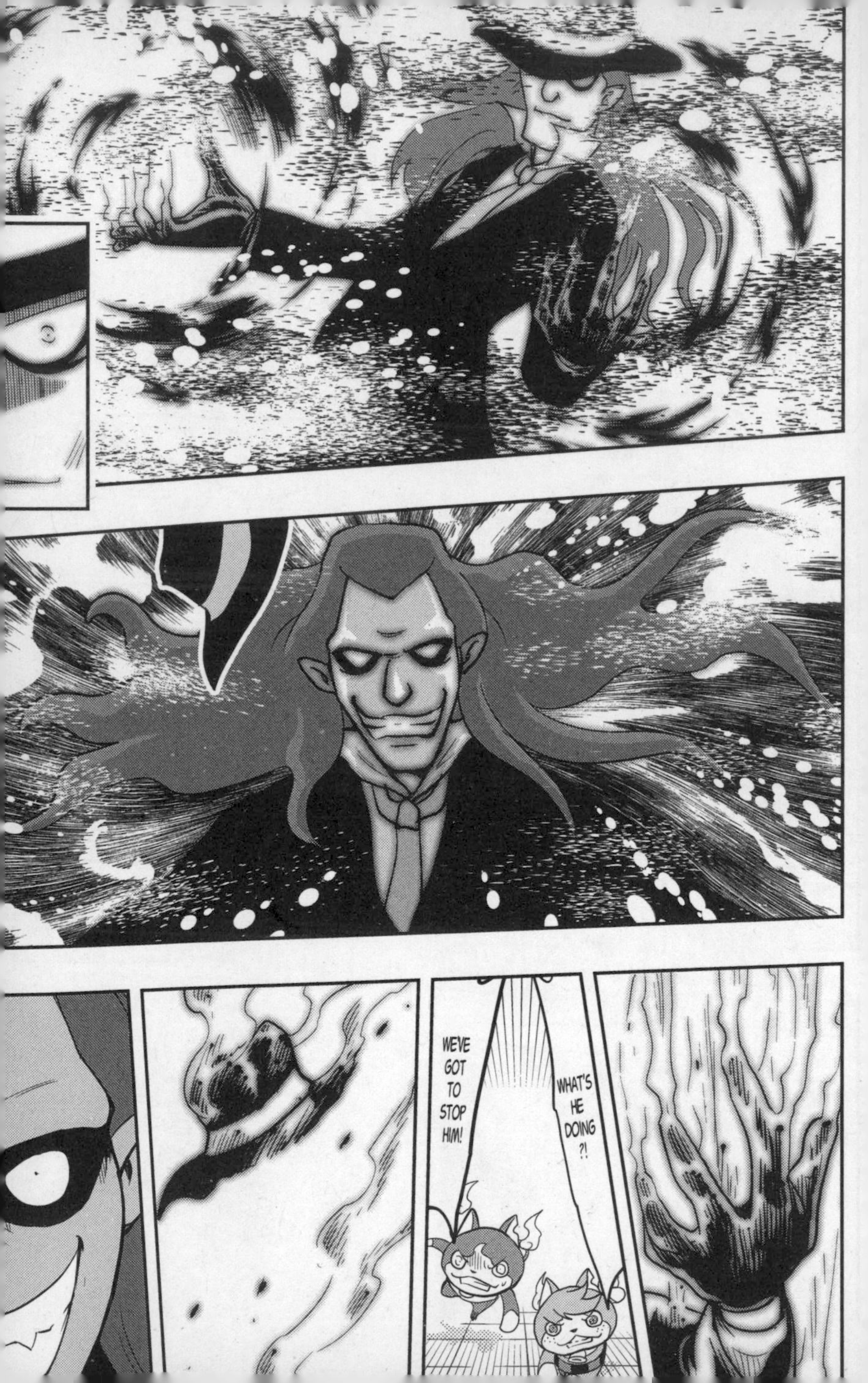
WHAT'S HE DOING ?!
WE'VE GOT TO STOP HIM!

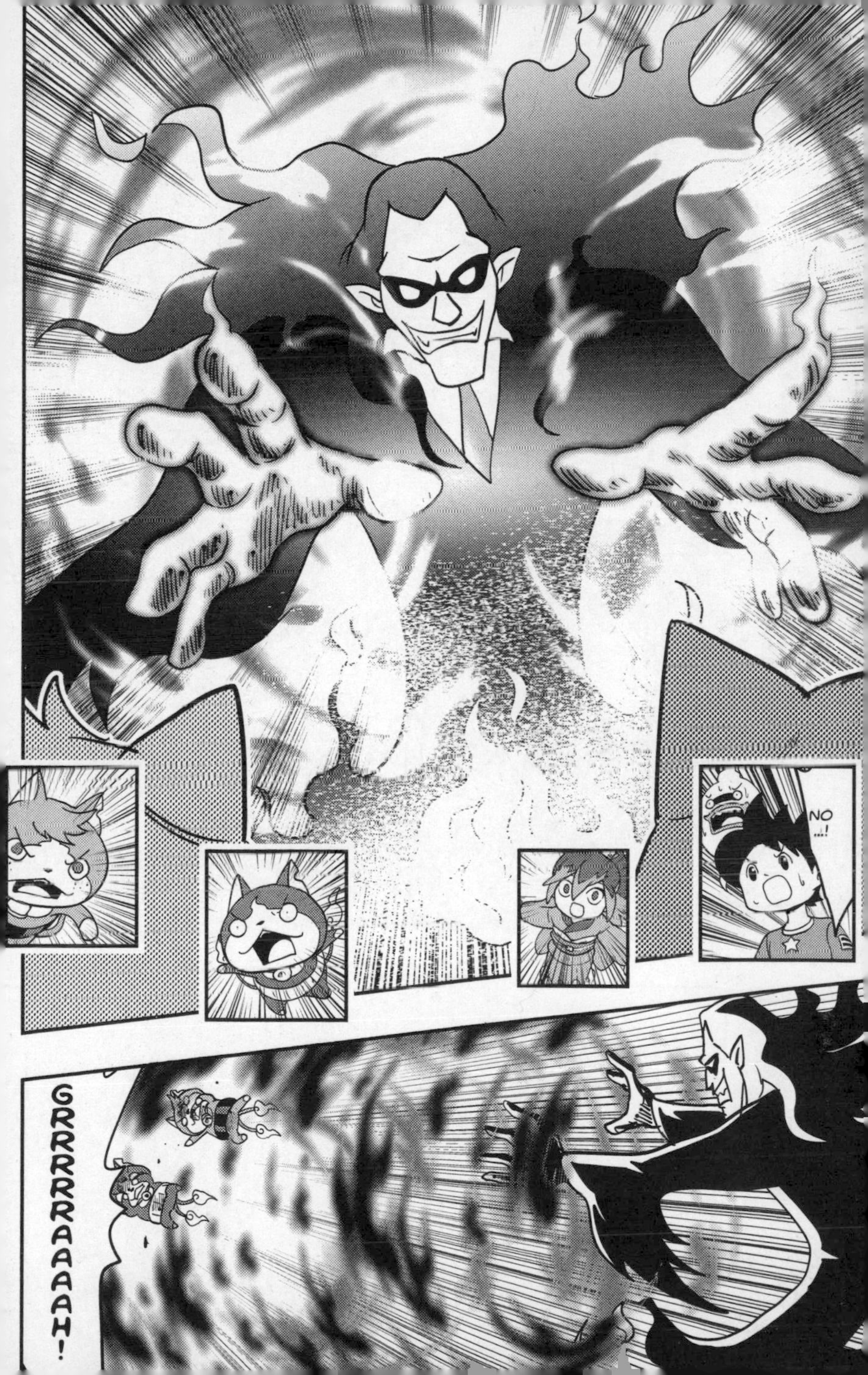
NO ...!
GRRRRRAAAAAH!

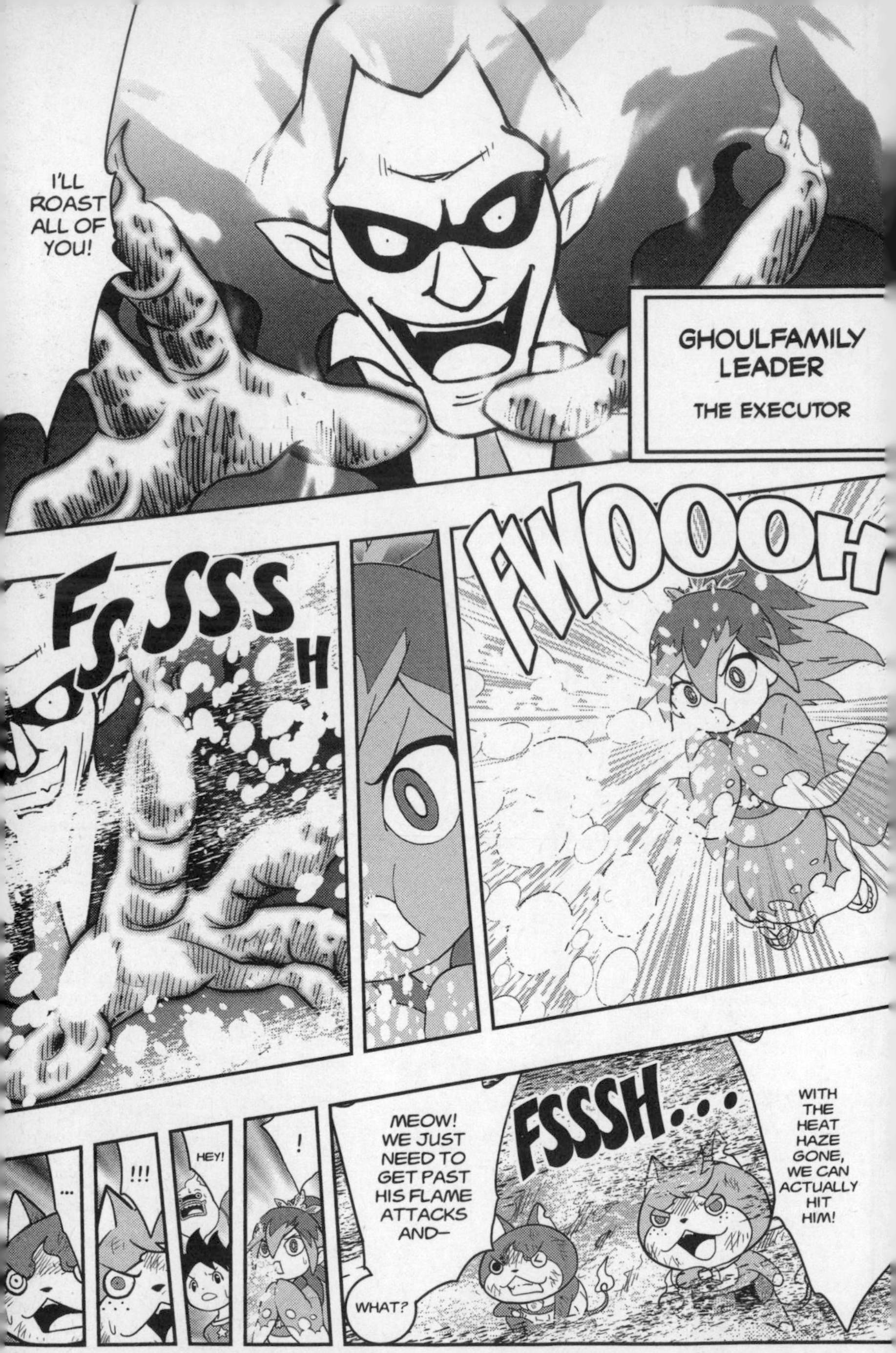
GHOULFAMILY LEADER
THE EXECUTOR
I'LL ROAST ALL OF YOU!
FWOOOH
FSSSSH
WITH THE HEAT HAZE GONE, WE CAN ACTUALLY HIT HIM!
FSSSH...
MEOW! WE JUST NEED TO GET PAST HIS FLAME ATTACKS AND—
WHAT?
!
HEY!
!!!
...

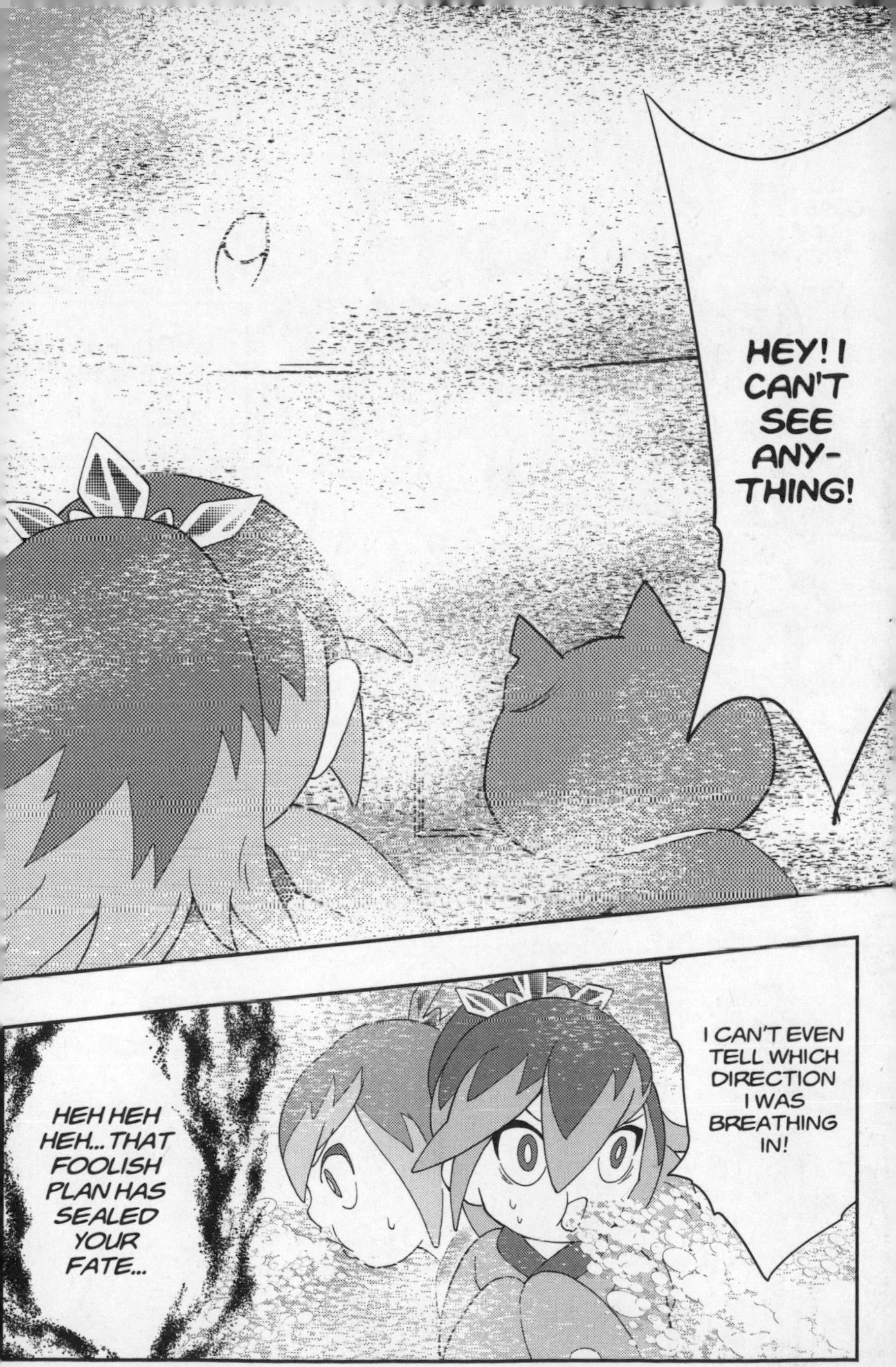
HEY! I CAN'T SEE ANY-THING!
I CAN'T EVEN TELL WHICH DIRECTION I WAS BREATHING IN!
HEH HEH HEH... THAT FOOLISH PLAN HAS SEALED YOUR FATE...

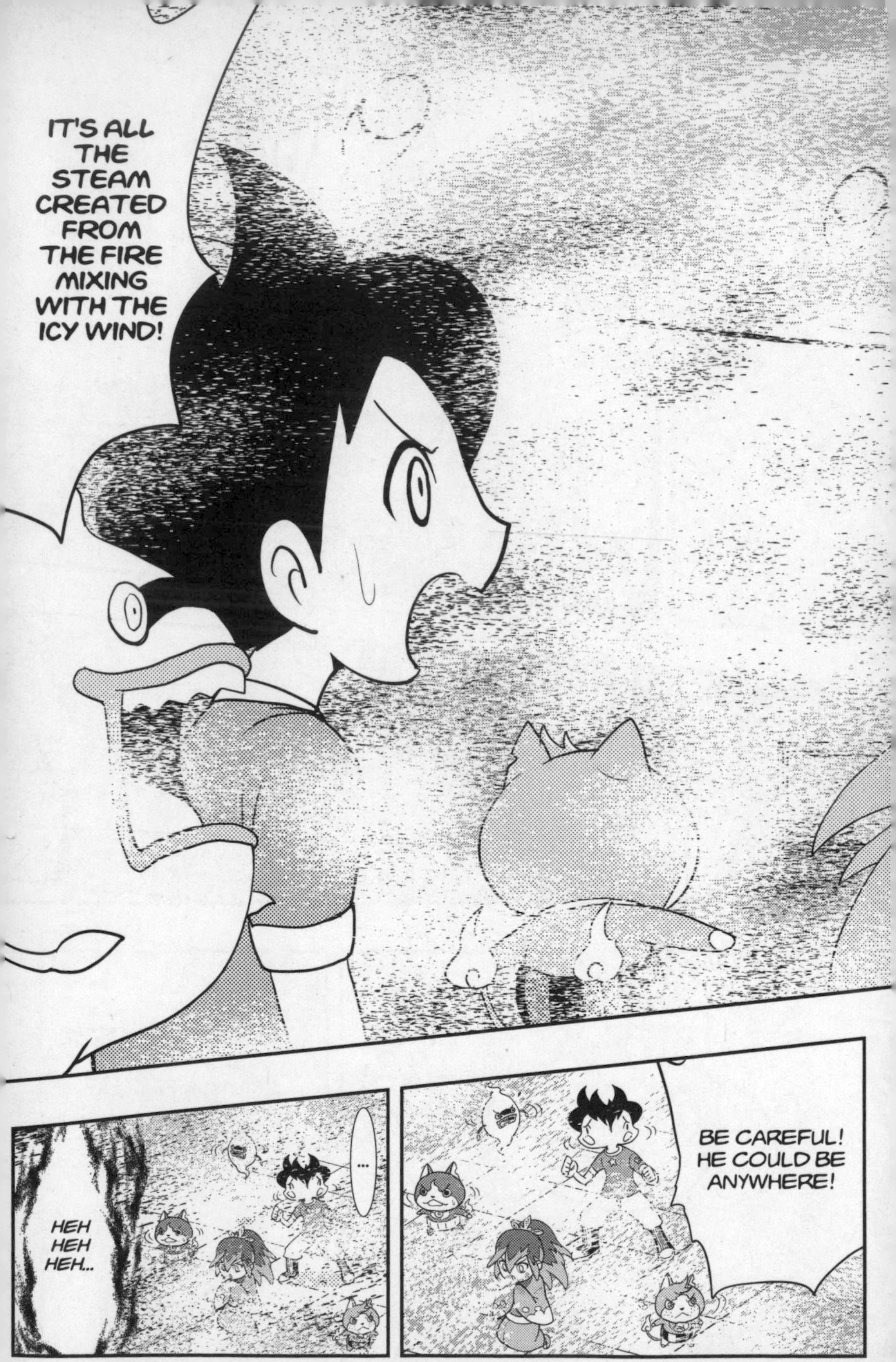
IT'S ALL THE STEAM CREATED FROM THE FIRE MIXING WITH THE ICY WIND!
BE CAREFUL! HE COULD BE ANYWHERE!
...
HEH HEH HEH...

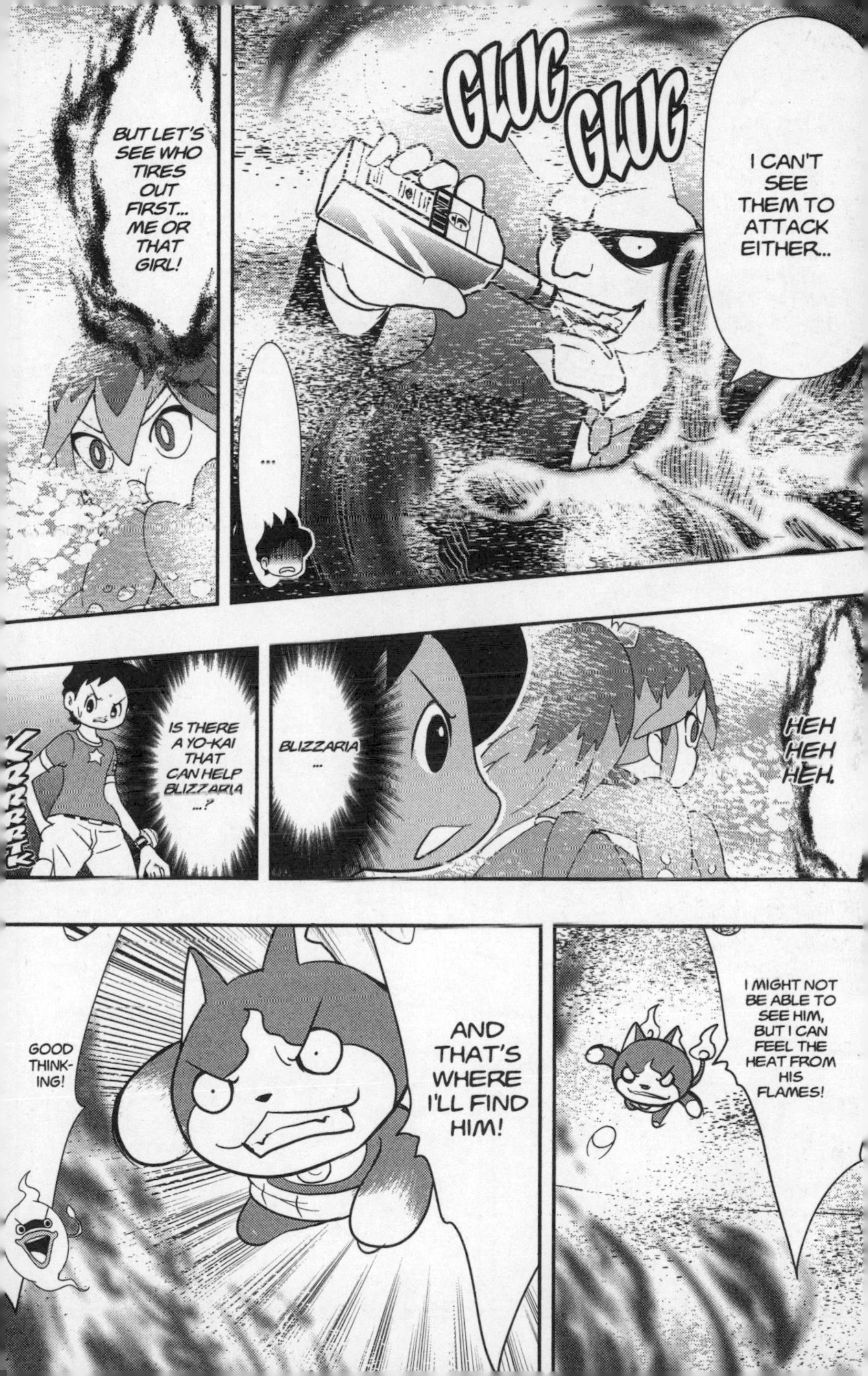
I CAN'T SEE THEM TO ATTACK EITHER...
GLUG GLUG
...
BUT LET'S SEE WHO TIRES OUT FIRST... ME OR THAT GIRL!
HEH HEH HEH.
BLIZZARIA ...
IS THERE A YO-KAI THAT CAN HELP BLIZZARIA ...?
I MIGHT NOT BE ABLE TO SEE HIM, BUT I CAN FEEL THE HEAT FROM HIS FLAMES!
AND THAT'S WHERE I'LL FIND HIM!
GOOD THINKING!

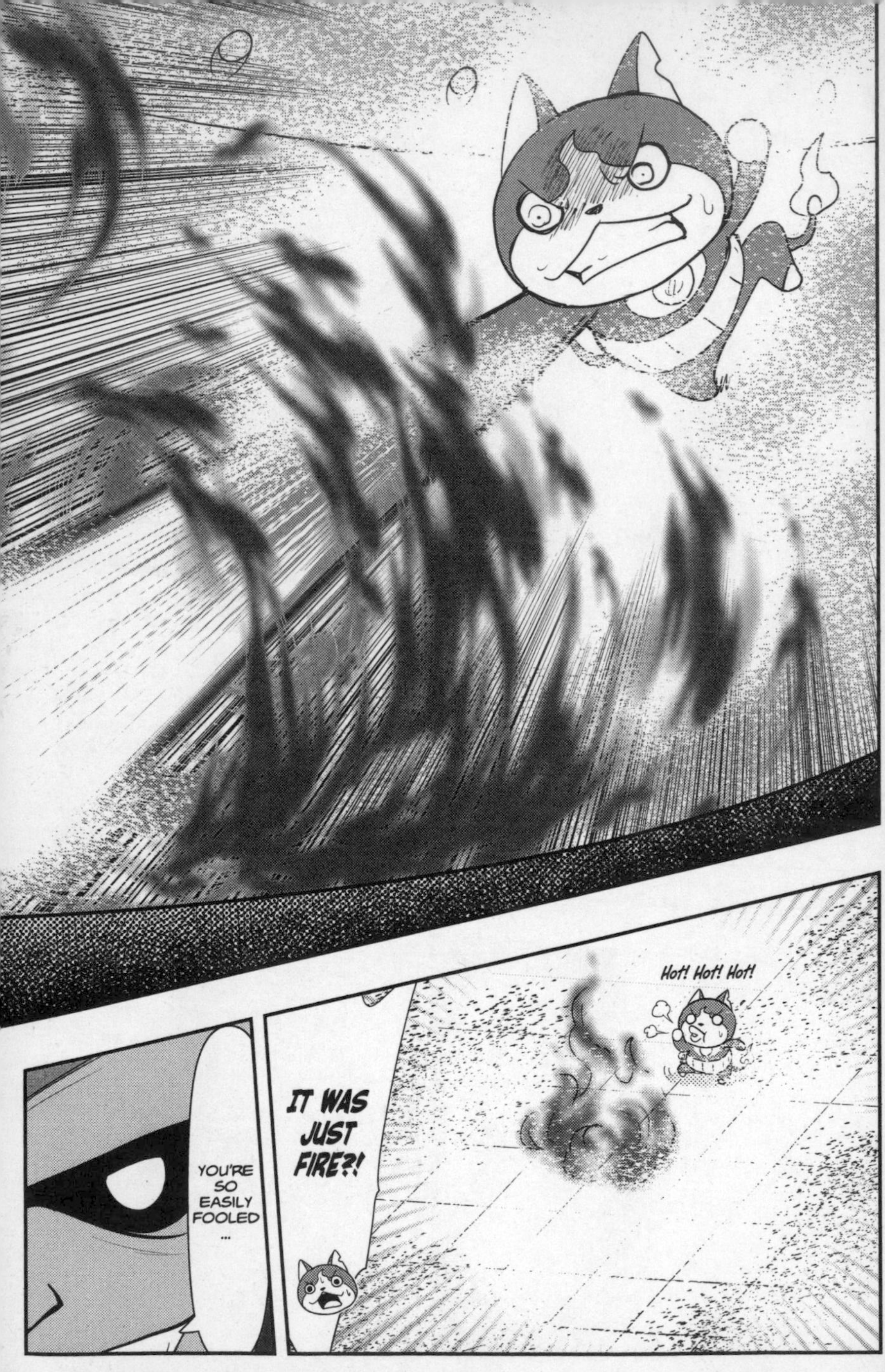
Hot! Hot! Hot!
IT WAS JUST FIRE?!
YOU'RE SO EASILY FOOLED ...

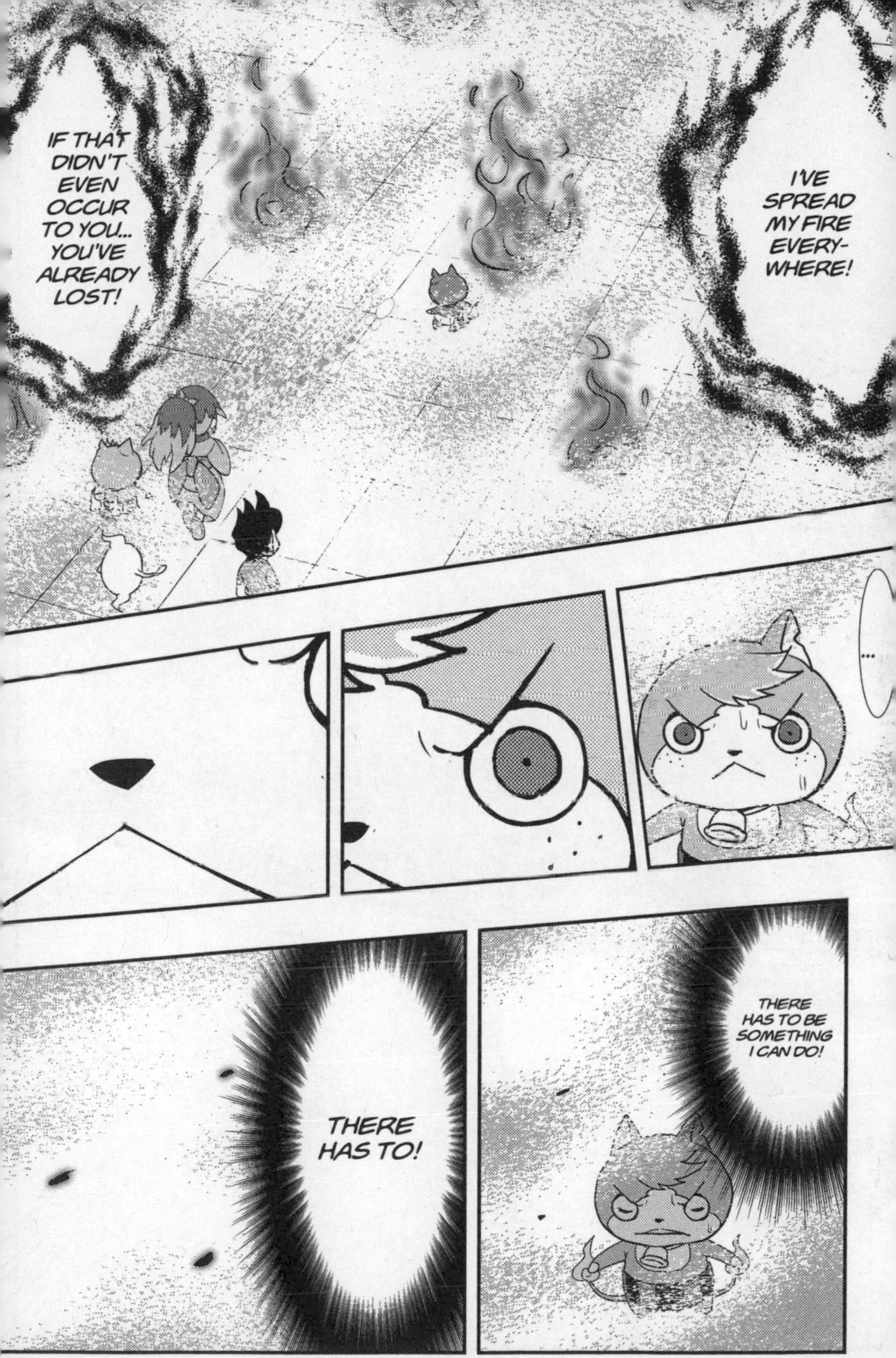
I'VE SPREAD MY FIRE EVERY-WHERE!
IF THAT DIDN'T EVEN OCCUR TO YOU... YOU'VE ALREADY LOST!
...
THERE HAS TO BE SOMETHING I CAN DO!
THERE HAS TO!

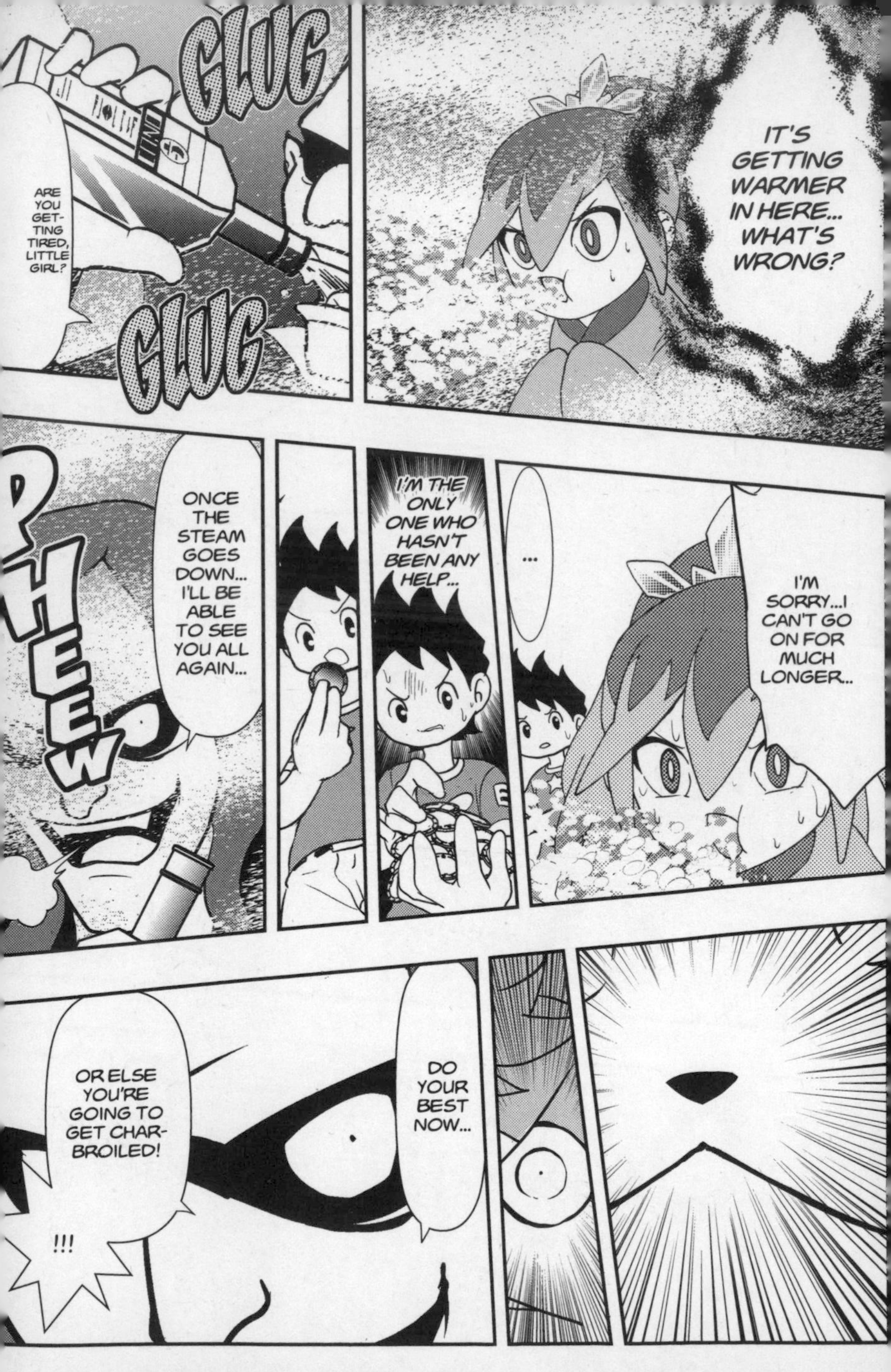
IT'S GETTING WARMER IN HERE... WHAT'S WRONG?
GLUG
GLUG
ARE YOU GET-TING TIRED, LITTLE GIRL?
I'M SORRY...I CAN'T GO ON FOR MUCH LONGER...
...
I'M THE ONLY ONE WHO HASN'T BEEN ANY HELP...
ONCE THE STEAM GOES DOWN... I'LL BE ABLE TO SEE YOU ALL AGAIN...
PHEEW
DO YOUR BEST NOW...
OR ELSE YOU'RE GOING TO GET CHAR-BROILED!
!!!

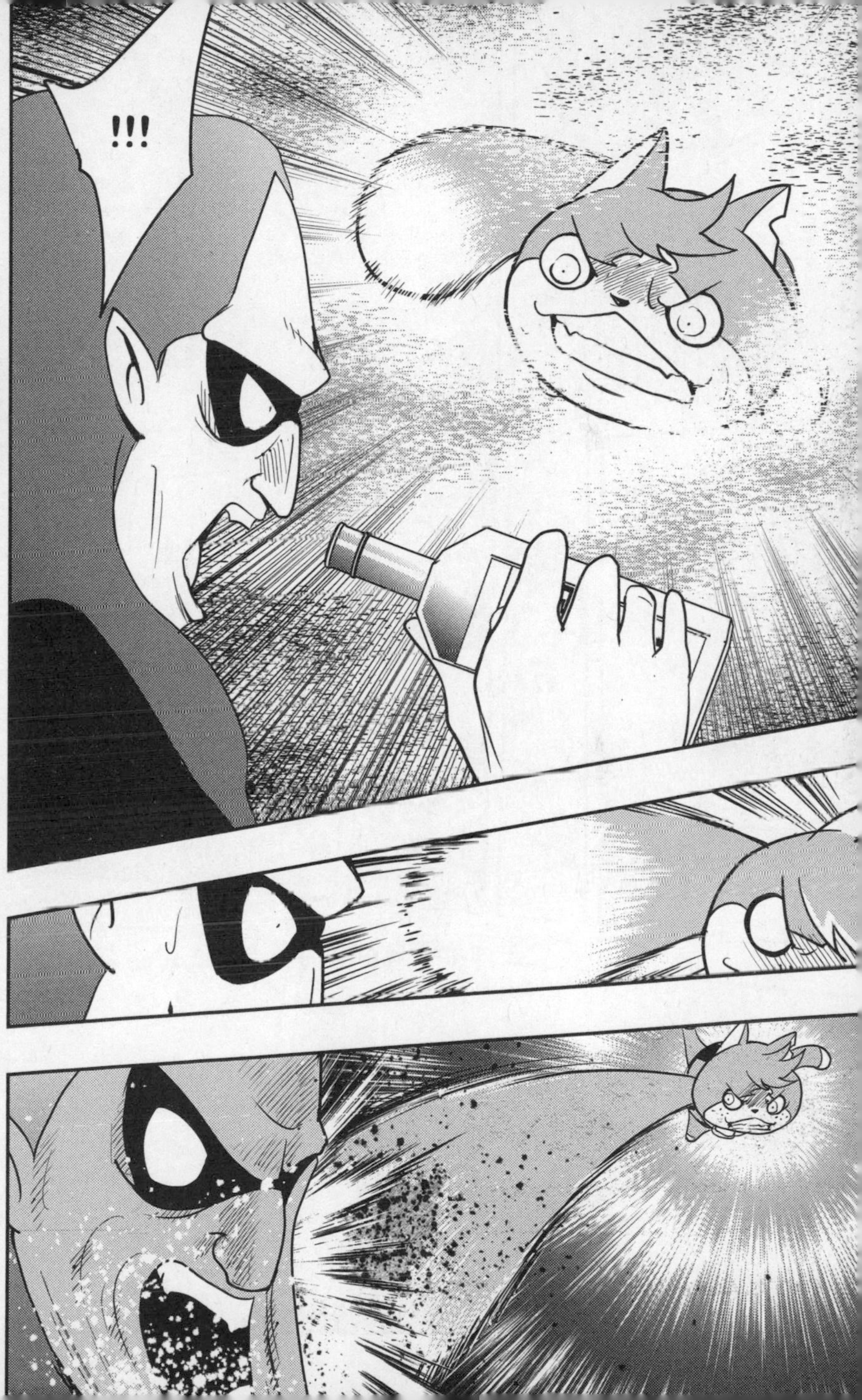
!!!

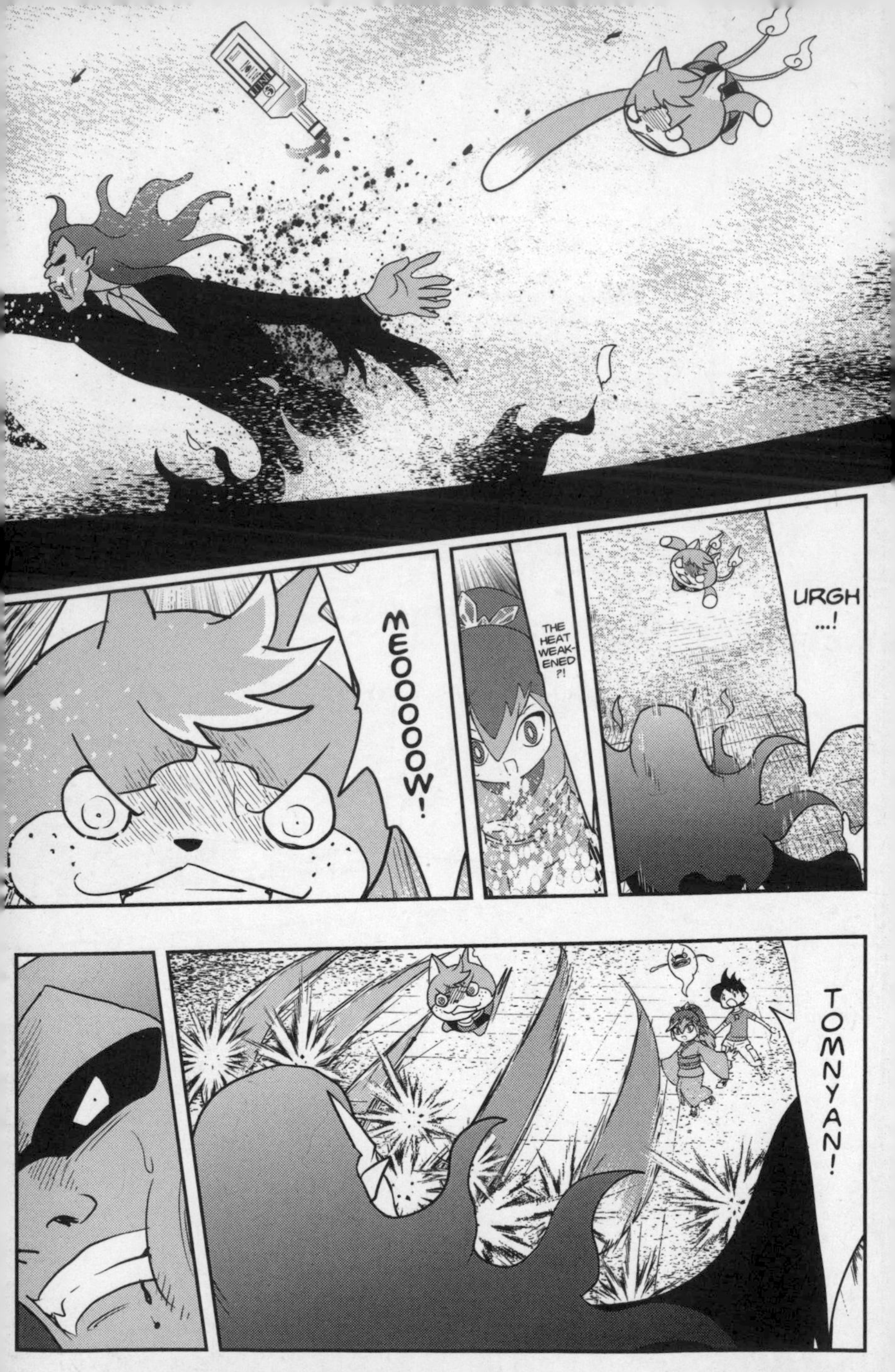
URGH ...!
THE HEAT WEAKENED ?!
MEOOOOOW!
TOMNYAN!

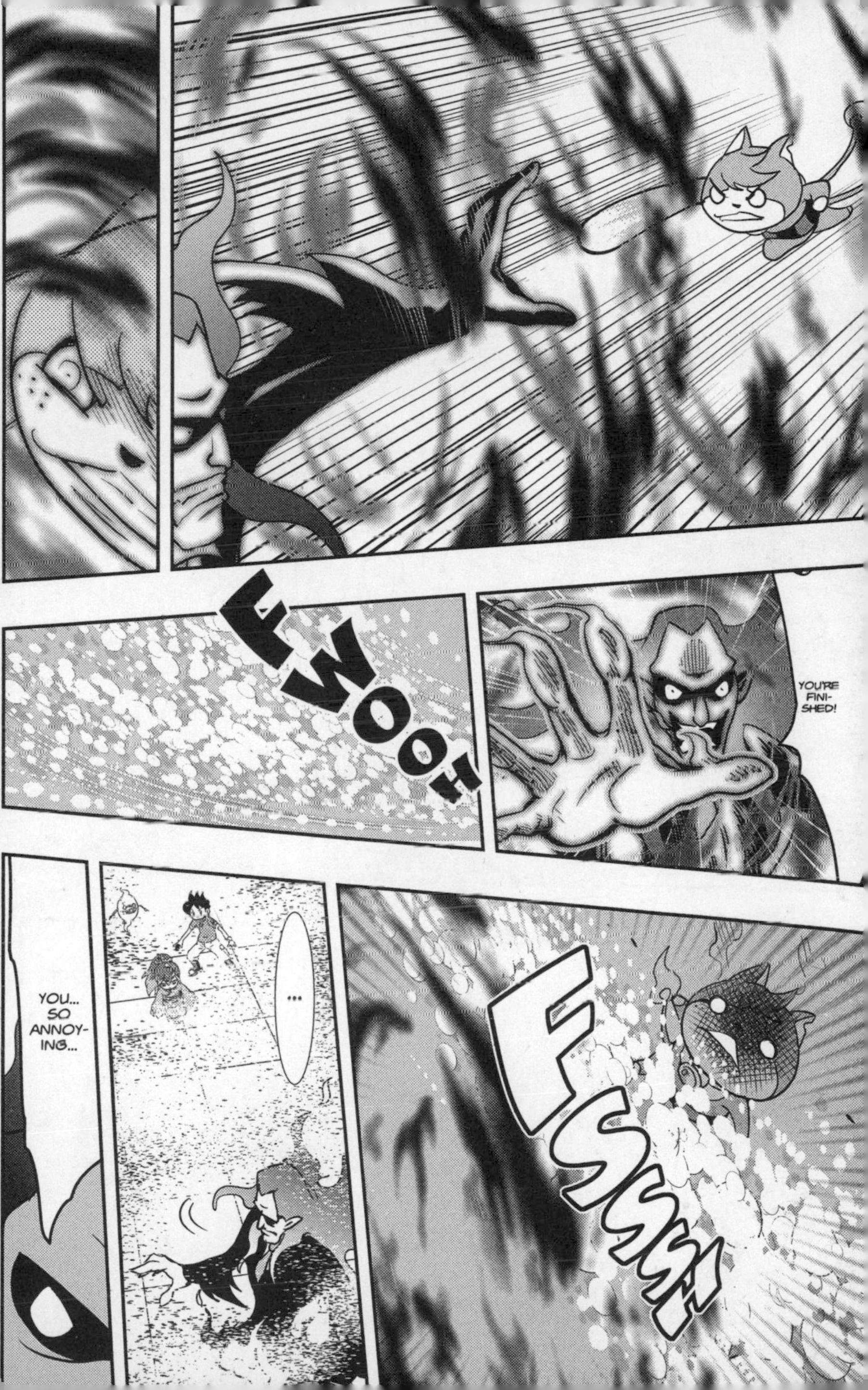
YOU'RE FINI-SHED!
FWOOH
FSSSH!
...
YOU... SO ANNOY-ING...

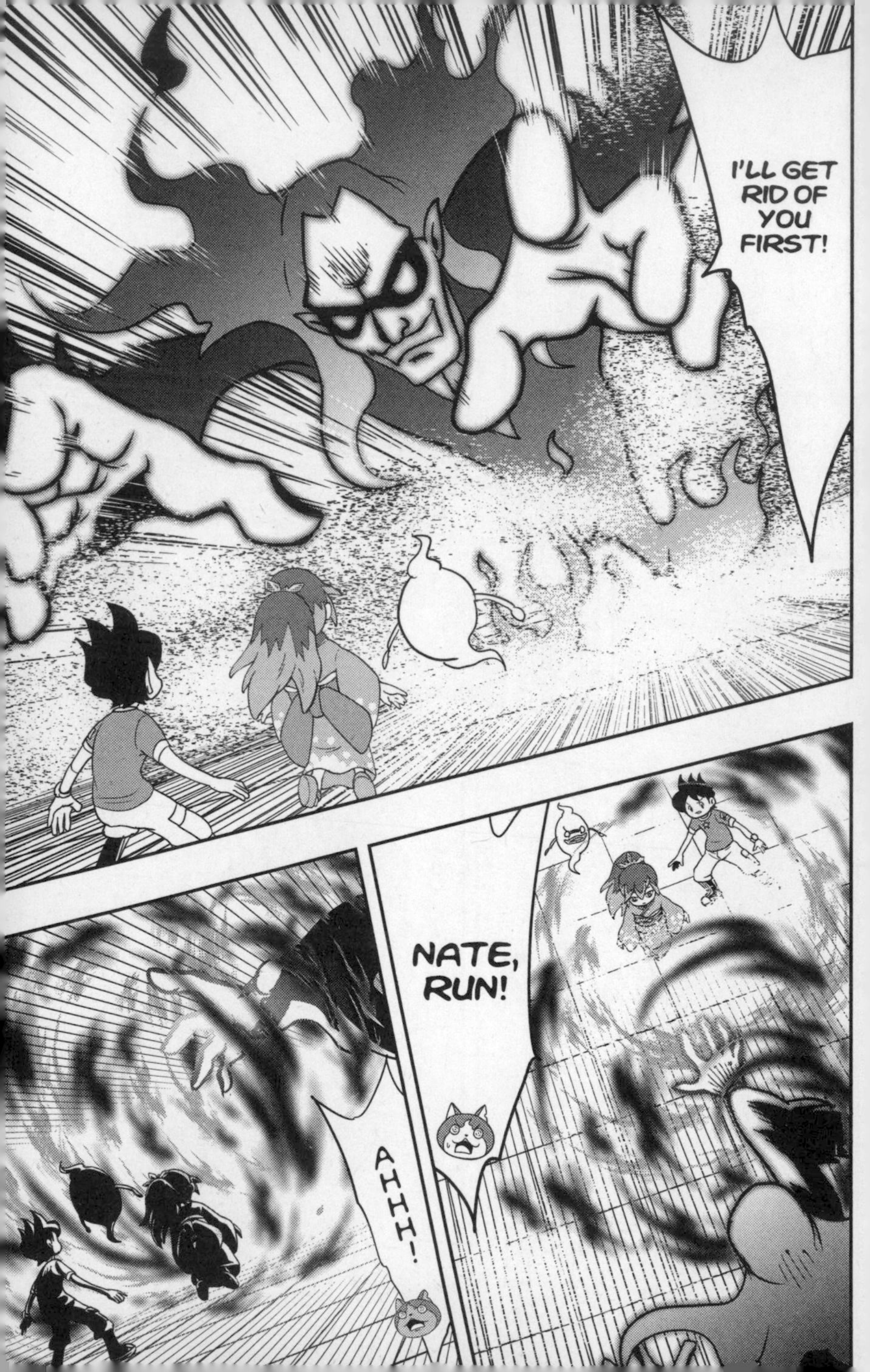
I'LL GET RID OF YOU FIRST!
NATE, RUN!
AHHH!

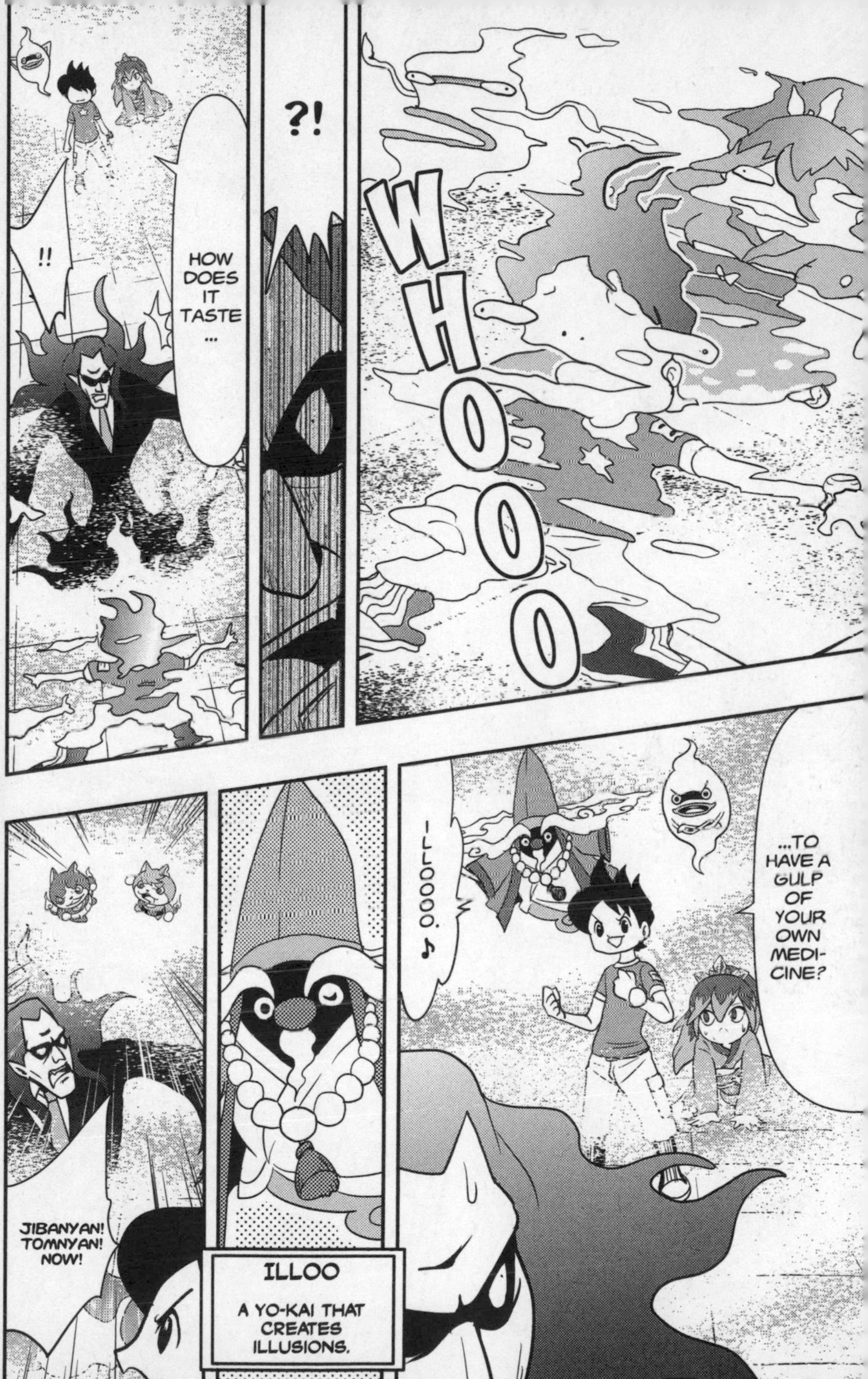
WHOOOO
?!
HOW DOES IT TASTE ...
!!
...TO HAVE A GULP OF YOUR OWN MEDICINE?
ILLOOOO ♪
ILLOO
A YO-KAI THAT CREATES ILLUSIONS.
JIBANYAN! TOMNYAN! NOW!

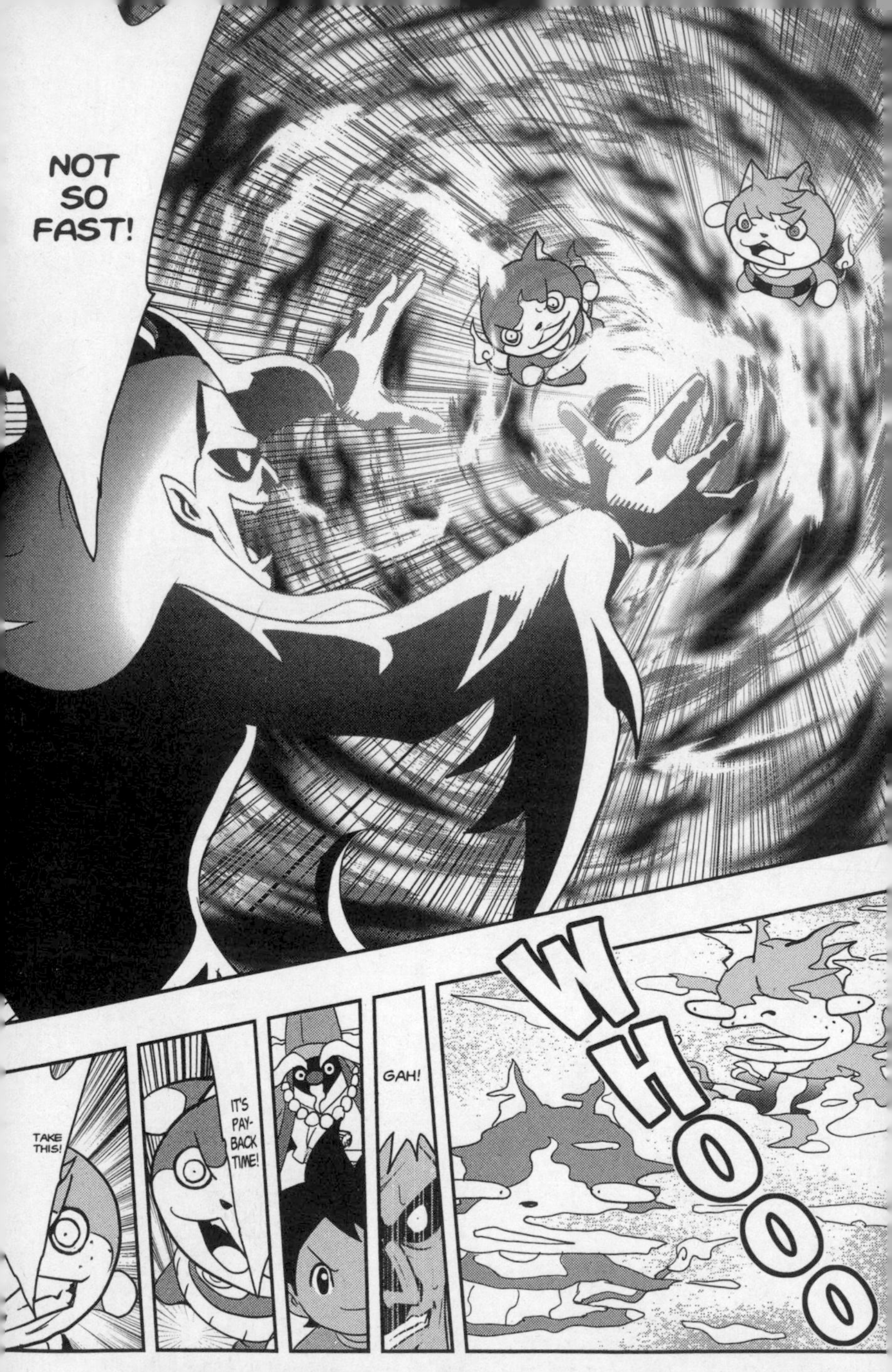
NOT SO FAST!
WHOOOOO
GAH!
IT'S PAY-BACK TIME!
TAKE THIS!

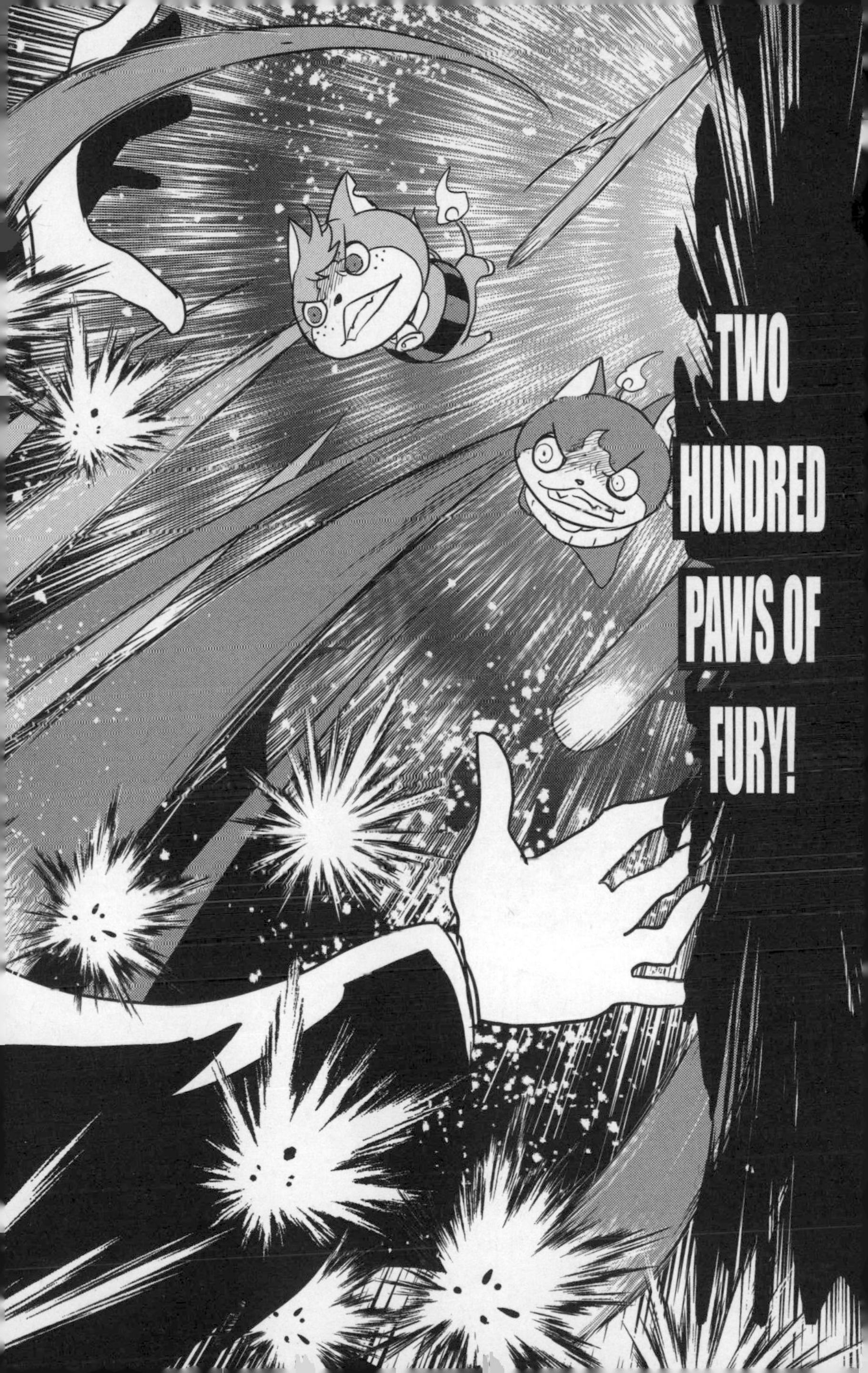
TWO HUNDRED PAWS OF FURY!

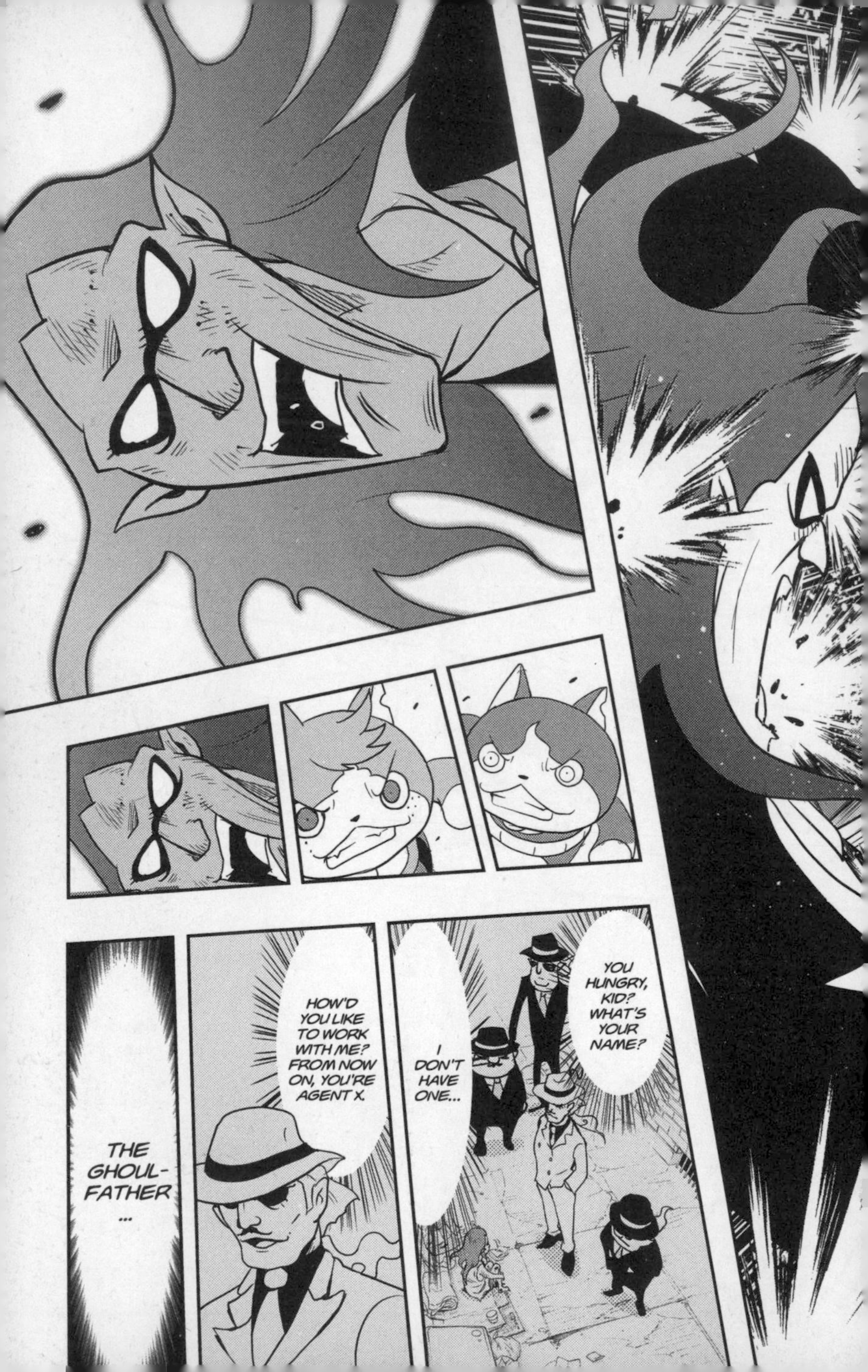
YOU HUNGRY, KID? WHAT'S YOUR NAME?
I DON'T HAVE ONE...
HOW'D YOU LIKE TO WORK WITH ME? FROM NOW ON, YOU'RE AGENT X.
THE GHOUL-FATHER...

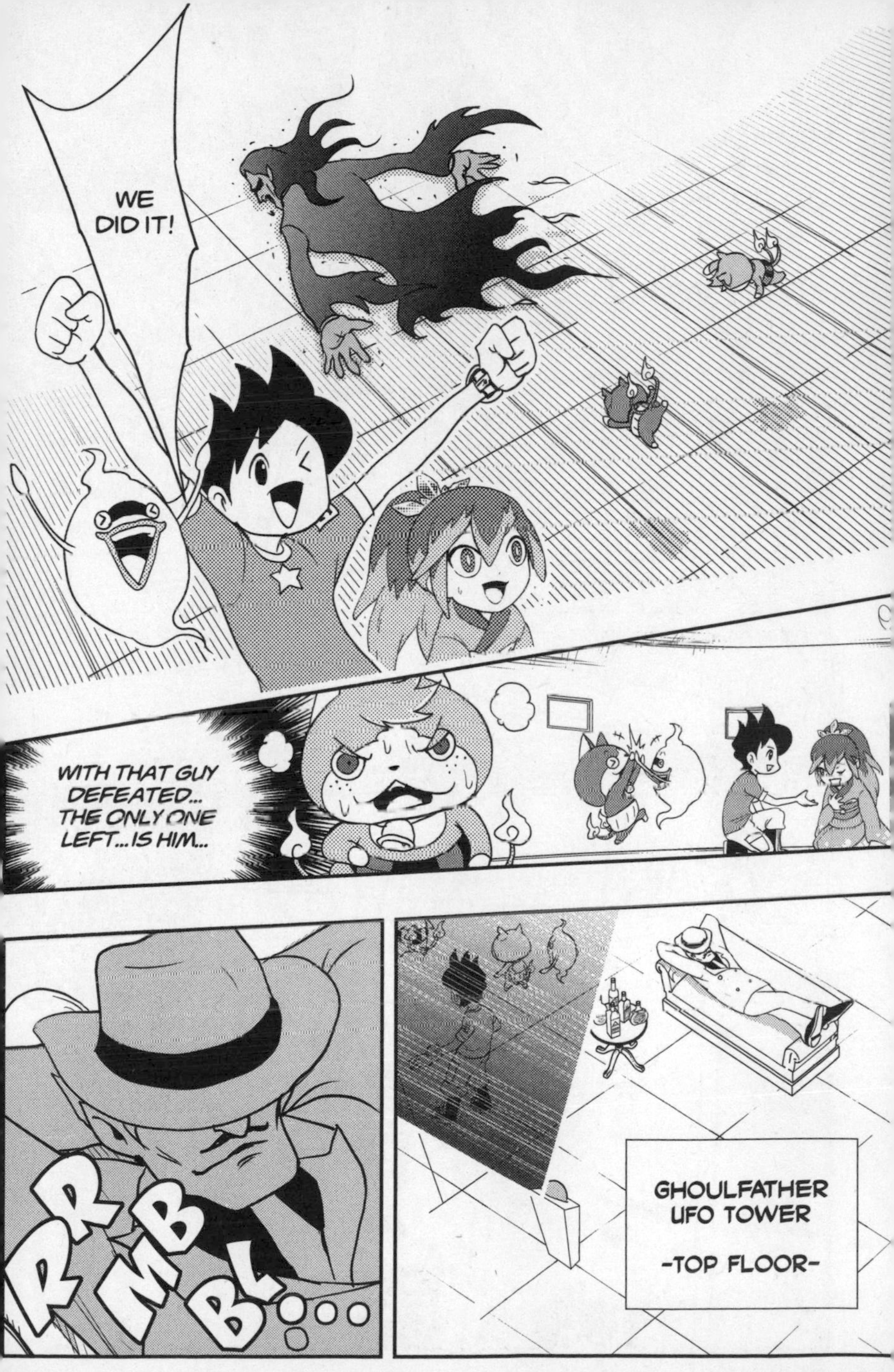
WE DID IT!
WITH THAT GUY DEFEATED... THE ONLY ONE LEFT...IS HIM...
GHOULFATHER UFO TOWER
-TOP FLOOR-
RRMBBL...

## THE GHOULFATHER ARC ④

# VS THE GHOULFATHER

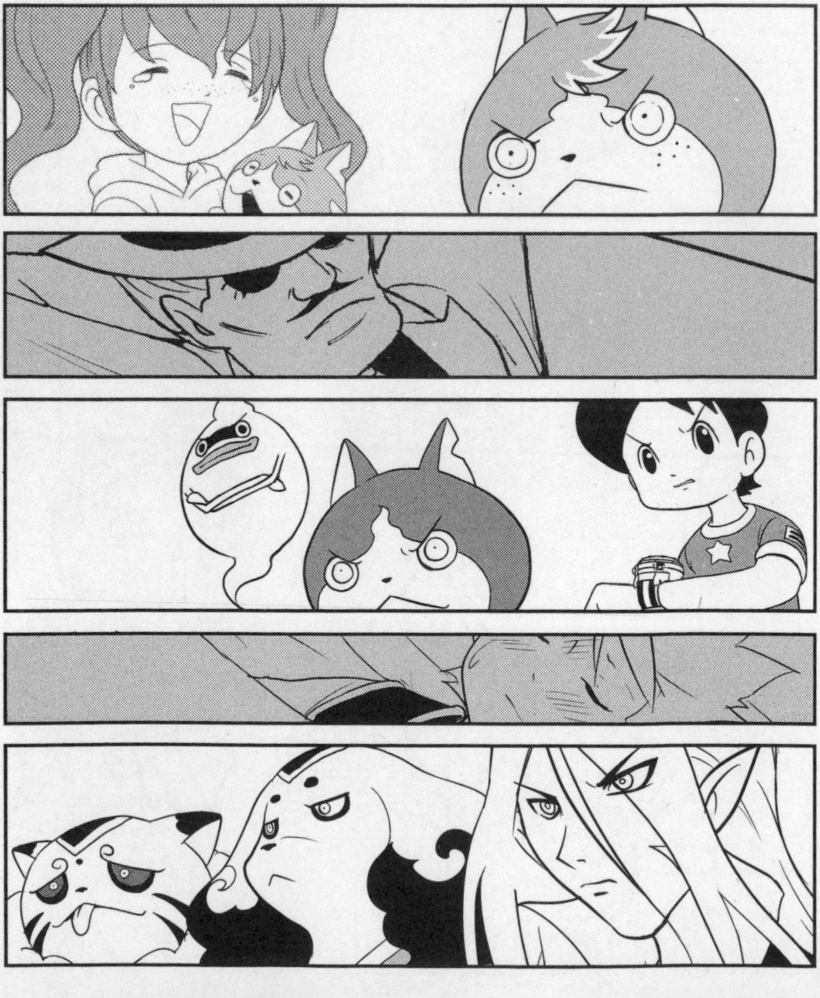

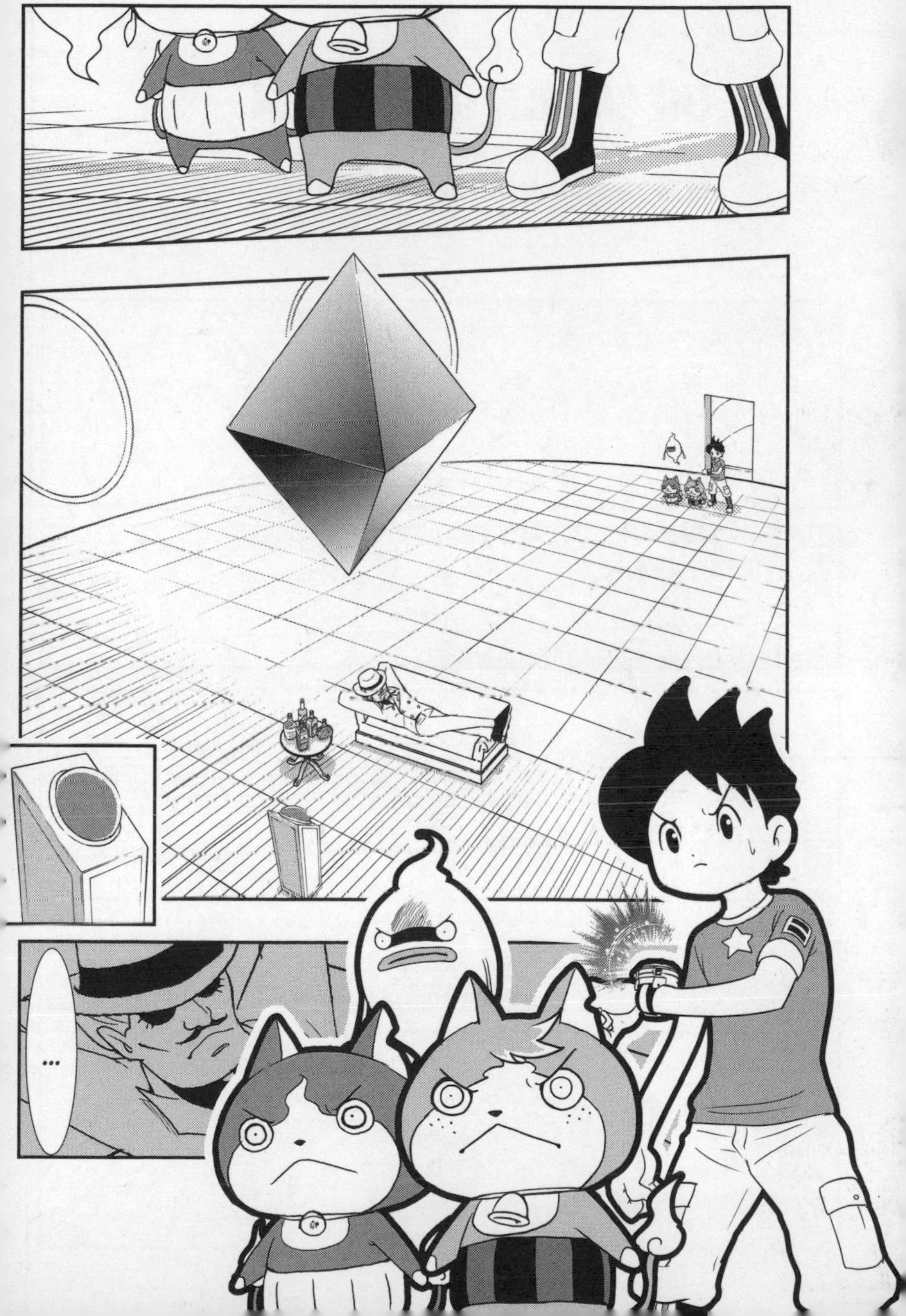
...

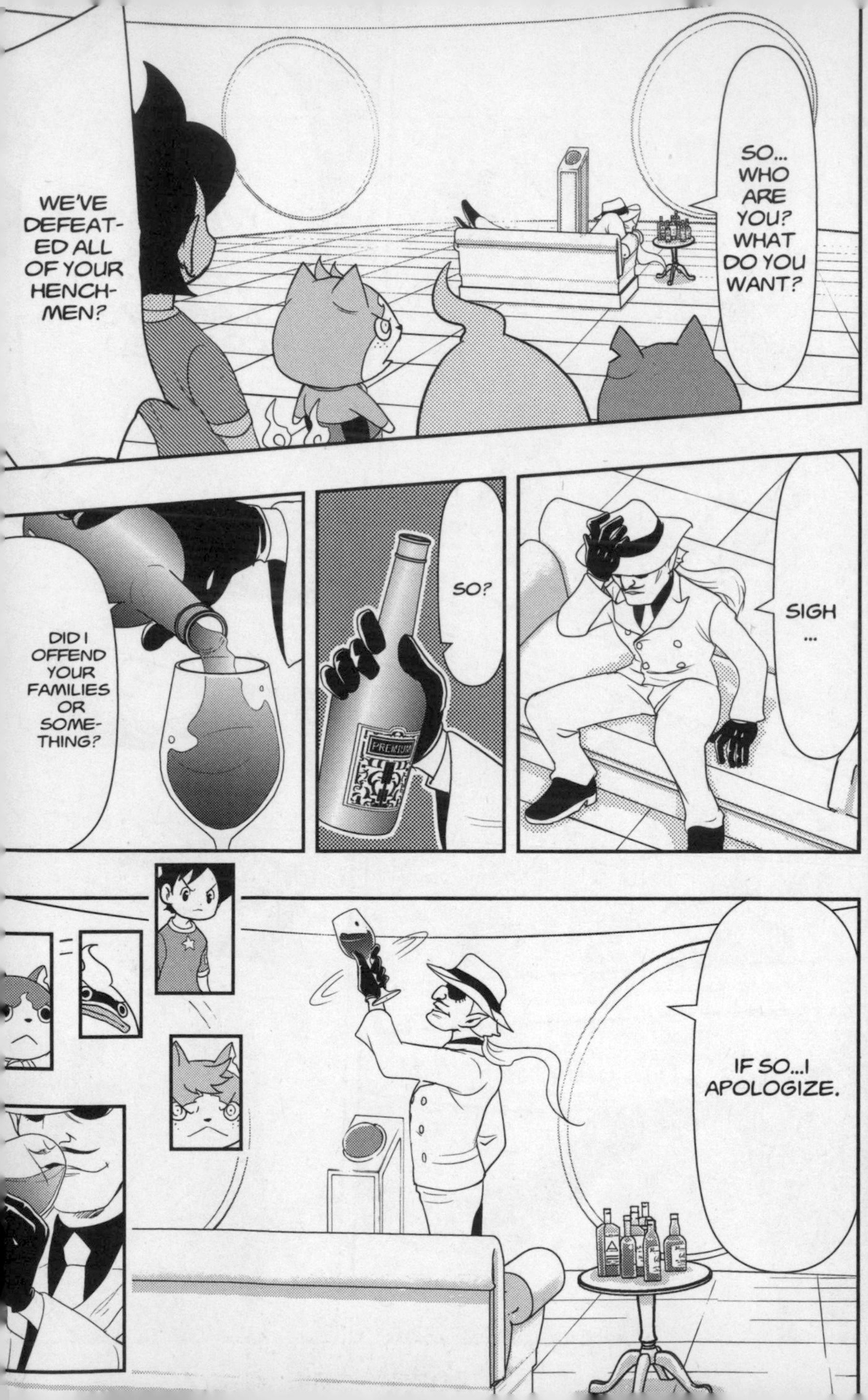
SO... WHO ARE YOU? WHAT DO YOU WANT?
WE'VE DEFEAT-ED ALL OF YOUR HENCH-MEN?
SIGH ...
SO?
DID I OFFEND YOUR FAMILIES OR SOME-THING?
PREMIUM
IF SO...I APOLOGIZE.

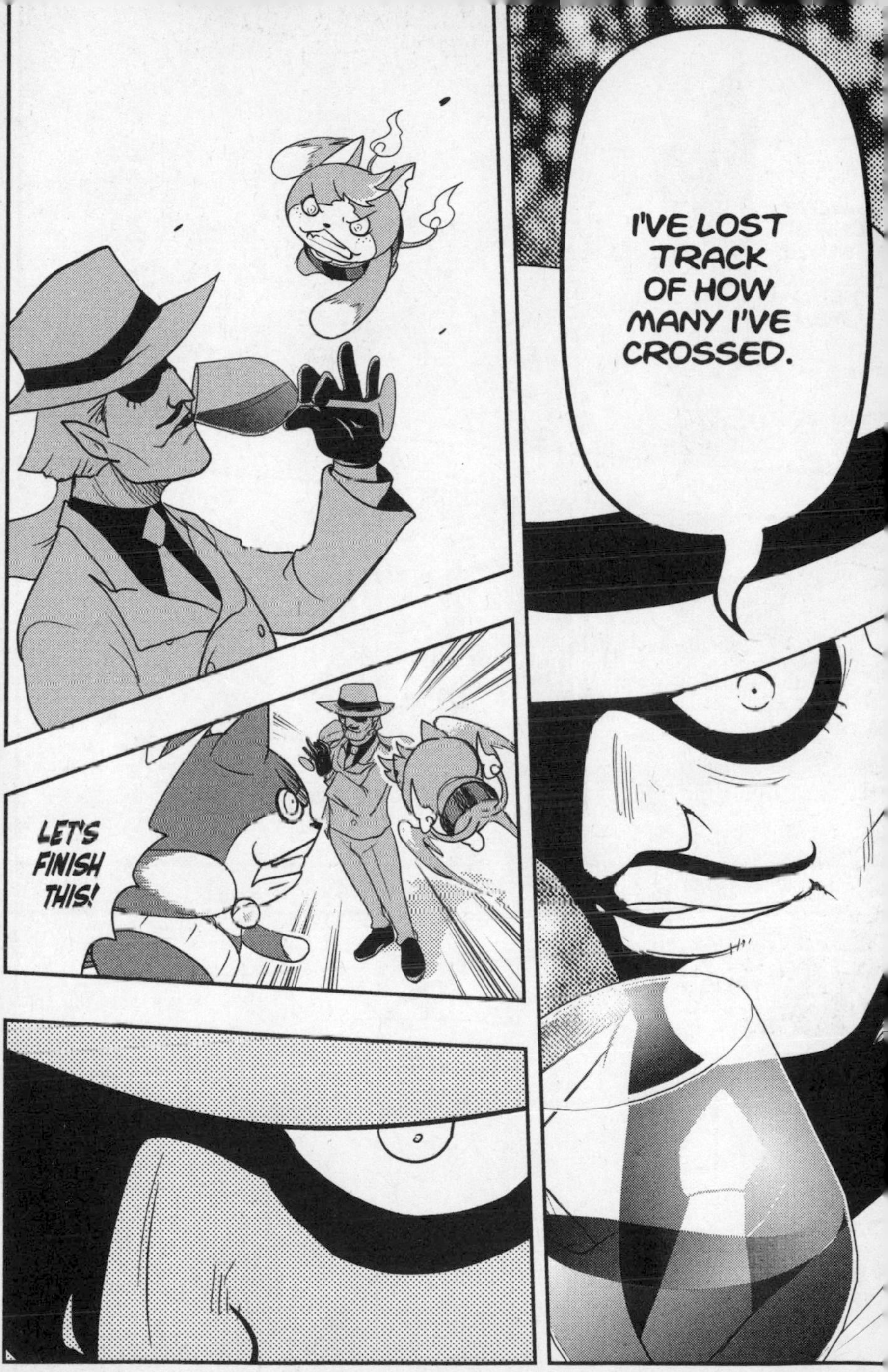
I'VE LOST TRACK OF HOW MANY I'VE CROSSED.
LET'S FINISH THIS!

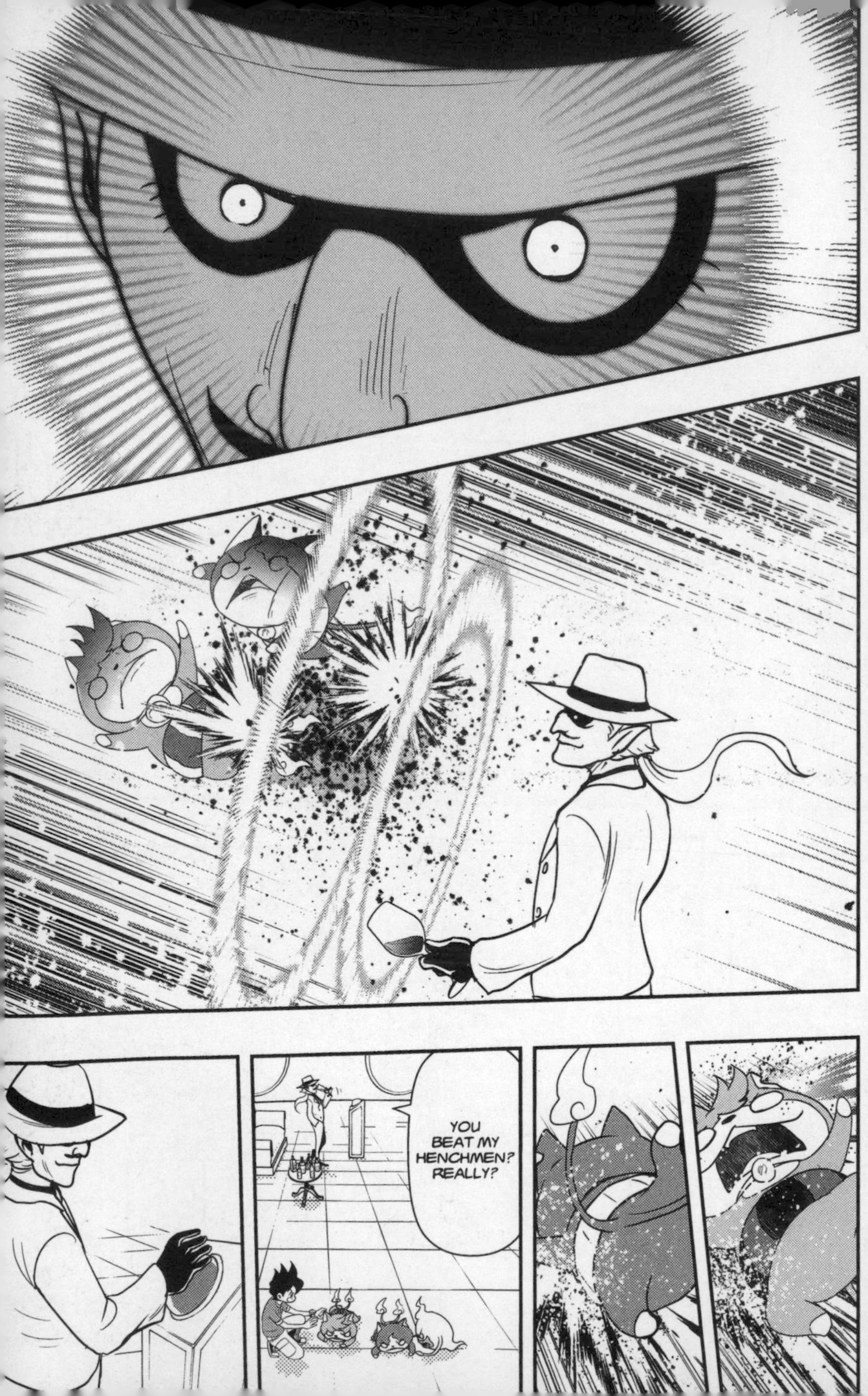
YOU BEAT MY HENCHMEN? REALLY?

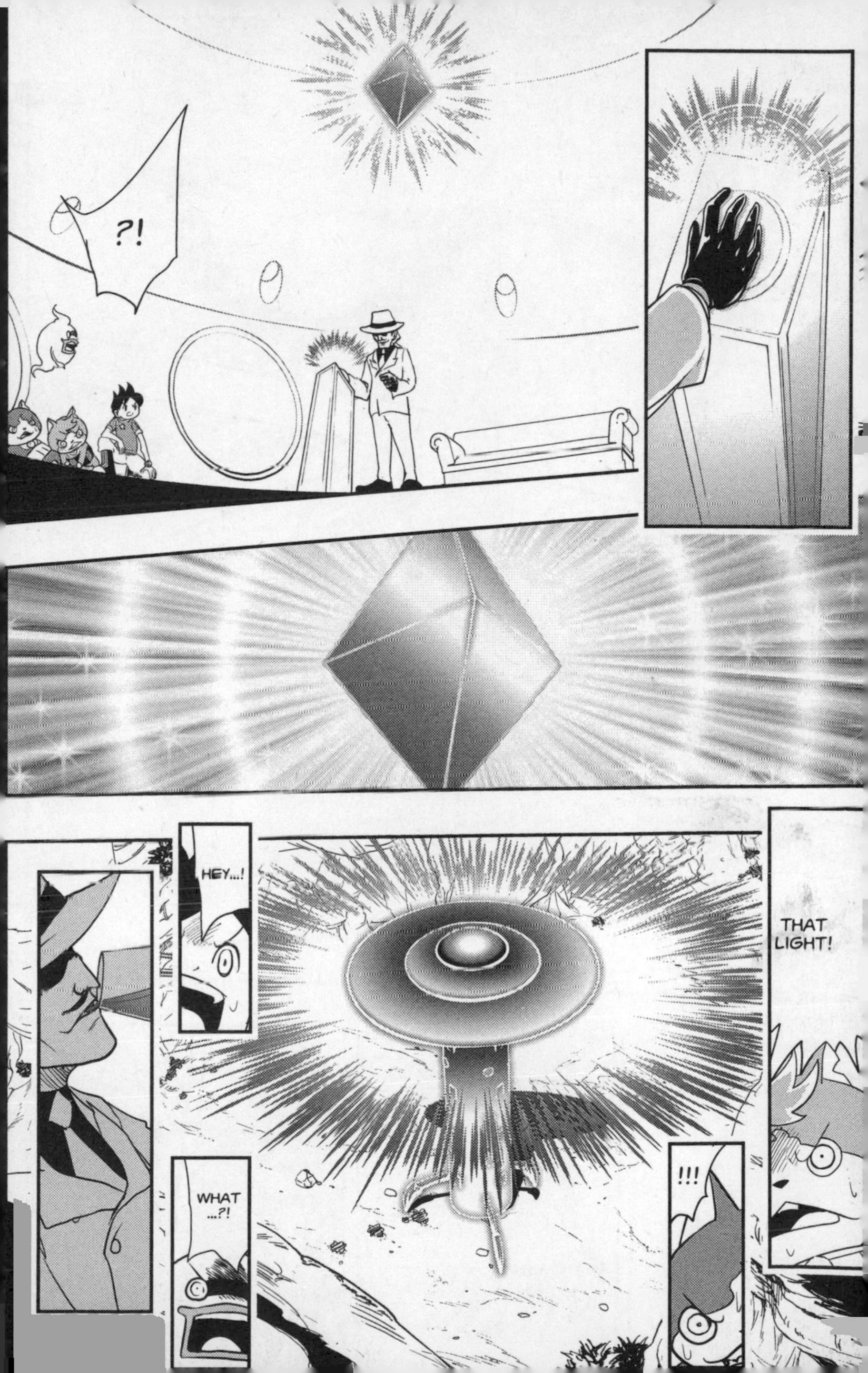
?!
THAT LIGHT!
!!!
HEY...!
WHAT ...?!

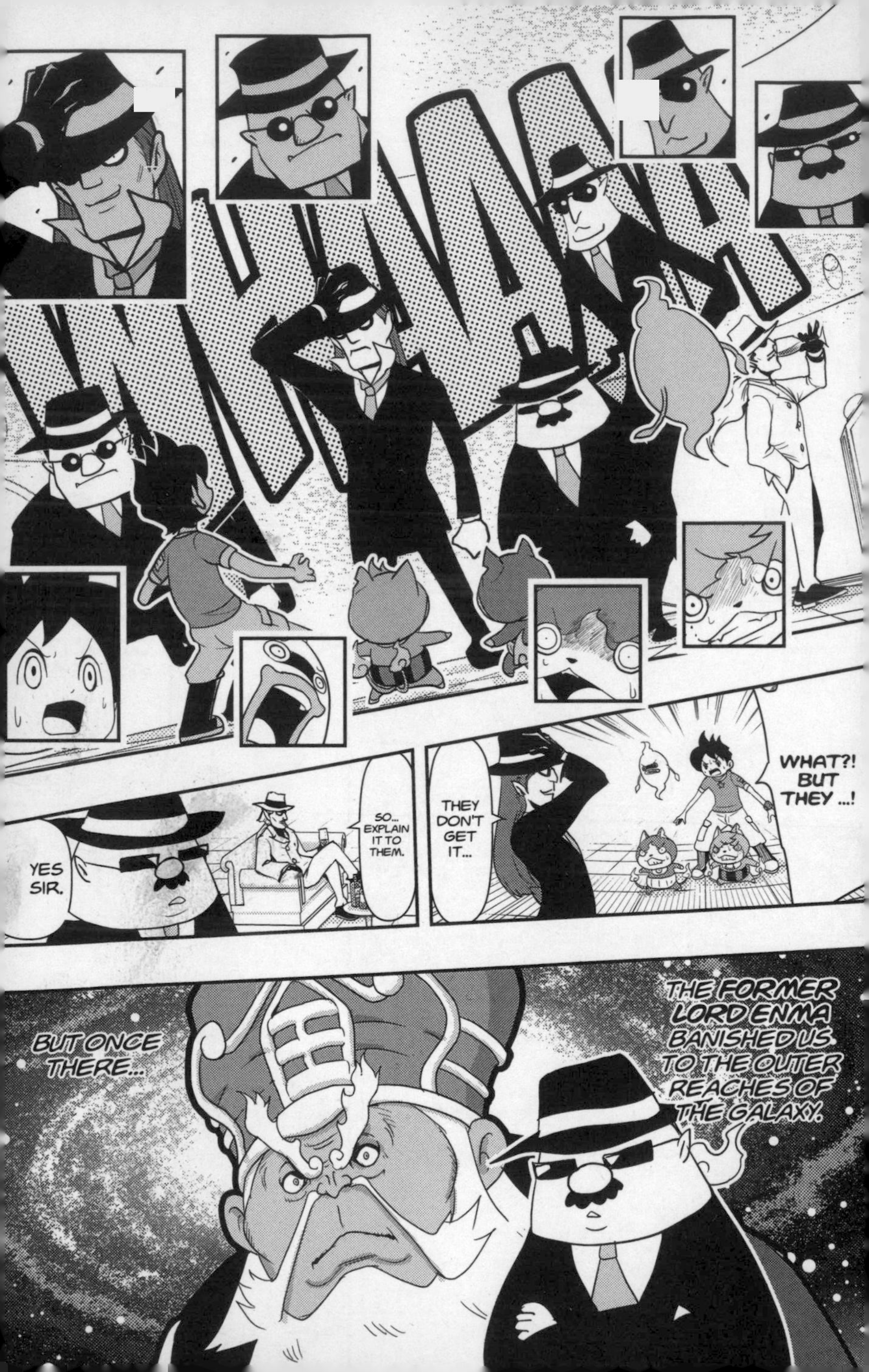
WHAT?! BUT THEY ...!
THEY DON'T GET IT...
SO... EXPLAIN IT TO THEM.
YES SIR.
THE FORMER LORD ENMA BANISHED US TO THE OUTER REACHES OF THE GALAXY.
BUT ONCE THERE...

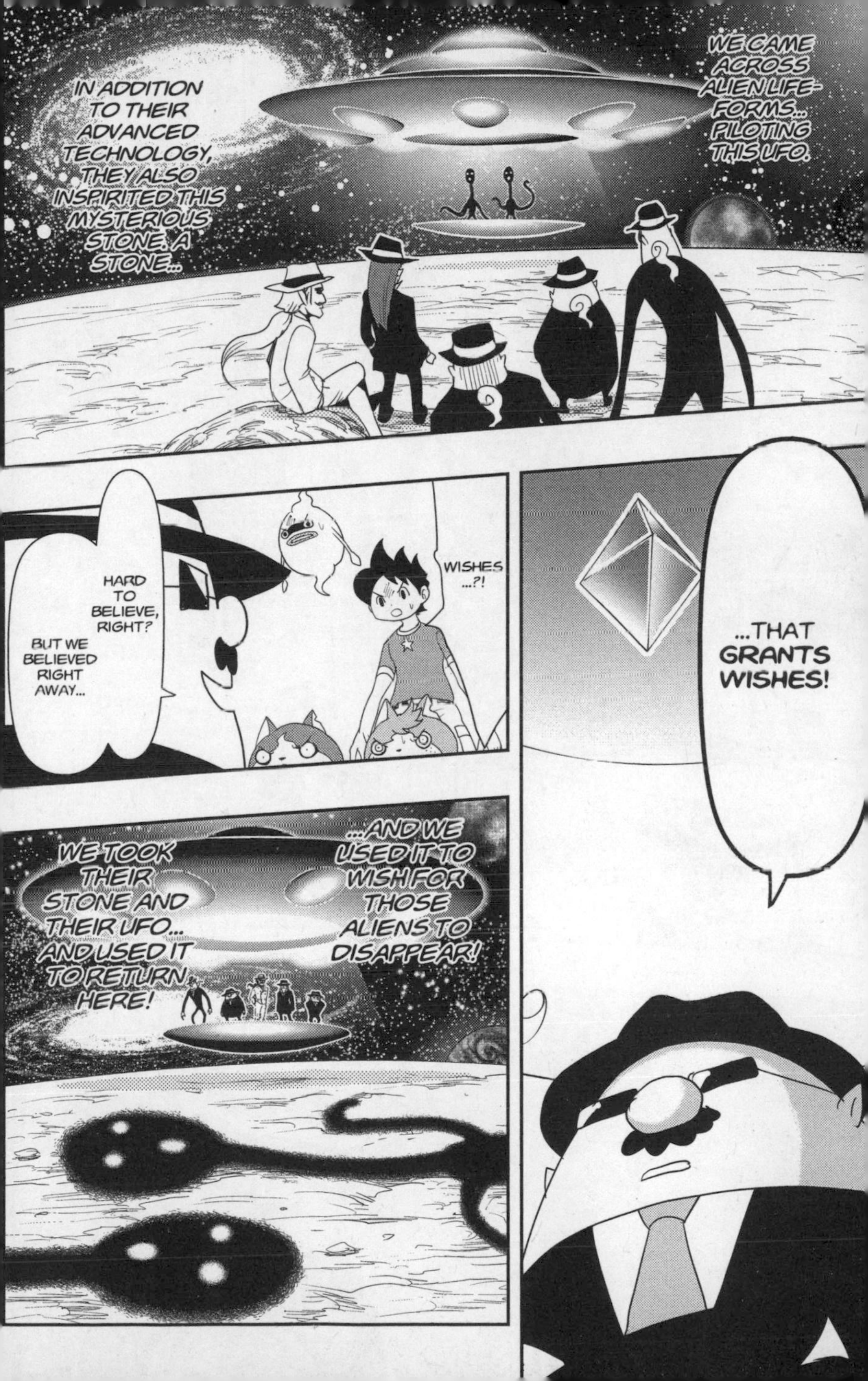

WE CAME ACROSS ALIEN LIFE-FORMS... PILOTING THIS UFO.
IN ADDITION TO THEIR ADVANCED TECHNOLOGY, THEY ALSO INSPIRITED THIS MYSTERIOUS STONE. A STONE...
...THAT GRANTS WISHES!
WISHES ...?!
HARD TO BELIEVE, RIGHT?
BUT WE BELIEVED RIGHT AWAY...
...AND WE USED IT TO WISH FOR THOSE ALIENS TO DISAPPEAR!
WE TOOK THEIR STONE AND THEIR UFO... AND USED IT TO RETURN HERE!

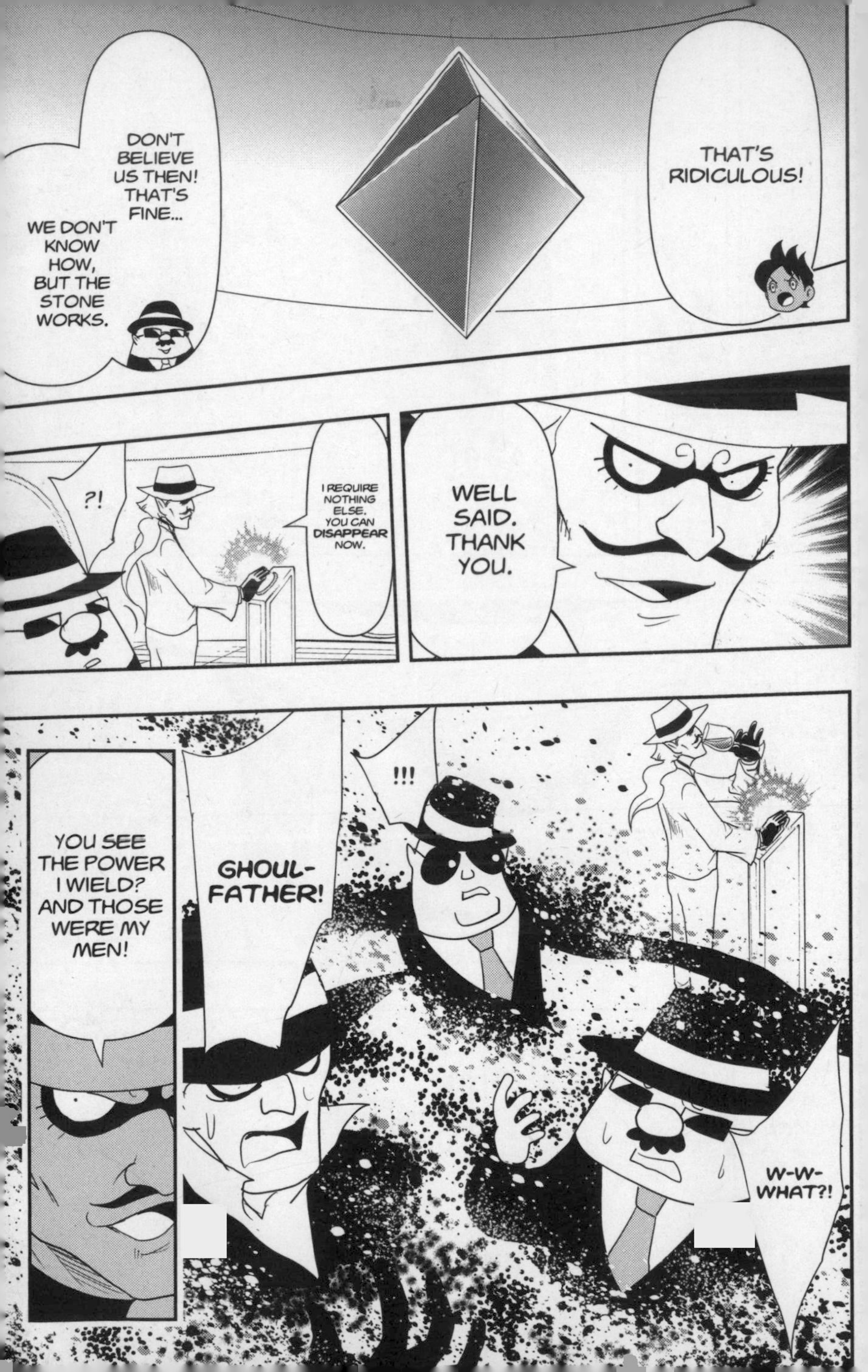
THAT'S RIDICULOUS!
DON'T BELIEVE US THEN! THAT'S FINE...
WE DON'T KNOW HOW, BUT THE STONE WORKS.
WELL SAID. THANK YOU.
I REQUIRE NOTHING ELSE. YOU CAN DISAPPEAR NOW.
?!
W-W-WHAT?!
!!!
GHOUL-FATHER!
YOU SEE THE POWER I WIELD? AND THOSE WERE MY MEN!

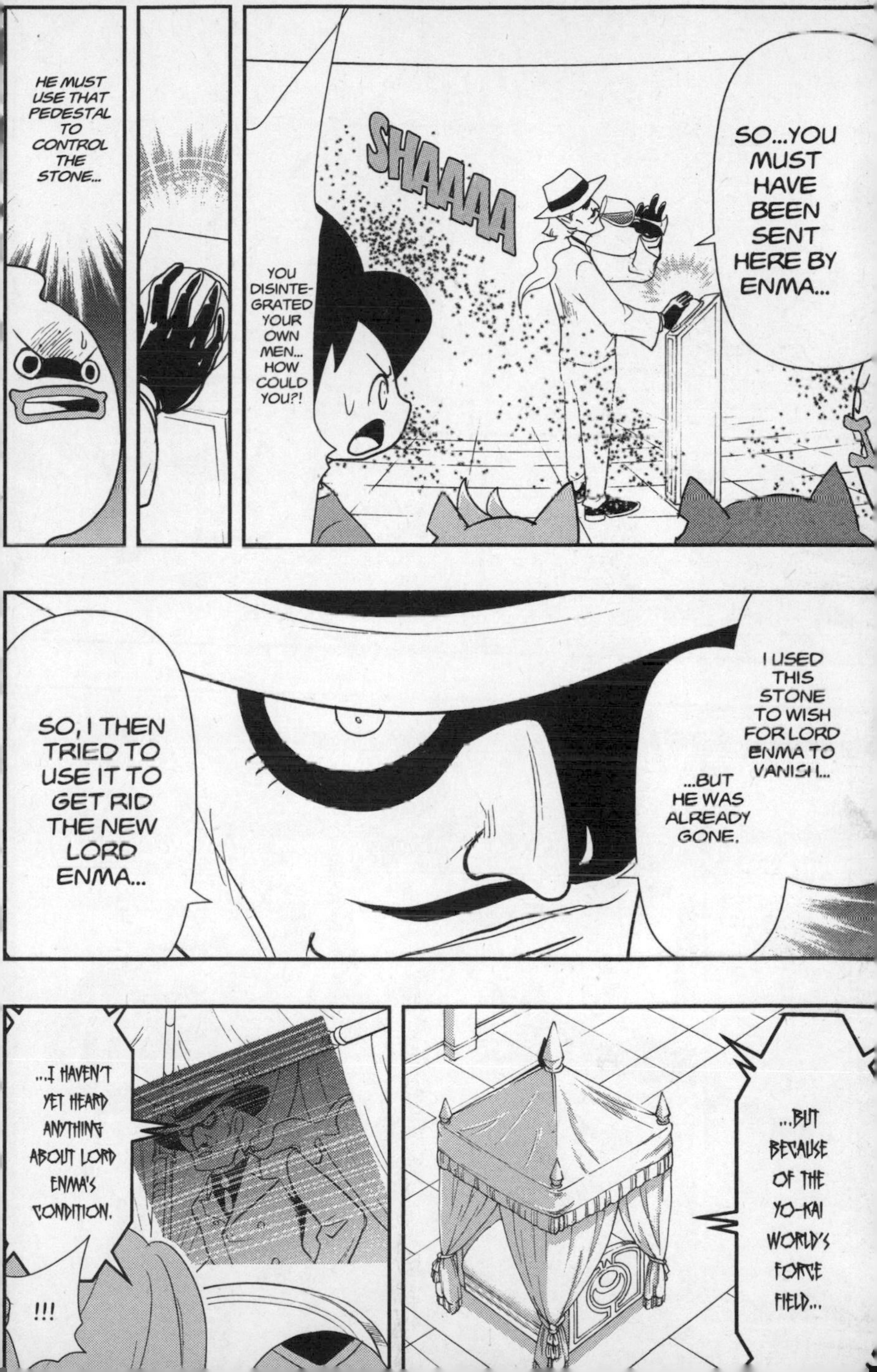
SO...YOU MUST HAVE BEEN SENT HERE BY ENMA...
SHAAAAA
YOU DISINTEGRATED YOUR OWN MEN... HOW COULD YOU?!
HE MUST USE THAT PEDESTAL TO CONTROL THE STONE...
I USED THIS STONE TO WISH FOR LORD ENMA TO VANISH...
...BUT HE WAS ALREADY GONE.
SO, I THEN TRIED TO USE IT TO GET RID THE NEW LORD ENMA...
...BUT BECAUSE OF THE YO-KAI WORLD'S FORCE FIELD...
...I HAVEN'T YET HEARD ANYTHING ABOUT LORD ENMA'S CONDITION.
!!!

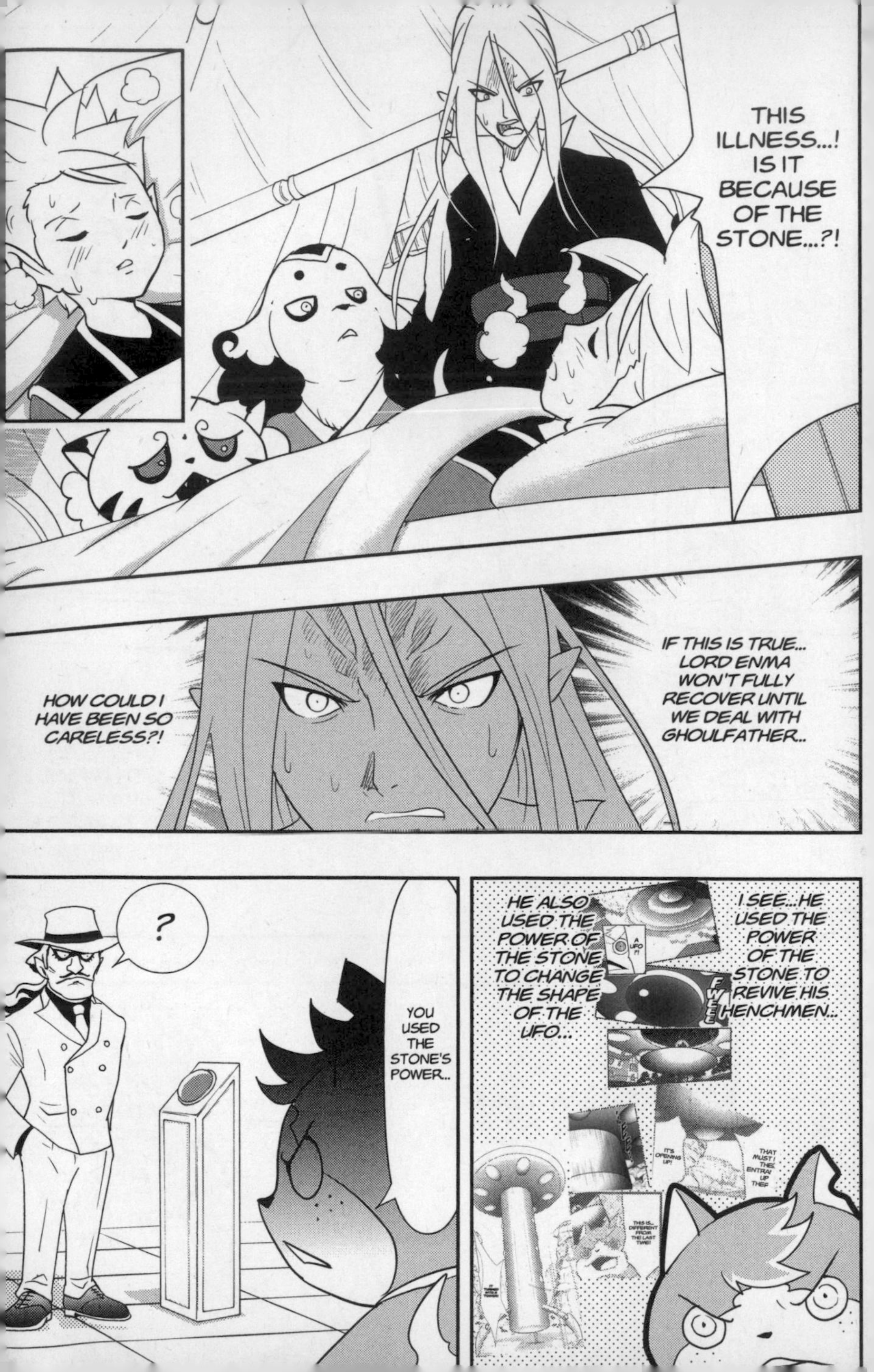
THIS ILLNESS...! IS IT BECAUSE OF THE STONE...?!
IF THIS IS TRUE... LORD ENMA WON'T FULLY RECOVER UNTIL WE DEAL WITH GHOULFATHER..
HOW COULD I HAVE BEEN SO CARELESS?!
I SEE...HE USED THE POWER OF THE STONE TO REVIVE HIS HENCHMEN...
HE ALSO USED THE POWER OF THE STONE TO CHANGE THE SHAPE OF THE UFO...
A UFO?!
FWEE
IT'S OPENING UP!
THIS IS... DIFFERENT FROM THE LAST TIME!
YOU USED THE STONE'S POWER..
?

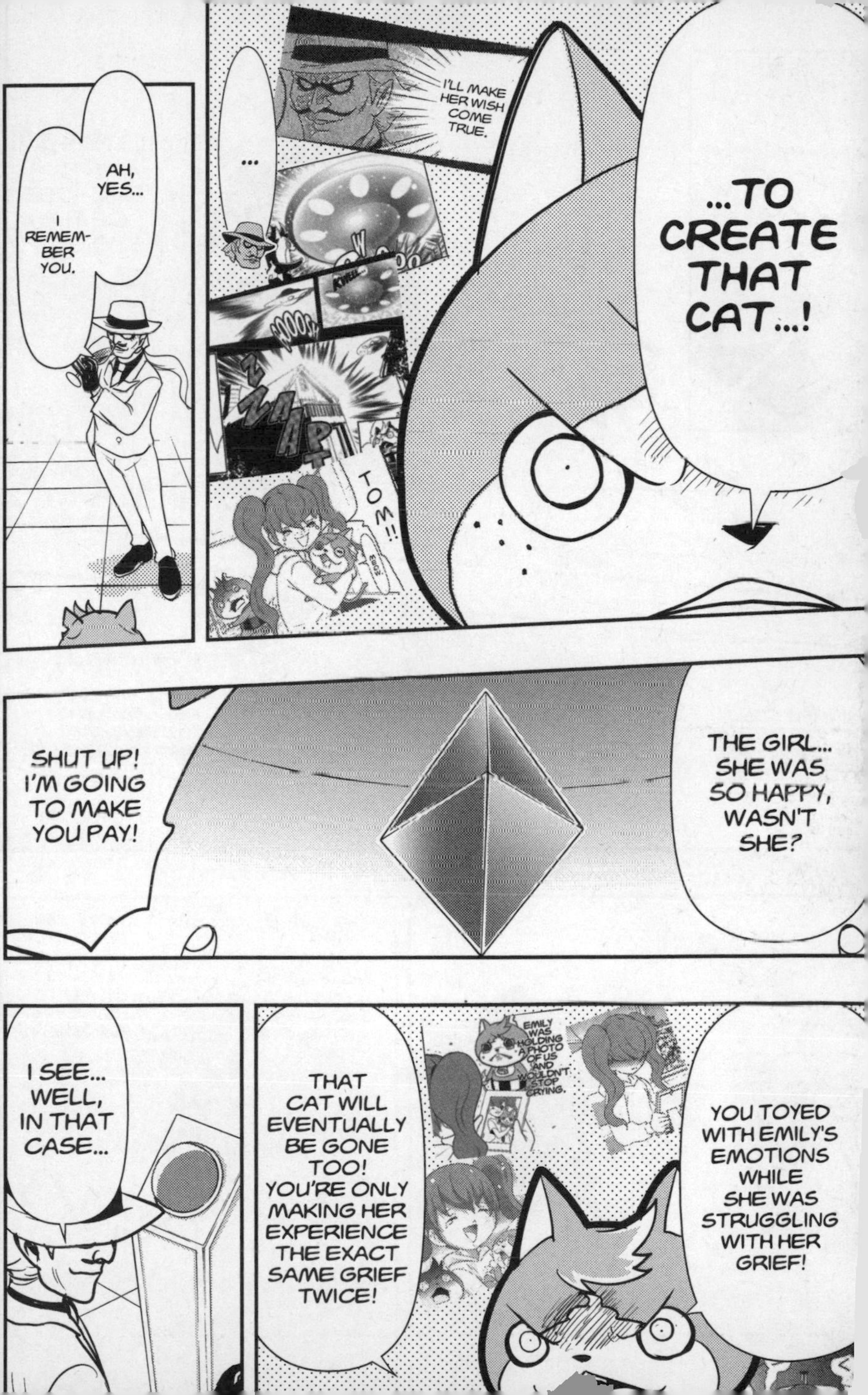
...TO CREATE THAT CAT...!
...
I'LL MAKE HER WISH COME TRUE.
TOM!!
AH, YES... I REMEMBER YOU.
THE GIRL... SHE WAS SO HAPPY, WASN'T SHE?
SHUT UP! I'M GOING TO MAKE YOU PAY!
YOU TOYED WITH EMILY'S EMOTIONS WHILE SHE WAS STRUGGLING WITH HER GRIEF!
EMILY WAS HOLDING A PHOTO OF US AND WOULDN'T STOP CRYING.
THAT CAT WILL EVENTUALLY BE GONE TOO! YOU'RE ONLY MAKING HER EXPERIENCE THE EXACT SAME GRIEF TWICE!
I SEE... WELL, IN THAT CASE...

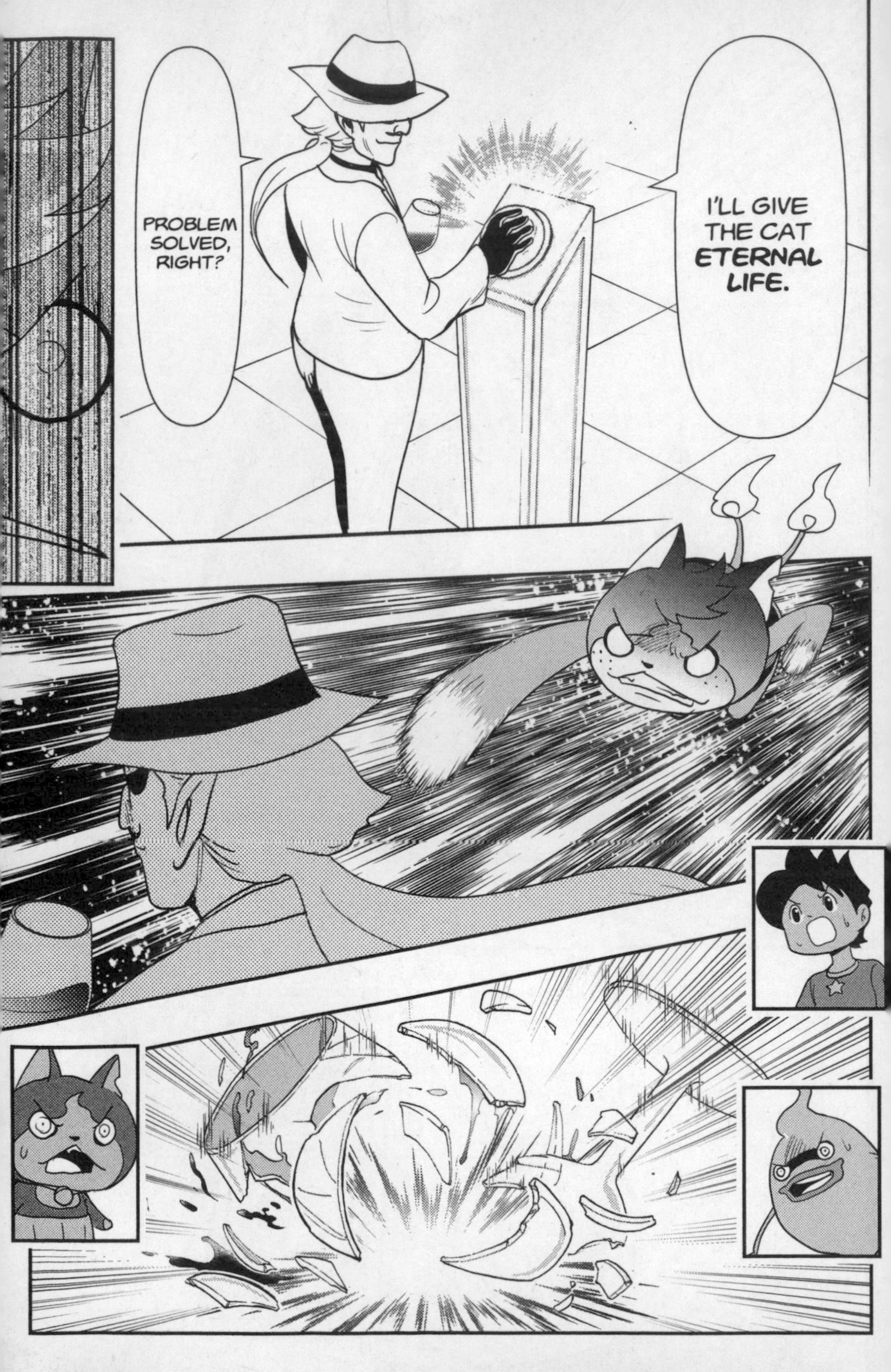
I'LL GIVE THE CAT **ETERNAL LIFE.**
PROBLEM SOLVED, RIGHT?

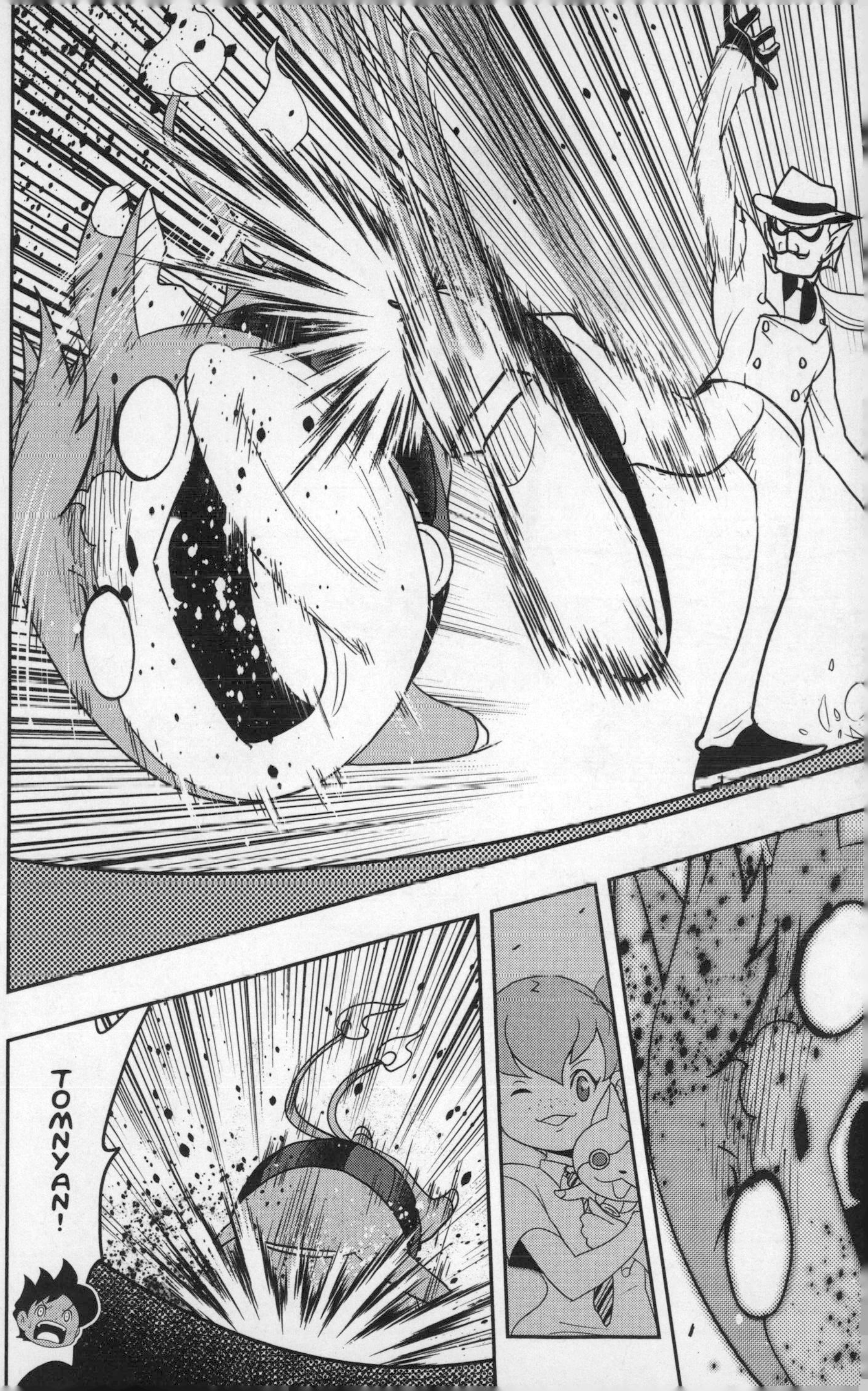
TOMNYAN!

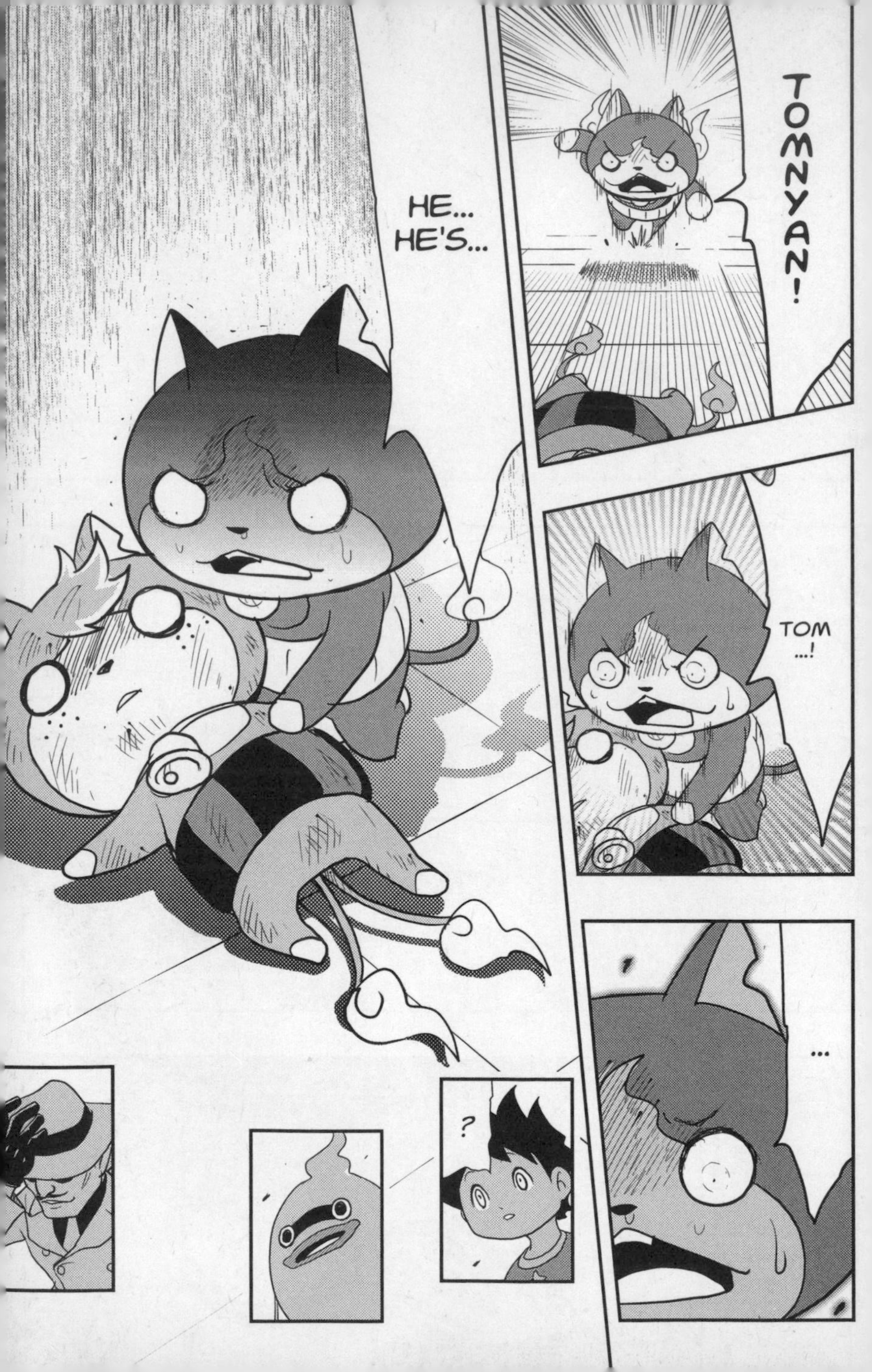
TOMNYAN!
HE... HE'S...
TOM ...!
...
?

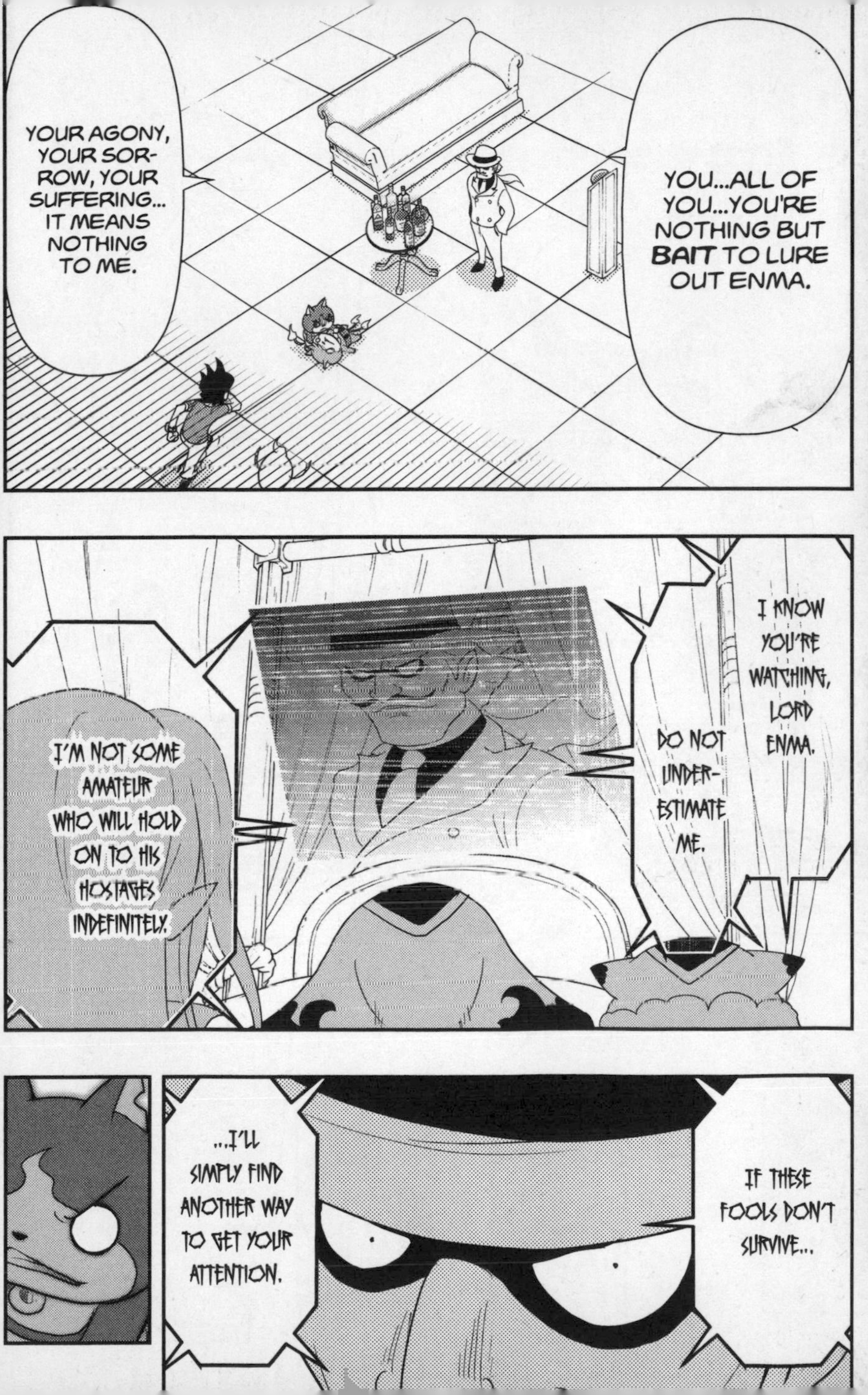
YOU...ALL OF YOU...YOU'RE NOTHING BUT BAIT TO LURE OUT ENMA.
YOUR AGONY, YOUR SORROW, YOUR SUFFERING... IT MEANS NOTHING TO ME.
I KNOW YOU'RE WATCHING, LORD ENMA.
DO NOT UNDERESTIMATE ME.
I'M NOT SOME AMATEUR WHO WILL HOLD ON TO HIS HOSTAGES INDEFINITELY.
IF THESE FOOLS DON'T SURVIVE...
...I'LL SIMPLY FIND ANOTHER WAY TO GET YOUR ATTENTION.

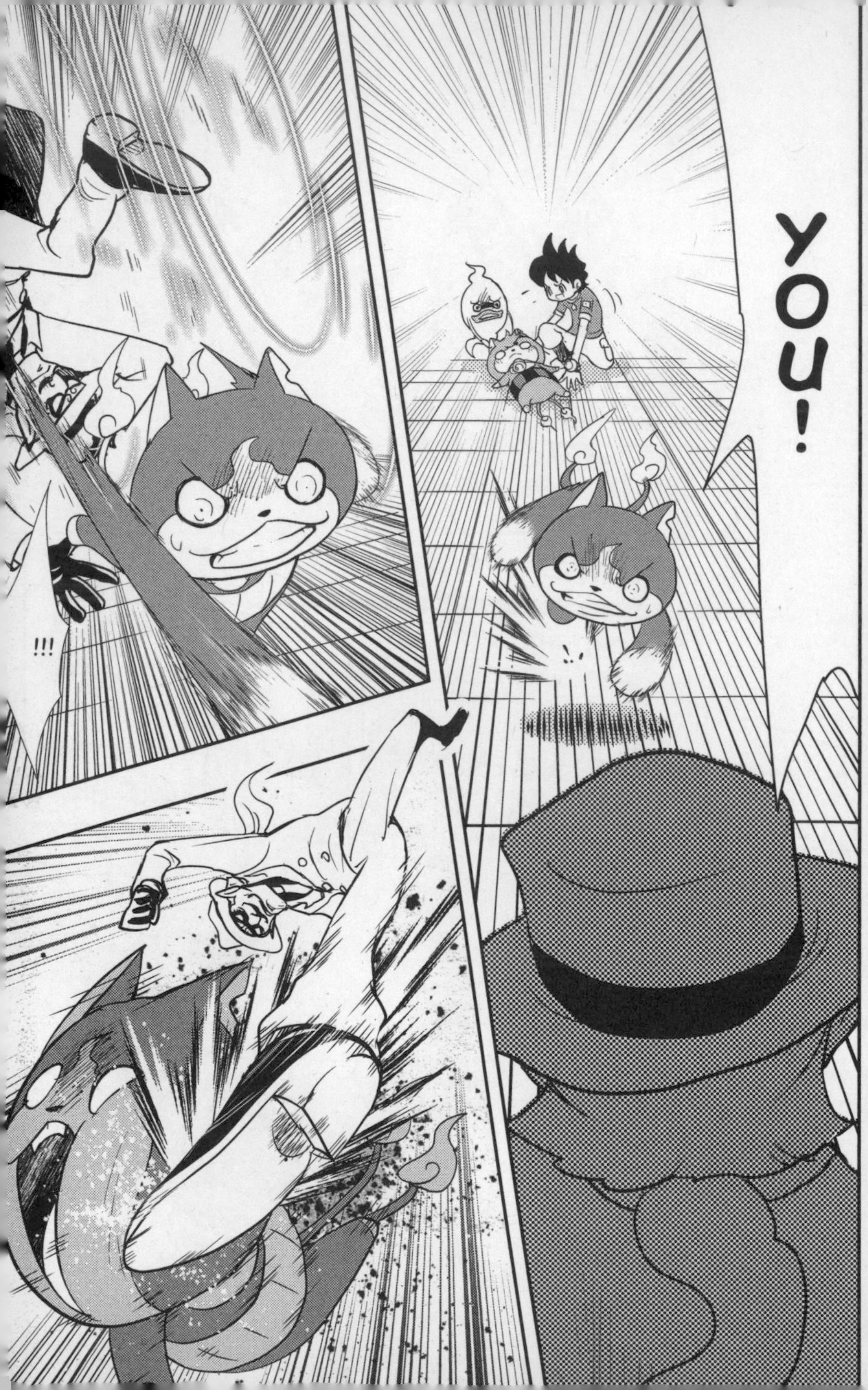
YOU!
!!
!!!

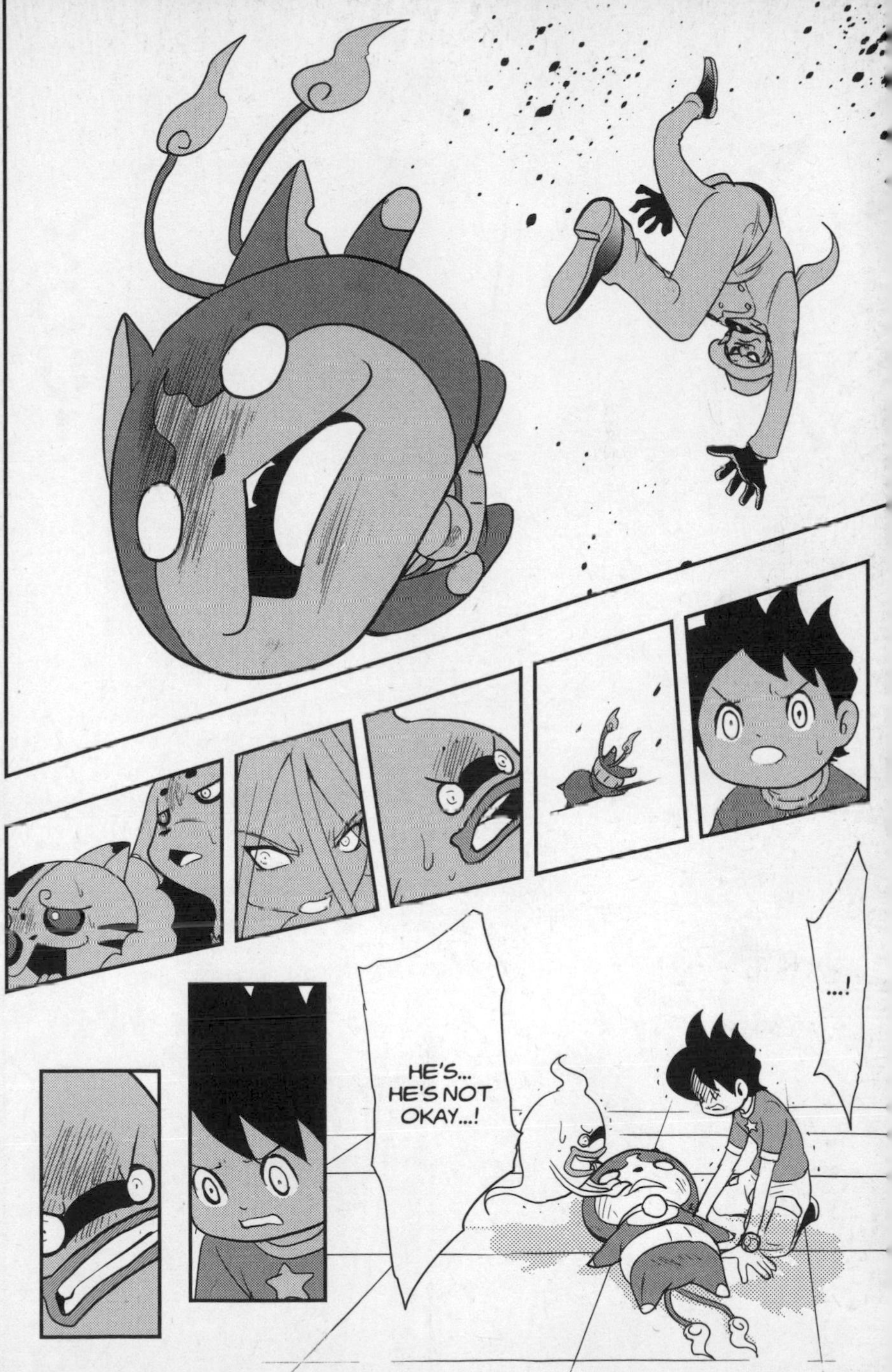
...!
HE'S... HE'S NOT OKAY...!

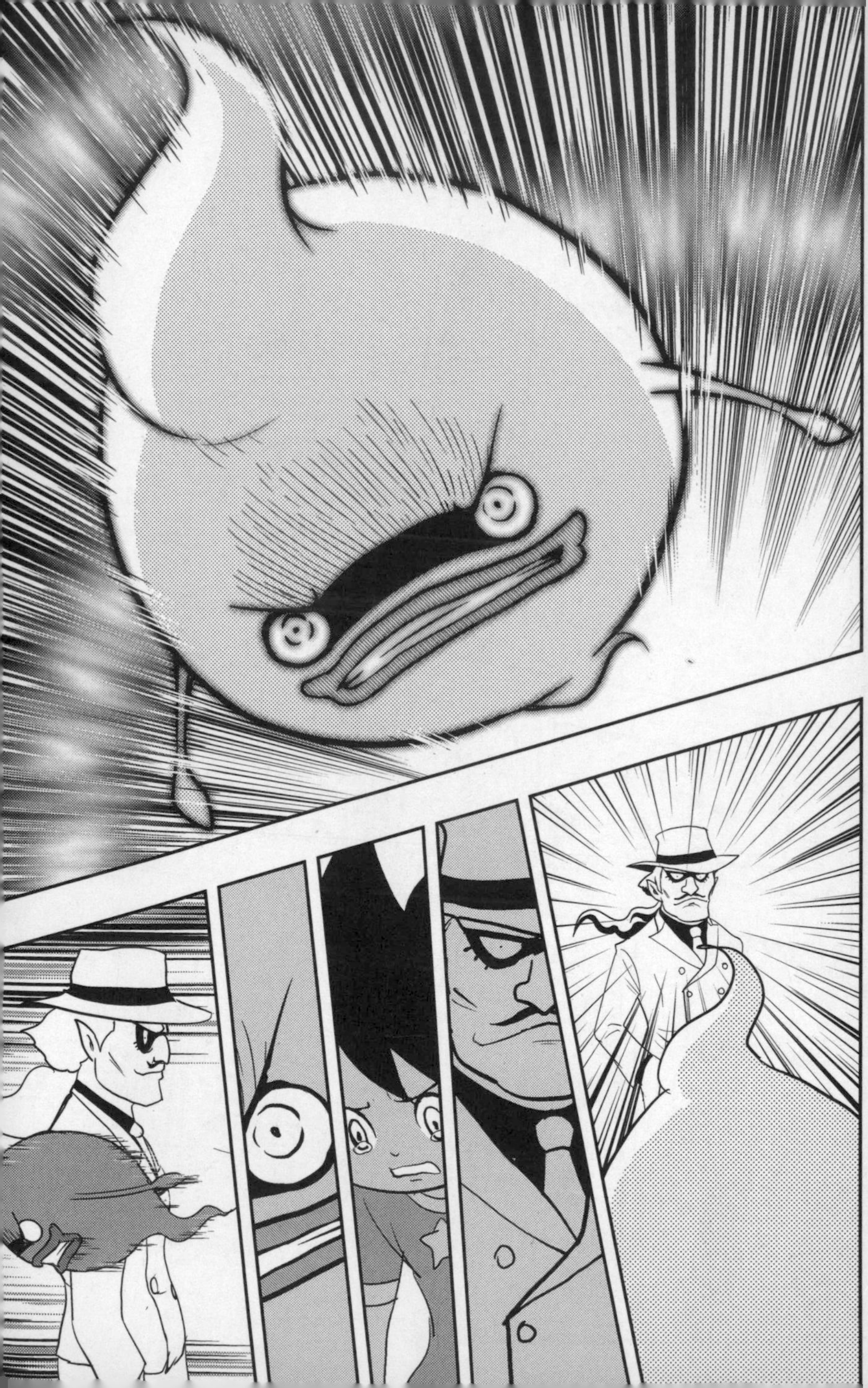

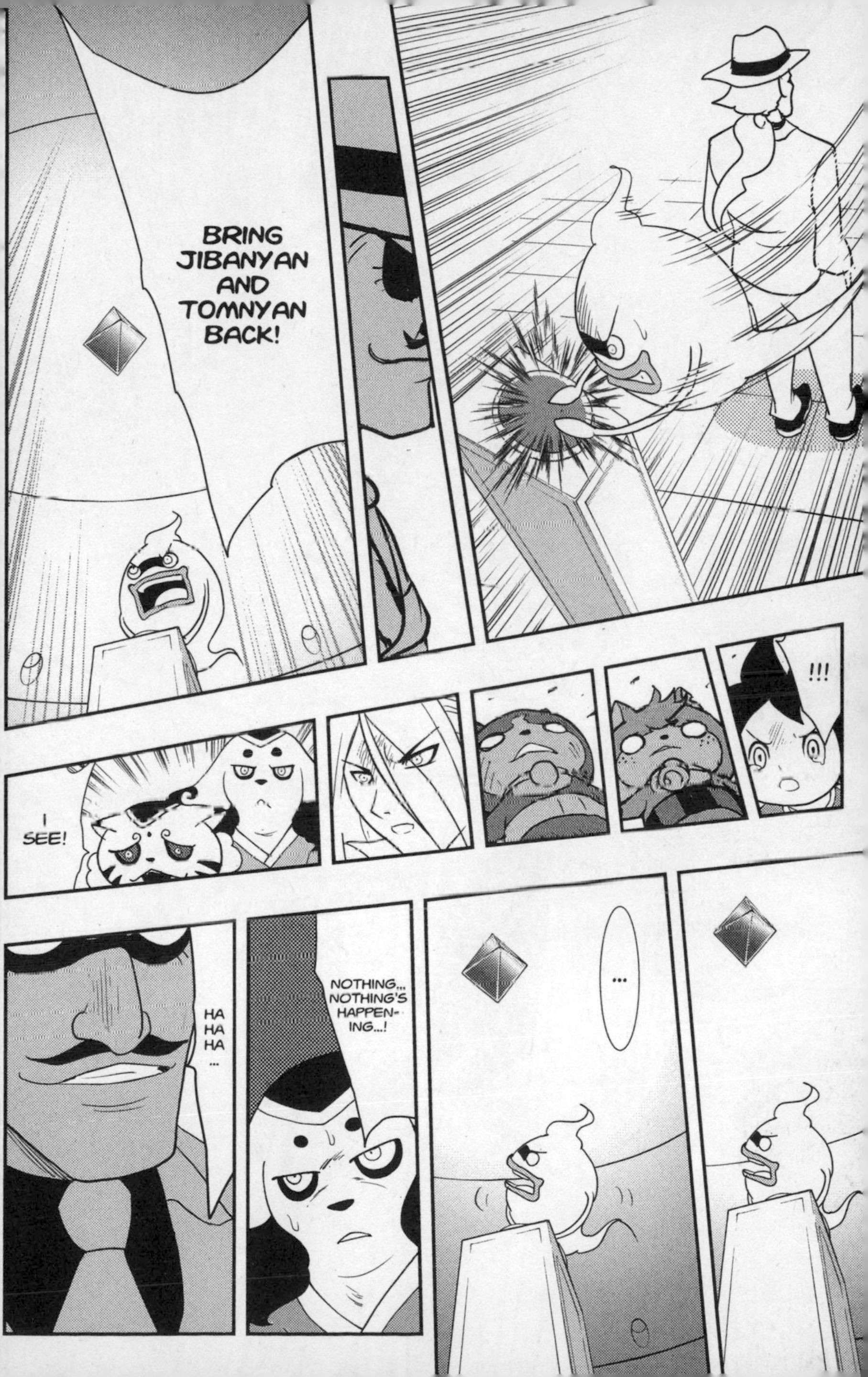
BRING JIBANYAN AND TOMNYAN BACK!
!!!
I SEE!
...
NOTHING... NOTHING'S HAPPEN-ING...!
HA HA HA ...

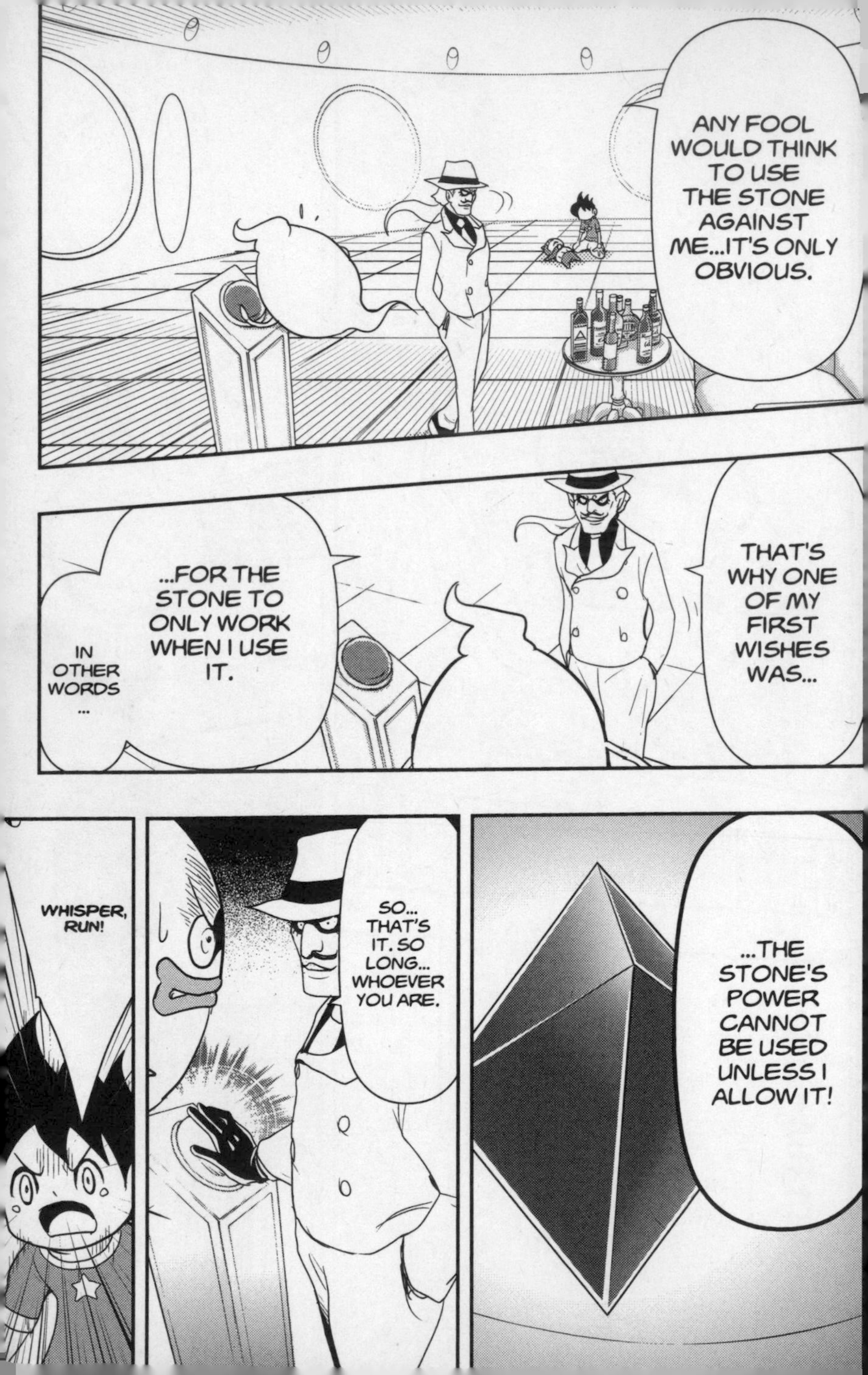
ANY FOOL WOULD THINK TO USE THE STONE AGAINST ME...IT'S ONLY OBVIOUS.
THAT'S WHY ONE OF MY FIRST WISHES WAS...
...FOR THE STONE TO ONLY WORK WHEN I USE IT.
IN OTHER WORDS ...
...THE STONE'S POWER CANNOT BE USED UNLESS I ALLOW IT!
SO... THAT'S IT. SO LONG... WHOEVER YOU ARE.
WHISPER, RUN!

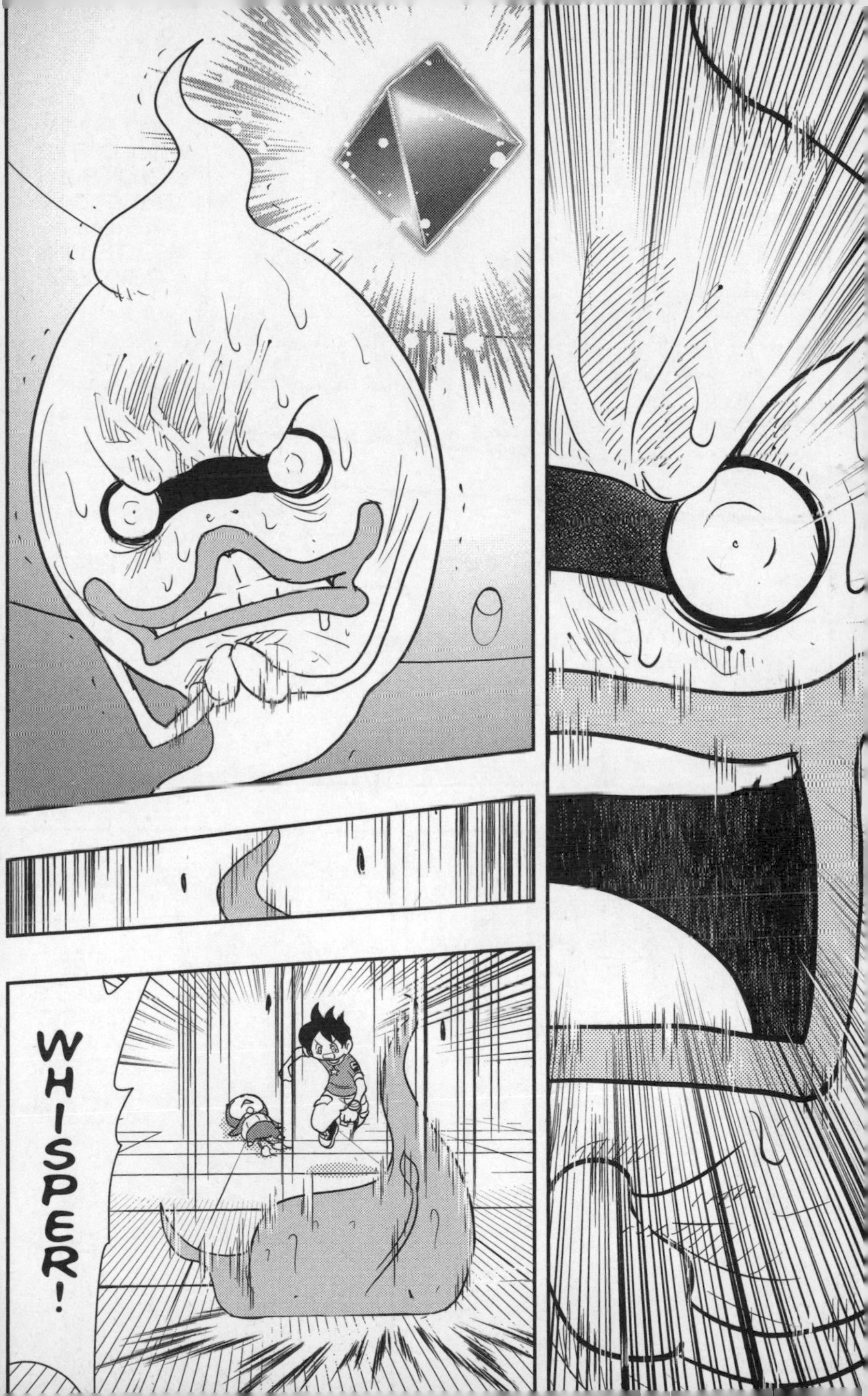
WHISPER!

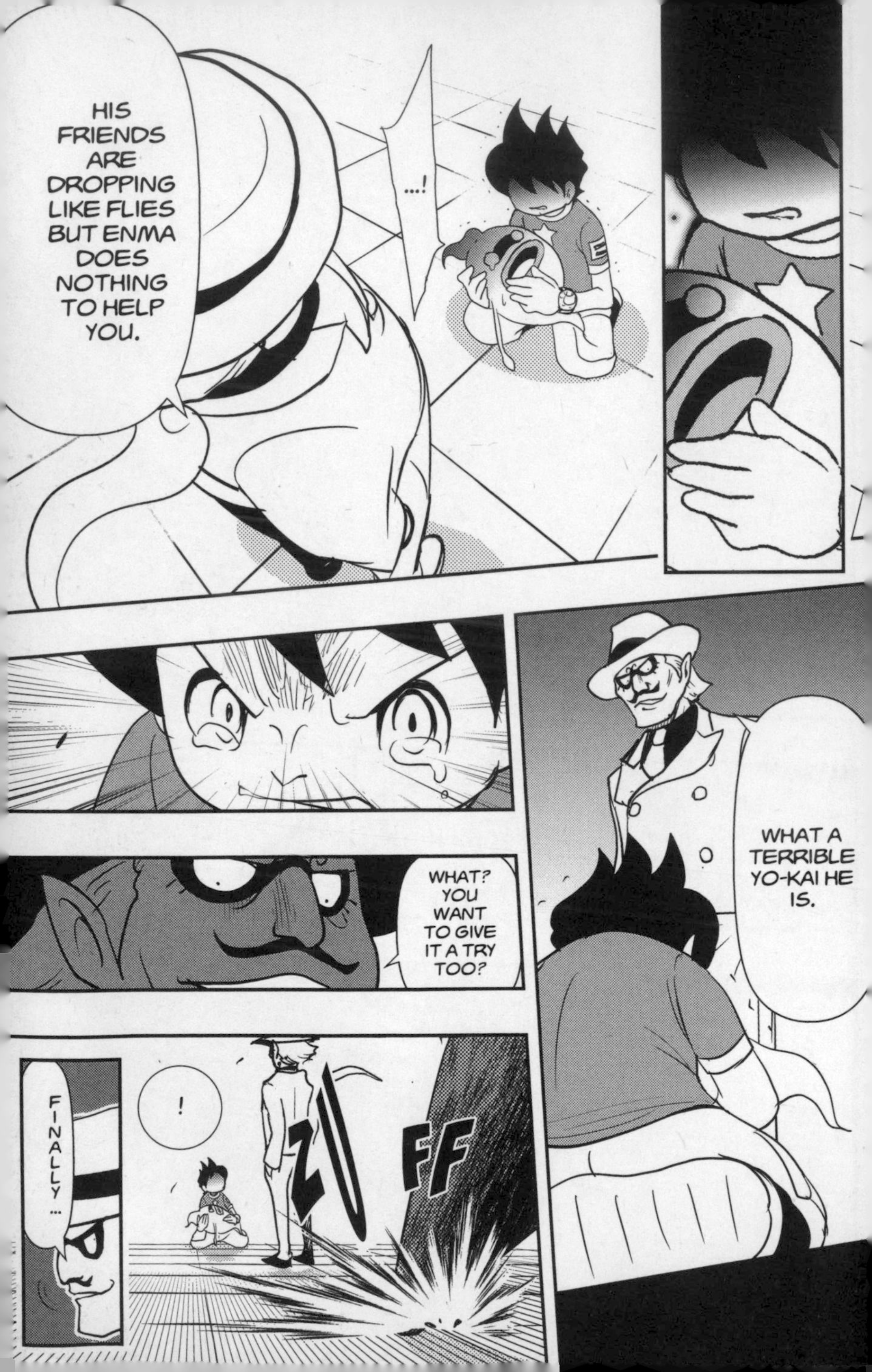
HIS FRIENDS ARE DROPPING LIKE FLIES BUT ENMA DOES NOTHING TO HELP YOU.
...!
WHAT A TERRIBLE YO-KAI HE IS.
WHAT? YOU WANT TO GIVE IT A TRY TOO?
!
ZFF
FINALLY...

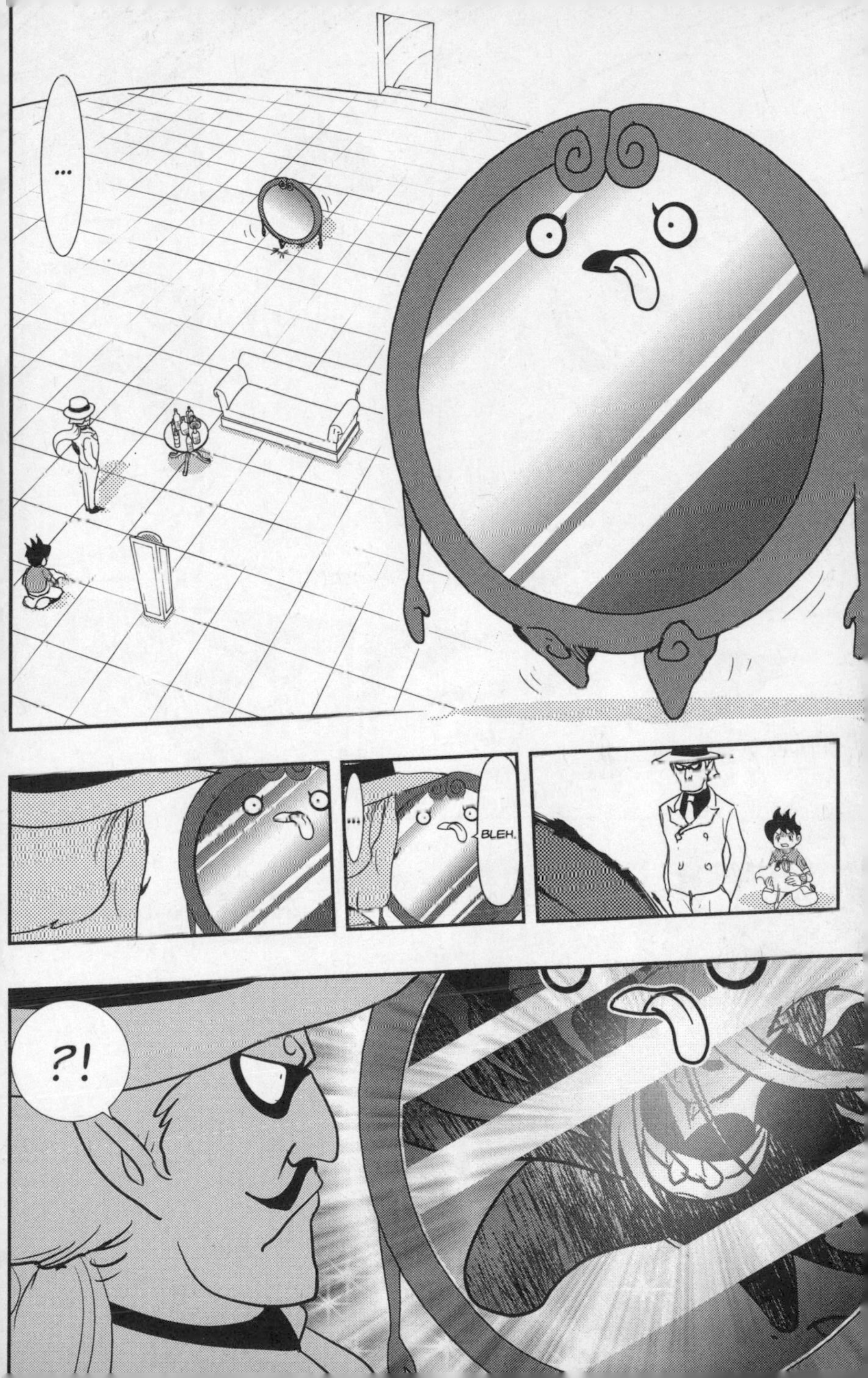
...
BLEH.
...
?!

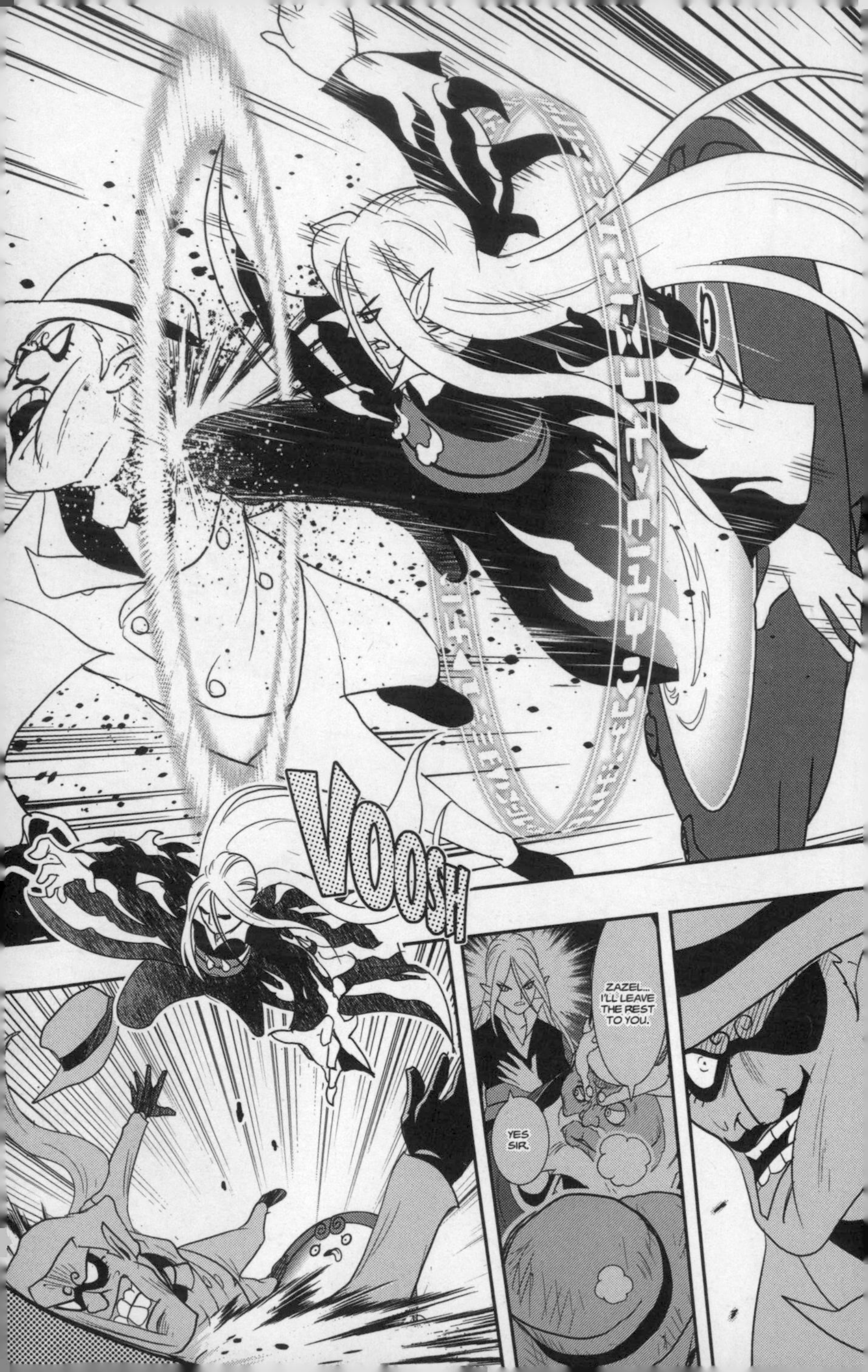
VOOSH
ZAZEL... I'LL LEAVE THE REST TO YOU.
YES SIR.

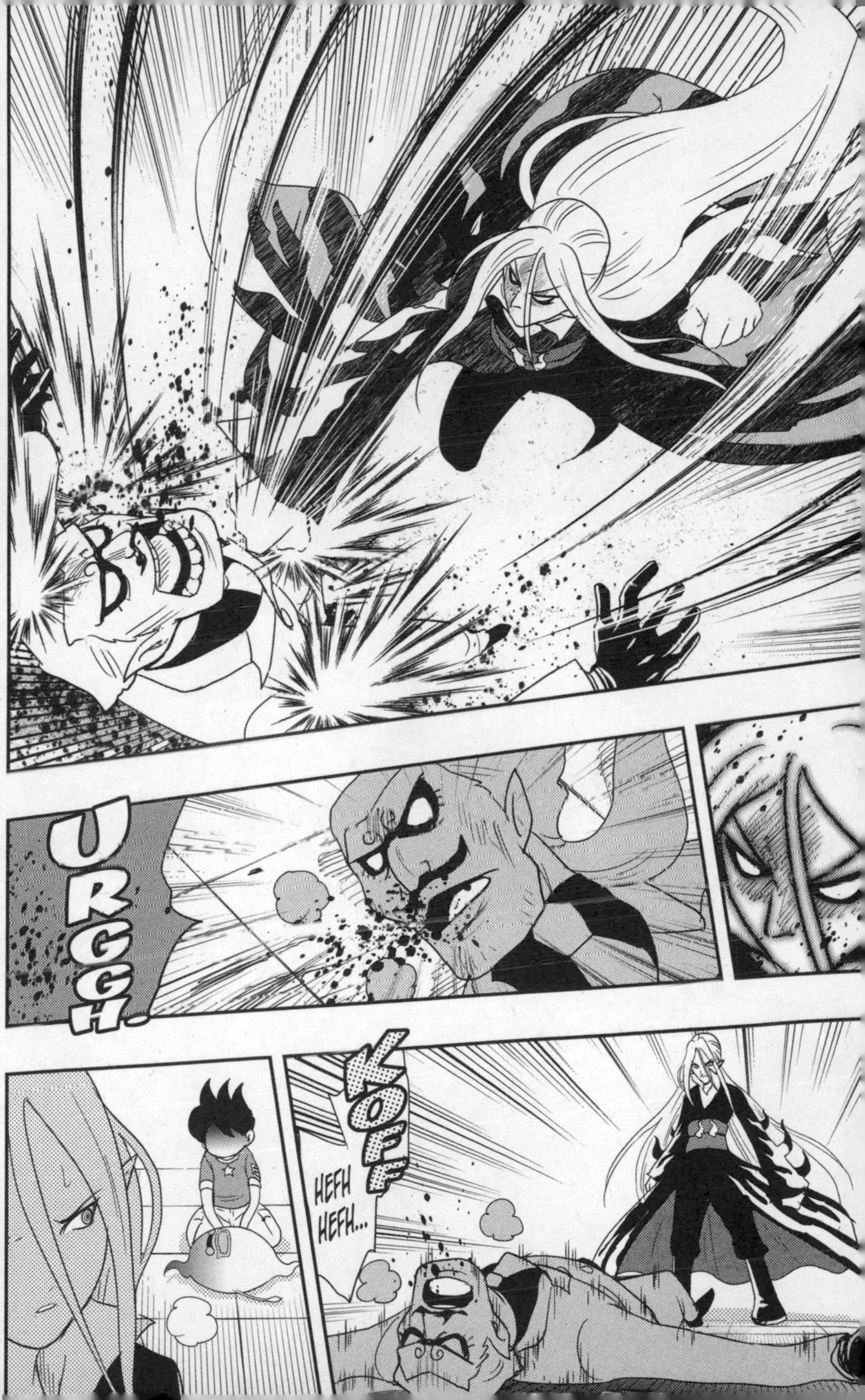
URGGH...
KOFF
HEFH HEFH...

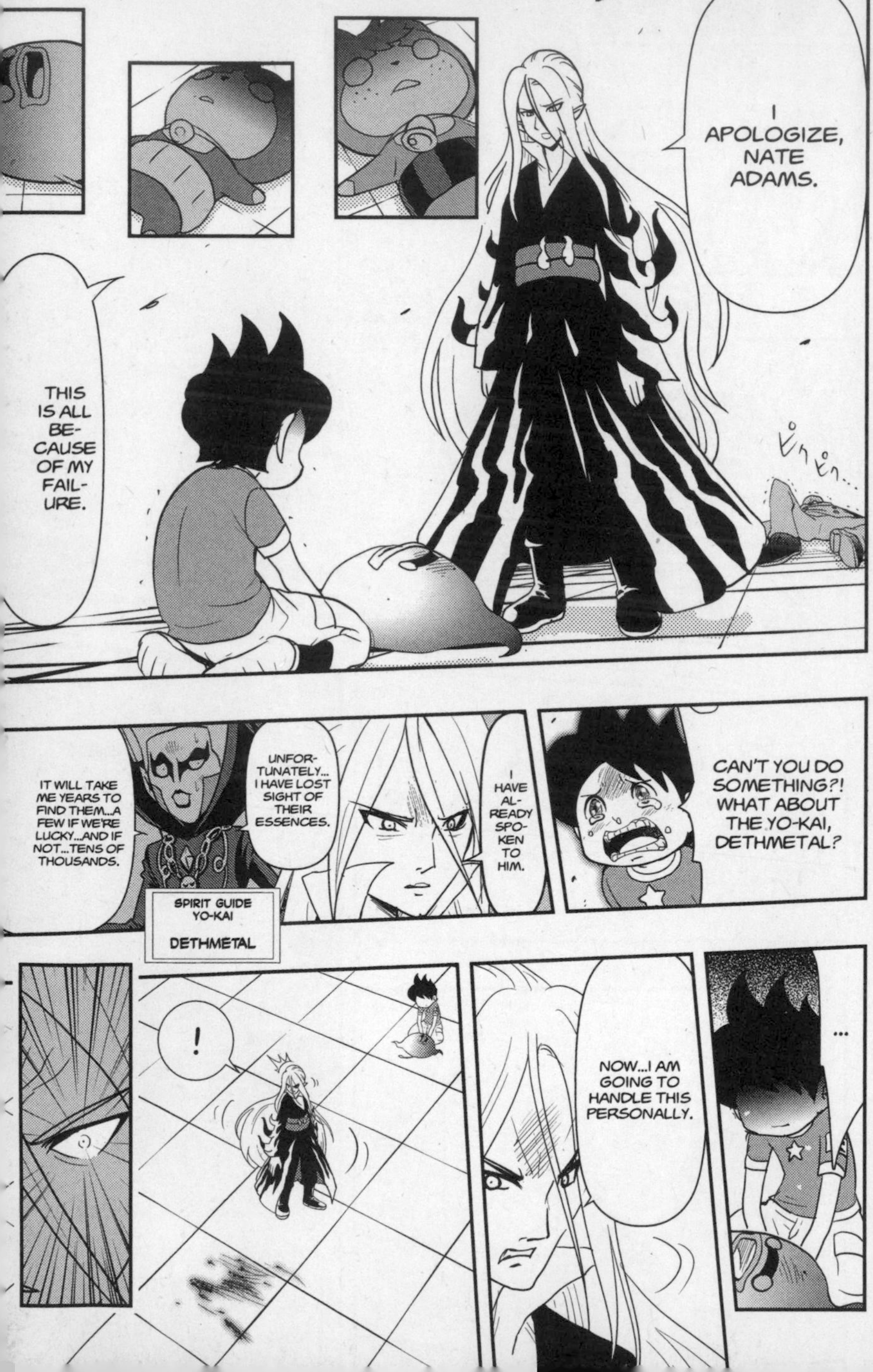
I APOLOGIZE, NATE ADAMS.
ピクピク...
THIS IS ALL BECAUSE OF MY FAILURE.
CAN'T YOU DO SOMETHING?! WHAT ABOUT THE YO-KAI, DETHMETAL?
I HAVE ALREADY SPOKEN TO HIM.
UNFORTUNATELY... I HAVE LOST SIGHT OF THEIR ESSENCES.
IT WILL TAKE ME YEARS TO FIND THEM...A FEW IF WE'RE LUCKY...AND IF NOT...TENS OF THOUSANDS.
SPIRIT GUIDE YO-KAI
DETHMETAL
...
NOW...I AM GOING TO HANDLE THIS PERSONALLY.
!

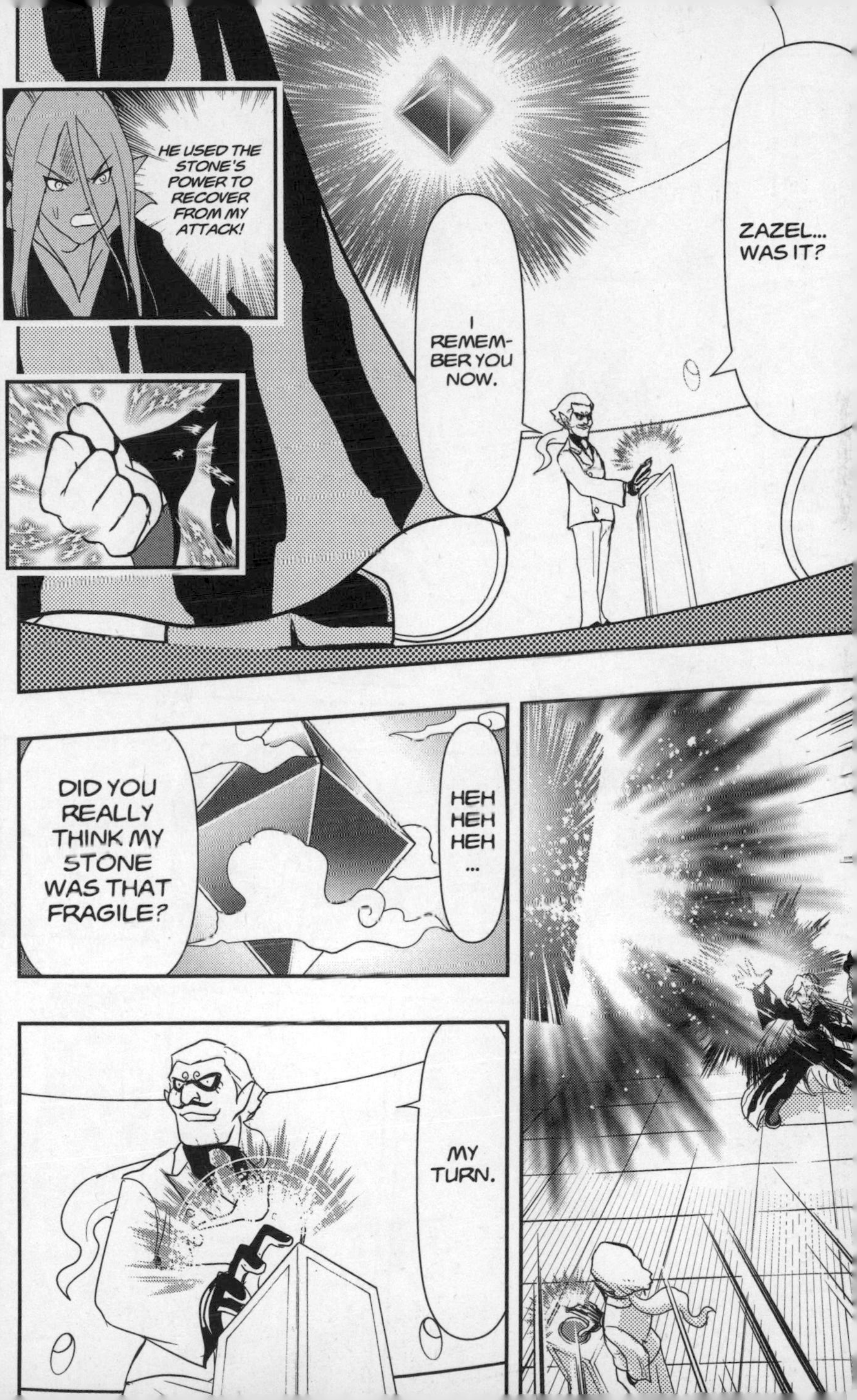
ZAZEL... WAS IT?
I REMEMBER YOU NOW.
HE USED THE STONE'S POWER TO RECOVER FROM MY ATTACK!
HEH HEH HEH ...
DID YOU REALLY THINK MY STONE WAS THAT FRAGILE?
MY TURN.

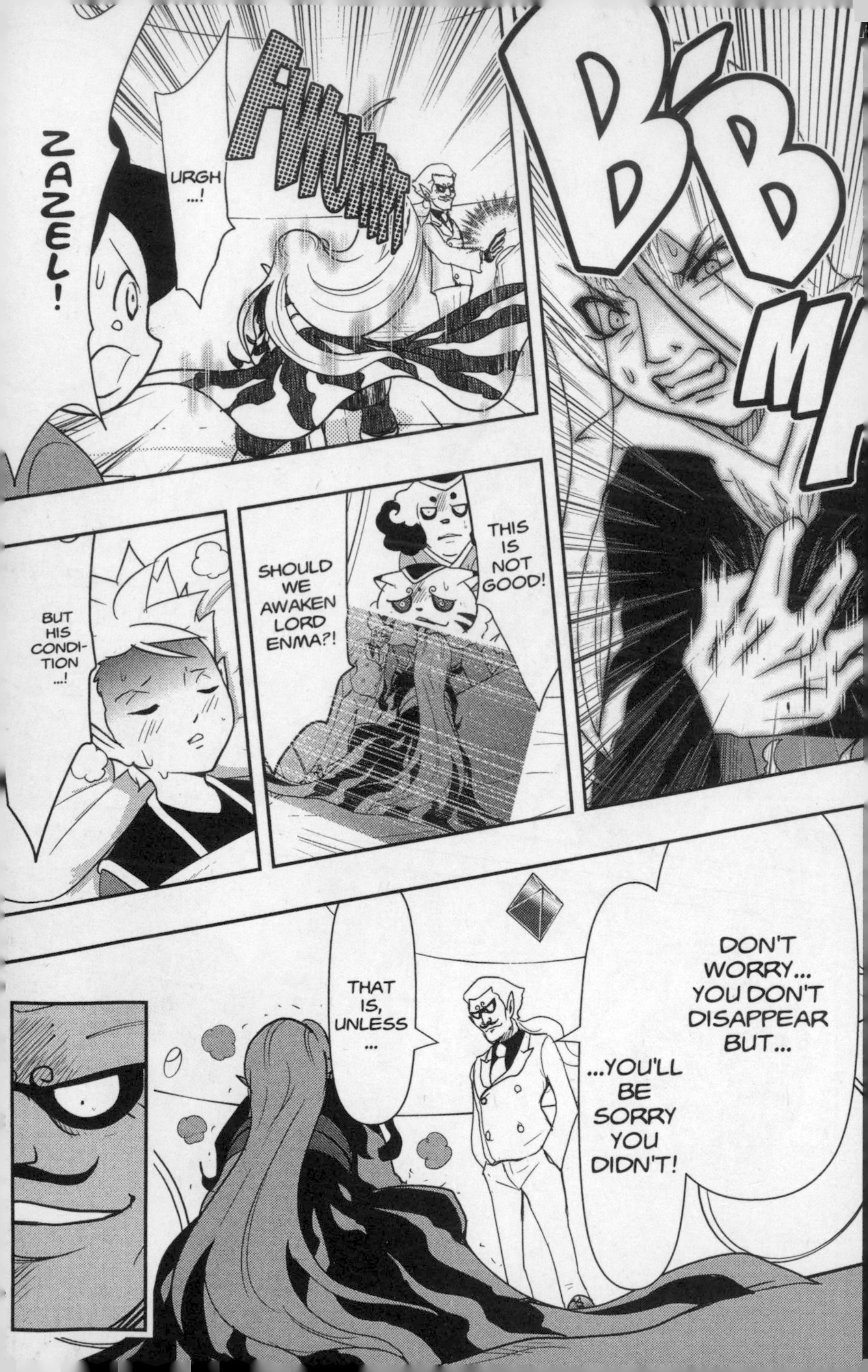
URGH ...!
ZAZEL!
THIS IS NOT GOOD!
SHOULD WE AWAKEN LORD ENMA?!
BUT HIS CONDITION ...!
DON'T WORRY... YOU DON'T DISAPPEAR BUT...
...YOU'LL BE SORRY YOU DIDN'T!
THAT IS, UNLESS ...

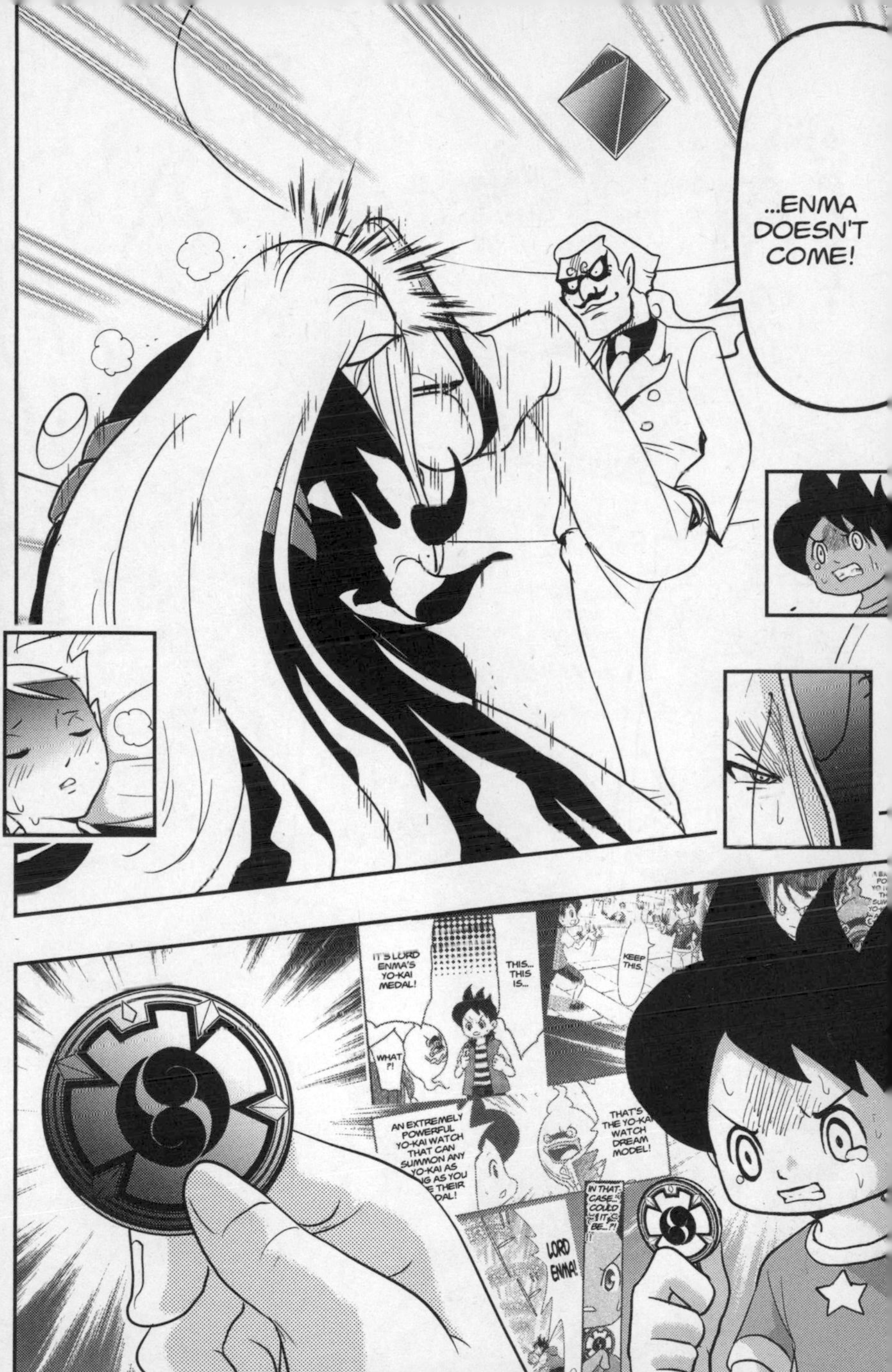
...ENMA DOESN'T COME!
KEEP THIS.
THIS... THIS IS...
IT'S LORD ENMA'S YO-KAI MEDAL!
WHAT ?!
THAT'S THE YO-KAI WATCH DREAM MODEL!
AN EXTREMELY POWERFUL YO-KAI WATCH THAT CAN SUMMON ANY YO-KAI AS
IN THAT CASE... COULD IT BE...?!
LORD ENMA!

# THE GHOULFATHER ARC ⑤
# FRIENDSHIP WINS OVER ALL ELSE

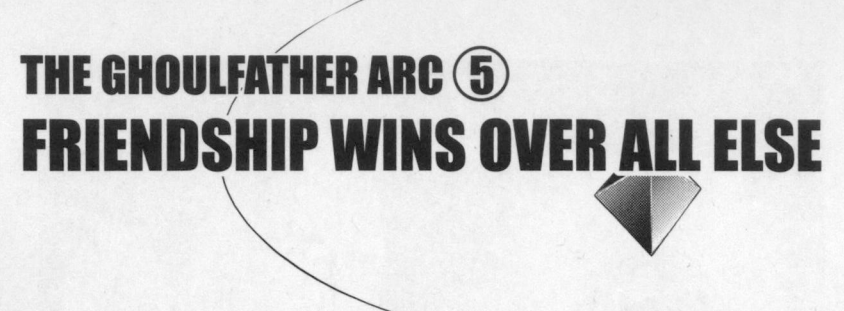

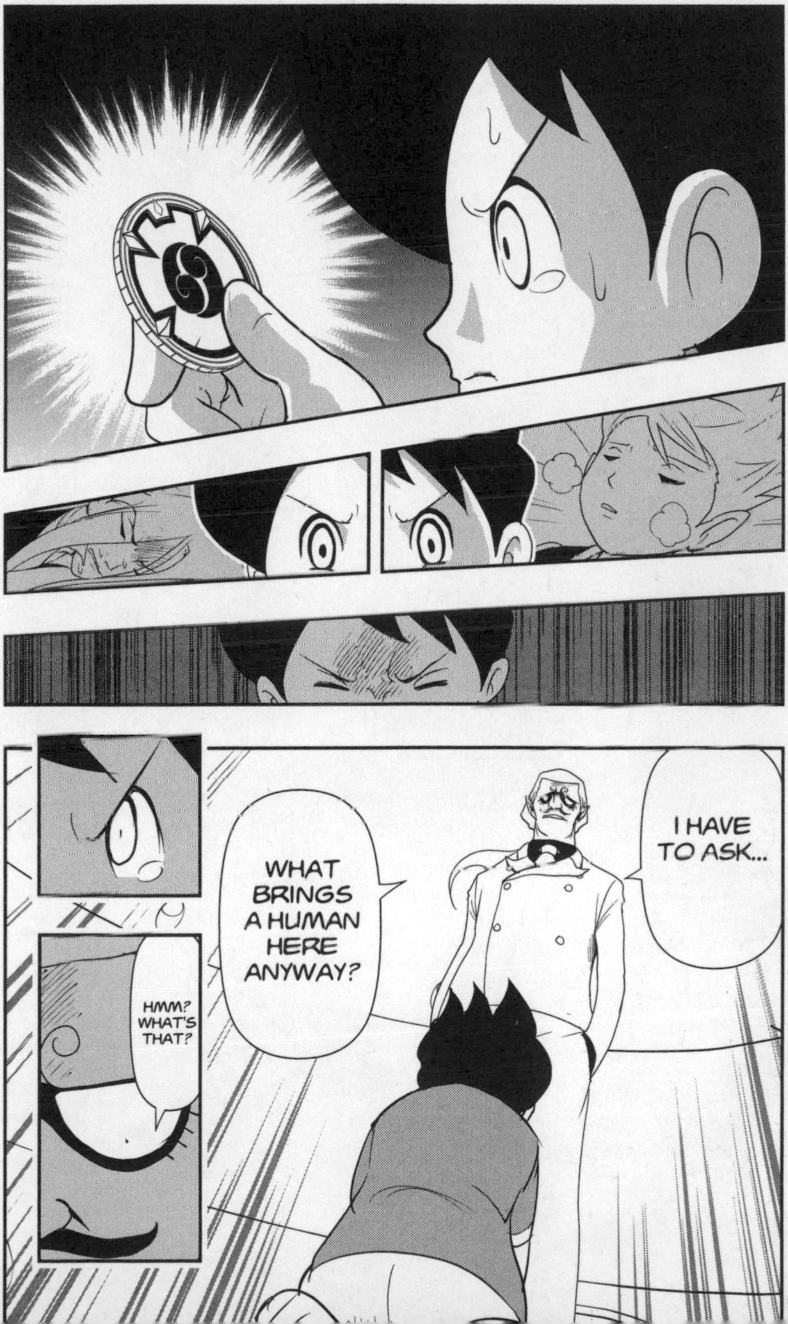
I HAVE TO ASK...
WHAT BRINGS A HUMAN HERE ANYWAY?
HMM? WHAT'S THAT?

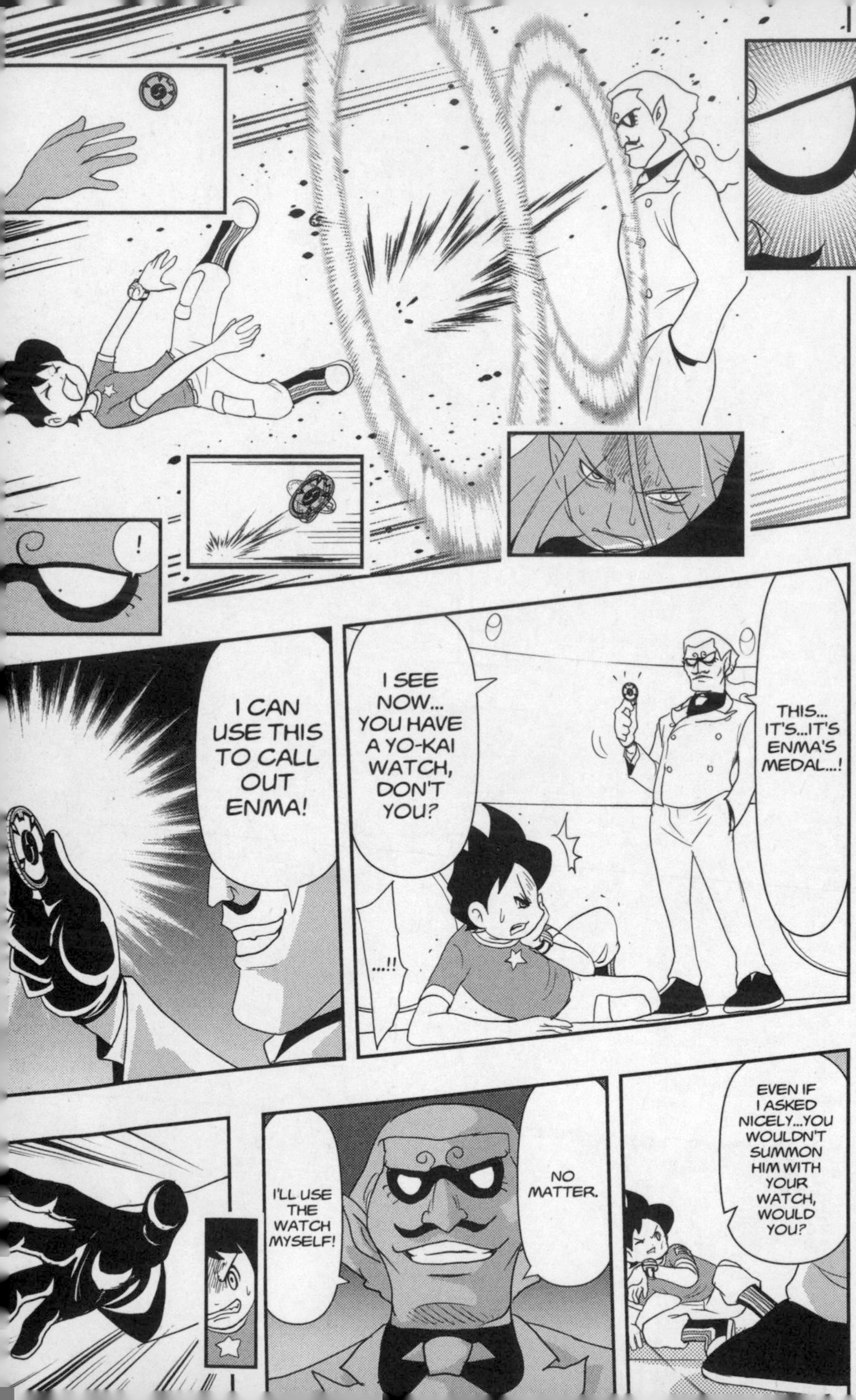
!
THIS... IT'S...IT'S ENMA'S MEDAL...!
I SEE NOW... YOU HAVE A YO-KAI WATCH, DON'T YOU?
...!!
I CAN USE THIS TO CALL OUT ENMA!
EVEN IF I ASKED NICELY...YOU WOULDN'T SUMMON HIM WITH YOUR WATCH, WOULD YOU?
NO MATTER.
I'LL USE THE WATCH MYSELF!

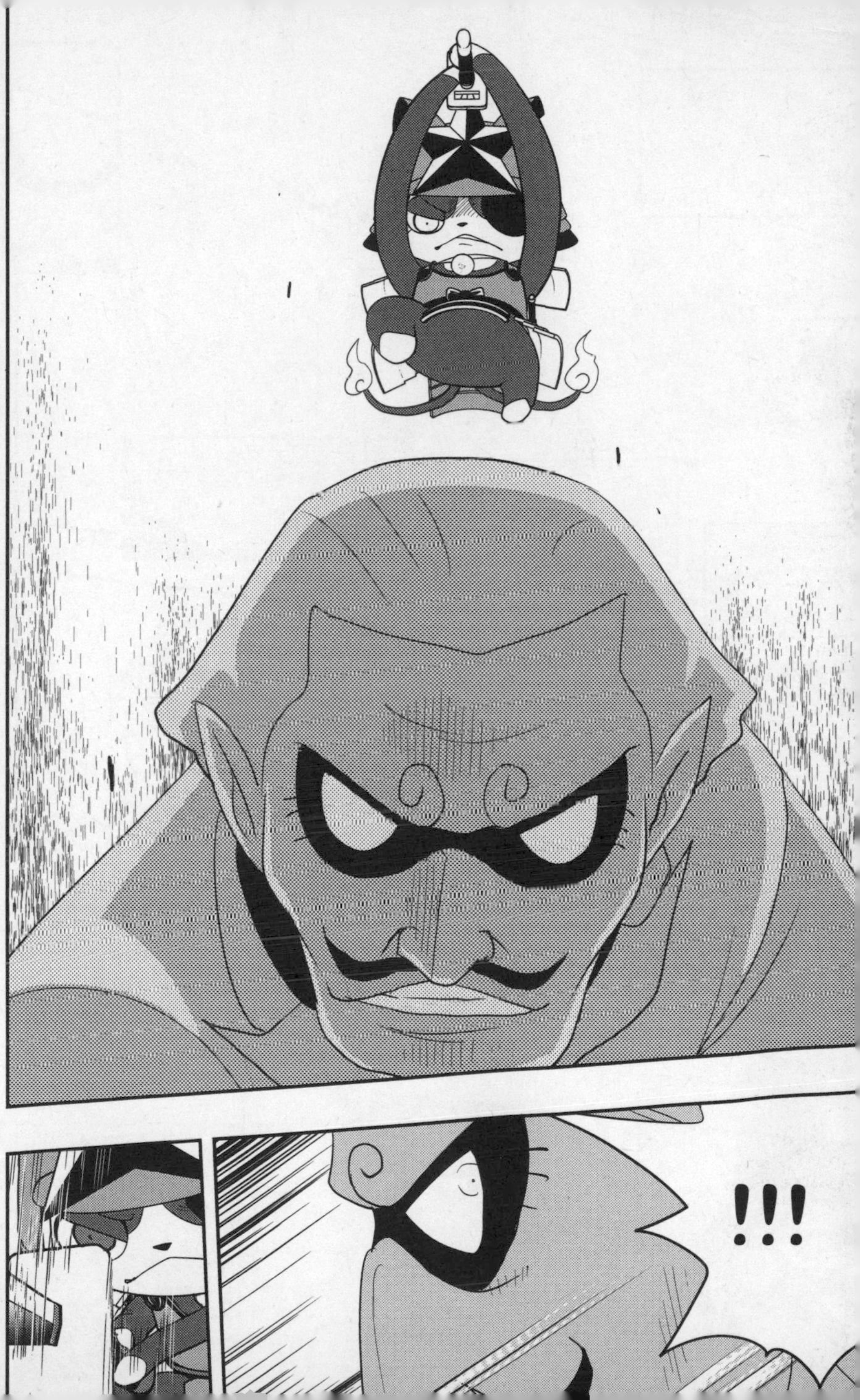
!!!

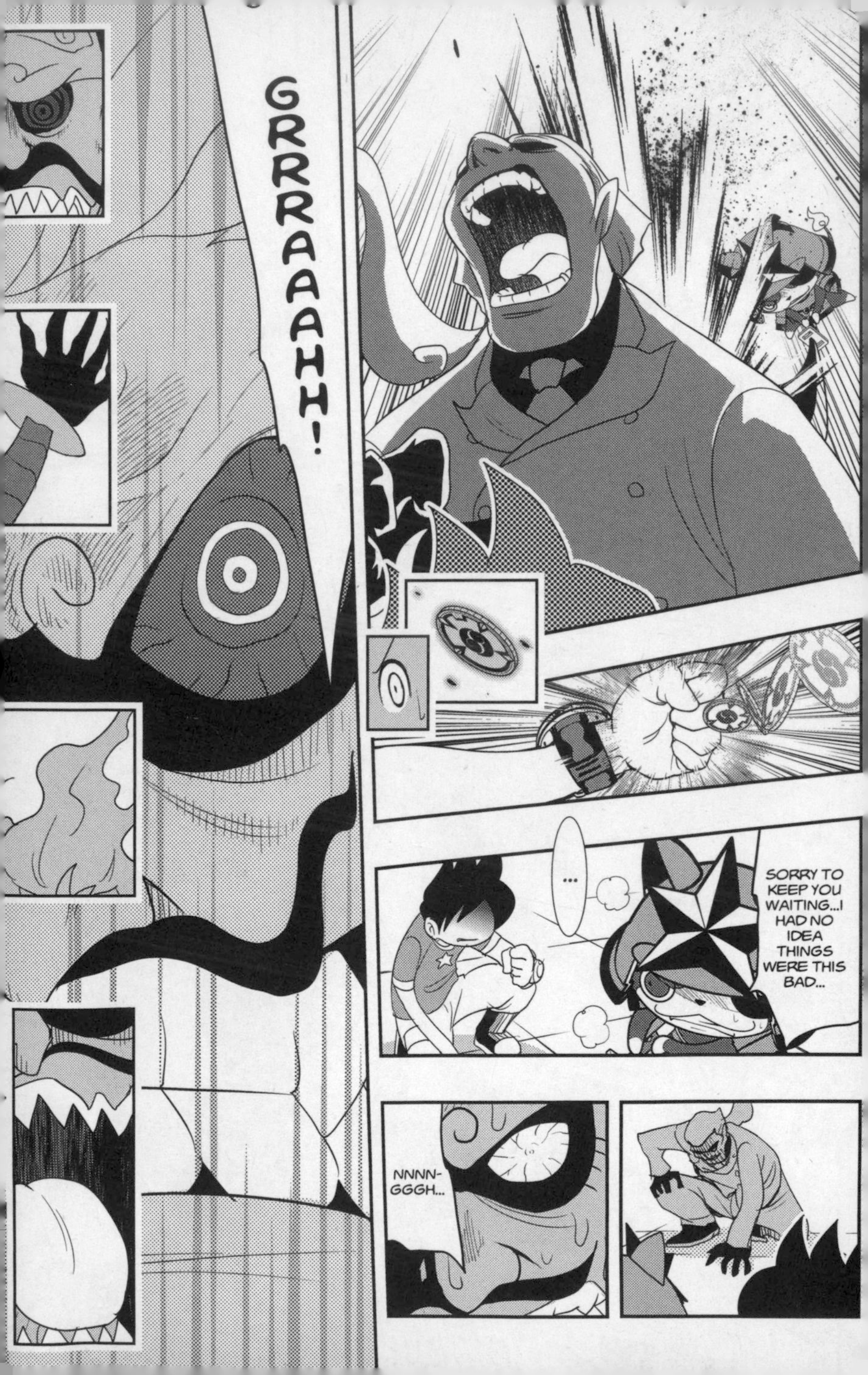
GRRRAAAAHH!
SORRY TO KEEP YOU WAITING...I HAD NO IDEA THINGS WERE THIS BAD...
...
NNNN-GGGH...

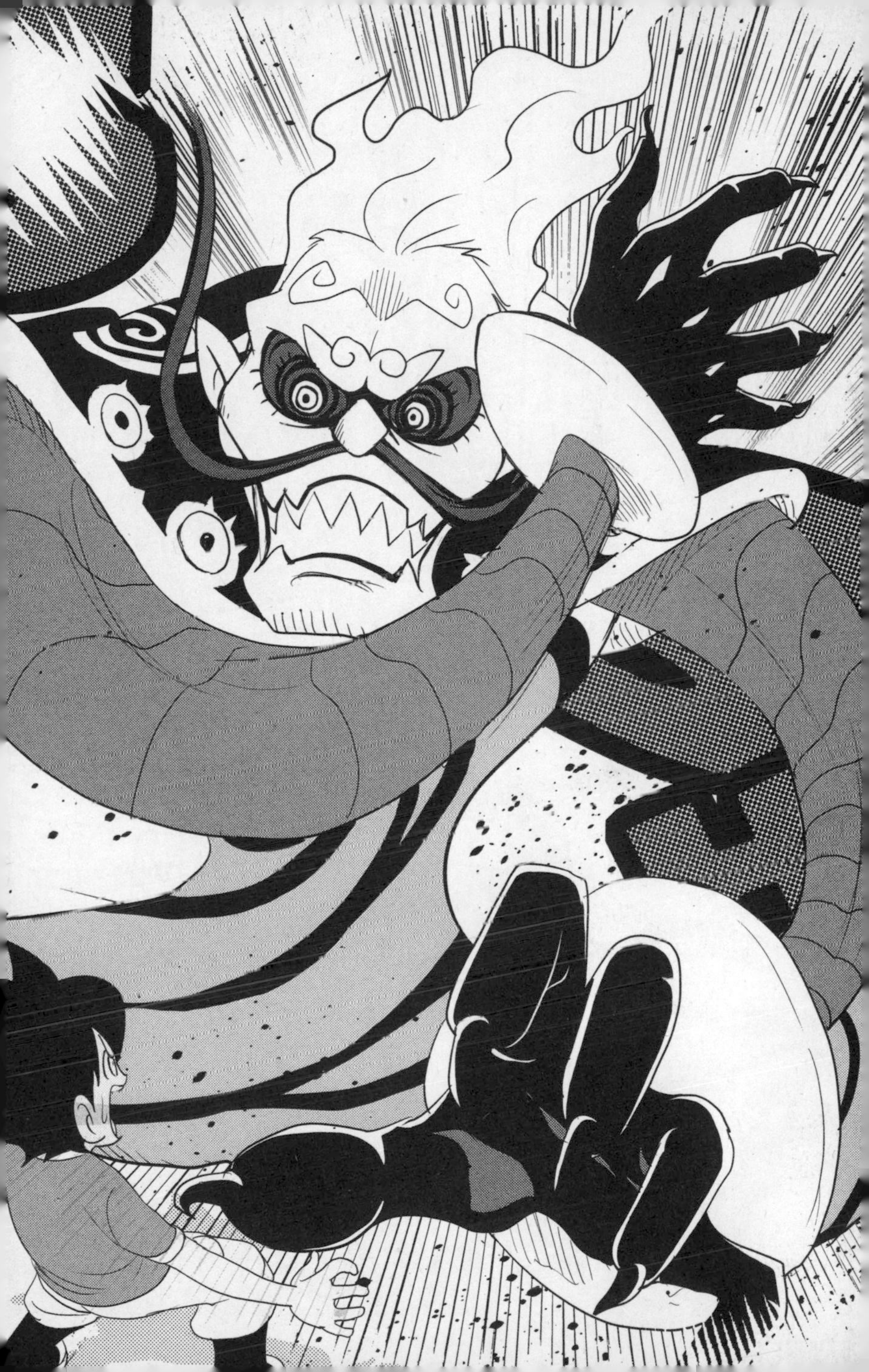

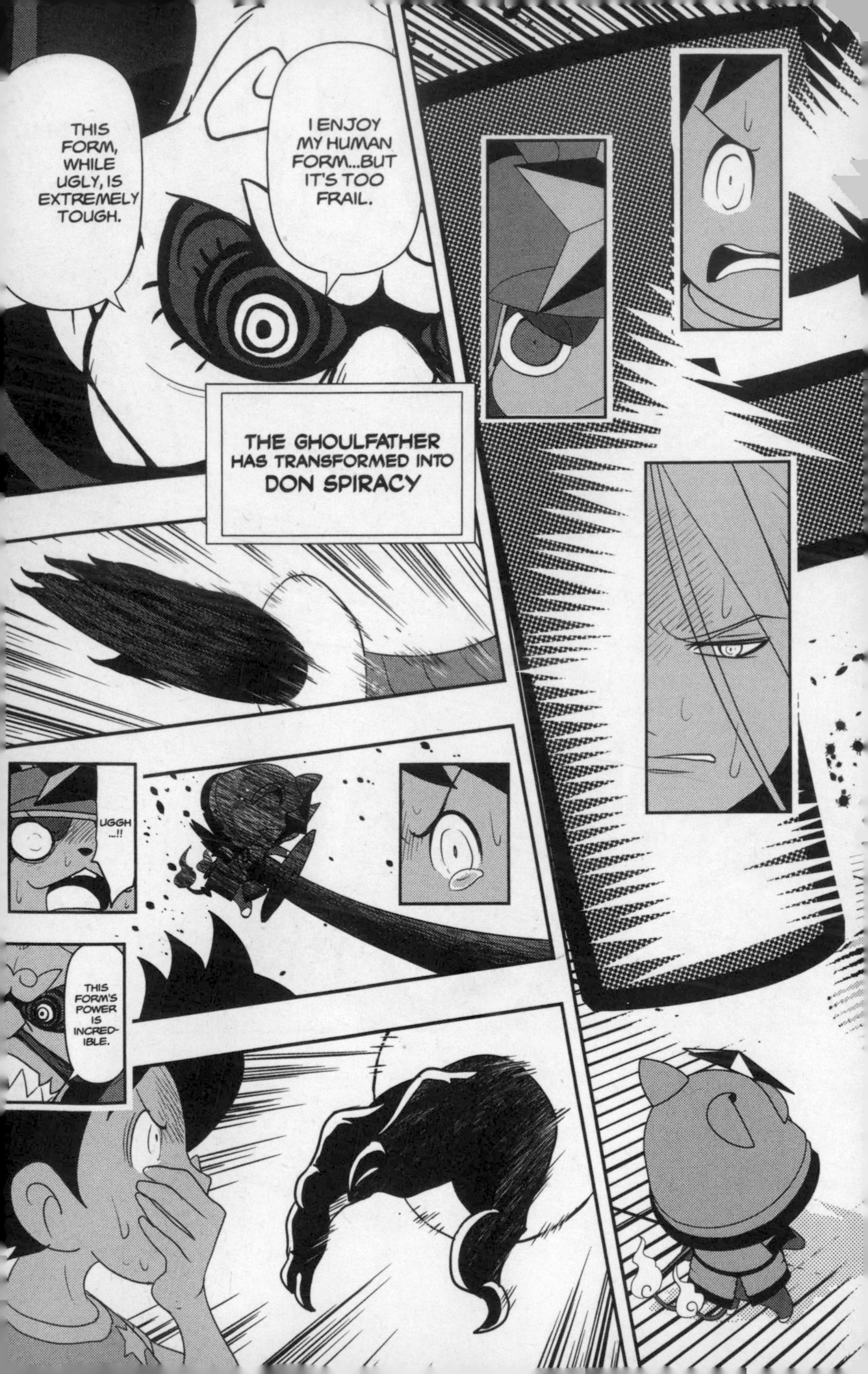
I ENJOY MY HUMAN FORM...BUT IT'S TOO FRAIL.
THIS FORM, WHILE UGLY, IS EXTREMELY TOUGH.
THE GHOULFATHER HAS TRANSFORMED INTO DON SPIRACY
UGGH ...!!
THIS FORM'S POWER IS INCRED-IBLE.

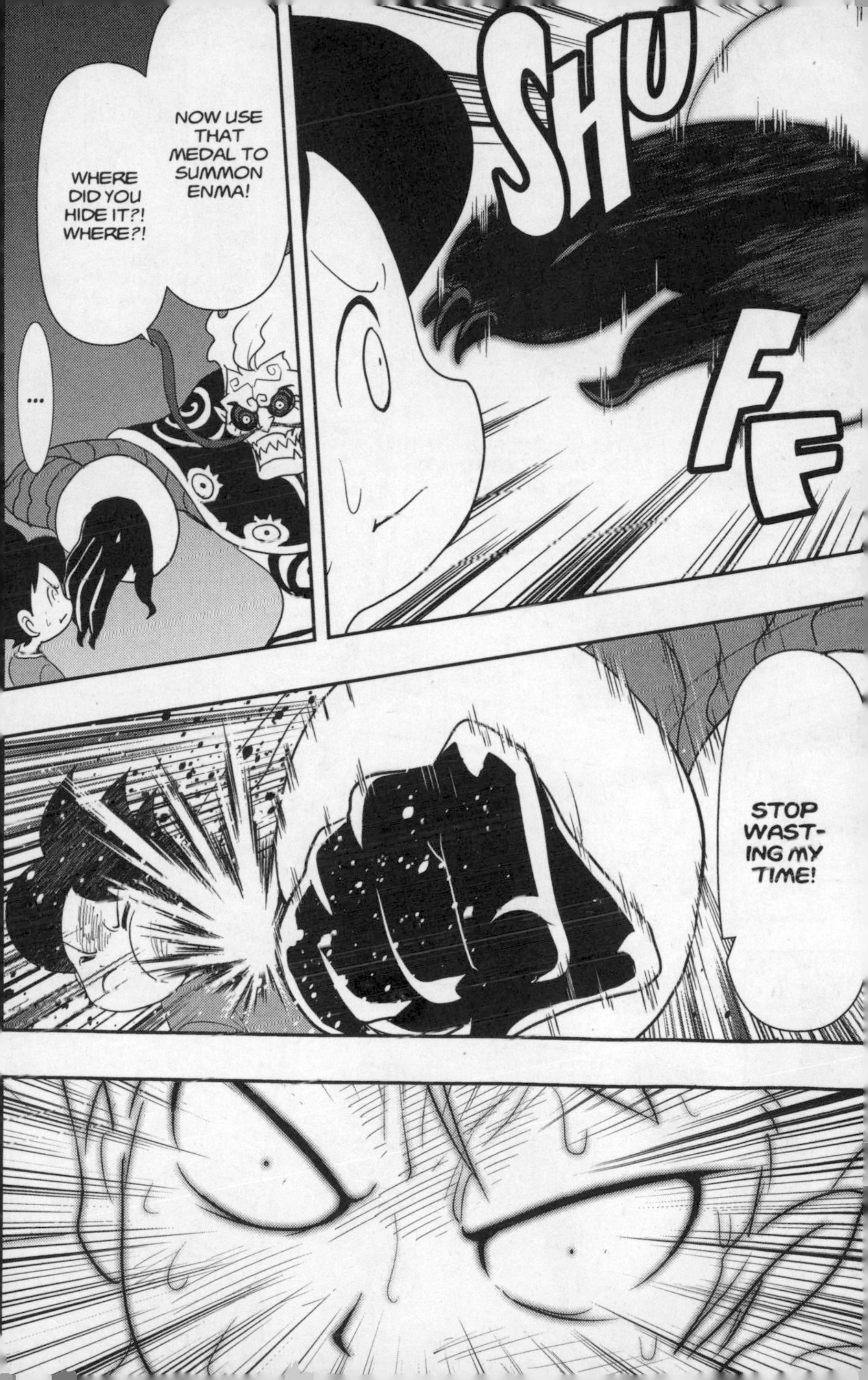
SHUFF
NOW USE THAT MEDAL TO SUMMON ENMA!
WHERE DID YOU HIDE IT?! WHERE?!
...
STOP WASTING MY TIME!

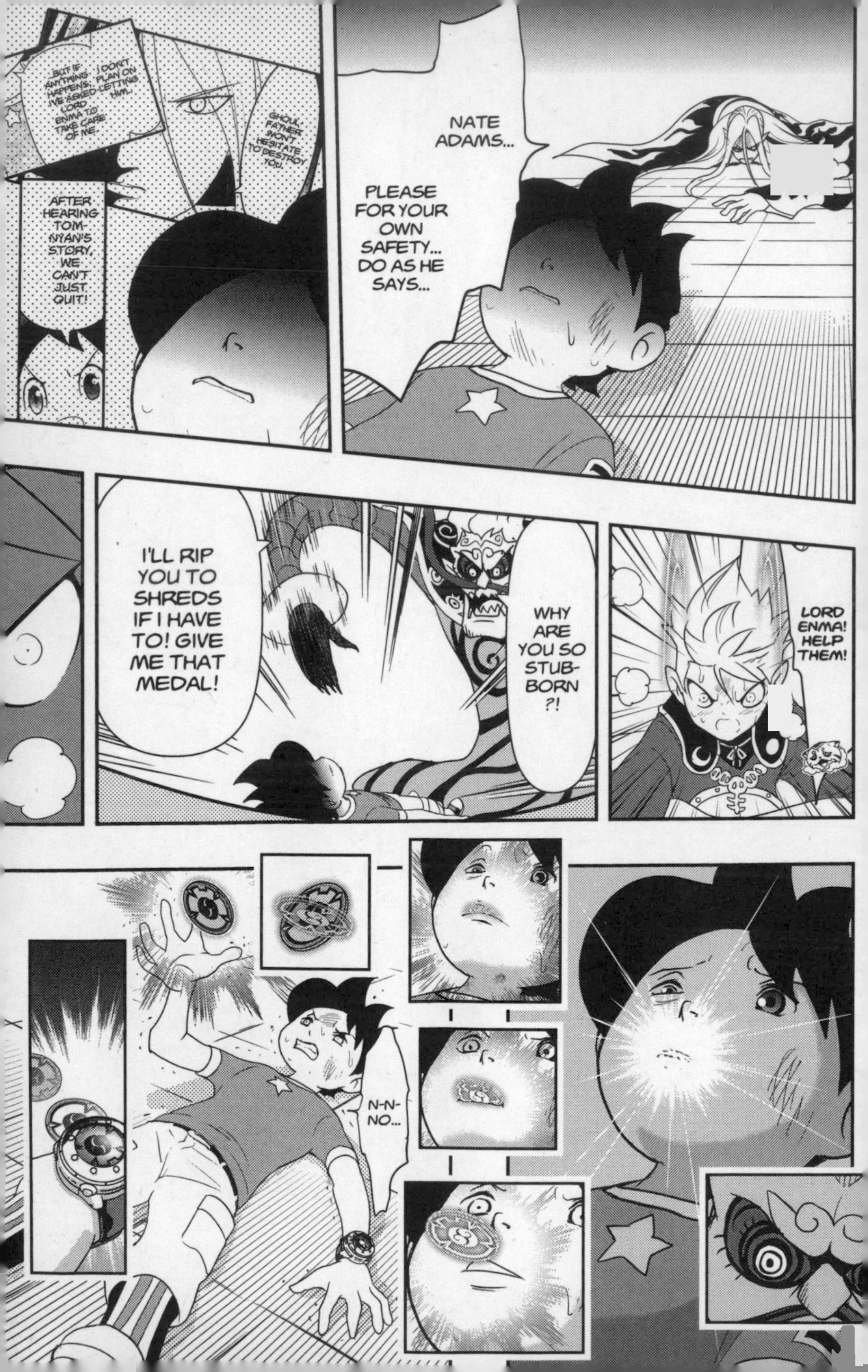
NATE ADAMS...
PLEASE FOR YOUR OWN SAFETY... DO AS HE SAYS...
I DON'T PLAN ON LETTING HIM.
...BUT IF ANYTHING HAPPENS, I'VE ASKED LORD ENMA TO TAKE CARE OF ME.
GHOUL-FATHER WON'T HESITATE TO DESTROY YOU.
AFTER HEARING TOM-NYAN'S STORY, WE CAN'T JUST QUIT!
LORD ENMA! HELP THEM!
WHY ARE YOU SO STUBBORN?!
I'LL RIP YOU TO SHREDS IF I HAVE TO! GIVE ME THAT MEDAL!
N-N-NO...

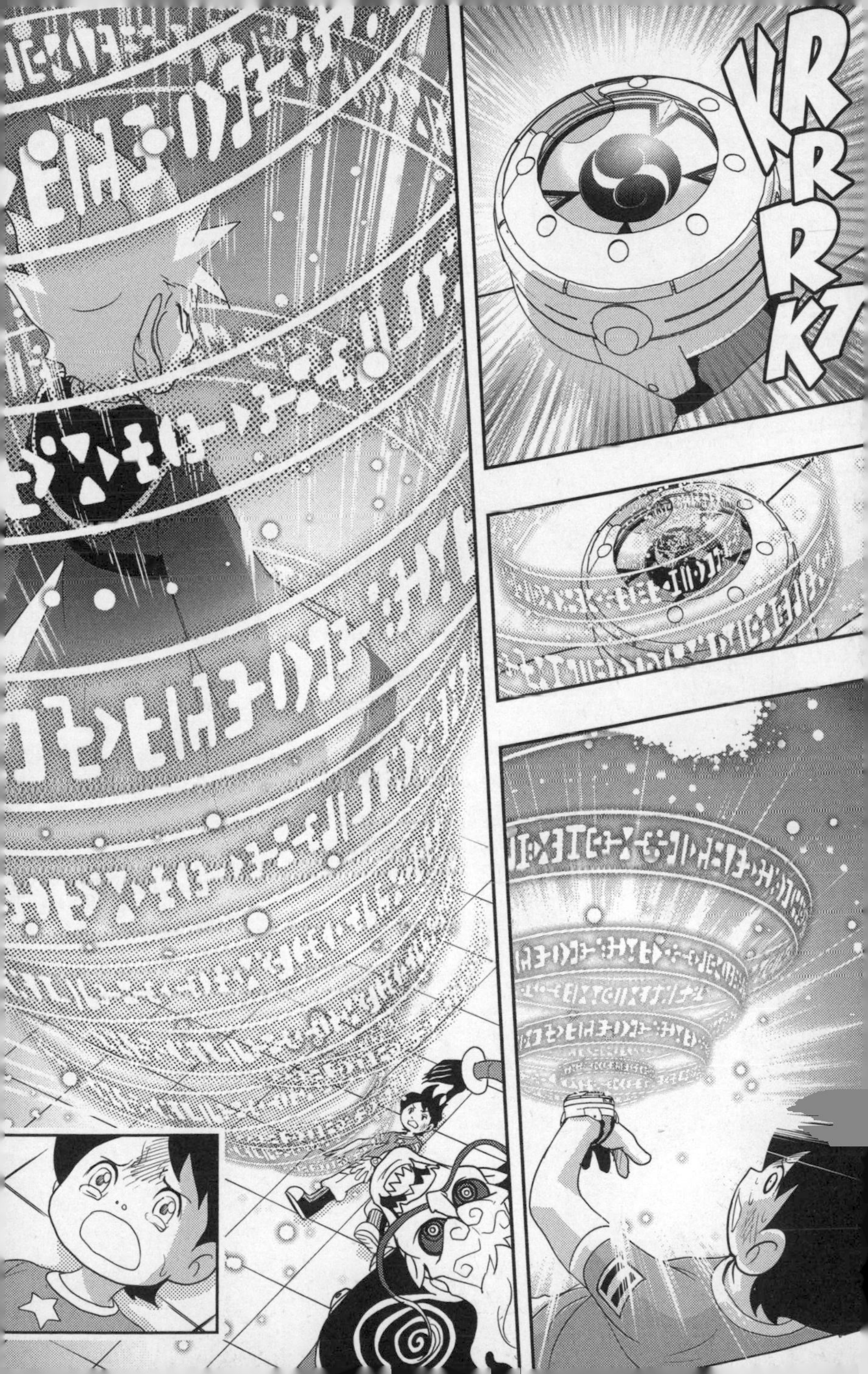
KRRRK

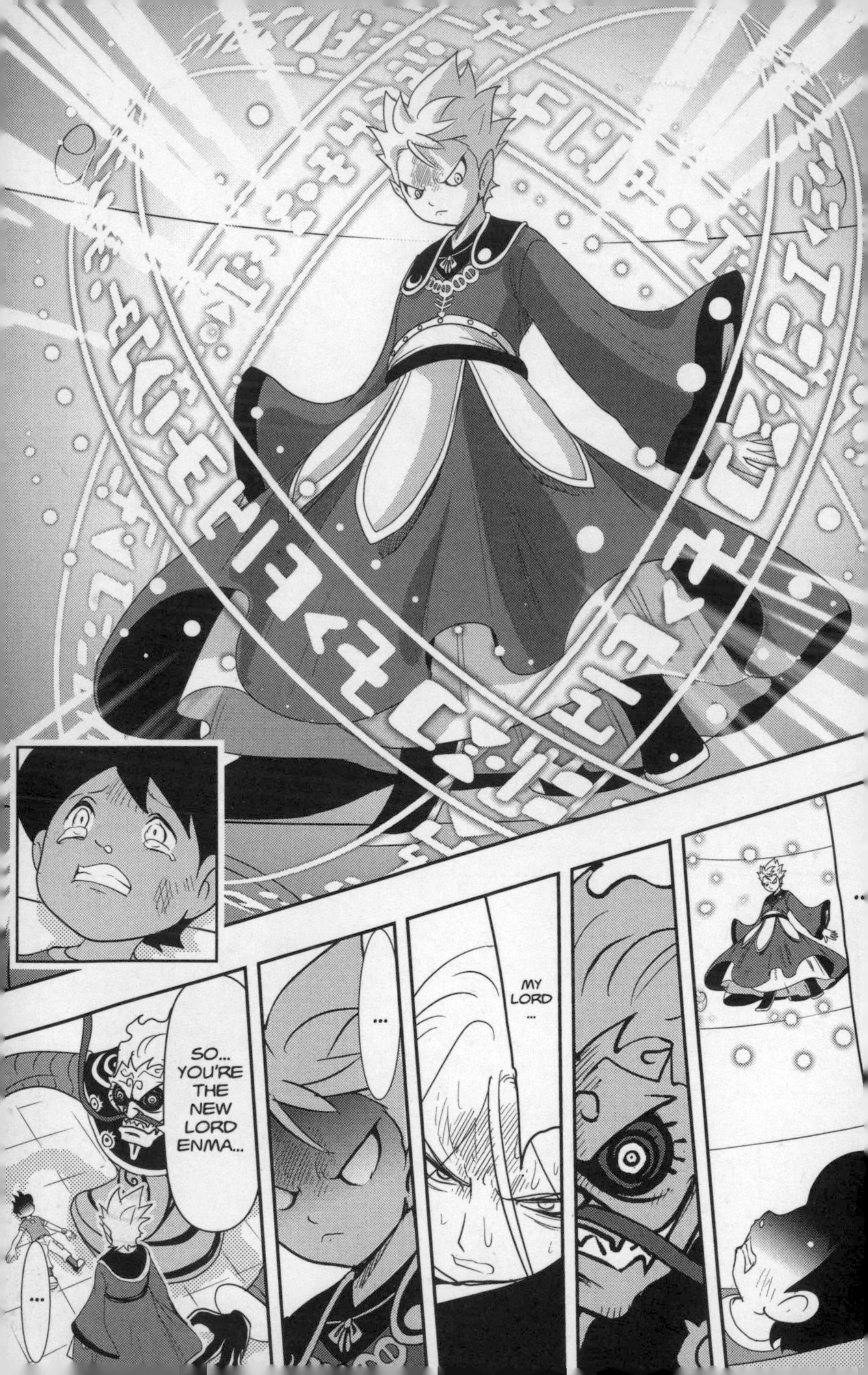
MY LORD ...
...
SO... YOU'RE THE NEW LORD ENMA...
...

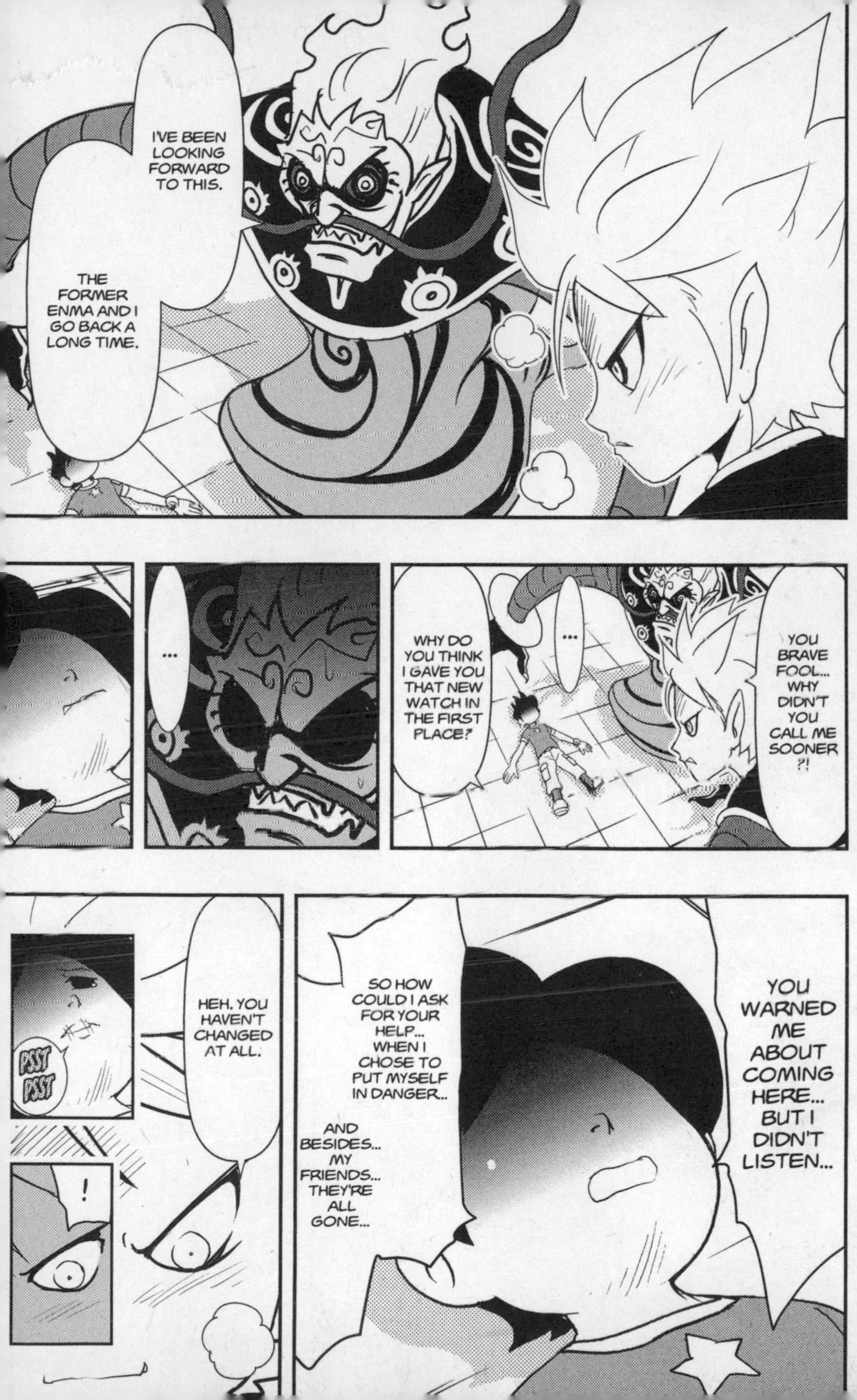
I'VE BEEN LOOKING FORWARD TO THIS.
THE FORMER ENMA AND I GO BACK A LONG TIME.
YOU BRAVE FOOL... WHY DIDN'T YOU CALL ME SOONER?!
...
WHY DO YOU THINK I GAVE YOU THAT NEW WATCH IN THE FIRST PLACE?
...
YOU WARNED ME ABOUT COMING HERE... BUT I DIDN'T LISTEN...
SO HOW COULD I ASK FOR YOUR HELP... WHEN I CHOSE TO PUT MYSELF IN DANGER...
AND BESIDES... MY FRIENDS... THEY'RE ALL GONE...
HEH. YOU HAVEN'T CHANGED AT ALL.
PSST PSST
!

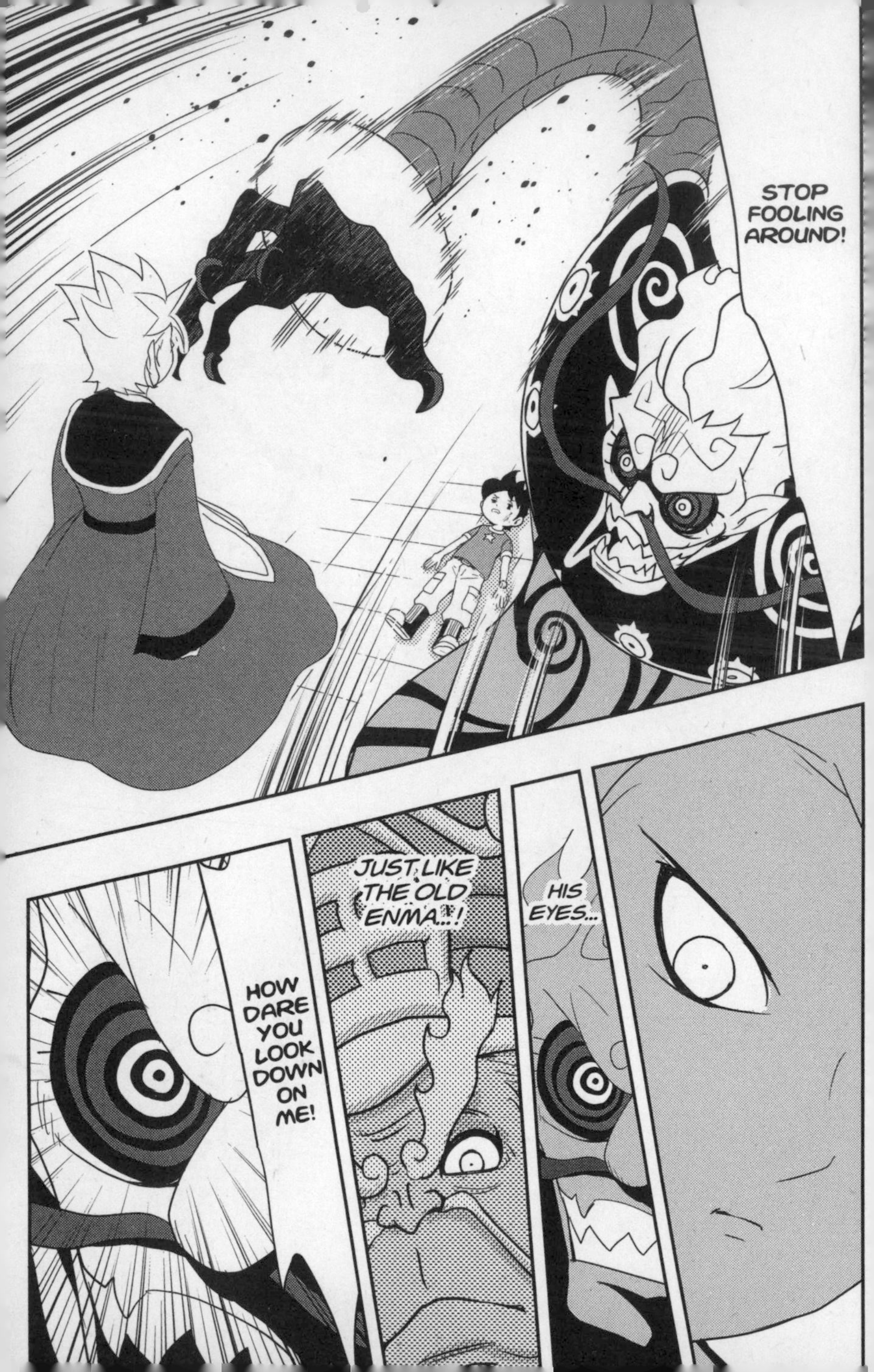
STOP FOOLING AROUND!
HIS EYES...
JUST LIKE THE OLD ENMA...!
HOW DARE YOU LOOK DOWN ON ME!

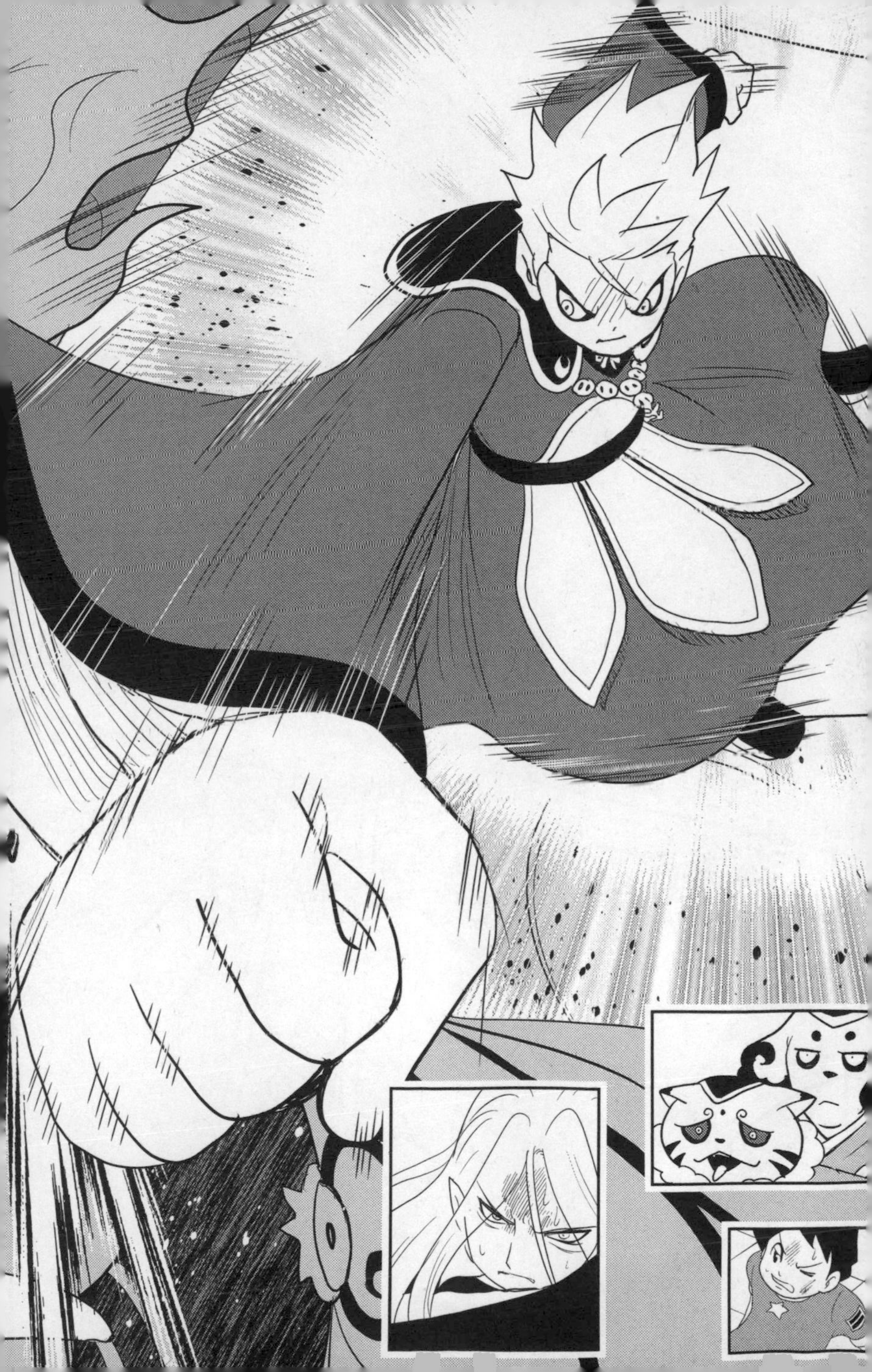

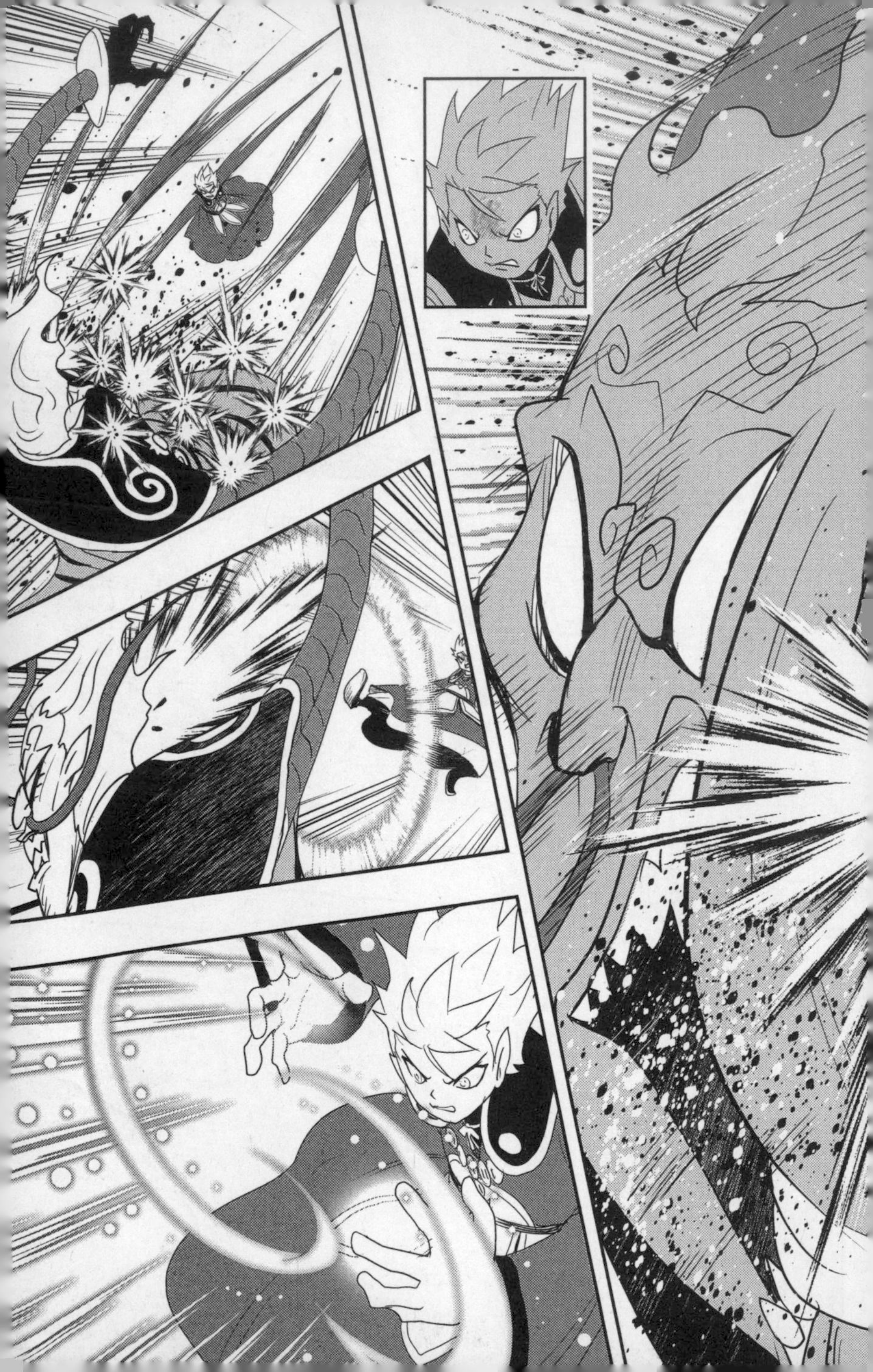

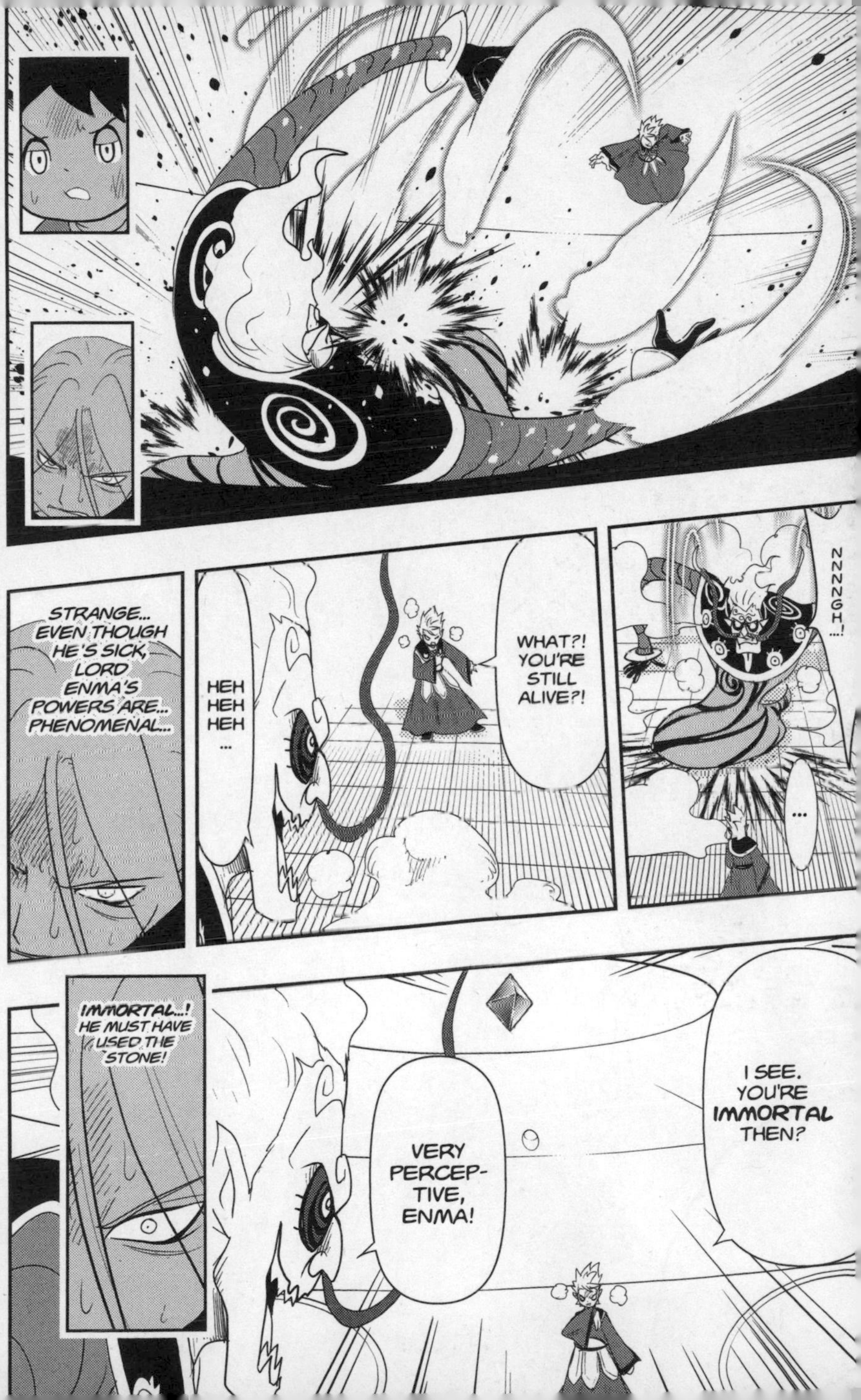
NNNNGH...!
...
WHAT?! YOU'RE STILL ALIVE?!
HEH HEH HEH ...
STRANGE... EVEN THOUGH HE'S SICK, LORD ENMA'S POWERS ARE... PHENOMENAL...
I SEE. YOU'RE IMMORTAL THEN?
VERY PERCEPTIVE, ENMA!
IMMORTAL...! HE MUST HAVE USED THE STONE!

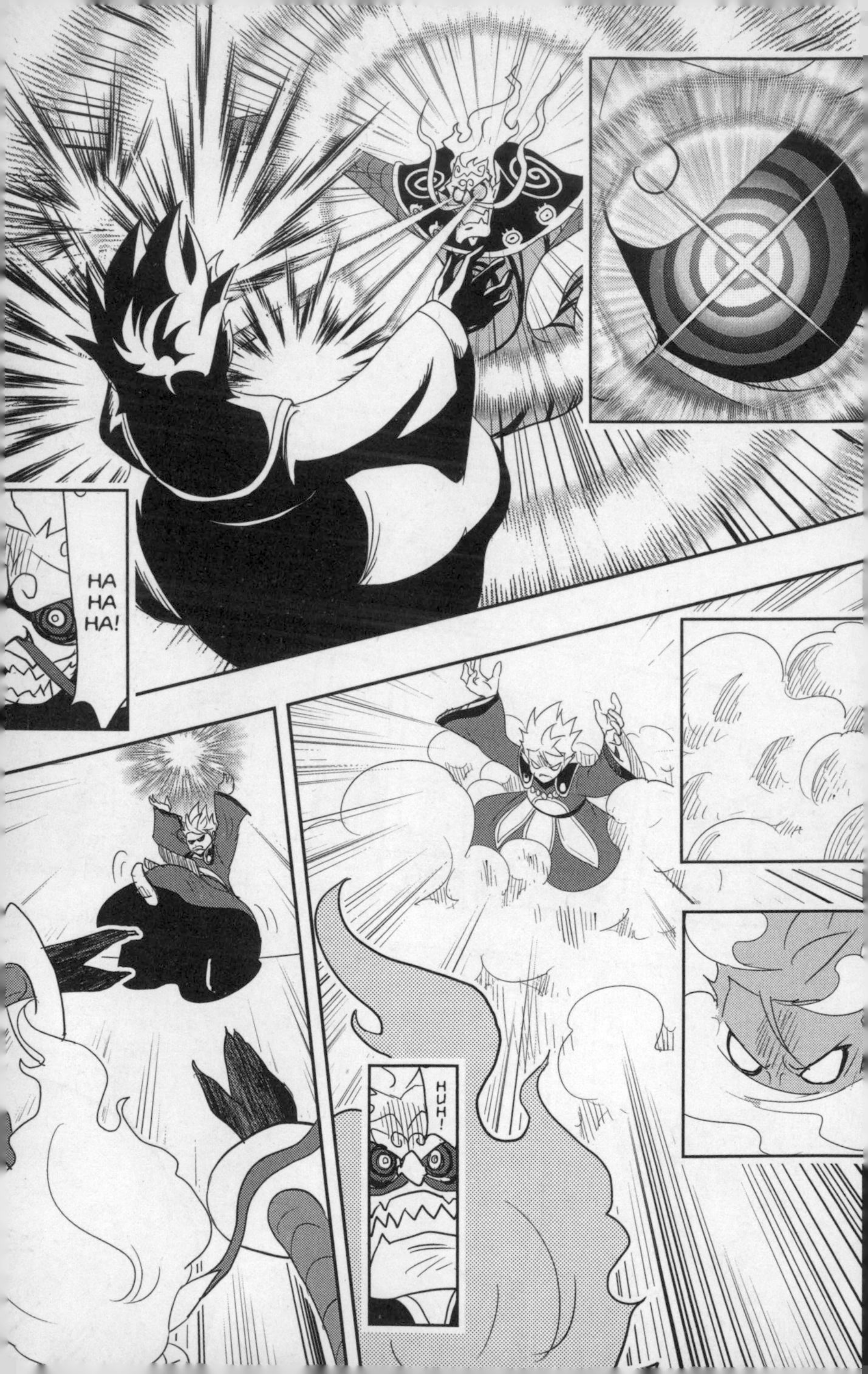
HA HA HA!
HUH!

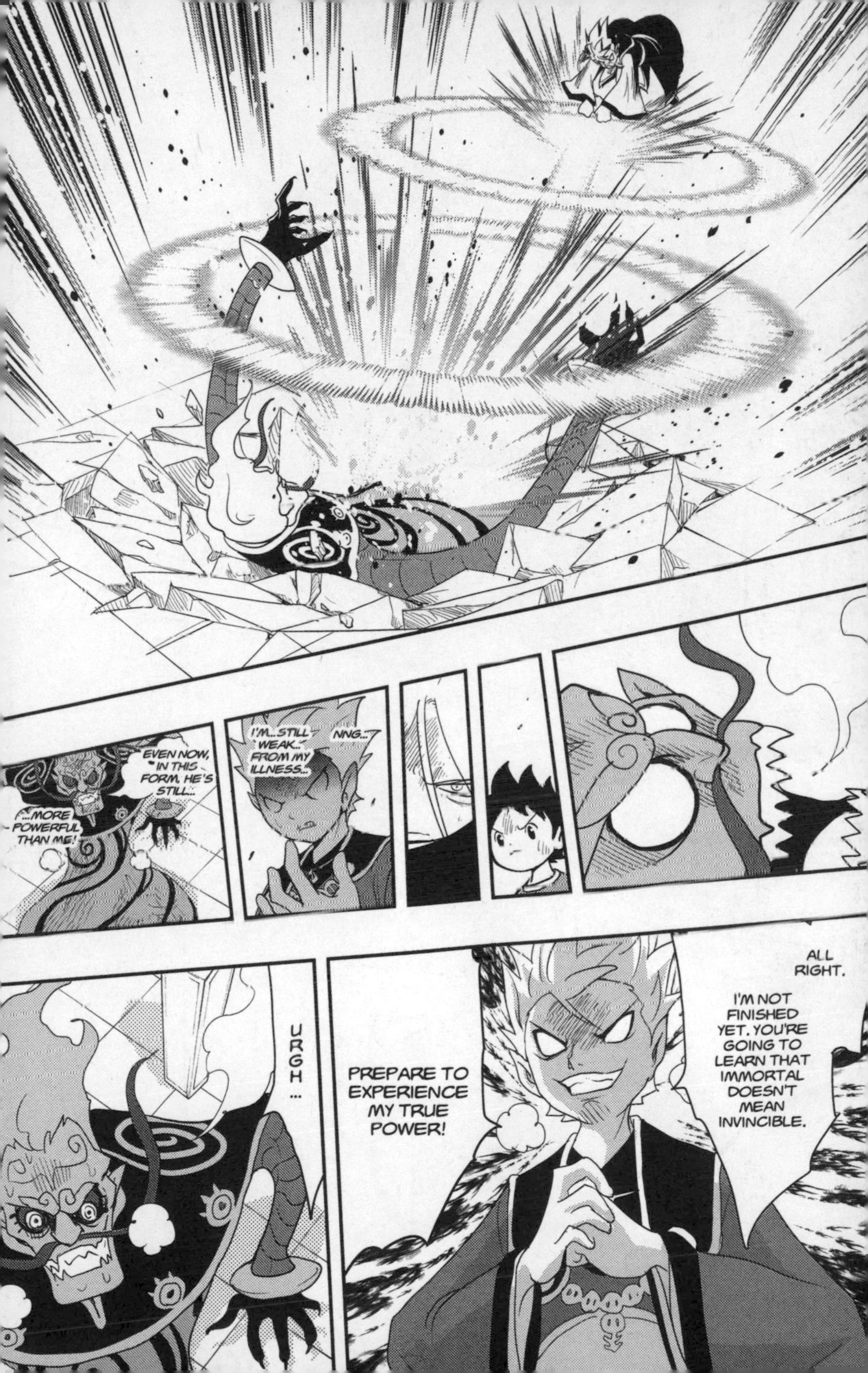
NNG...
I'M...STILL WEAK... FROM MY ILLNESS...
EVEN NOW, IN THIS FORM, HE'S STILL...
...MORE POWERFUL THAN ME!
ALL RIGHT.
I'M NOT FINISHED YET. YOU'RE GOING TO LEARN THAT IMMORTAL DOESN'T MEAN INVINCIBLE.
PREPARE TO EXPERIENCE MY TRUE POWER!
URGH...

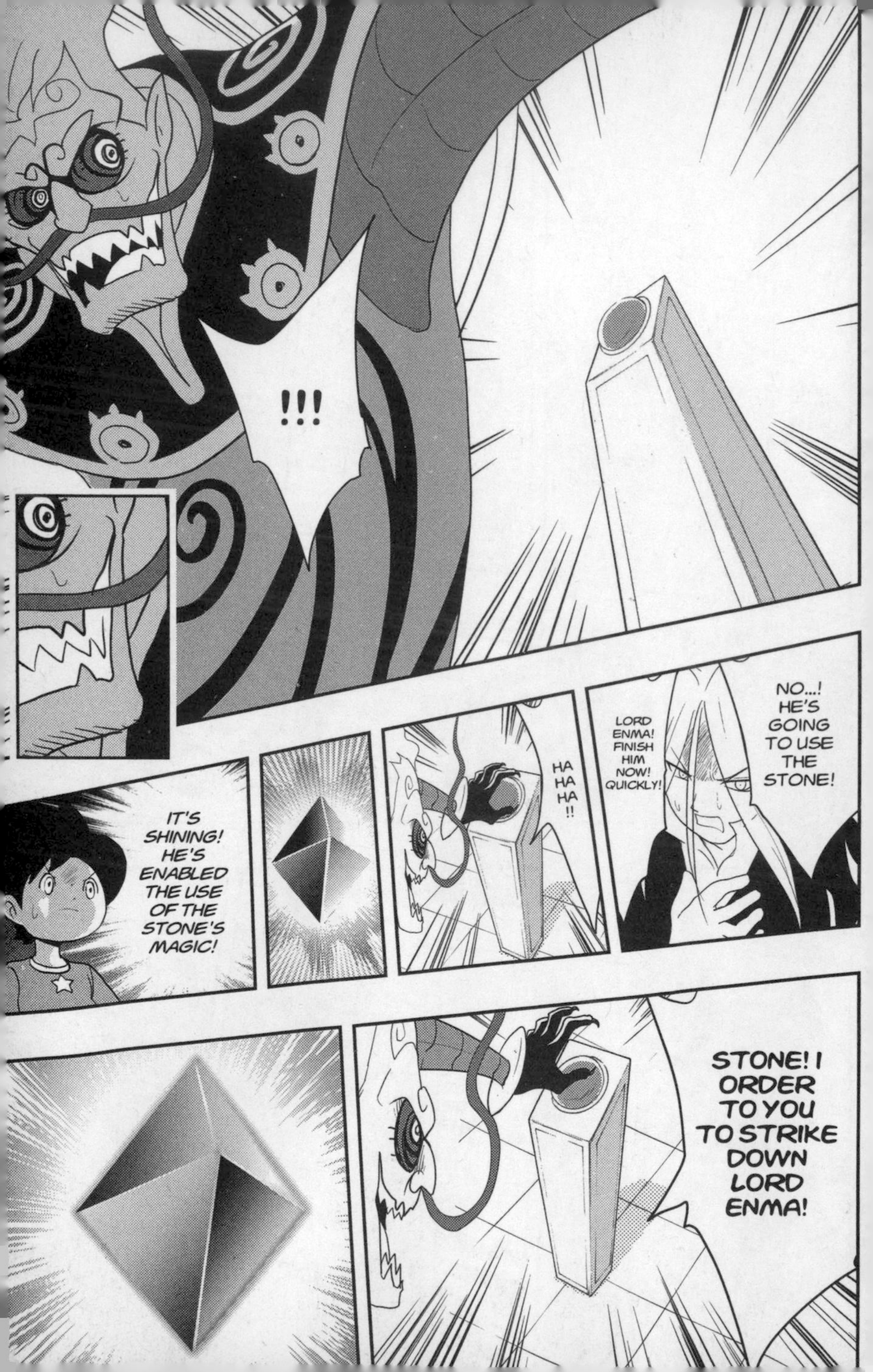
!!!
NO...! HE'S GOING TO USE THE STONE!
LORD ENMA! FINISH HIM NOW! QUICKLY!
HA HA HA !!
IT'S SHINING! HE'S ENABLED THE USE OF THE STONE'S MAGIC!
STONE! I ORDER TO YOU TO STRIKE DOWN LORD ENMA!

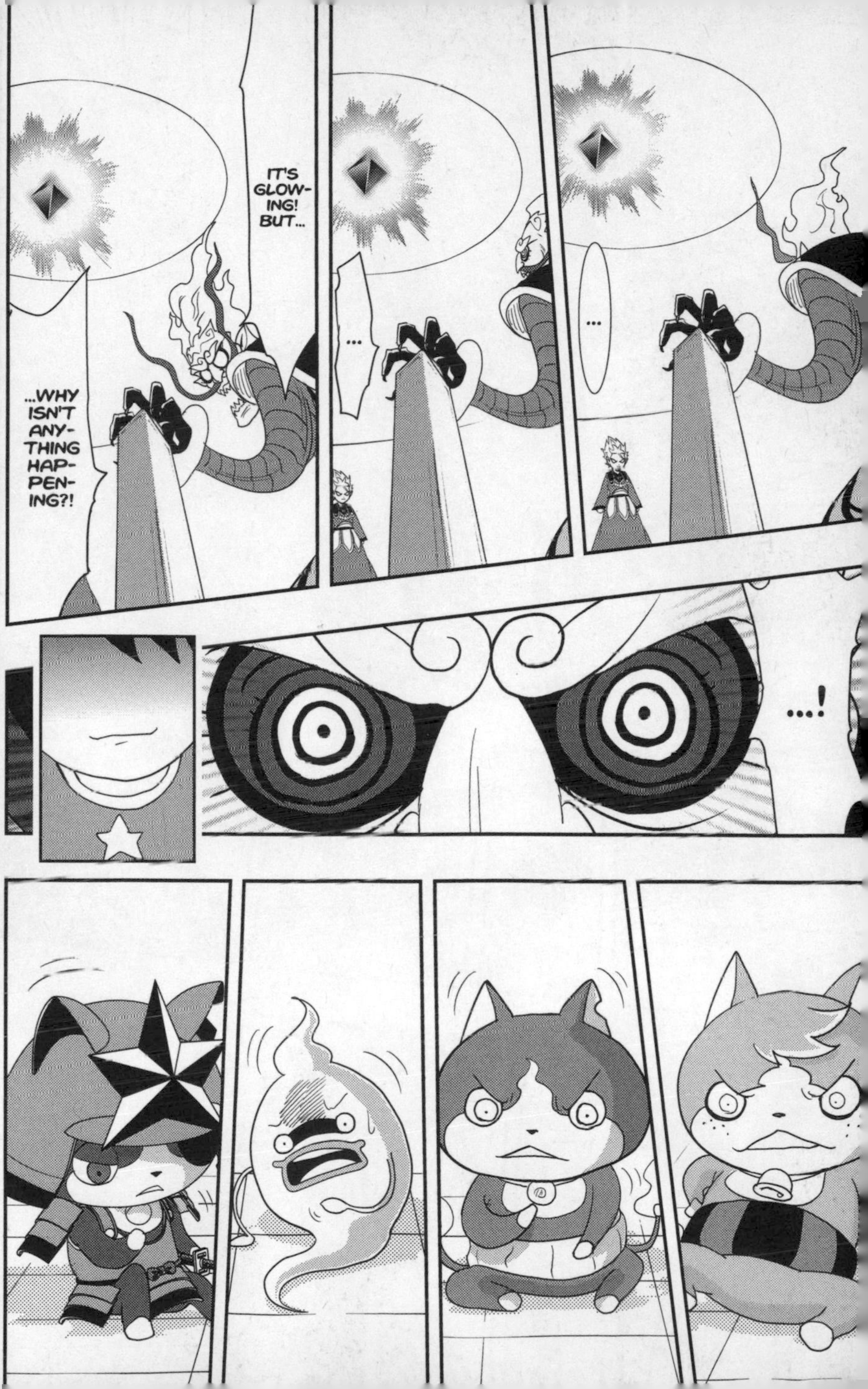
...
...
IT'S GLOWING! BUT...
...WHY ISN'T ANYTHING HAPPENING?!
...!

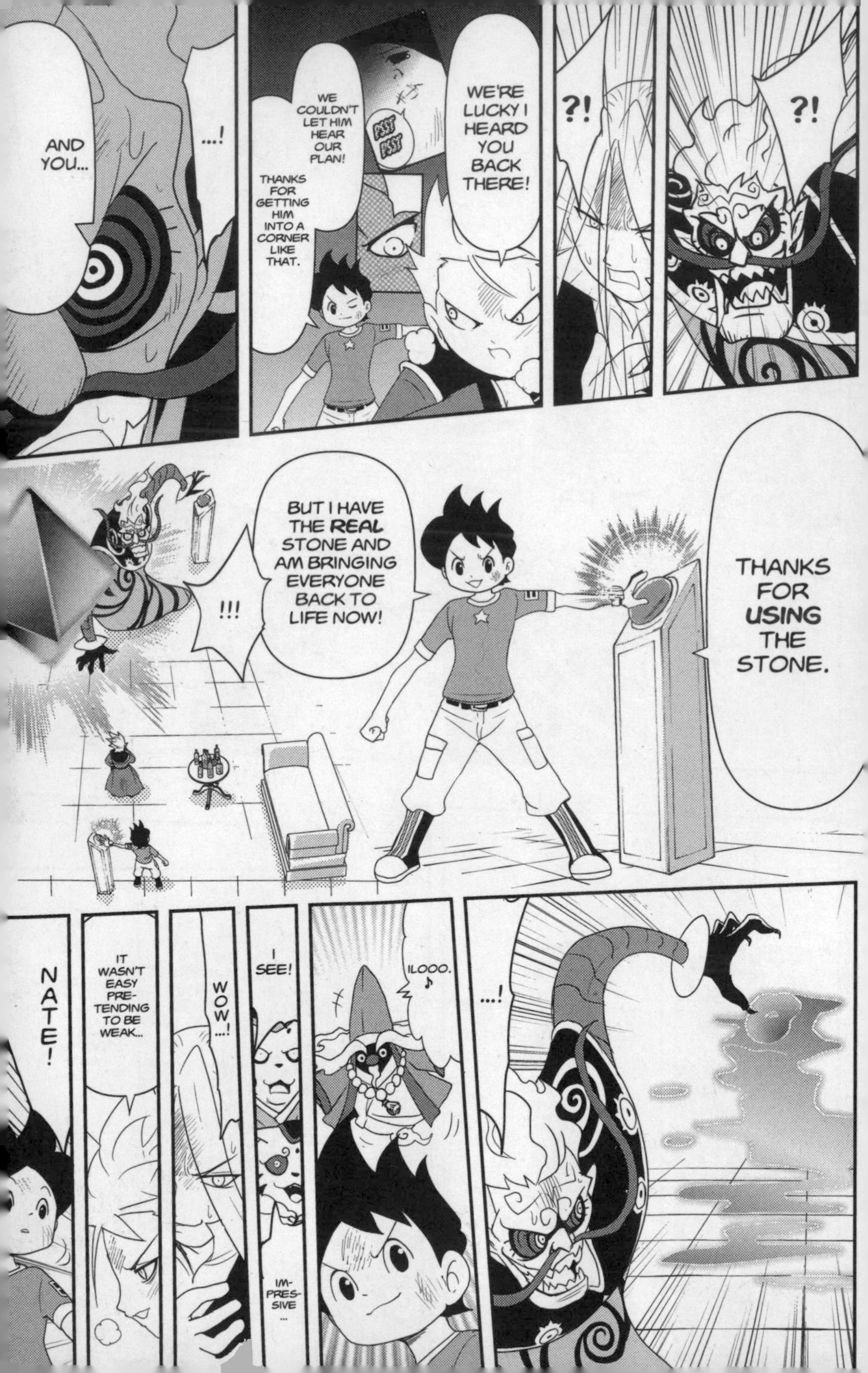
?!
?!
WE'RE LUCKY I HEARD YOU BACK THERE!
WE COULDN'T LET HIM HEAR OUR PLAN!
PSST PSST
THANKS FOR GETTING HIM INTO A CORNER LIKE THAT.
...!
AND YOU...
THANKS FOR USING THE STONE.
BUT I HAVE THE REAL STONE AND AM BRINGING EVERYONE BACK TO LIFE NOW!
!!!
...!
ILOOO. ♪
I SEE!
IMPRES-SIVE...
WOW...!
IT WASN'T EASY PRE-TENDING TO BE WEAK...
NATE!

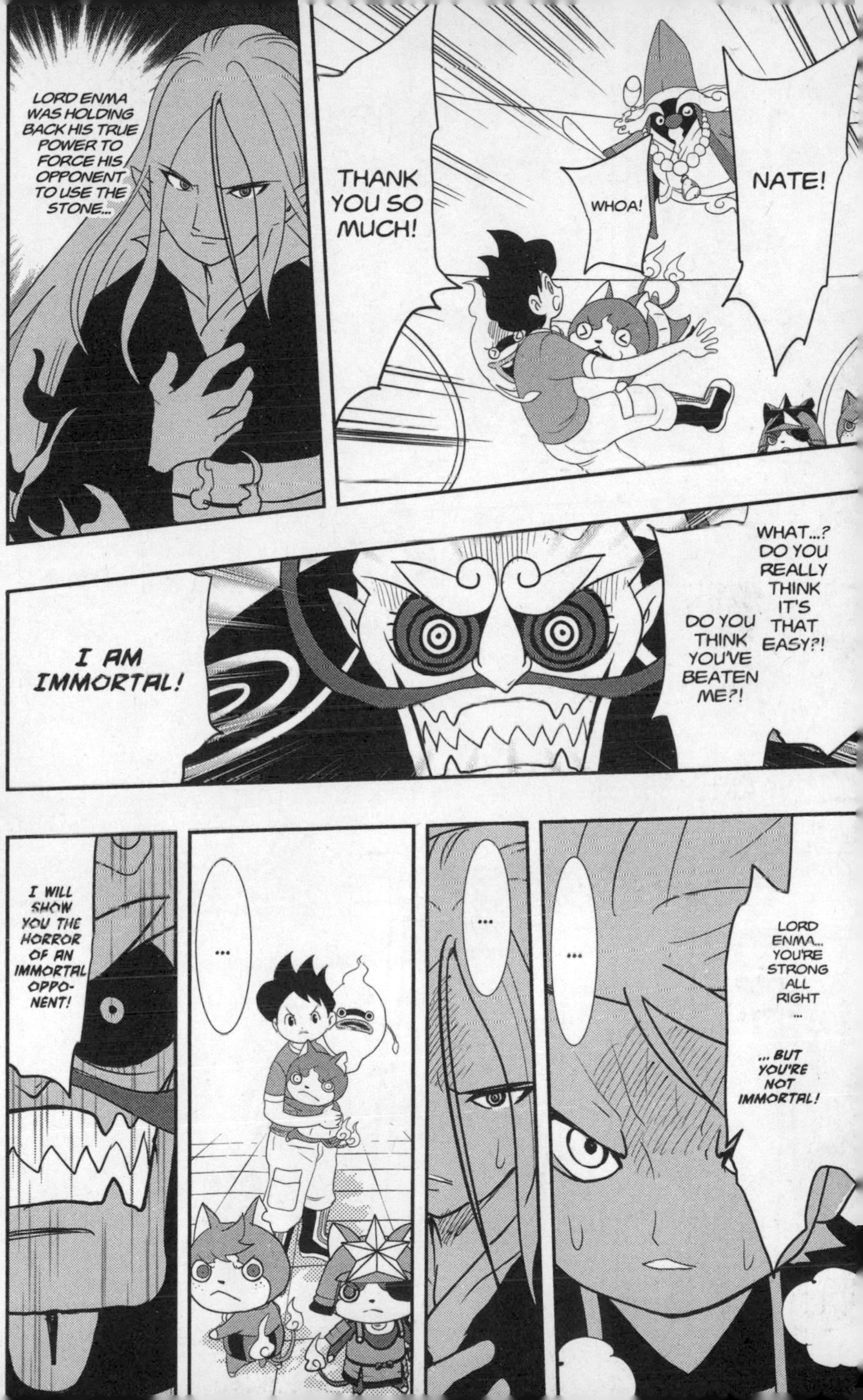
NATE!
WHOA!
THANK YOU SO MUCH!
LORD ENMA WAS HOLDING BACK HIS TRUE POWER TO FORCE HIS OPPONENT TO USE THE STONE...
WHAT...? DO YOU REALLY THINK IT'S THAT EASY?!
DO YOU THINK YOU'VE BEATEN ME?!
I AM IMMORTAL!
...
LORD ENMA... YOU'RE STRONG ALL RIGHT ...
... BUT YOU'RE NOT IMMORTAL!
...
...
I WILL SHOW YOU THE HORROR OF AN IMMORTAL OPPO-NENT!

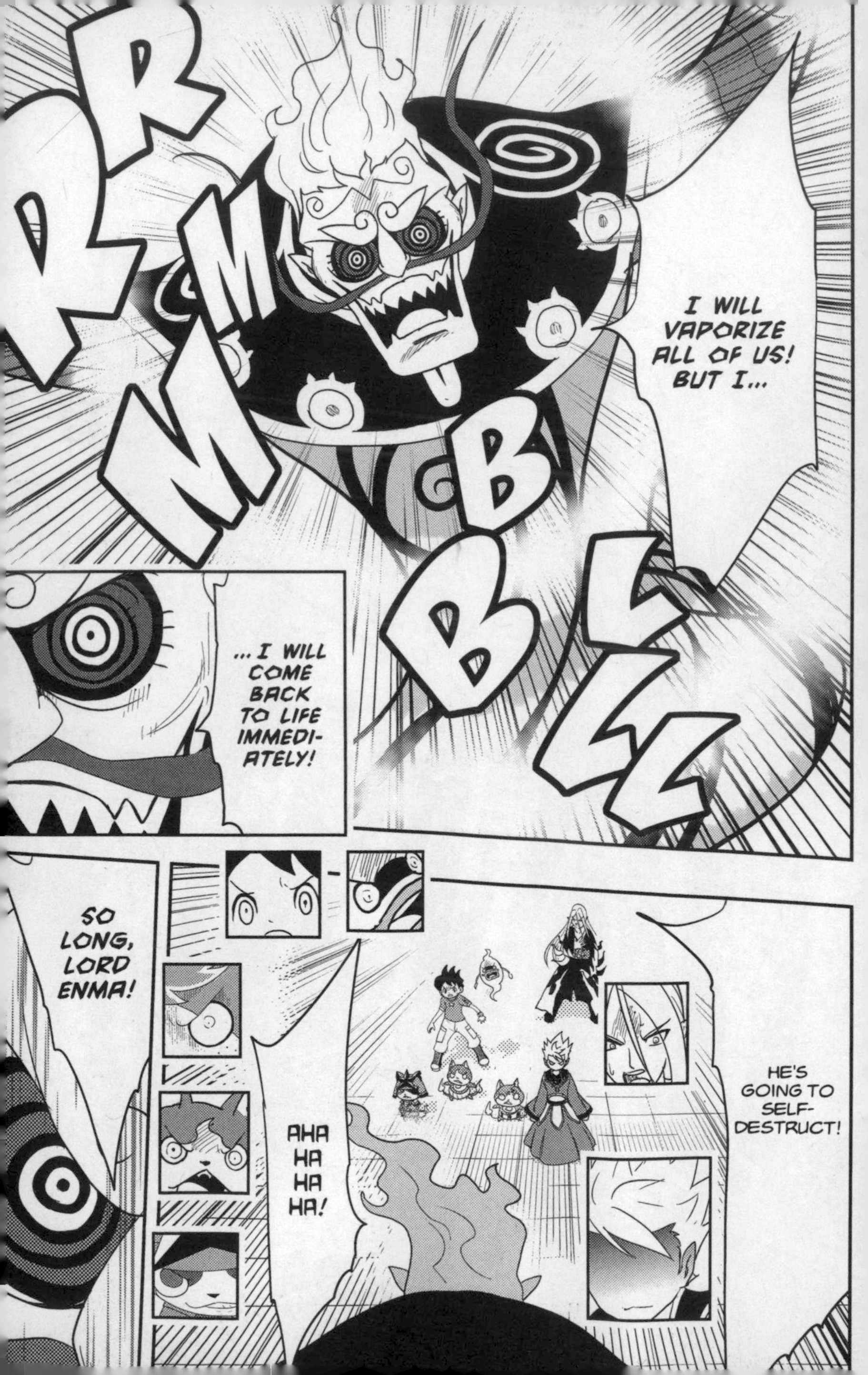
I WILL VAPORIZE ALL OF US! BUT I...
RRMMBBLLL
...I WILL COME BACK TO LIFE IMMEDI-ATELY!
HE'S GOING TO SELF-DESTRUCT!
AHA HA HA HA!
SO LONG, LORD ENMA!

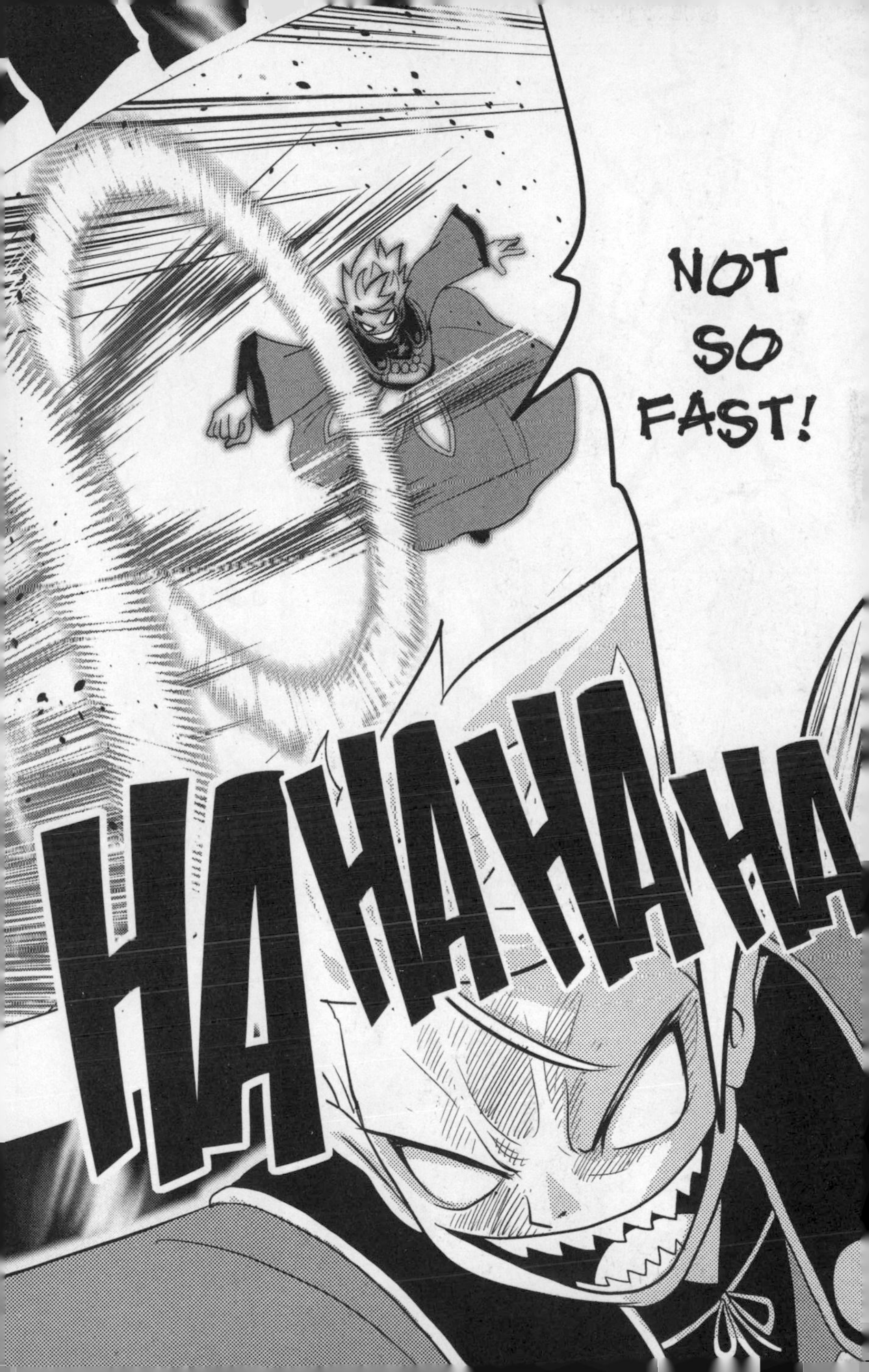
NOT SO FAST!
HAHAHAHAHA

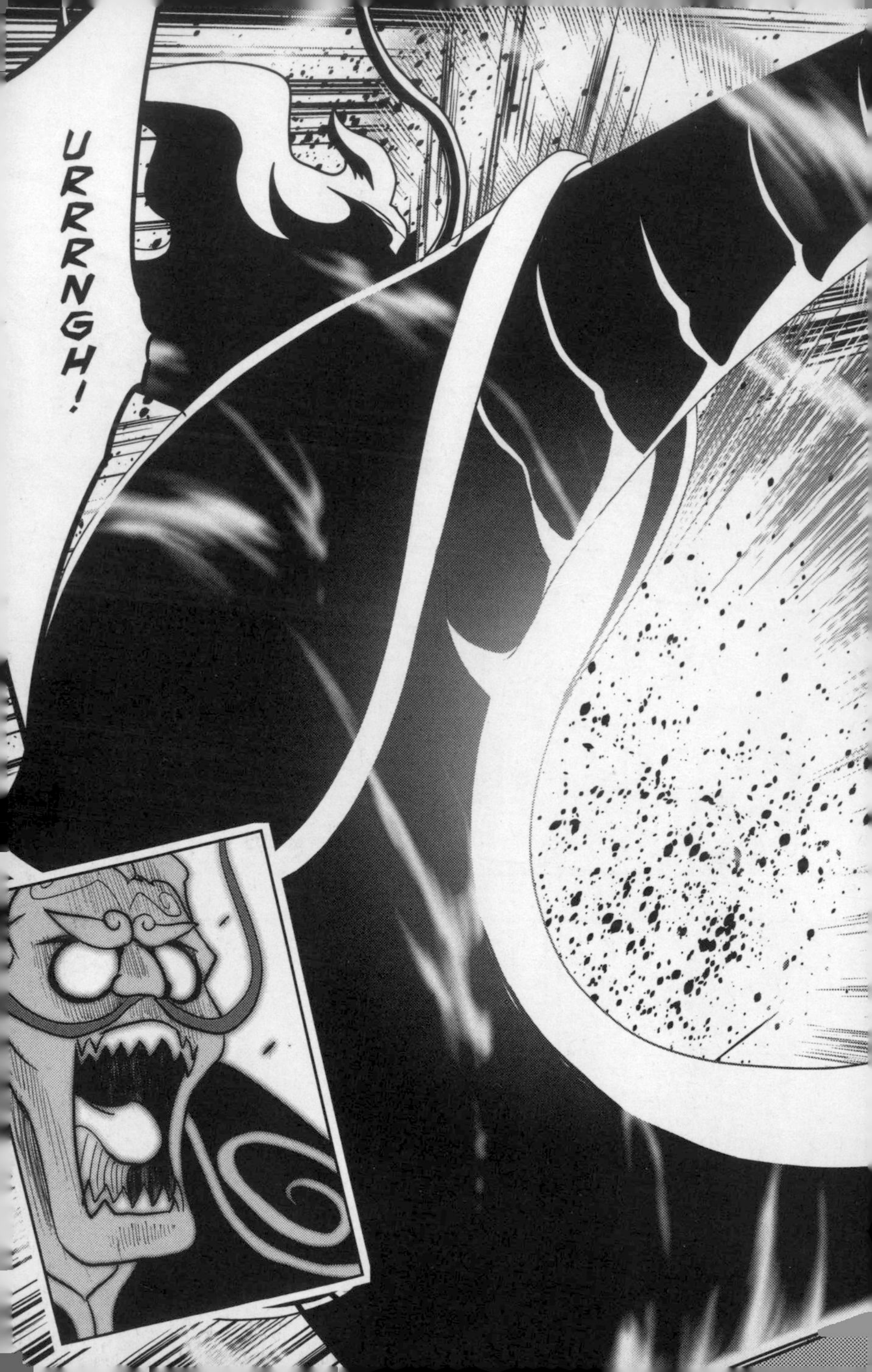
URRRNGH!

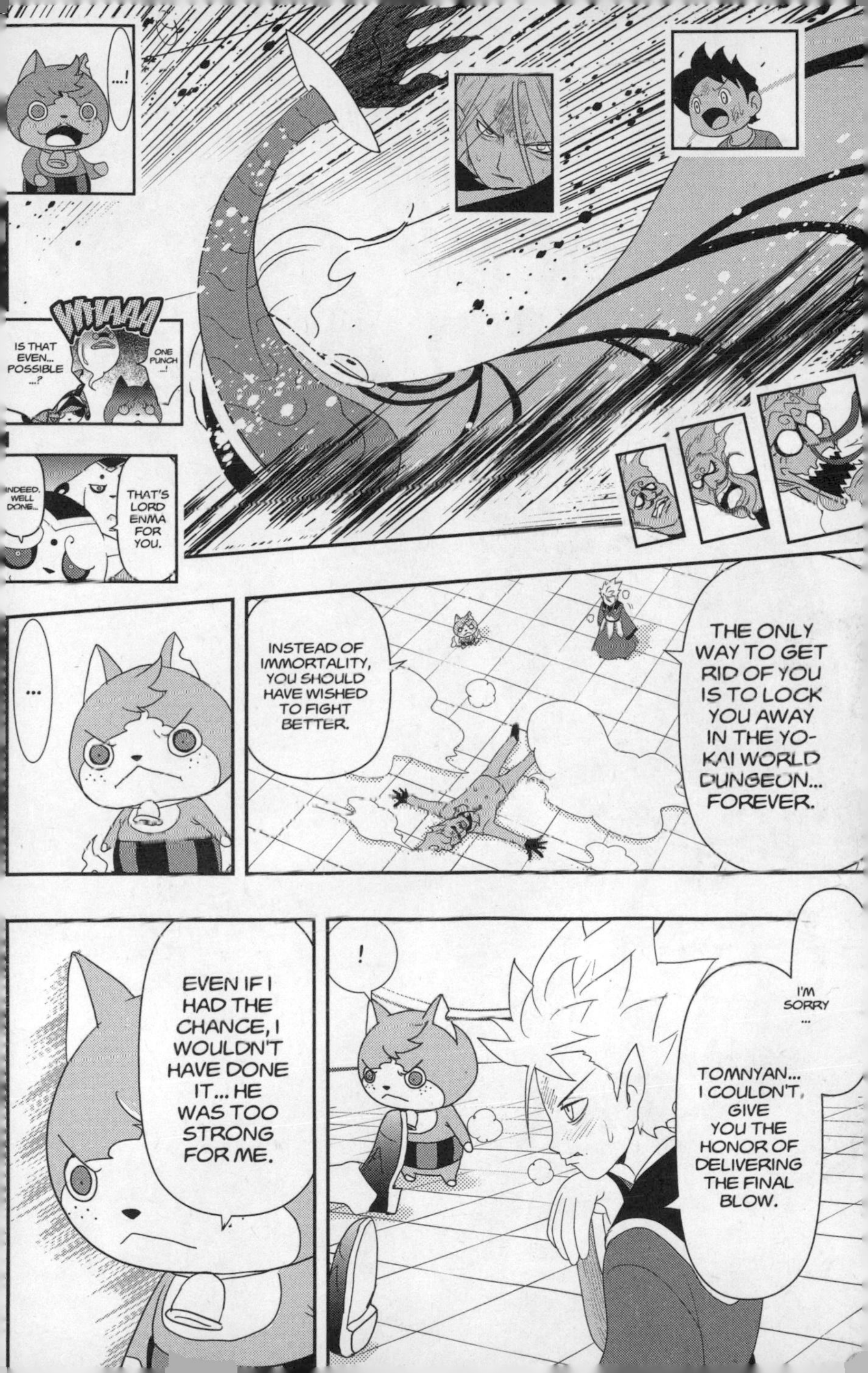
...!
WHAAA
ONE PUNCH ...!
IS THAT EVEN... POSSIBLE ...?
THAT'S LORD ENMA FOR YOU.
INDEED, WELL DONE...
THE ONLY WAY TO GET RID OF YOU IS TO LOCK YOU AWAY IN THE YO-KAI WORLD DUNGEON... FOREVER.
INSTEAD OF IMMORTALITY, YOU SHOULD HAVE WISHED TO FIGHT BETTER.
...
I'M SORRY ...
TOMNYAN... I COULDN'T GIVE YOU THE HONOR OF DELIVERING THE FINAL BLOW.
!
EVEN IF I HAD THE CHANCE, I WOULDN'T HAVE DONE IT... HE WAS TOO STRONG FOR ME.

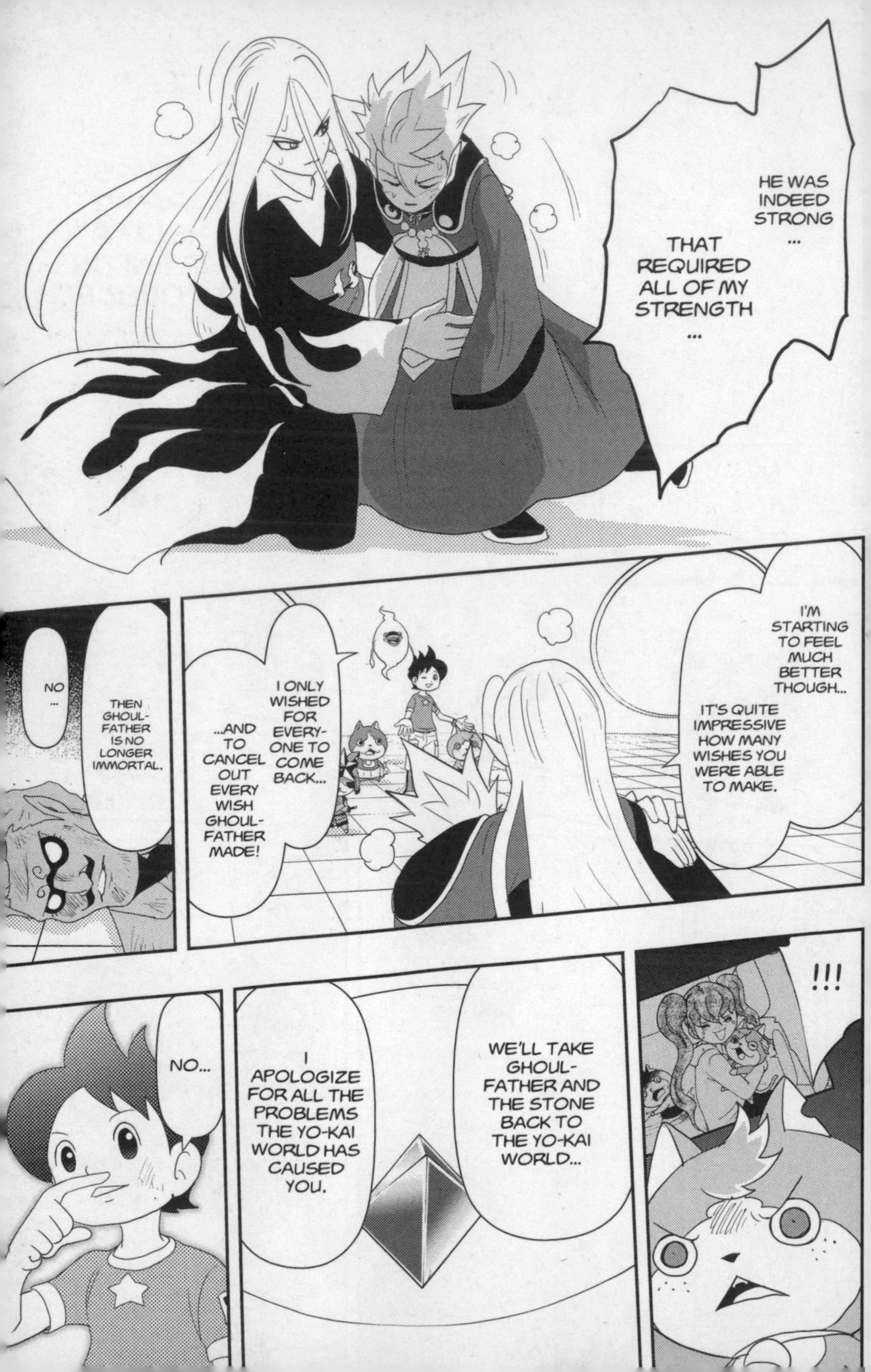
HE WAS INDEED STRONG ...
THAT REQUIRED ALL OF MY STRENGTH ...
I'M STARTING TO FEEL MUCH BETTER THOUGH...
IT'S QUITE IMPRESSIVE HOW MANY WISHES YOU WERE ABLE TO MAKE.
I ONLY WISHED FOR EVERYONE TO COME BACK...
...AND TO CANCEL OUT EVERY WISH GHOUL-FATHER MADE!
THEN GHOUL-FATHER IS NO LONGER IMMORTAL.
NO ...
!!!
WE'LL TAKE GHOUL-FATHER AND THE STONE BACK TO THE YO-KAI WORLD...
I APOLOGIZE FOR ALL THE PROBLEMS THE YO-KAI WORLD HAS CAUSED YOU.
NO...

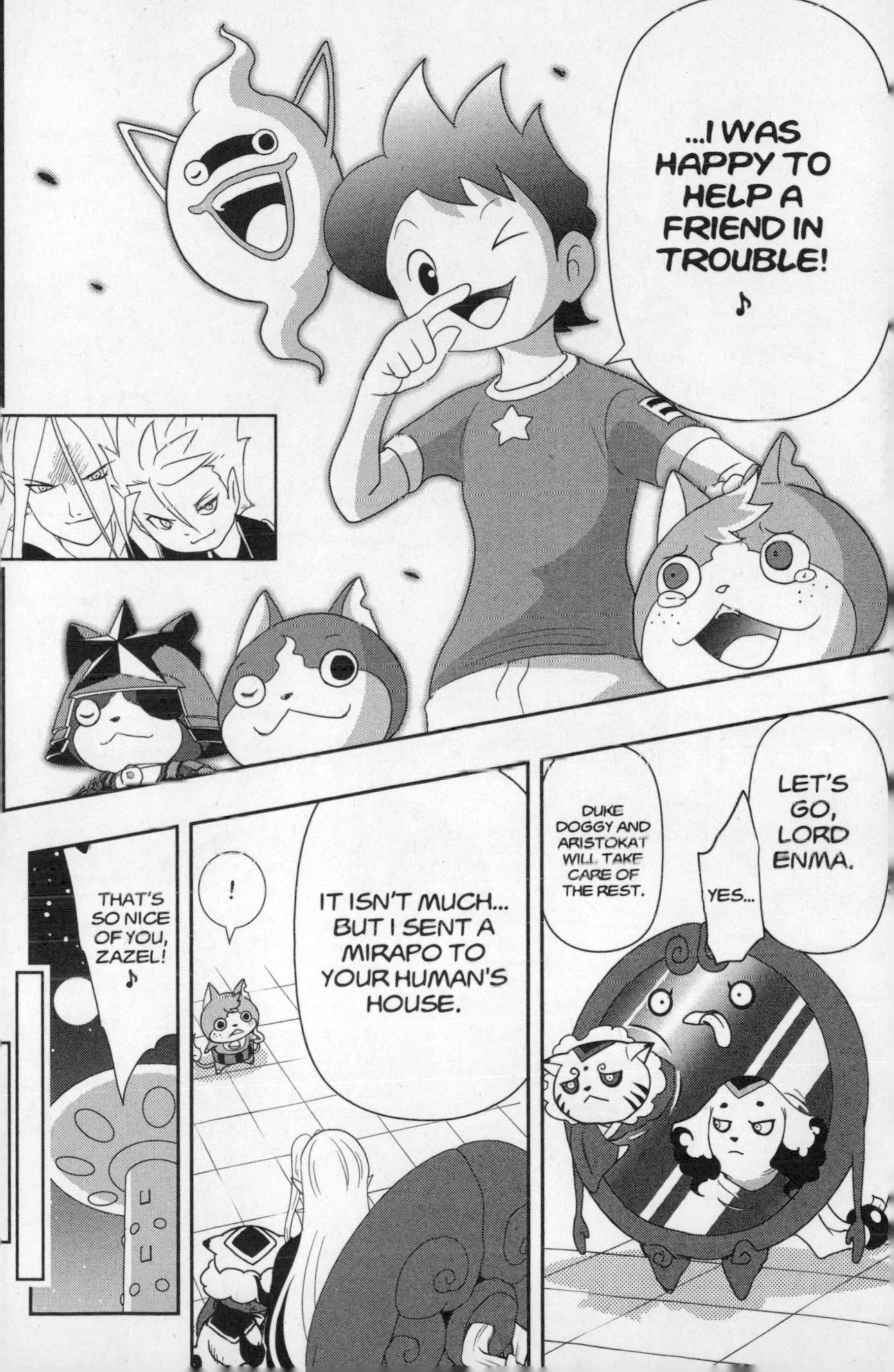
...I WAS HAPPY TO HELP A FRIEND IN TROUBLE! ♪
LET'S GO, LORD ENMA.
DUKE DOGGY AND ARISTOKAT WILL TAKE CARE OF THE REST.
YES...
IT ISN'T MUCH... BUT I SENT A MIRAPO TO YOUR HUMAN'S HOUSE.
!
THAT'S SO NICE OF YOU, ZAZEL! ♪

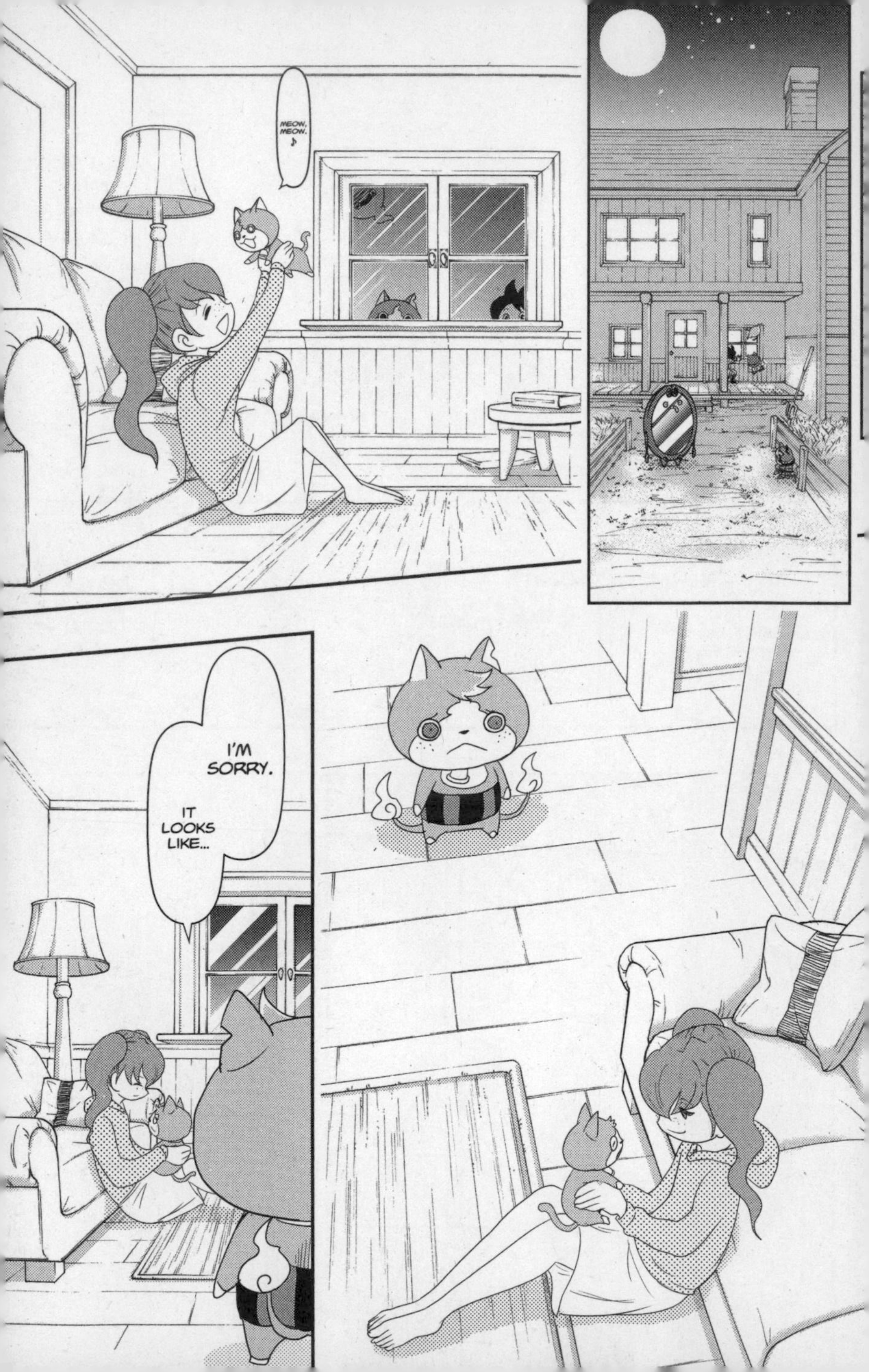
MEOW, MEOW. ♪
I'M SORRY.
IT LOOKS LIKE...

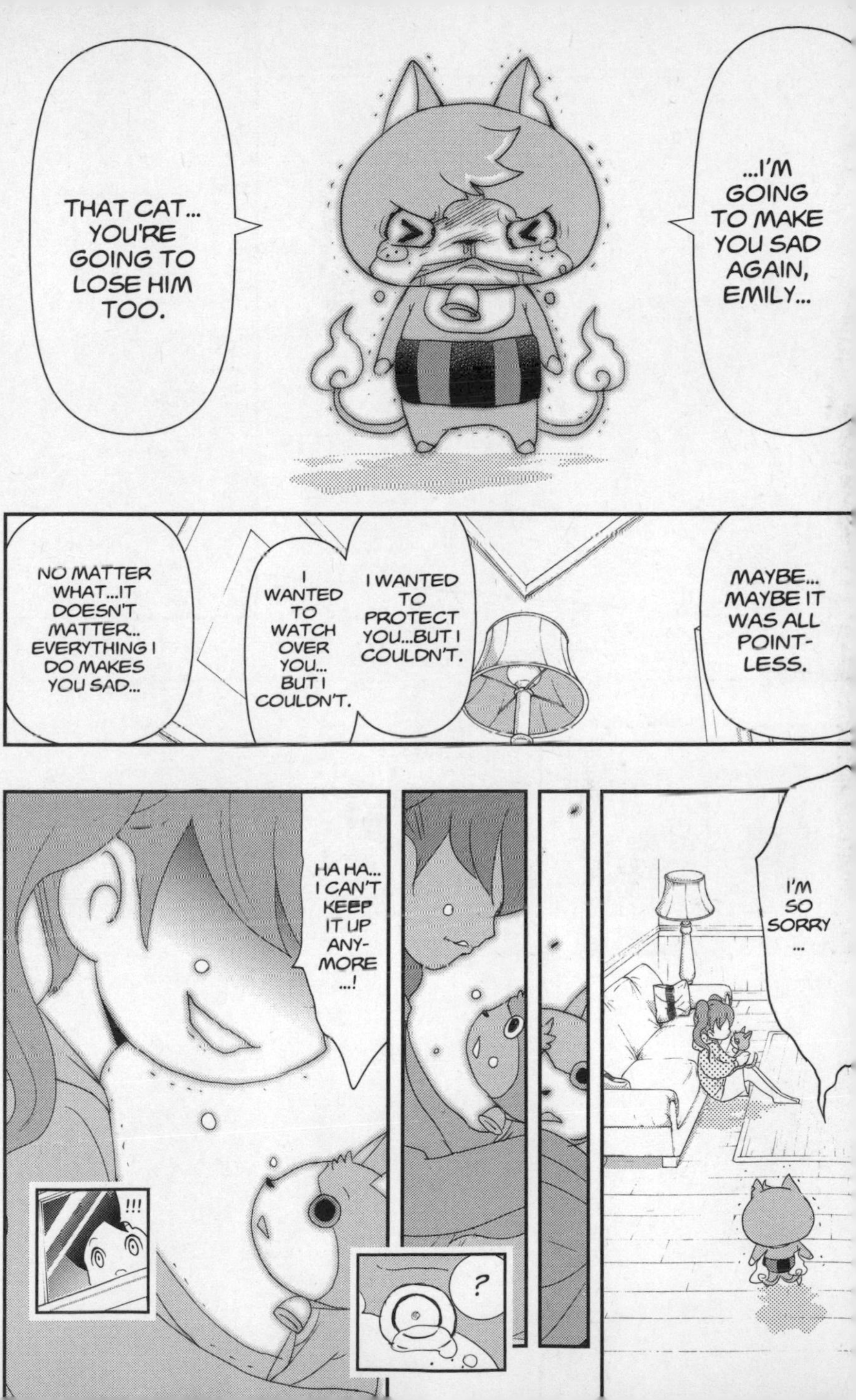
...I'M GOING TO MAKE YOU SAD AGAIN, EMILY...
THAT CAT... YOU'RE GOING TO LOSE HIM TOO.
MAYBE... MAYBE IT WAS ALL POINTLESS.
I WANTED TO PROTECT YOU...BUT I COULDN'T.
I WANTED TO WATCH OVER YOU... BUT I COULDN'T.
NO MATTER WHAT...IT DOESN'T MATTER... EVERYTHING I DO MAKES YOU SAD...
I'M SO SORRY ...
HA HA... I CAN'T KEEP IT UP ANYMORE ...!
?
!!!

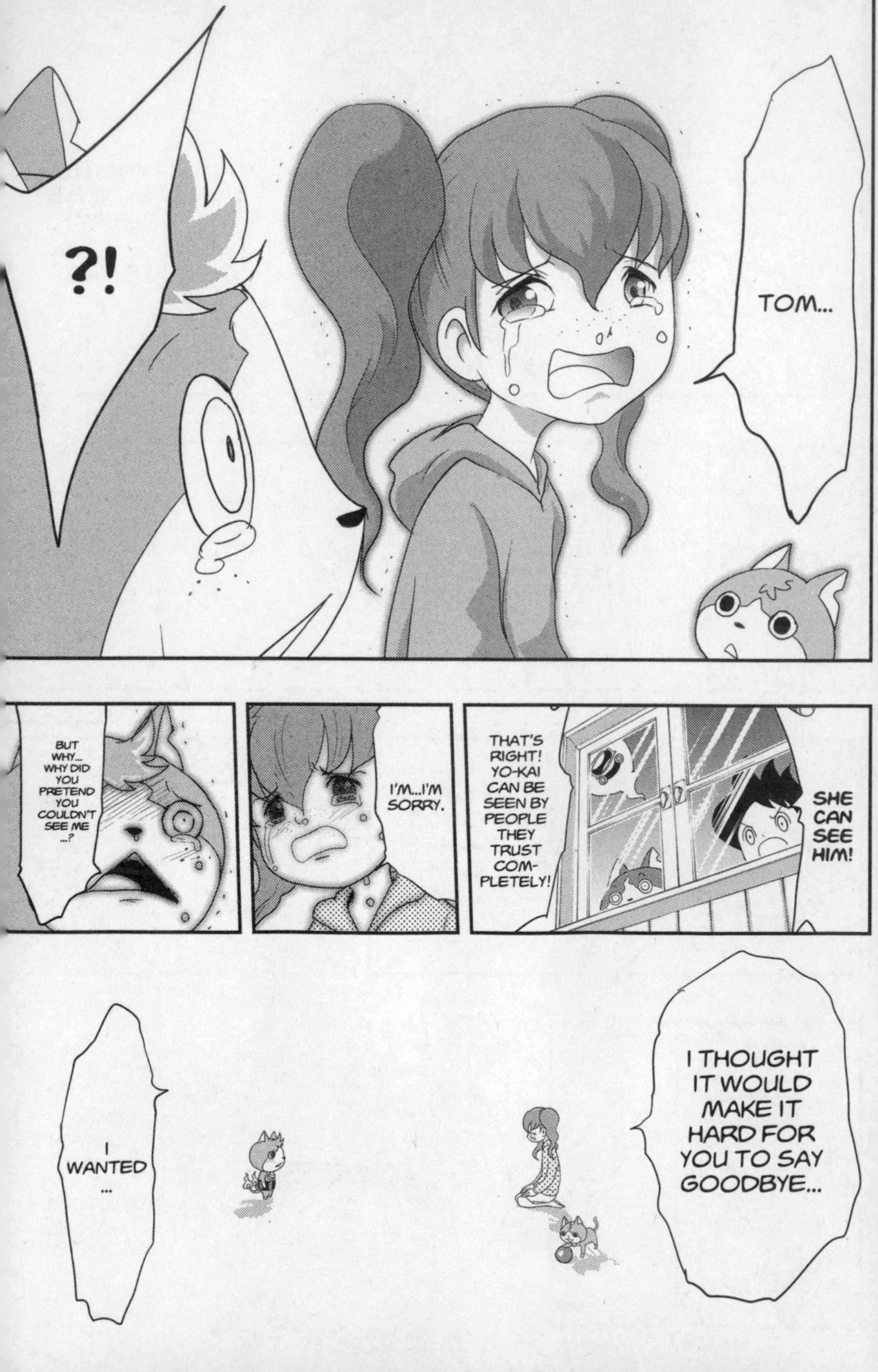
TOM...
?!
SHE CAN SEE HIM!
THAT'S RIGHT! YO-KAI CAN BE SEEN BY PEOPLE THEY TRUST COMPLETELY!
I'M...I'M SORRY.
BUT WHY... WHY DID YOU PRETEND YOU COULDN'T SEE ME ...?
I THOUGHT IT WOULD MAKE IT HARD FOR YOU TO SAY GOODBYE...
I WANTED ...

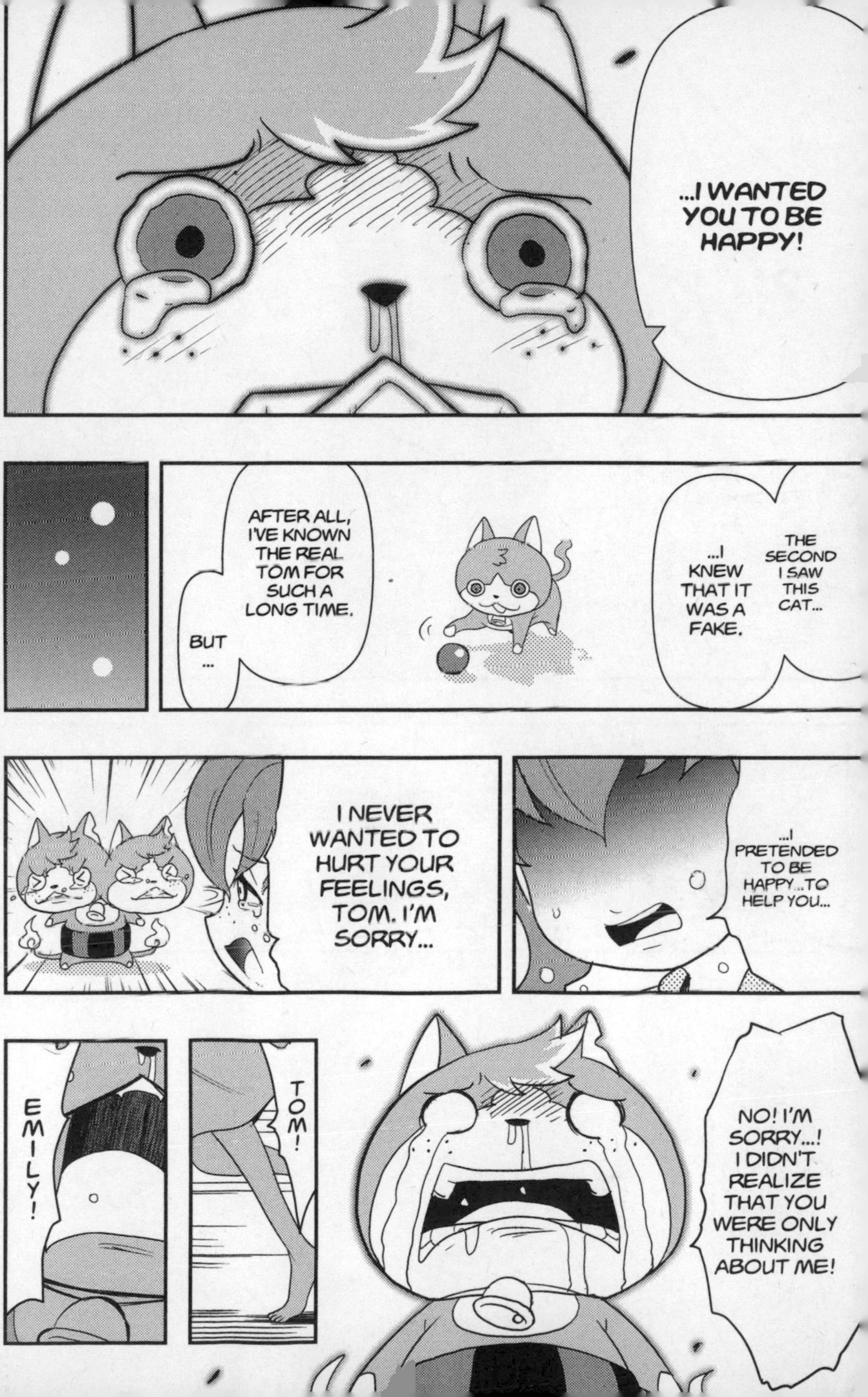
...I WANTED YOU TO BE HAPPY!
THE SECOND I SAW THIS CAT...
...I KNEW THAT IT WAS A FAKE.
AFTER ALL, I'VE KNOWN THE REAL TOM FOR SUCH A LONG TIME.
BUT ...
...I PRETENDED TO BE HAPPY...TO HELP YOU...
I NEVER WANTED TO HURT YOUR FEELINGS, TOM. I'M SORRY...
NO! I'M SORRY...! I DIDN'T REALIZE THAT YOU WERE ONLY THINKING ABOUT ME!
TOM!
EMILY!

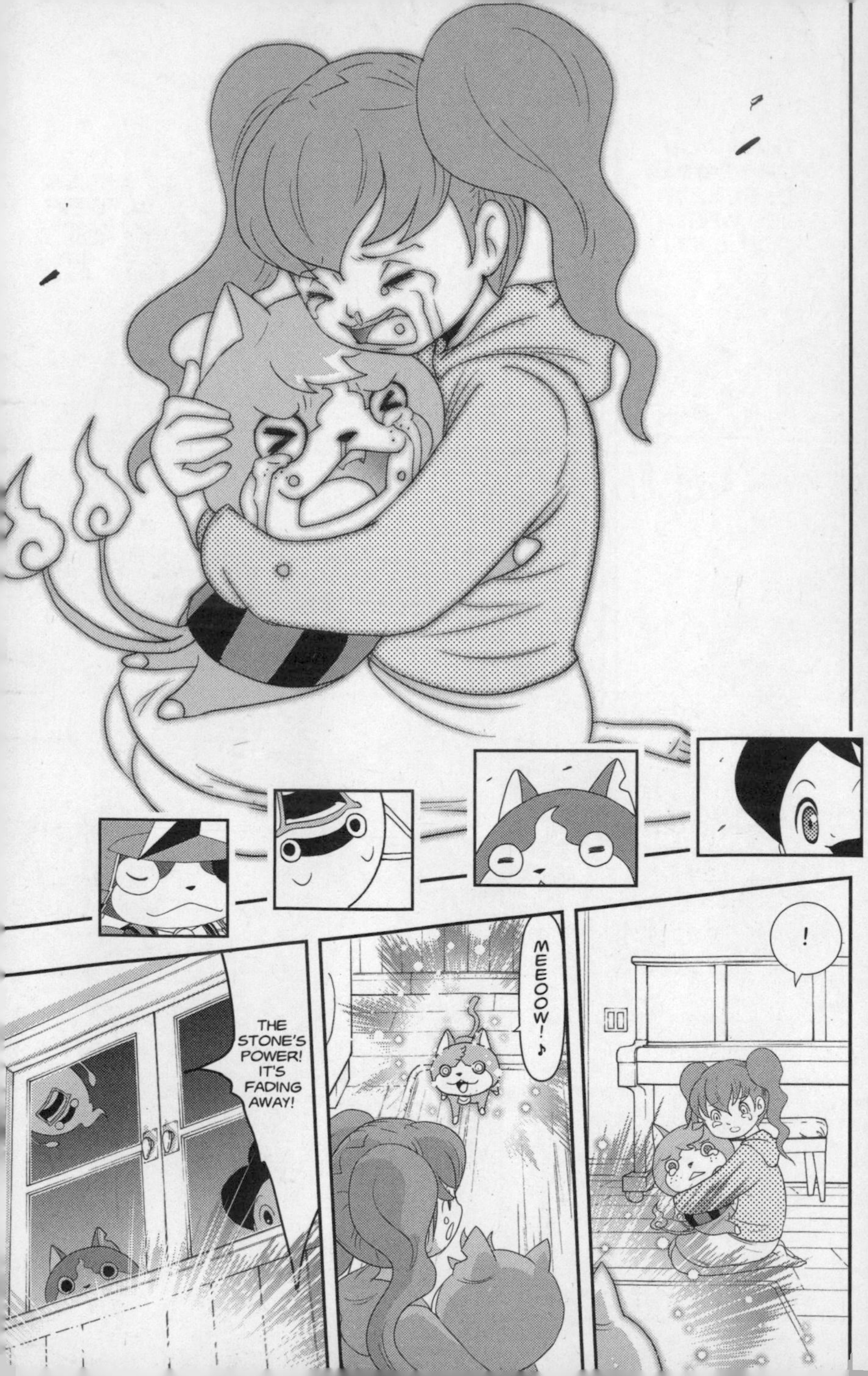
!
MEEOOW! ♪
THE STONE'S POWER! IT'S FADING AWAY!

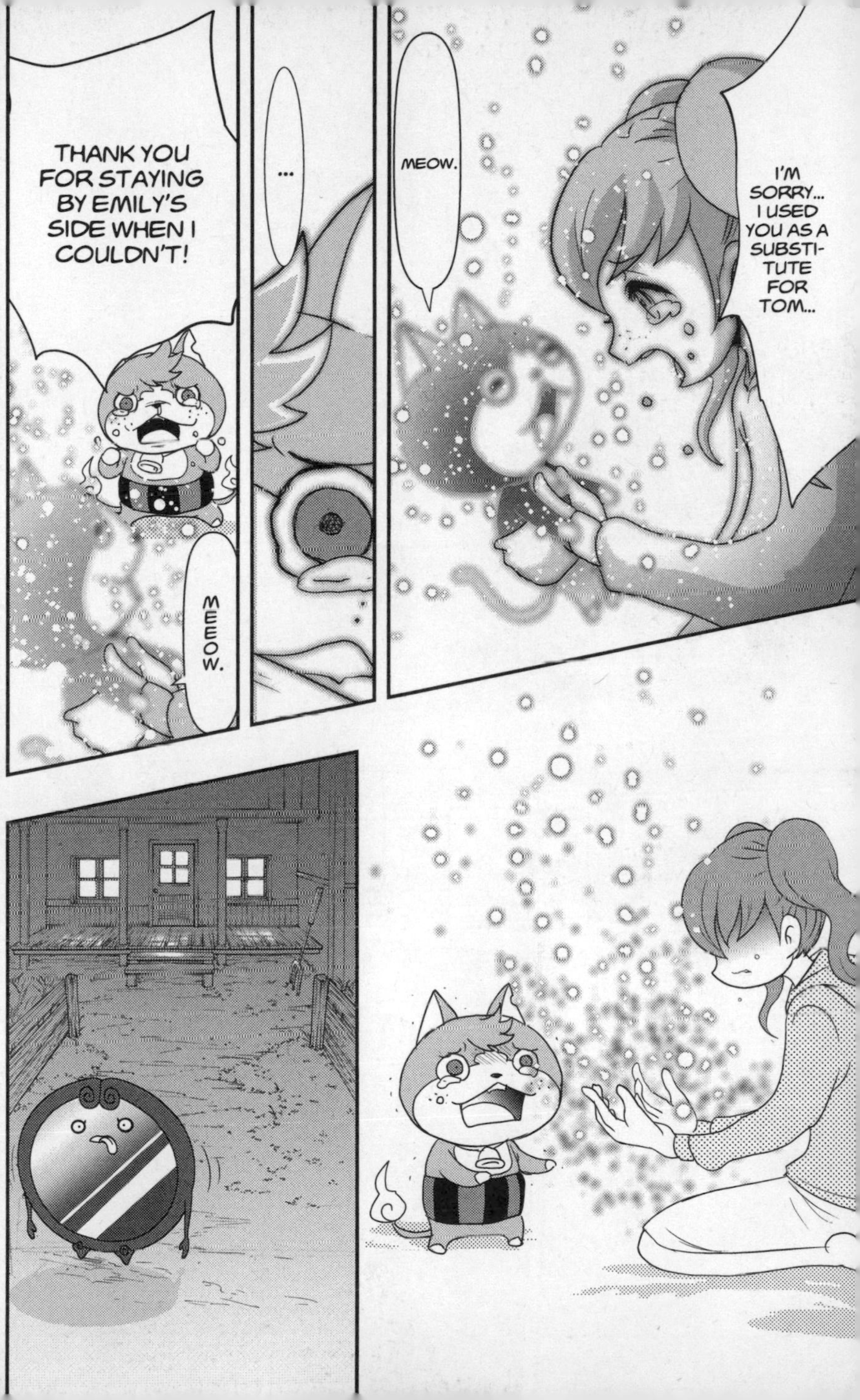
I'M SORRY... I USED YOU AS A SUBSTITUTE FOR TOM...
MEOW.
...
THANK YOU FOR STAYING BY EMILY'S SIDE WHEN I COULDN'T!
MEEEOW.

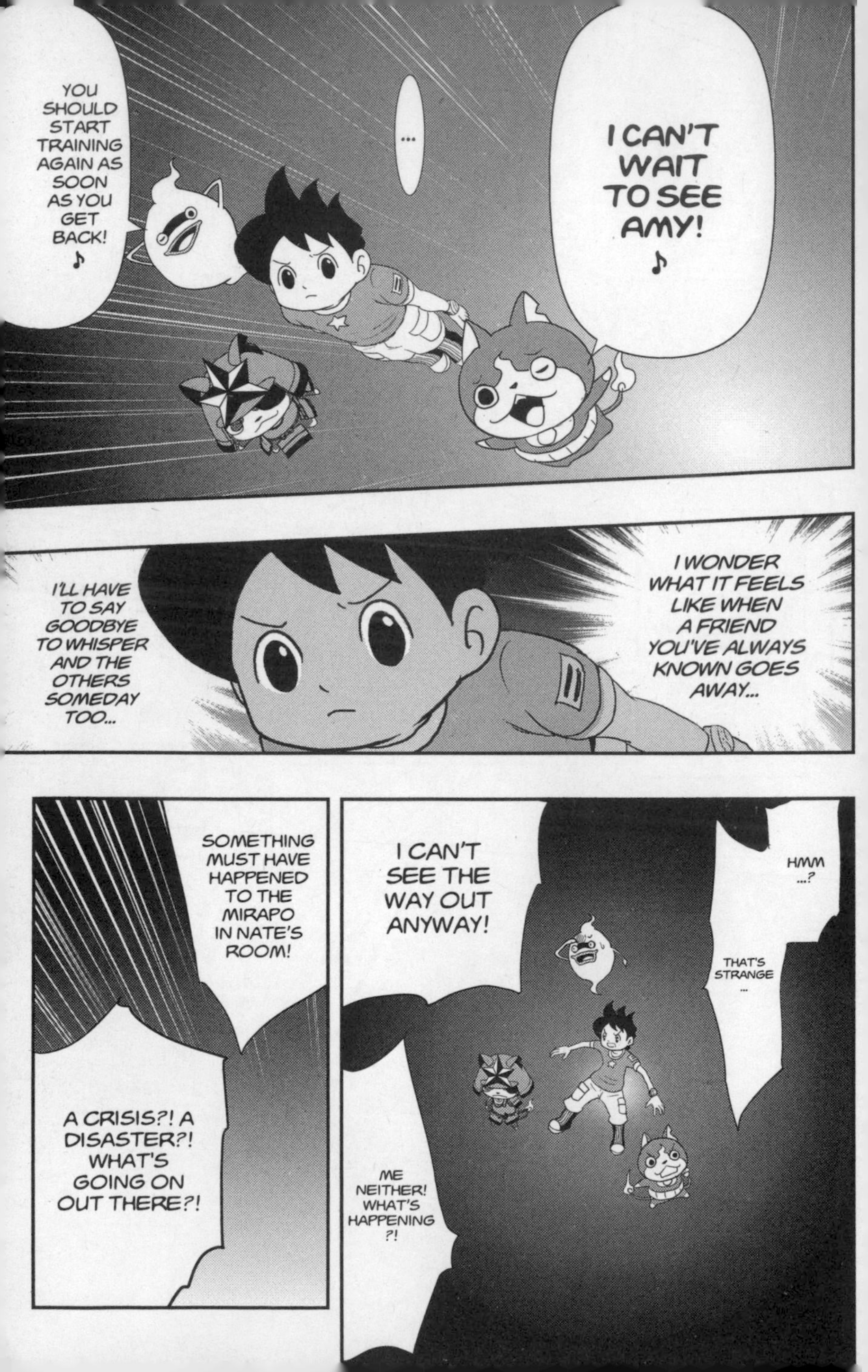
I CAN'T WAIT TO SEE AMY! ♪
...
YOU SHOULD START TRAINING AGAIN AS SOON AS YOU GET BACK! ♪
I WONDER WHAT IT FEELS LIKE WHEN A FRIEND YOU'VE ALWAYS KNOWN GOES AWAY...
I'LL HAVE TO SAY GOODBYE TO WHISPER AND THE OTHERS SOMEDAY TOO...
HMM ...?
THAT'S STRANGE ...
I CAN'T SEE THE WAY OUT ANYWAY!
ME NEITHER! WHAT'S HAPPENING ?!
SOMETHING MUST HAVE HAPPENED TO THE MIRAPO IN NATE'S ROOM!
A CRISIS?! A DISASTER?! WHAT'S GOING ON OUT THERE?!

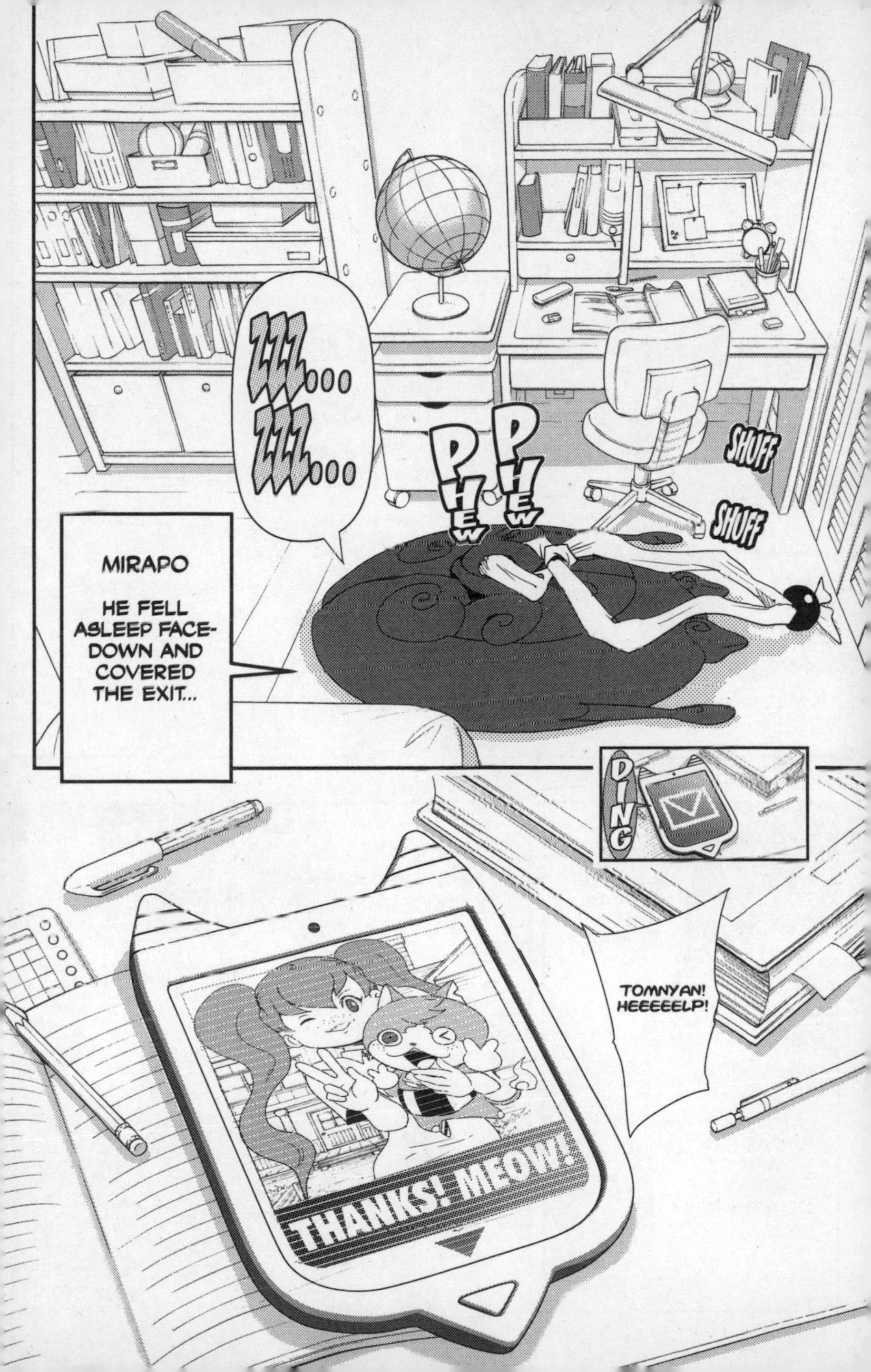
SHUFF
SHUFF
PHEW
PHEW
ZZZ... ZZZ...
MIRAPO
HE FELL ASLEEP FACE-DOWN AND COVERED THE EXIT...
DING
TOMNYAN! HEEEEELP!
THANKS! MEOW!

Welcome to the world of Little Battlers eXperience! In the near future, a boy named Van Yamano owns Achilles, a miniaturized robot that battles on command! But Achilles is no ordinary LBX. Hidden inside him is secret data that Van must keep out of the hands of evil at all costs!

All six volumes available now!

DANBALL SENKI
© 2011 Hideaki FUJII / SHOGAKUKAN
©LEVEL-5 Inc.

# Little Battlers eXperience LBX LITTLE BATTLERS EXPERIENCE

## Story and Art by HIDEAKI FUJII

GODFATHER ARC
-SPINOFF-

NATE?
NATE? AREN'T YOU IN?
I'M COMING IN.
KRCHK
NATE?
GK
THUN
TMP
WHERE HAS HE GONE?
FWUMP
AND NOW YOU KNOW HOW MIRAPO ENDED UP IN THIS STORY!
SHF
SHF
SHF

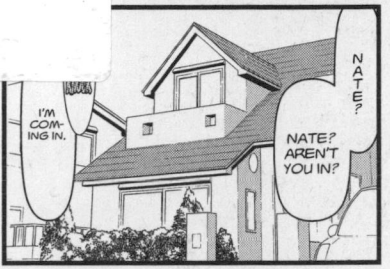

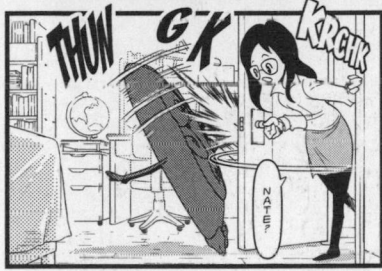

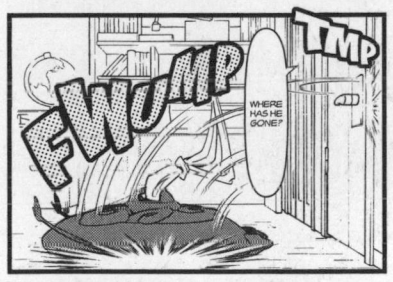

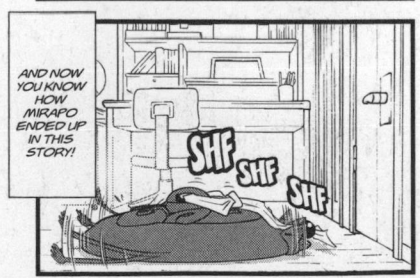

# AUTHOR BIO

Instead of a bunch of separate chapters,
this volume is all one story. It's something
a little bit different and I hope you enjoy it!
I've also added a bunch of ideas that are
different from the game and anime.

—Noriyuki Konishi

Noriyuki Konishi hails from Shimabara City in Nagasaki
Prefecture, Japan. He debuted with the one-shot *E-CUFF*
in *Monthly Shonen Jump Original* in 1997. He is known
in Japan for writing manga adaptations of *AM Driver* and
*Mushiking: King of the Beetles*, along with *Saiyuki Hiro
Go-Kū Den!*, *Chōhenshin Gag Gaiden!! Card Warrior
Kamen Riders*, *Go-Go-Go Saiyuki: Shin Gokūden* and
more. Konishi was the recipient of the 38th Kodansha
manga award in 2014 and the 60th Shogakukan manga
award in 2015.

# THIS IS THE END OF THIS GRAPHIC NOVEL!

FOLLOW THE ACTION THIS WAY.

**To properly enjoy this graphic novel, please turn it around and begin reading from right to left.**

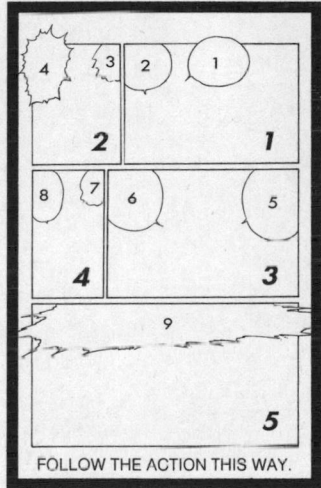